A TANGLED VISION

BOOK TWO OF THE RUNEBOUND

LINDSEY S. JOHNSON

ARUS
ENTERTAINMENT

BOOKS BY LINDSEY S. JOHNSON

A Ragged Magic

A Tangled Vision

A Jagged War (coming soon)

Published by ARUS Entertainment (Seattle, WA).

This book is catalog #ARUS3002, and has ISBNs of 978-1-954394-05-6 (print) and 978-1-954394-06-3 (ebook)

Edited by Marti McKenna and Scott James Magner

Cover art and design by Angie Abler

ARUS
ENTERTAINMENT

www.arusentertainment.com

A TANGLED VISION

For Angie: the bestest best friend that ever was, ever since that fateful day you knocked on our back door and asked if there were any kids your age to play with. Every friendship I ever write is secretly about you, at least a little bit, because with you I learned how to be a friend at all. Your imagination and kindness and laughter have been a gift ever since. Thank you for all of it.

And for Medea T. Cat: You were the smartest, cuddliest, most determined furry baby, and we'll miss you forever.

THE STORY SO FAR...

Rhiannon Owen had the Sight, visions of the future or glimpses into the minds of others. In her country of Talaria, that was dangerous, as the leaders of the Kirche believe that people with magic should be kept under strict supervision as acolytes.

Despite her relatively weak gifts, Rhiannon was accused of being a witch and calling demons to bring a sickness called The Wasting to her hometown of Haverston. Rhiannon was captured trying to escape, and in retribution for her supposed crimes her mother, father, and brother Keenan were all hanged, and her younger sister imprisoned.

The reason? Bishop Gantry, a powerful—and corrupt—sorcerer wanted someone with the Sight for a dangerous spell, and carved runes into the captive Rhiannon's flesh so he could have a repository of demonic power available to him at all times. The spell went badly awry, and Rhiannon was left for dead in the kirche's dungeons.

Princess Julianna, the wife of the crown prince,

rescued Rhiannon with the help of Earl Connor Fitzwellan. Rhiannon tried to tell them of Gantry's plans, but the spells he carved into her skin prevented her from even saying the word "demon," much less what he wanted with them. Although Julianna is an accomplished healer and a skilled spy working on behalf of the crown, she is also very pregnant, and enlists Rhiannon's help with maintaining her many deceptions.

Rhiannon joined Julianna as her lady's maid and went with her Haverston Castle, the home of her mother and brother, the Duchess Marguerite and Duke Hugh Theroux. While learning her new duties, she encountered Bishop Gantry in the castle. He did not recognize Rhiannon, although his new acolyte, Orrin Beaudreau, did. Orrin was once Rhiannon's brother's lover, and kept Rhiannon's secret and became her friend.

Hugh frees Rhiannon's sister Linnet and brings her to the castle. Linnet, furious and frightened, takes out her frustrations on Rhiannon, blaming her for all their problems. But Linnet's magic interacts with and amplifies Rhiannon's, causing problems for them both.

On the morning of the Summer Solstice, Gantry attempted a spell targeting Julianna, using Orrin's magic much as he'd intended to use Rhiannon's. It failed, but Rhiannon and Connor were independently wary of another attempt, and each managed to thwart a similar spell cast at sunset.

Now aware of her true identity, Gantry made several attempts to discredit Rhiannon, but was unable to muster enough political support to override Julianna's influence. Frustrated and afraid, Rhiannon attempted to poison Gantry, but nearly killed Duchess Marguerite instead. A quick-thinking Orrin spilled the wine intended for Gantry, and Rhiannon accidentally revealed her powers—and her intent—to Connor and Hugh.

Julianna, Connor, and Hugh pleaded with Rhiannon to make no further attempts, since they needed Gantry alive to expose a plot by Archbishop Montmoore against the crown. While investigating, Connor and Hugh overhear a rumor blaming Julianna for the Wasting, which Rhiannon knew from her visions was actually being spread by Gantry, using magic drawn from Orrin. While she couldn't relate the information directly, Hugh was able to deduce the truth, and vowed to protect Orrin and Rhiannon at all costs.

The Guildmasters of Haverston fell sick from the Wasting, as did Archbishop Montmoore and many residents of the castle. Montmoore admitted Gantry was behind the Wasting spell but has since disappeared.

Julianna went into labor and gave birth to twins, but the boy died. The girl lived, but showed signs of demonic influence, which Hugh and his ally Asa, an agent of the Indrani empire, worked to remove with a spell powered by Rhiannon's magic.

Alerted by her use of power, Gantry arrived at the castle with Orrin in tow, hoping to claim the children for his nefarious ends. Rhiannon used her power to call for help, summoning Connor, Hugh, his ally and accomplished kirche healer Cardinal Robere, and Linnet to the castle chapel. In the resulting battle, both Gantry and Linnet draw on Rhiannon's power, but instead being drained she learned to tap even more power, summoning up the strength to topple a statue onto Gantry, killing him.

Gantry's spells spiraled out of control, summoning demons and nearly killing Orrin. Attempting to save him, Rhiannon pushed herself even farther, seizing control of the spell and dissipating it, while at the same time changing the runes carved into her skin, unlocking even more magical potential in both herself and Orrin.

CHAPTER 1

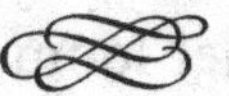

Spring means war. I can feel it coming in the warming air and the melting snow. Messenger birds bring news tied to their legs from Fanthas, while couriers and soldiers bring similar reports back to Haverston from the north.

My visions bring news of war more regularly than any messenger or ship in the harbor. They knock me sideways when walking down hallways or sitting in chapel, while everyone stares at the witch with confusion and distrust.

I try to keep my mouth shut unless I'm alone with my sister Linnet, Hugh, or Orrin, but the Sight is brutal, and hard, and sometimes shouting is the only way to handle the pain.

Orrin and I often have the same visions at the same time. Arriving without warning, leaving us staggering in hallways or yelling in the courtyard.

To most people, we seem like mad creatures, dangerous and untamed. They don't See the way we do, and they don't want to.

There's a reason oracles live on mountaintops or hard-to-reach caves.

That's thirty-two, I send to Orrin, looking down from Linnet's bedroom window at the bay below. The morning sun shines through scudding clouds as we sit curled up on her wine-colored couch. My sister sits with her back to us at her loom and does not look up as Orrin speaks.

"Thirty-two what, Rhiannon?" he asks, his nose in a book of poetry.

"Thirty-two wounded soldiers off that transport ship. They're hurrying to load supplies and more troops to go back north."

"More wounded," he mutters. "We know where the duchess will be this afternoon, then."

"Maybe I'll go with her to the hospice today," I say quietly, picking at my nails.

"Probably not," Linnet says through her teeth, biting through a pale blue thread. "They don't want you there."

They don't want any of us there, Orrin adds bitterly, his sending stinging a little.

I glance back at him, but rather than meet my eyes he glowers at the page. His dark skin glows in the sun, a pretty contrast to his pale linen shirt. I send a little nudge and he reaches out to hold my hand lightly.

"You could work in the still room," Linnet says, focusing on the pattern in front of her—a seascape. "There's plenty to do in there, and at least no one will make a sign against evil at you."

I grimace and look out the window again. "I don't think the new cook likes me in there, either."

"The new cook is stupid," Linnet snaps. "And Duchess Marguerite says she appreciates our help. So there."

"The cook isn't so new anymore," Orrin mutters. "She shouldn't be surprised by the duchess. Or us."

"Whatever," Linnet says. "Why are you two even in here, anyway?"

"We ate breakfast with you," I point out. "You asked us."

"Breakfast is over. I'm busy. Go away."

"Why, when you're such great company?" I tease. "Look at you, all sunshiny and pleasant. Who would ever want to leave?"

Linnet looks over her shoulder and wrinkles her nose. "Go do something useful, like write another sappy letter to your lovverrr," she mocks. "'Oh, dearest Connor, why have you not responded to my last kissy face note?'"

"Shut up!" I yelp, my face burning. Just because she saw one letter—that I didn't even send. "You're such a brat. He's not my lover. He's just...whatever."

"Mm-hmm," she sniggers.

I scowl at her. "His Grace will be here soon anyway, and then I'll go to chapel with him and leave you alone. Can you try not being rude?"

"Can you try not being so annoying?"

"No. I've decided annoying you is my only purpose."

"Well good job—you did it! Get a new purpose."

I stick my tongue out at her. She sticks hers out right back.

Orrin breaks into our bickering with a laughing "All right, that's enough, you two."

I lean my forehead on the window's glass, looking back down at the harbor.

"Do you still plan to look for the spy again today?" Orrin asks.

I've been looking for Fanthan spies in Haverston since the war was only a rumor. We know Archbishop Montmoore and his allies in exile must have some here in Haverston. I thought chapel might be a good time to try. It's a time of meditation and prayer, and though not everyone attends, those who do are a nice sampling of who's who in the castle. Servants, soldiers, castle guards, even the gentry who come and go at will. I've tried for weeks, and though I've found thoughts that "seem" suspicious, I can't tell yet who's doing the thinking.

I shrug. "I know I've felt something in chapel before. If I can just focus, I'm sure I can figure out who it is. Then we can actually do something about it." Orrin snorts at my half-hearted confidence. "It's better than sulking," I mutter.

"Why does Hugh think you will be able to find them? He keeps telling us spies are hard to read, how they're trained to keep their minds closed off from the Sight and other magic," Linnet asks as she starts a new row.

"Not against our Sight."

Linnet's withering glare over her shoulder says she doesn't find that impressive. Orrin's lips twist and he raises an eyebrow at me.

"Not always," I mumble. "We have to do something," I insist, feeling defensive.

"I am doing something," Orrin replies. "I'm looking, too. I just won't spend time in that...the chapel." Jaw clenching, he glares at me. "You know I'm looking, too. Just because I'm not following your lead doesn't mean I'm not doing something. You're so much like your brother sometimes." He sighs. "He was always so sure he was right."

"She's not like Keenan," Linnet grumbles. "He was a lot nicer."

"You used to be nicer," I snap.

"We all used to be a lot nicer," Orrin mutters into his book.

We all used to be happier, too. Sometimes—a lot of times—I wish everything would go back to how it was before. Before Bishop Gantry, before Mum and Da and Keenan were executed, before the guilds conspired against my family. Before the torture and pain, the scars that ache and burn and fill with untamed, unwanted magic.

I ache for that before. I'd give up every thread of my magic to go back. Even if it meant never meeting Connor, or Hugh, or Princess Julianna. I stare out the window, wishing for mornings with Mum singing to herself, Da teasing us, Keenan coming home from the monastery, Linnet carefree and laughing.

I wish for everything that was destroyed when Bishop Gantry needed someone with the Sight to power his demon spell. The runes carved into my skin—and Orrin's—transforming my simple magic talent into an uncontrolled well of power, all so Gantry could try to murder Princess Julianna and support Stephen Valcourt's bid for the throne.

I thought killing Bishop Gantry would stop the visions, that I wouldn't have to worry all the time. But that turned out to be naïve.

My mind turns in circles again, shows me Gantry dying, Cardinal Robere banishing the shrieking demons, the leftover power in the air that I pulled into myself and Orrin to change the horrible runes we bear so we could be free of Gantry's magic—or as free as we can be.

Still changed. Still full of magic we can't control. But at least we're no longer linked to demons.

There's a knock at the door, which opens a second later to admit Hugh—or rather, His Grace the Duke Hugh Theroux, Lord of Haverston and older brother to her Royal Highness, Princess Juliana.

We still startle at his not waiting for acknowledgement before entering someone's private chambers. Although technically all the chambers do belong to him, I roll my eyes and stand up.

I'm ready to go, ready to stop remembering.

"Good morning, all! You're looking lovely today, Rhia." I curtsey to Hugh in my dark green and ivory chapel best. He smiles and bows. He's beautiful, as always, his blond hair gleaming in perfectly tousled waves and his soft blue tunic somehow making him seem affable yet so very much a Duke. He turns to look at Linnet's work. "Linnet, gorgeous as always. As is that ocean study—I love it. Stunning, my dear," he raves. Linnet hums but doesn't look up. A slight smile plays on her lips, so I know she's pleased he likes it.

"Orrin, good morning. That is a lovely shire, er, shirt you have, um, on. It l-looks very nice on you," Hugh stammers a little, clears his throat, glances away from Orrin, who also seems to be nervous suddenly, blinking and running one hand over the front of his shirt. I raise my eyebrows at Orrin, but he pointedly ignores both of us, going back to his book.

"Are you ready to go, Rhia?"

"Good morning, Your Grace. Yes, I'm ready," I say and start toward the door.

"Are you coming, Orrin?" Hugh asks.

I sigh and shake my head at Hugh. He knows better.

Orrin doesn't look up from his book, but his eyebrows furrow in an angry frown. "Am I coming to the place in this castle where I was tortured and abused? No, I think not, Your Grace."

Hugh opens his mouth, but I shake my head at him and wave my hand toward the door.

"As you wish," he says quietly. "Linnet?"

"Mmm busy," she mutters. "Go away."

I roll my eyes and take Hugh's arm to steer him out. "Let's go, Your Grace," I insist.

"Please remind me," I say as we walk down the hall. "Did we not discuss how Orrin feels about the kirche and all kirche-related activities?"

Hugh winces. "I just...it just slipped out. I'll apologize."

"Just leave him alone about it," I chide, but let it go at that. "Do you have anyone in particular you'd like me to focus on today?"

"There are some soldiers coming. Special invitation. One of them could be our spy, but I don't have the proof needed to accuse anyone specific. If you discover something we can use, let me know. But try not to go into a trance this time. You weren't exactly subtle last week."

Hugh isn't entirely happy with our spy discovery plan, but he's gone along with it so far. I want to find everyone who could hurt us and stop them before they can.

"Rhia, I wish you wouldn't..." he starts, but sighs and reverses our arm placement to escort me instead. "I don't want you to risk yourself when Connor and I may have other ways of finding out this information. He's worried about you, too, you know."

I blush and look away. "Is he? He hasn't written lately."

Hugh clears his throat. "Ah, well, he's kept very busy in Corat. But he asked me to look out for you, which I'm trying to do. Searching for the minds of spies can be dangerous—you almost lost yourself in Montmoore's mind when you tried last year. You and Orrin are too..." he trails off again, searching for a word.

"What? Precious a resource? Useful as tools?" I sneer.

"No, Rhiannon. No." He stops and turns to me, his face so beautiful, so wounded. He cups my cheek with a soft, warm hand. "You are both too likely to be hurt, and I would be devastated if you were. Please be careful. If you must try, then I will help to keep you safe as best I can. Don't push too hard, don't get lost in the minds of others, don't get trapped or lose control. You are precious to me because you are precious. I want you to be safe."

He blinks at me for a moment, dropping his hand from my face. "Tell me, if you would. Can you hear my thoughts when I'm not sending them?" His voice is maybe a little nervous. I pat his arm.

"Your barriers are very good," I tell him. I don't tell him that those barriers aren't always good enough to keep me from hearing very strong thoughts. I don't want to worry him, and there's nothing he can do about it anyway.

We walk into the small castle chapel together, my arm through his. The morning light through the west facing windows, highlighting the golden wood of the pews and the lacy stonework, bright on the whitewash and the colorful murals. The smell of burning candles, an affectation since most of the walls hold glowsand lamps, wafts over the smell of perfumed people, sweating in their worship finery. The air is a little damp with the spring chill, the stones only reluctantly heated by the steam heat that moves through the walls, and a few braziers in the corners.

Hugh escorts me to the front pew of the gentry box and sits at my side, showing support. He often sits with me rather than up in the balcony with his mother, the Duchess Marguerite. He smiles at everyone around us – the soldiers off to our right in the main pews, a few servants with them, and the Duchess' ladies. The ladies head for the second pew of the gentry box and leave us on our own. Hugh reaches for the book of Dorei in front of us and thumbs through it, waiting for the pastor to begin. I take a deep breath and try to get comfortable on the hard, wooden pew. The sermons aren't terribly long, but it should be enough time to start my search.

Chapel isn't the ordeal it was when Bishop Gantry was leading it, but it still isn't my favorite. I don't feel close to either Dorei or the Star Lord. I don't feel that my prayers mean anything, and I don't like the way everyone looks sidelong at me. But Marguerite pointed out that my going makes me look normal, relatable, and safer.

I know—better than anyone—how people feel about us. That Marguerite supports us helps a bit because everyone trusts her. But what if she's wrong? I can hear them thinking it at me. What if she's wrong and this magic brings ruin?

Minds are like buzzing bees—a flower garden of thoughts, all whizzing around, some lazy, some with purpose, and far too few of them very important. As many minds as are in the castle, it's like hundreds of hives trying to pollinate the same garden.

When you're trying to hear just one set of wings amongst the swarm.

Often I hear thoughts from the people passing by, and even if they aren't physically making a sign against evil, inside their minds they're wondering if they should. Their thoughts are full of fear or disgust, certain I'm contaminated by what happened last year.

Contaminated by demons, or the demon-wrought Wasting plague that Gantry caused with his spells. Even though we've been declared innocent victims of his plans, we're still forever tied to Bishop Gantry, who everyone knows was working with the enemies of Talaria.

King Peter formally declared war against Fanthas, again, naming Archbishop Montmoore as a traitor to the crown—along with his nephew Stephen Valcourt, Connor's brother. Hugh, as the Duke of Haverston, placed Linnet and Orrin and I under the protection of Haverston Duchy. We live in the castle as ourselves, not pretending to be servants or hiding. Not pretending we don't have magic.

Sometimes I wish I were still pretending. People don't like us having this power, even if they don't exactly know what the power is. And the thoughts of people who are frightened of you are so tiring, even if you only catch them in bits. Sifting through those frightened fragments to find someone who is plotting to hurt you and not just thinking you're a monster is not a task I've excelled at so far. But I'm determined, even if Hugh thinks it's too dangerous for someone so...precious.

It's hard to match specific thoughts to a specific

person, especially since I don't know who I'm looking for. But I do hope I'll know it when I find it.

... Please, Lord of stars, of skies...

... I hate this gown...

... look at her there, looking like butter wouldn't melt...

... What are we having for lunch...

... I don't like being this close. Witches are dangerous...saw what happened with that Gantry...demon tainted, all of them, including his exiled bishopness...

I close my eyes tighter to try to focus on just those last thoughts. They feel close by, so I push a little harder, open myself to just a little more magic, which in turn flows up to me from the power well deep below the castle. It fills my runes, gently buzzing.

...money's not good enough to...want to get out of this country. I don't care what...

I narrow my focus to that mind, trying to navigate the swirling thoughts around me. So much anger, so afraid of everything.

...getting out as soon as we can...run to Fanthas...as soon as we take them...what—what is happening? Who is—get out! Get out of my head!

Too much magic—they feel me in their head! I flinch and gasp as a barrier pushes back against me, jerking my head up to see who it might be. Behind me I hear a scrape and a rustle, harsh breathing, and I twist around in time to see a soldier two rows behind me grab a knife from somewhere on her uniform and lunge across the pews.

I fall against Hugh, summoning more power in desperation. It burns quick and hot, a stomach-churning rush up my spine, and I try to find something to do with it. Hugh grabs my arm, turning as I pulse with magic.

"Rhiannon, what –" he says as people shout and scatter.

The attacking woman screams, "Stay out my head, you witch!" and stabs at me, barely missing as Hugh pulls me away. I throw a Book of Dorei at her head, try to use the magic to make a physical shield, but everything burns too hot. Hugh shouts something and shoves me down, stepping over me to grapple with the soldier over the back of the pew.

"To me! To me! Stop her!" Hugh roars, his parade-ground voice punching through all the noise, and the other soldiers in chapel react and rush to help him. Curling into a ball, I roll under the pew with the magic burning under my skin. I grab for the spy's leg and try one of Hugh's defensive spells against her. It's supposed to confuse and weaken a target, but instead she screams as the magic pours from me like a molten river, and her knees buckle.

Hugh catches her as the other soldiers yank her knife hand back. I let go of her leg but hesitate to crawl out from under the pew. Hugh glares down, sending me a warning I can't ignore.

Release the magic back into the power well before you hurt yourself. You're going to set the chapel on fire, he snaps into my mind. Underneath, I can hear a faint *this won't help convince people she's harmless*. I don't let him know I hear that, concentrating on pushing the magic out of my runes and letting it drain away. It grumbles and swirls and looks for purpose, but quickly settles to a manageable level.

Captain Nerishe, commander of the Haverston guard, arrives at a run, her expression fierce as she demands reports from her soldiers. Sweat sheens her dark skin. Word either got out of the chapel very quickly, or she was close enough to hear the commotion. Hugh waves her to him, then hands the now unconscious spy to her.

"Take her to the barracks and put a guard on her," Hugh orders. He reaches down and helps me to my feet. "Are you hurt?" he asks.

I shake my head. Looking around at the damage, I notice everyone staring at me, at my disheveled state, at the long scratch on my neck from the soldier's knife. Their thoughts are loud in my head, and through the din of them I understand a few.

... Look at her, in shock, poor thing ...

... pulled a knife in chapel, how could anyone...

... Barely more than a child, really ...

... Why would a soldier attack her ...

Captain Nerishe lifts the unconscious spy onto her shoulder, and then I see it. On her right trouser leg, a scorched burn mark in the shape of a hand. My hand.

Voices and thoughts around me stutter to a stop as others notice as well. The smell of burned fabric mingles with candle wax, overwhelming my stomach for a moment. I swallow hard and take a step back. I didn't know my magic would do that. I didn't know it would burn hot outside of me, as well as inside. I clench my trembling hands together and try to keep outwardly calm.

"I want a report from every soldier here, and I want to know her schedule and duty partners. I'll be with you shortly," Hugh snaps, his arm around my shoulder. "Quickly, Captain." Nerishe nods and starts away, guards following at her command.

The thoughts around us are not so forgiving, now.

...I knew she was a witch...
...What did she do to that soldier...
...What will she do to us...

Duchess Marguerite, who must have come down from the balcony where she usually attends chapel, glides to the front of the congregation and calls for quiet. Because she's the duchess, everyone stops to listen.

"I know this was all very upsetting," she says. "Please everyone, stay calm. Everything is under control now." She turns to the priest and smiles at him. "Thank you, pastor. Your service was lovely, before it was disrupted so terribly. We will have to check everyone for shock or injuries." She walks to Hugh and me, still smiling, and takes my arm. "Come with me, my dear. We'll take a turn in the garden, I think, while Hugh carries on here."

I look at her uncertainly. She pats my arm lightly, but the pull of her tiny hands is inexorable. I don't resist. My shaking is likely apparent to everyone. Hugh bows to his mother and stands with the priest to answer questions while we walk serenely out the door. Rather, Marguerite seems serene. I am a sweaty mess.

I'm sure she'd rather stay and take charge of the chapel instead of Hugh. I'm sure there are many things she'd rather do about this situation than this. Her taking my arm and leaving is a move to keep sympathy with me.

I don't think it's going to work.

CHAPTER 2

I head back to my room after my turn in the garden with the Duchess. Her soothing talk helps, but underneath it is a thread of worry I can almost taste, souring the sweet fresh smell of the flowers beginning to bloom.

"I know things are hard right now, but you'll find your footing. I do think perhaps you should not search for spies during chapel, however. I think we can work more subtly than that. I'll have a talk with Hugh."

She wants us here, she's sincere about that, but she has an entire castle, not to mention a duchy, to worry about. We complicate things for her, whether or not she wants to tell us so.

Hours later, Linnet hands me a book and sits on my bed. I don't know when she came in, or how long she's been waiting to talk to me. "You're in a mess," she says.

"Thanks."

"Again."

"I know, Linnet."

She pats my leg. "It's not like you can help it. Messes

find you. She gets up to leave. "Oh, and Hugh says to stay here until he can come up. And to mind your own business. Hah. He's funny." She smiles, but it doesn't help, so she shrugs and leaves.

Orrin comes to see me, too. "Maybe chapel isn't the best place for either of us," he says.

I swat him with a pillow. "I found a spy," I say. "I did what I meant to do."

He nods. "Maybe we're better off focusing on the magic and ways to get shut of this whole business—and letting Hugh find the spies."

"Hugh, huh?" I nudge him. He presses his lips together.

"His Grace has asked me to call him Hugh. You too. You were there."

I smirk at him. He's never called Hugh by his given name that I can remember.

"I don't want to seem overly familiar. Besides, his insistence that's he's right all the time gets...annoying."

"So now you're going to trust him to find the spies and not go looking on your own at all? That's a lot of trust in a man you've been so annoyed with." I keep my tone bland, but my smile betrays me.

Orrin's cheeks grow darker. "He's a competent man. He's just—sometimes he's overbearing. And pushy. And self-righteous." He glares out the window. "But he knows what he's doing. I mean in this instance," he finishes hotly.

I hold my hands up. "You're right. He is competent. And pushy. And self-righteous."

"Thank you both," Hugh says from the doorway, and we jump. Hugh shakes his head, smiles, but his face looks strained. "I did knock."

"No one heard it—it doesn't count," I snap, a little embarrassed. But Hugh is all those things, and he knows it.

Hugh sighs and pulls at his collar. Orrin fidgets, his cheeks still burnished a darker brown.

"I would like you two to stop looking for spies," Hugh says. "You've found one, but I was right when I cautioned you. It's too dangerous. Your magic is too unpredictable at the moment, and I don't want either of you hurt. Using it in front of people like that just makes them afraid of you."

I raise my eyebrow, and his mouth twists in acknowledgment.

"More afraid of you. But please try to keep the magic to just our practice sessions for now. Just until we can get things under better control. Hmm?" He runs his hand through his hair, smiling beguilingly at us. I know he's working his charm like a spell, as he often does. It often works. I scowl at him anyway, and see Orrin do the same.

"What happens to the spy Rhia found," Orrin asks.

Hugh's face loses its smile. "I don't know. We may transport her to Corat, but that's a difficult proposition right now. I'm still pondering the logistics, but I've sent a bird to the king for advice. Orrin, if you would work with me to send to Cardinal Robere, we could ..." He stops at Orrin's glare. "Ah, no. Well, Rhiannon and I will work on that."

Orrin's expression goes distant, and I feel a deep tug of magic from him. His eyes flash with power. He looks at Hugh. "I don't think that spy will be a problem for much longer," he says, and then I feel it, too. The pull of a vision.

"What do you mean?" Hugh asks.

"Poison," I say, the vision wavering around me. Hugh swears and runs out of the room, but it will be too late when he gets there. I can't tell if she took it herself or if she was forced to take it, but she is dying now, her fear reaching for us, reaching for me, to tell me it's my fault. I shudder, retreating from the vision, from Orrin—from everything.

Sometimes I really don't like having the Sight.

CHAPTER 3

The tower room is much the same as it was when I first saw it—small bed, table, some chests, the thick, curved walls and narrow windows. When I woke up here last year after Gantry tortured me, after the guilds conspired to hang my parents and my brother, I thought I would die here. I thought I'd never want another vision again. I suppose I still don't. But here I am actively chasing one.

Hugh and Linnet stand waiting for Orrin and me as we try for a clearer vision. We've both been having the same one of a battle in the capitol for a few weeks, but the details remain vague. Hugh wants more information. We're going to try to have the same vision on purpose. We sit down in chairs next to one another and reach out. I look Orrin in the eye, take a deep breath. His hand grasps mine, and I fall into the vision that I've been fighting off until I was ready.

As though I am ever ready.

It overtakes me all at once, like a wave crashing down, though at least this time I called it. But this isn't the vision I thought would appear—not the one we've been chasing. I lose sense of Orrin's hand, of the chair beneath me, of anything but the vision all around me.

A vortex of wind swirls with colors of magic, like a storm over the sea. It threads around me, through me, rich with the scent of hot metal. My pulse pounds in my throat and temple, and I See.

It's like watching the vision through a hailstorm at first. I See a courtyard in a palace, with pillars and arches and grand steps. A dome rises behind a tower, and beams of weak daylight breaking through a humid, cloudy sky.

The stones of the courtyard are painted, and beneath the colors are worn carvings of faces and runes. I can feel the stone through my slippers. I still feel Orrin's hand in mine, anchoring me, but it seems very far away.

In the courtyard people fight with swords and knives and bayonets, brawling—guards in royal blue and red, others in brown leather and canvas, or Fanthas green. Amorphous demons swirl overhead, forms blending and shredding in the wind from a vortex of their own making.

I See Connor's face too near them, fighting to push Fanthas soldiers away from the king. He turns to fight someone new, whose face is so like his it must be his brother Stephen. Their swords flash, and they disappear in a crowd of other soldiers. I cry out but my voice turns to nothing in the gale.

There is movement on the magical plane, and in the swirling fog of the maelstrom I See Archbishop Montmoore, his face pale and his eyes narrowed in concentration. He stands across from...himself.

Montmoore stares at himself kneeling on courtyard

stones, marking runes and chanting a spell that encircles the courtyard, the vortex, all of it. I can feel it forming in my bones.

I See future Orrin and future me, blood-spattered, hand in hand, pulling magic and chanting. Trying to push back the demons, I think. Tears run down our faces and magic pours from us and into the other vortex.

Montmoore draws his runes on the flagstones, with blood drawn from a too-still form crumpled before him. Linnet, downed by a sword stroke. A scream I can barely hear rips from my throat, and I break free from where I stand rooted by Orrin's anchoring grip, frantically to try to reach Linnet and stop this.

I trip over uneven paving, and as I hit the ground I can feel it all now; the warm, sticky stones under my feet, the magic rushing through my body, the hot, thick air of a sultry summer afternoon. The smell of sweat, blood, metal and musty stone sink heavy on me as I rise and stagger to Linnet's side.

Montmoore—both of them—glares at me, the one from the future doggedly chanting, although he looks bone tired and haggard.

The other Montmoore stands in the magical plane where I was—where I should be—caught in a vortex and staring with wide and greedy eyes. I swallow my fears with my heart and stumble to Linnet's side.

I throw myself down next to Linnet's crumpled, gory form. My hands touch her, I can feel the blood on her skin, the limp lifelessness of her. I try to hold the wound in her chest closed.

Montmoore's arms rise as he calls to something, somewhere—I recognize neither the spell nor the runes he's drawn. I look over my shoulder into my own eyes. That me stares back, straining at the magic, tears and blood and sweat dripping, and then that me looks past me toward Montmoore.

I don't follow her gaze. I get back to trying to save Linnet somehow, from the past. I can't pull on any magic, can't find a healing chant, I'm gasping for Linnet to wake up and look at me.

Out of the corner of my eye, I See a flicker of me, but not where I thought I was. I look up, feel more magic surrounding me, pulling at me. I hear chanting, and I know it's my own.

At that moment I feel arms around my waist, the dark, slicing wind of the vortex, and the rush of time. I fall backwards into a heap on the floor of the tower room, tangled up with Orrin and my own screaming.

I'm in a heap on the floor with Orrin and Linnet on the rug before the hearth. The wool is dry and thick—not at all like blood, but my hands still feel wet. I hold them up, trembling, and force myself to stop screaming with a choked inhale. We all stare at my hands, at the blood and gore, as it starts to disappear.

"What was that?" Linnet demands, her voice shaky. I struggle to sitting so I can grab her, half-sobbing, and pull her across Orrin to me. She squawks, falling back into our heap. Orrin groans behind me as I hold onto Linnet and shudder.

"Quit it, you're strangling me," she croaks, and wriggles away. Hugh stands in front of me, ready to help us all up. He lifts Linnet to her feet easily, then hesitates a moment before taking my hand. I can't blame him.

Orrin scrambles up on his own, wipes his hands on his shirt, rights the much-abused chairs. He looks at me sidelong, his head lowered, his expression as desperate and disturbed as I feel.

I try to quiet my gasping. Wobbling over to the bed, I sit heavily, put my head in my hands. "Let's not do that again," I whisper.

"What was it exactly that we did?" Linnet asks, her face paler than usual, her eyes angry. "I want to know where you went."

"I would like to know that, too" Hugh says. "Did you feel yourselves disappear? Can you tell what happened?"

I reach for the cup on the table next to the bed, gulping down cool water with trembling hands. I touch my face, wipe my mouth. With every touch, I'm trying to reassure myself that I'm here. Here and now—I hear *that* sound; the water feels *this* way; *this* is how the skin of my face feels; this is the sound of my own breath. I stare at my hand, to make sure it isn't covered in gore.

"I..." I start, stop, swallow. My voice is hoarse, throat raw, even after the water. Orrin walks to the bed, sits next to me with a soft groan. I take his hand. "We Saw...somewhere else this time. Not the battle in the harbor. It was...a courtyard somewhere. A castle? There was fighting all around, Connor and other people in Talarian uniforms against Fanthas forces. Montmoore was there, working a ho...horrible spell. Demons. There were...there will be demons, and a lot of blood, and I Saw...I Saw us," I shudder, forcing the words out.

"Orrin and I were there, trying to fight the demons. I Saw people dying all around us—Linnet was dying, and Orrin and I were chanting and working some kind of spell. But it looked...it looked really desperate. Then I felt Orrin grab me and we came back," I say.

"Demons," Hugh breathes. "Again."

"You faded," Linnet says, her voice flat and accusing. "You faded and disappeared, the both of you! And when you faded back in, I jumped on you." She glares at me, as if I'd planned it all along. She almost always reacts with anger first anymore, to anything unexpected. "And I felt...I felt the spell. A spell, coming back through with you. It was really strong, but I didn't understand it."

I look at Hugh, his face grave. Small lines frame his eyes and mouth that I don't remember seeing before.

"You did disappear. There wasn't time for me to do much, but the amount of magic the two of you were drawing and using—and bringing back—was...disturbing."

"More than usual?" Orrin asks.

"Much more."

"I don't know why it was so different this time. I don't know why we went...into the vision," Orrin says. He sighs, rubs his hand over his eyes. "I don't know why the magic was so strong. But Rhi is right. Montmoore was—will be—using demon magic again. If that's why..."

Hugh swears. "Tell me. What was Montmoore doing?" he asks.

"Did you see the runes he drew?" I ask him.

"Some of them. Montmoore was doubled, too. He was there, in the future, and he was watching from inside another—we were in one magic storm, and he was in another. He watched everything, Saw it. And the Montmoore who was there in the future, he Saw the magic storms. He was working a spell—something with the demons. The runes looked like ours—like how they used to. He was drawing them with blood, the blood of the dying. That's why they were...everywhere." Orrin shivers, and hunches his shoulders.

"I could feel them, the crawl of them along my spine. But the rest—I felt the stones, the air, could smell the blood. I felt the magic around us. But it was at a distance. Nobody but Montmoore seemed to notice us. And at the end, I felt more versions of us—as if we went back again." He shakes his head, sweat still beading on his brow.

I nod, closing my eyes. "I felt that too, at the end. I've never felt anything like it before. Any of it. So much magic." I gulp in a breath. "I don't know if we made it worse." I whisper it, but Linnet hears me.

"What do you mean?" Linnet's voice is sharp.

"What do you mean, Montmoore saw you?" Hugh interrupts. "Saw you how? His vision-self saw you? And another version of him? I don't understand." He brings a chair over. "Explain again. Send it to me," he demands.

I squeeze Orrin's hand. He leans into me a bit more.

"The magic surged when we touched, in the vision. The future us."

"Possible future," Hugh says.

Orrin shudders and looks at Hugh. "I Saw," he gulps, "I Saw you, too. You were fighting. You weren't...winning," he whispers. I realize tears are trickling down his cheek. I reach into my skirt pocket and pull out a handkerchief. When I hand it to him, he smiles weakly and shakes his head, but takes it.

Hugh sits in the chair, rakes his hands through his hair, leans his elbows on his knees. "Do you know when this is supposed to occur?"

We both shake our heads, but "The air was warm," I say. "Heavy and wet, like a summer storm."

Orrin nods. "It smelled like summer, under...everything else." We both hunch a little closer to one another.

"So we are all going to die in a few months, then," Linnet growls, and Hugh sighs and shakes his head.

"Not if we can figure out how to stop it. This spell, Orrin, Rhia—could you sense anything about it?"

Orrin shakes his head. "Just that it was powerful—so much power. There were spells on some of the soldiers and spells in the air outside in the other visions we've had. And the demons were...everywhere. They would need to gather a tremendous amount of magic to cast so many spells. Rhi and I were—we must have drawn on them—on the demons," he chokes out, disgust in his face.

Hugh looks at us both sharply. "Do you think you could use demon power if it were there? Do you know what you were trying to do?" We just shake our heads, shuddering. "Do you know if Montmoore ever saw the spell Gantry used on the two of you? Or if he was duplicating it?"

I shake my head, but Orrin might know. We all look at him, but he doesn't look up. He almost never talks about what happened with Gantry or what Gantry might have told anyone. I can't really blame him.

"Are we going to talk about how you both disappeared?" Linnet demands. "Because I think that's pretty important, magically speaking. And then you had blood on your hands! And feet—it was all over your slippers. And then it went away. Isn't that...new?" Linnet's sarcasm doesn't hide her fear and she does have a point.

"I've never—I don't think that's ever happened to me before," I venture.

Orrin shrugs, still staring at his own feet. I bump his shoulder with mine, but he just grips his hands together tighter.

"Link with me, one of you. Send me your memory of this vision." He reaches out, takes Orrin's hands in his. He looks in my eyes, since Orrin's gaze is steadfastly on the ground. "Rhia, will you?" He lets go of Orrin and takes my hand. I take a deep breath and link to him softly, softly, try to send softly. My magic is surging now, too giddy to be coherent in the sending, but he gets it.

Hugh leans back, lets my hand go, shuddering. "I...I don't know what any of that means." He rubs his face, takes a deep breath. "But we're going to have to find out. That looks like the main courtyard at the palace in Corat. I don't see how that's possible. How would Stephen get Fanthas forces into the very well-guarded palace grounds?"

We just shake our heads, exhausted.

Hugh reaches for our arms again. Orrin stares at the floor, his face tense and eyes red. Hugh lets go of me to pat his hand. "There was a huge power surge as your vision started. And you were linked even more closely than usual. I think I have some ideas that I'd like to send to Cardinal Robere, ask if he's heard of this before. But...the two of you are far stronger—each alone—than any Seer I've ever encountered. I can only imagine what that kind of magic can do.

"The fact that we're here, over the Seely Magan cliffs, definitely affects what you have access to," he says, reminding us of the natural magic that gathers under the castle, that is so easy to use for those who can access it. The reason why this castle was built, and why, last year, Gantry carried out his plans here. "But that doesn't explain what just happened."

Hugh angles his head, trying to look in Orrin's eyes.

"Perhaps by Dorei's grace, and with the cardinal's help, we can figure it out together," he starts, but Orrin stands abruptly and strides out of the room.

Linnet makes a face at Hugh. "Maybe you shouldn't tease him about religion, Your Grace," she mutters.

"I wasn't teasing," he protests.

"You weren't subtle, either," I say. "I'll go talk to him. Are we...are we trying again tomorrow? Because I think I'd rather look into it some more. Maybe we can...wait."

Hugh sighs. "Let's meet here, anyway. We can work out plans then."

I nod, standing up. I grab Linnet and hug her fiercely despite her protest, kissing her forehead. She shoves me away with a "gerroff" and glares. I give a trembling smile and wipe at my face with my sleeve. Orrin still has my handkerchief. I really ought to carry several, anymore.

CHAPTER 4

I don't send to Orrin to find out where he is, but I know where he's likely to go, and I can feel him if I try, anyway. Ever since the fight with Gantry when I pulled magic from the well under the castle to heal Orrin, it feels like our runes speak to one another. Sending mind-to-mind is almost as easy as thinking. But when he's upset like this I try not to push—it makes him feel trapped. After the way he was tortured by Bishop Gantry, I can't blame him. He doesn't like to talk about it, and I can't blame him for that, either.

I know he has good reasons. But we're the only two who can understand this feeling, and sometimes I wish we could talk about it more. It feels lonely inside this power, even though it keeps trying to listen to everyone's thoughts. Including each other's.

Orrin stands outside on the west barbican, staring out to sea. If he hadn't come here, I'd have found him in the library. He doesn't like the tower passage anymore, with the memories of Gantry attacking us there. Attacking him. I know he went through even worse torture than I did, so I keep my mind very firmly inside its boundaries as I walk to stand next to him. He looks over at me, then back out to sea.

"Hugh doesn't mean to hurt you," I say to start, but I'm not sure I should be apologizing for Hugh. Surely he can do that himself. "But it was an asinine thing to say. Linnet made sure he knows it."

Orrin shrugs, but the corner of his mouth turns up a little. The evening light turns his face a luminous reddish-brown. It's still chilly enough that I wish I'd brought my cloak. We stare out to sea together for a while.

"He liked birds," he says, startling me. He's been quiet for so long, our minds blocked from one another for privacy.

"Who liked birds?"

"G-, the bishop. He liked birds." I press my lips together and nod silently. What can I say, that isn't "why are you thinking about him?" I know why. Of all the things between us, I most definitely know that.

"He used to watch them from here." Orrin points up at a hawk floating high over the cliffs. "He liked hawks best of all, but he knew every kind. He could make bird calls that were astonishingly accurate.

"I used to think—at first, when I was first assigned to him—that he couldn't be all bad, someone who loved birds so much." He shakes his head, tears barely grazing his cheeks as they drop onto the wall, his knuckles pale where he grips the stone. "He would stop and watch hawks in flight and say 'Look at that magnificent crea-ture. Only a truly magnificent deity could create such animals.' And I thought—surely I can learn to under-stand him."

I start to reach out to him, but I pull my hand back as his shoulders hunch.

"But I never did. Even after...with all the time I spent in his demon-addled mind, and I saw what he wanted and why, and how—I never understood him. I did try. I thought I could convince him. To stop. To renounce. But I couldn't. I couldn't do anything. And now—Hugh wants too much. He wants me to understand Montmoore, and Stephen, and find out how their minds work and what they plan. He wants me to use my faith–" Orrin spits the word, his mouth screwing up into disgust, his repudiation of everything about the word clear from his expression, the hard lump of rage I can feel through our barriers.

"Orrin," I start, but not sure what else to say, I just cover his hand with mine. I let my heart show my love and acceptance, but I won't push it on him. We already had that fight.

"I have no faith. There is no deity, no bright Lord of Stars. There is nothing but the demons and the darkness."

I do not mention my brother Keenan—his first love, an acolyte, murdered along with most of my family. I do not mention Keenan's calling, or Orrin's own call to be an acolyte years ago. I do not mention Cardinal Robere, or his letters. We've had that fight, too. And I don't want to fight about faith. I don't know what I believe, either.

"Have you heard from your family?" I ask instead, but he is not in the mood to be comforted.

"They keep thanking Dorei and the Star Lord for miracles. I am not a miracle," he spits.

"You are my friend, though. And I'm glad you're here."

He breathes a sigh, presses his lips together. "I'm glad you're here, too." He pulls his hand from mine. "I'm not a good friend."

"Neither am I." We smile at each other.

"I'm not giving you this handkerchief back. You owe me at least ten."

I kick him lightly with the side of my foot. "Fine. But I'm keeping that pretty embroidered one. You weren't taking proper care of it, anyway."

"You just want it because it was Connor's, you big fake."

I blush, stick my tongue out. He isn't wrong, but I don't want to talk about Connor, either. Especially not after that vision. I look back at the water, the sinking sun.

"Has he written?"

"Not for a while. But he's rather busy. I understand."

"Have you written to him?

"I don't know what to say."

Orrin rolls his eyes. "Well, maybe he's waiting to hear from you. Write him a note. You don't have to declare undying love like some kind of poet, just to say hello."

I think of him fighting, bleeding, his face a rictus of fury in the vision, shudder. I don't know if I feel undying love, but I desperately want the battle to turn out differently than in our vision, for a lot of reasons.

"You'll never know what he's thinking if you don't ask," Orrin says. "You haven't even seen him in months."

"He has his orders. He hasn't been able to come to Haverston."

"And the king doesn't want either of us anywhere near Corat." Orrin's mouth twists. "We're a miraculous political embarrassment, you and I. Distrusted in two countries, and wanted as pawns in a third. Perhaps we should take to sea. Become pirates."

"You don't know the first thing about being a pirate, Orrin. Have you ever even sailed?"

"My family came to this country from the Southern Empire. We sailed here, all the Beaudreaus, in three ships. Weeks of travel."

"A century before you were born. You've never been on more than a rowboat."

"Not the point."

"Well, I'm unlikely to embark on a career in piracy that has so little chance of succeeding. Besides, Linnet would make a better pirate than either of us."

"So we'll take her along. She can be the captain."

I roll my eyes and laugh. "Save me from such a fate as piracy under Linnet." But at least he's trying to laugh, bitter as it is.

I feel some bitterness, myself.

Orrin sighs and shudders, rubs his arms. "I'm heading inside for dinner," he says. "Don't stay out here too long. It's cold."

I stare out over the barbican wall as he walks away, sunset painting the water crimson and gold. The ache of magic stirs still in my bones, leaking up at me from the power well. I wonder if I will ever learn to control it—if I'll ever get used to it. The sweet fresh breeze flutters my hair, smelling of brine and growing things.

The breathing ocean disguises the sound of footsteps on flagstones, and for some reason I don't notice their emotions or thoughts until they are almost on me—two men, full of fear and determination, anticipation, and disgust. I turn sharply, but too late.

One man clamps a big, gloved hand over my mouth

from behind, lifting me off my feet, his other arm tight around my middle. The second man in a mask yanks my hands out in front of me, wrestles something onto my wrists as I thrash, kick to get away. A sharp click, and a burning pain flares up my arms, into my blood. My angry yells turn to harsh screams, muffled by the hand on my face. He drags me toward the stairs that lead to the castle harbor.

I struggle past the pain that wants me to curl into a ball. I work my mouth wider to bite the man holding me, but he grinds my lips down against my teeth. Kicking back, I connect with a leg, and I smash my head back into my abductor's chin. He growls a curse in my ear, and the other man grabs my legs to hoist me up.

By now I've reached past the pain to the magic. Whatever is on my wrists drains it, but I can draw more. The burning in my arms makes it hard. They might have planned to catch a witch with this spell, but these men are ill-prepared for me. I have access to a lot more power than they've bargained for.

They start down the stairs as I flail and try to kick. I strain past the spell from the manacles, the pain, yank as much power as I can, drawing it in over my own shuddering breath in my lungs, my writhing. I pull power from everywhere, from every link I can find. My skin flushes hot—hotter—I am a furnace, and the men drop me as the manacles on my wrists flare red-hot.

I hear their footsteps running away this time as I tumble to the stairs, gasping, crawling up past the top step to lie on my back, off my bound wrists.

The spell tries to eat my magic, but I'm too much for it. The manacles burn hotter, burn my skin as my skin burns them back, the runes flaring to anger at being thwarted. I hear myself shouting.

Through the hair plastered over my sweaty face, I look up in the dusk at the Haverston guards appearing around me, unwilling to approach too closely while I'm burning with magic.

"Got to get them off," I wheeze. The stone beneath me starts to heat and steam, power pouring off me, overloading the spell on the manacles.

"Rhia! Shut it down!" Hugh shouts, his magic scrabbling at mine, try to find a way in. I feel Orrin in my mind—and the binding spell, too. I yank on my wrists, trying to pull them apart. Hugh slides to his knees in front of me reaching for the manacles but winces away.

"Get back," I gasp. I can feel a pulse building—the manacles warp and buckle. The spell can't hold. Hugh backs away and I roll to face the wall.

The manacles explode with a sharp clang and crack, spraying the wall with hot metal shards, steaming in the spring air. I turn my face to the ground as the pieces fly.

So much shouting everywhere as I try to cool the magic in my blood, the air, the angry broken spell, and let it drain back into the power well. It grumbles and shimmies down my runes, thwarted of purpose, and I can't shake the feeling it is alive somehow.

I've been feeling that way for a while now, and I don't know why.

"Rhia!" Voices out loud, voices in my head. Something is wrong with Linnet. I can feel it, deep in my runes. Got to turn over. I flop toward the people gathering, careful of my burned wrists.

"Got your breath back yet, girl?" Captain Nerishe kneels over me. "Is that the last of the fireworks?"

"I think so, yes," I pant.

"Are you hurt?"

"I—don't know."

"Can you stand?" Her brown eyes are kind but assessing under her helmet.

"Maybe."

She gingerly puts her arm around me to help me up. "Easy, now. That magic looked nasty to me." She looks over to Hugh. "Sent four guards after the villains, Your Grace. But it looks to me like they had an exit planned."

"Have the guards report directly to me when they return, Captain."

"Yes, Your Grace."

She helps me to stand, a strong arm and a comforting presence. She makes sure I'm steady before she lets me stand on my own, Hugh hovering in front of us.

"Where is Linnet?" I ask, trying to send to him, but everything hurts.

Hugh grimaces. "Whatever spell they used on you ended up affecting her. She's all right," he assures me as I start to try to go to her, his arm and Nerishe's holding me still. "She's fine. Orrin is with her. You aren't able to hear what he's sending?"

I feel in my head for Orrin, and there he is—faint, words buzzing at me from far away, and it hurts. The spell hurt me on the inside, too. I wince away from the sending, shut down my barriers. Hugh watches me.

"Don't try any sending right now. We'll need to check you out, first. But Orrin is with Linnet, and they're both all right. They were together. There were men coming for him, too, but they hit just after yours, and he was calling for help for Linnet. It's lucky I was close—I got there in time to run the kidnappers off. We have people searching for them now.

"Speaking of guards," he says, "where are the guards who were supposed to be at the harbor entrance, Captain?" His voice has suddenly gone ducal, and his eyes are colder than usual.

"I will find out, Your Grace," Nerishe says, and nods at the guards nearest her, who salute and march off. "I'll have a report to you as soon as possible. I don't like this timing," she says.

I gather my strength for the short walk into the hall. "I don't either," I grumble.

"No, I don't suppose you would," she smiles gently. Hugh takes my arm to lead me toward the Great Hall. She bows to him and strides away, barking orders.

Hugh has me sit on a bench in the hall, then calls for a servant to send to the Inquisitor's building for a Healer, or further to the hospice or the town fisicus if none are available. I'd rather the fisicus—she knew me as a child and doctored our family. Although that might make it worse; she might hate and fear me as much as everyone else from town does. Maybe I don't want any of them. I wish Julianna was here.

"We have salves and herbs here at the castle, Your Grace. The hospice Healers are busy with wounded soldiers. It's hardly worth the bother," I say, trying to put him off, but he overrules me.

"You need someone to look at your wrists—those burns are nasty. There may be other injuries related to the spell on those...manacles. Don't be foolish." Hugh raises his eyebrows in his stern look.

I glare at the floor. I don't trust any of the Healers

among the kirche brethren. I don't trust anyone in the kirche at all. Not here.

Orrin comes into the hall with Linnet. He doesn't trust those Healers, either.

"Are you all right?" He asks, his arm around Linnet's shoulders.

"I'm fine," I say, and Hugh snorts. "I'm a little bruised and burned, but mostly fine," I amend. "Linnet, are you all right? What happened?"

She looks angry and upset. "I don't know what happened," she mutters. "I'm all right now."

Orrin rubs her shoulder and turns to Hugh. "I'll go see if there's something for burns in the herbarium," he says, and hurries off.

"What happened, Linnet? Were you hurt?"

"I dunno," she says, looking away from me. "I just, I felt it all, that's all."

"What did you feel?" I ask Linnet.

She glowers at me. "Pain. I felt you, I felt pain, I felt the magic draining away. You were draining me, too." She shrugs as though she's trying to brush it off. "I couldn't shut the link down."

Hugh frowns at us both. "I thought you had. We worked on that. Keeping that link open all the time is dangerous for you both."

"I did! I thought I did. I can barely form a candle flame now, so I thought it was closed." She folds her arms, her chin out. "It's not my fault."

When Linnet pulls enough power from me, she can create fire, we learned last year at a dramatic moment. Linnet with that kind of power terrified all of us enough that we've worked hard to keep her magic separate; keeping her to her own natural talents to send to minds and some small ability to move objects. I thought the link was closed, too—I don't want to hurt her, or for her to hurt anyone else.

"I didn't mean to—I was just trying to get away. I didn't know I pulled power from you," I say, but I probably wouldn't have noticed.

"Well, I didn't ask for you to do that. I tried to stop it! This isn't my fault!"

"No one is blaming you, Linnet." Hugh says.

"It feels like you are," she grumbles.

"I just want to know how to fix it," Hugh soothes. "Can you feel the link now? Either of you?"

"All I feel is a cracking pain all inside my head and body," she snarls. "Aren't you supposed to be some scary mind reader? Why didn't you know they were coming?"

I resist the urge to kick her. "You know it doesn't work like that," I mutter.

"Some Seer you are."

"Enough." Hugh sighs, crossing his arms. "You all are to keep a guard detail with you at all times you're not in a secured area, until I can figure out a more permanent solution."

"What defines a secured area?"

"What about Orrin?"

"Orrin, too. Orrin especially."

"Why me, especially," Orrin asks as he walks up behind Hugh.

Hugh flinches a little but smiles as charmingly as only he can. "Because I'm afraid they'll try harder to get you, now. Because they might think you need extra containing, as a man. Because I..." he stops talking and clears his throat, smile fading. "I think it's wise, that's all."

"I'm not sure dragging guards around all day even inside the castle is a good solution," Orrin says mildly.

"Well, I do," Hugh snaps. "Just...indulge me."

"There has to be a better way," I say.

"Then tell me what it is, and I'll entertain the idea," Hugh says, his temper still prickly. "But otherwise, this is my order. You are all to have bodyguards from now on, until I decide otherwise."

We all blink at him. "Do you have enough guards for that?" I venture.

"I'll make sure we do," he says darkly.

"But...if you hire people you don't trust, or if we don't know who the spies are, doesn't that make all of the guards a potential threat, too?" Linnet asks. "That spy was a guard, wasn't she?"

Hugh glowers at her.

"I'm just asking," she says, glowering back. "You're the one who is paranoid."

"My own people were just attacked in my castle! Again! Of course I'm paranoid!" he shouts. Everyone bustling through the hall stops to look at him. He runs his hands through his hair and groans.

"Fine! Fine—I will choose your bodyguards for specific purposes, and you're to have a guard detail if you leave this castle at all—which I wish you would not do right now. And I'm scrutinizing the guard, yes, of course I will be doing that. I have some scrying techniques I can try, as well. But you are all under orders to stick together as much as possible and guard each other's backs."

I nod and Orrin puts his hand on my shoulder. "Of course, Your Grace. We always do."

Hugh mutters about upstart children as he stalks

away. But I know we'll talk about this again. And I still must suffer through an exam with an untrustworthy Healer. Which reminds me.

"Orrin, a Healer's coming. Probably from the kirche. If you want to avoid them."

His mouth folds in grim lines. "Ah." He glares at everyone while we wait. It's simply a lovely day.

CHAPTER 5

The sun has long set, and the glowsand lamps in my room burnish the walls with greenish gold. I'm tired, and the lamplight hurts my eyes. I sit wincing against my headboard, waiting for the Healer's examination to be over.

The Healer is neither as competent nor powerful as Princess Julianna. He has a nervous grimace of a smile, a quiet voice, and seems harmless enough. Hugh's made it clear that we're not to show off our power if we can help it, so although I would very much like to I don't help him help me as he blunders around with his magic. But his efforts are clumsy, and painful, and I find I miss her more than usual.

He hovers over me making tisking noises, trying not to stare at the scars that wind along my arms, my sleeves pushed up to show the new burn marks. He is tallish and roundish and owlish, a priest wearing a healing blue surplice over his robes.

Orrin glared at him as he walked in the room. Orrin doesn't want anything to do with him but decided he didn't want to leave me alone with him, either. He stands, a brooding presence beside me, making the priest nervous. Perhaps that's why he's so clumsy.

"Ha...have you always had trouble with sendings?" he asks, his voice quavering.

"No," I answer, trying to hedge what he might not know against getting proper healing. "Not since I first got these." I indicate my scars. As if he hadn't noticed them.

"Yes, yes, of course, but o...otherwise you haven't been having trouble? And now it seems to be coming back to you?"

I sigh, send to Orrin *Can you hear this?* Which hurts like pushing on a bruise.

With no trouble at all, he answers. *And if he hurts you again I will punch him in the face.*

I clear my throat. "Yes, it seems to be coming back," I answer.

"Well then. It doesn't seem as though the spell has hurt your magic, uh, from what I can tell, um, yo...lady, er, Miss Owen. And the burns are superficial, enough so that they should heal on their own." He glances up at Orrin, and blanches a little. "I mean, with some ointment, of course! To protect the skin! You seem, um, otherwise fine," he stammers. "I don't understand your, er, your magic ru...that is, your markings, er, the uh..."

"Yes, I realize that," I murmur. "It's fine. No one does."

It doesn't seem to reassure him. "Well, then, I will have an ointment sent over right away, and that should help with the pain of the burns and keep away infection." He stands and brushes at his robes, keeping his head down and eyes away from both of us. "If there's nothing else..."

"There is something else," Hugh says, leaning in the open doorway. "Rhiannon, I see you're finished with him, yes?" I nod. "Good. Father, follow me, please. I have something for your superior. Rhiannon, take some time to rest. I will see you later."

"Yes, rest is a...good idea," the priest murmurs, happy to escape Orrin's glares.

"I don't think you were very helpful, Orrin," I say as the door closes behind them. "It might have been better if you'd avoided him after all."

"We need to be careful of strangers now," he says in response. I look up at him, but he's turned to stare out the window. "We have to make plans. Use our heads."

"I don't see how using my head would have stopped any of this from happening," I mutter.

He shrugs. "It happened, and now we know to be on the lookout for it. So now we use our heads. We should use our magic with more precision—keep a closer look out for spies."

"That doesn't always work," I protest. "I didn't notice them coming—they had strong barriers and kept quiet until they were right there. We can't even choose what visions we have, or when. The visions choose us."

"But we can try," he insists, turning to me. "We can practice more, learn ways to make it work. We have to try harder to protect ourselves."

I wince as he sits down beside me on the bed, jostling my sore head. "I thought that's what we've been doing." He sighs, and I put up a hand. "All right, we'll try harder. But...not right now, all right? I don't feel very heroic tonight, and the only thing I want to do is sleep."

He smiles, leans forward to kiss my forehead. "We'll

start on it after you've recovered. I know you're hurting. That priest was terrible. He made everything worse."

I roll my eyes. "You made him nervous."

"He should be nervous. He should know better than to get anywhere close to me. He knew what Gantry was doing and he didn't stop him."

My stomach lurches at Gantry's name. "He—how do you know he knew?" I ask.

"I remember him," he mutters. "I remember him staring at me, at Gantry, and shuddering away, like I was some kind of monster. He was terrified of Gantry, but he never did anything to stop him."

"I'm sorry." I take Orrin's hand, grip it hard. I am so much more than sorry. I wish I could take everything back, take away our pain and this impossible power and go back to a year ago—before a year ago. Before we were carved into magic tools for a power-hungry bishop. "I'm so sorry."

His smile turns brittle, and he squeezes my hand and stands up. "We both are. Look what happened to us— that man's terror was justified. But my opinion of him doesn't change. He's a terrible priest and a worse Healer, and I hope I never see his living face again."

He turns and walks out the door, closing it quietly behind him. I bite my lip, taste salt, and wipe my face. Weeping again. I sigh and dig in my bedside table for a handkerchief. It would be nice to not have so many reasons to weep.

CHAPTER 6

The insistent pounding of my head rouses me into reluctant lethargy. The light through my window says morning, but I'm irritated at the thought of it.

Nightmares and pain kept me from real rest, and when I try to sit up, I let out a yelp of pain and fall back. I'm nauseated and exhausted, but I have to pee. My muscles shriek in protest, and I would, too, if only the sound wouldn't hurt my head.

I roll to the side of the bed and let the weight of my legs pull my feet to the floor. I lie sideways, panting, with my face in the covers, trying to make myself finish the movement until Linnet opens the door.

She turns her head sideways and looks at me. "Were you trying to go somewhere? Because you didn't make it."

"Thanks ever so," I mumble over my headache. "You're too kind."

"Well, just in case, because you might have thought you made it."

"Shut up and help me," I growl.

She sets the tray she's carrying on the table and walks to my side. "So you're hurt more than you let on yesterday. I'm sooo surprised." She pulls me upright to sit, and I bite back a yelp. My arms and back ache like they've been bludgeoned, and the burns on my skin itch and sting. The channels of magic along my skin, along my bones, feel scorched and swollen, and my eyes hurt. I glare out of them at my sister. She glares back. "Maybe if you'd let that Healer do his job..."

"He wasn't any good at it." To my exasperation, tears prick my eyes. "Just let me alone. I want to sleep."

"Do you need to pee?" I groan in response, and Linnet shakes her head. "So why don't I help you up and you can have a quick wash, eat something, then go back to sleep after. Don't be pig-headed. Let me help you."

I let her muscle me across the hall to the bathing chamber in Julianna's unused rooms, and she wrestles me back when I'm done.

"You're heavy," she grumbles. I'd take a swipe at her, but I'm too tired.

"Shut up and go away," I mutter, but I can't be too angry. She's spent a lot of time taking care of me this last year. I only wish I didn't keep needing it.

"Ah, you're back," Hugh says, striding into the room. "Good, I have questions for you. What is it? You don't look well. Are you worse? Is it the spell?" He takes over from Linnet and helps me into bed.

"Sore, headache, burns," I list in a surly voice.

"Some backlash from too much magic, I'd wager," he says with a sympathetic wince. "But you haven't noticed anything stranger happening with your magic since?

Nothing that would suggest you're more deeply injured?"

I shrug, shake my head. I'm not sure I could tell right now, but I don't feel as terrible as I have in the past, so I'm probably all right.

Hugh pats my shoulder as he pulls the covers back up to tuck me in. "That Healer wasn't very good, was he? He didn't do nearly as much for you as he should have. Can Orrin help you? I know he doesn't have the same abilities you learned helping Julianna, but maybe you could guide him."

"I think I'll just have to heal on my own. I'll try not to have any visions for a bit," I say, exhausted just being near him.

"Perhaps Orrin can send to the cardinal about this," Hugh says softly, but I shake my head.

"Don't ask him to do that, Your Grace," I warn.

"Don't ask who to do what?" Orrin asks, as he steps into the room.

"Nothing," Linnet snaps. "We weren't talking about you." She glares at Hugh. Hugh presses his lips together in annoyance but shrugs nonchalantly when Orrin glances at him.

"It's nothing, as Linnet says."

Orrin looks us all over warily. "And how are you feeling?" he finally asks me.

"Terrible," I grumble.

"I knew it," he snaps. "That damn priest."

"Or, just throwing this out there, maybe it was the people who tried to kidnap us," I snap back. "It might be their fault."

"He still did a terrible job helping you. He's awful as a Healer. Priests always are," he mutters darkly.

I exchange a look with Hugh, and he sighs a little in defeat.

"I will heal on my own," I announce, although my headache is not being made better by everyone and their moods.

Linnet jostles the tray she brought earlier into my lap. "Have tea. It's probably cold now."

"Oh good, you've already brought her tea." Duchess Marguerite announces herself from the doorway, and I'm beginning to wonder why they ever keep it closed. "I was going to have some sent up for you. Will you need some more? And more importantly, how are you this morning, my dear? I bet you still feel awful, poor thing. Did cook use my headache tea?"

The duchess—Marguerite—approaches my crowded bedside, glancing at the tea Linnet brought. "Good, that should help. And I've the salve for burns. Good morning, everyone," she says, looking around pleasantly.

"Good morning, Your Grace," Linnet, Orrin, and I chorus.

"Good morning, Mother."

"Don't tire Rhiannon out, dear. She needs rest. You'll just have to question her later."

"Mother," Hugh groans.

"For pity's sake, Hugh, it's not like she's leaving here tomorrow," she says in an exasperated tone. "Speaking of going places, I think it's high time King Peter put an oar in, don't you? Orrin and Rhiannon need to go to Corat. The palace can protect them better than we can here."

"We don't know that the palace can protect them from Stephen, Mother. We don't even know how he got people in here."

"So you think Stephen is behind it," she says.

"Of course it was Stephen. Who else?" Hugh snaps.

"Do not use that tone with me, Hugh Reginald Theroux. I am aware of the situation. And you are aware that the news of these two and their abilities has gotten about to more than just His Majesty and Stephen. There are factions within court who might want a closer look at our magicians. Queen Esther and Empress Heroha have information and likely interest, as well."

I shudder at the idea of Queen Esther of Fanthas getting anywhere near us. I don't know what Archbishop Montmoore told her, but I imagine she'd use us as mercilessly as he would. Empress Heroha of Indranah might be just as terrifying—she's an empress. But the Indrani empire are supposedly Talarian allies, so I worry what the duchess is implying. Asa and the other Indrani agents who were here last fall knew about us. What would the empress gain by kidnapping us?

Hugh sighs. "Queen Esther is working with Stephen, and leaves all of the dirty work to him. And Empress Heroha would...approach us differently." Marguerite just looks at him. "All right, yes, someone else could have tried. Although I don't think this is the Butcher's style, either."

She raises her eyebrow, waiting.

"I apologize for my tone," he says, closing his eyes.

She nods, then turns to me. "What do you think, my dear? And Orrin—do you have any feeling about who was behind it?"

"It was the ex-duke," he says flatly. He turns from the window and looks at me. I don't know what he wants me to do about it.

"It seems like him," I temporize. Orrin shakes his head. "Well, what do you want? Without proof, we can only guess. Stephen makes the most sense. Or Mont-moore. No visions came to me to tell me otherwise, I can tell you that." Everyone raises their brows, I guess at my own snappish tone. "One would have been welcome, is all I'm saying," I mutter and fold my arms.

"What do you propose to do, then?" Duchess Marguerite asks us all. I can tell by how she asks it that she thinks there's a right answer and a wrong answer.

"Your Grace, I am just a humble citizen of Talaria. I cannot propose military action," Orrin says.

"Don't be sarcastic, dear. What do you think we, or the king, or anyone, should do?" Marguerite opens her hands and looks at both Orrin and me.

"About Stephen? Or about the kidnapping?" I ask.

"About any of it. About the two of you, for one thing."

"I would prefer the king not express any particular interest in the two of us," Orrin says.

Hugh sighs. "It's too late for that. I have already sent a bird to inform the king. And Connor as well, of course. He's been expecting an attack—we all have. I just thought we had Haverston more buttoned up than we apparently do." He rubs his hand across his forehead.

"How did they get away?" Orrin asks.

"How did they get in?" I ask.

"It seems they did both the same way—the harbor. There are gates and guards at the barbican stairs, of course." Hugh paused, and the weariness in his voice matched that in his eyes. "They shouldn't have been able to get in. But there are spies and then there are spies.

"At least one of Stephen's—or whomever's—is very good. Good enough to be on the inside, good enough to know when the guards move and where, and then to lie in wait for you both. They must have been tracking your movements, and when you were each alone they took the opportunity."

"What do you mean, tracking our movements?"

"Spies, Rhia. They watched, and waited, and figured out the best time to take you. We found a summoning stone, which allowed them minor communication. They likely have someone who can do sendings, and it stands to reason they must have had spells to keep them hidden as well.

"Stephen is not a stupid man, and he won't have hired incompetent people. He likely has other spies in place even now. If not in the castle, then nearby. I don't doubt there will be other attempts."

Fear floods through me. "Then—they always know where we are?"

"As much as anyone in this castle. They've probably been watching for a while. I don't know why they chose this moment to attack."

"There must be a reason, though," Marguerite says.

"There is always a reason," Hugh mutters.

"I'm well aware of that," she says. "But all these factors only strengthen the need for Rhiannon and Orrin go to Corat."

"I'm not sure King Peter is prepared..."

"Well, he's going to have to get over that. You leave him to me." She turns to Orrin and me. "Peter needs to meet you, and he needs to give you better protection. He has plenty of guards in the castle and a better network to watch over you both than we have here in Haverston."

"Corat is also a larger city, with more people," Hugh says, "which makes it harder to protect them. And speaking of the Butcher, this would put them right in her and her brother's grasp. I don't see how it's any safer than here."

"Stephen will only try again. You already know he has spies in place, and don't know who or how. And having these two in the hands of Stephen and Richard Montmoore can only bring harm, both to Talaria and to their own selves."

Marguerite pauses briefly, and Hugh tries to get a word in. But she waves him off and continues with even more passion. "Also, I don't know what those manacles were for, or how they came to be. I may not be a magician or a Healer like my children, but I know precisely how much a man like Stephen must want the magic of the kind Rhiannon and Orrin have. He must not get anywhere near them!" Marguerite argues.

Hugh's mouth closes, and I can almost hear his teeth grinding. He says nothing, though, and his mother nods.

"We cannot let them be harmed, Hugh. The king needs to see them as people, and right now he's thinking of them as either assets to be exploited or a strategy to deploy. He's tried to divert attention from them, but it obviously isn't working. I cannot in good conscience keep them here if they're not safe from Fanthas or Stephen's machinations. And to your other point, Yvonne Boucher is dangerous, yes, but she is loyal to the king. She's not the worst threat in this situation. I am convinced they will be safer in Corat than Haverston, and you know it too."

"Are we safe anywhere?", says Orrin. "As far as the kirche is concerned, we are abominations. As far as anyone who knows about it is concerned!" Orrin tosses the book in his hand to the table, leans back against the wall, a puckered line between his brows. "I'm not saying

I won't go to Corat. I'm saying I don't trust that we'll be any safer there."

I rub my eyes, exhaustion pulling at me. I am so tired of worrying about everything. "Who is this Butcher? Boucher?" I ask.

"Marchioness Boucher is the king's spymaster. She is..." Marguerite pauses, mouth pursing, "not a kind person. She already knows all about you. But you should avoid her as much as possible."

"Why would she wish us harm?" I ask.

"Oh, it won't be personal. But you represent a significant danger to the crown, which she considers hers to protect. Her job is to find threats and eliminate them, and she is very good at her job," she says grimly. "And then there's the fact that she doesn't care for me or my family. Or Connor, for that matter. She has specific grudges against all of us, and she nurses them as if her life depended on it. She might even attempt to harm you to do injury to myself or Connor. She would definitely harm you if she thinks it would serve the king.

"Try not to be alone with her while you're there." She raises her eyebrows and stares me in the eyes. "It will be difficult. Try anyway."

"Mother, I'm still not certain we should send them to Corat right now. They'll be right under Boucher's nose," Hugh points out.

"She's not any less dangerous to them while they're here, and you know it. If they're in Corat King Peter will be forced to see them as people, rather than pawns."

"There are other considerations –"

"Yes, yes, you told me about the visions. But those are all just possibilities, aren't they?" Marguerite asks.

"Strong possibilities," Hugh says.

"Visions that Orrin and Rhiannon had while here, in Haverston. And in those visions, you said Stephen and Richard Montmoore seemed to have taken them captive. Well, someone *has* tried to take them captive while they were here in Haverston. It's just as likely staying here will create the situation as sending them away.

"That's how visions work, Hugh. Don't be stubborn. Going to Corat is no more likely to cause a catastrophe than anything else. The smart thing to do is to get them to King Peter. Make him see their value, and their humanity. Make him pay attention."

"Mother –"

"Look at this child!" Marguerite insists, gesturing to me. "Can you honestly tell me that she's been safe here? Do you have any idea what was done to her by those spies? Who is going to help her here?"

I must look pretty pathetic. I do feel rather gray. I'm holding my head, fighting tears. Everyone stares at me.

"We do need to consult with someone about her injuries, and the visions," Hugh says gravely. "It would help if I could discuss what happened with Cardinal Robere."

I wince, and Linnet winces more. Orrin turns his glare onto Hugh. "Then consult him," he says very quietly.

"I sent a bird already. What I meant to say—it would be wise to discuss this more immediately."

"There are other magicians in the world, Your Grace. And there are many ways to consult with all of them," Orrin snaps. "You even know some of those magicians and how to contact them. Asa Siradhi was very helpful when she was here last year."

"Yes, she was," Hugh snaps back. "And she reported everything she saw and did to the Empress and her superiors, and a whole host of people you know nothing about now know far too much about you. You don't know even half of the players in all of the many games that are being played, Orrin Beaudreau. Cardinal Robere may not be your favorite person, and you might not trust him, but he's the safest option we have. And I need to speak with him urgently!"

"Your head is still inviolable—no one dares invade it," Orrin hisses. "I have reasons to keep all of the kirche out of mine."

"Please," I rasp, flinching, my head pounding from all of this noise and tension. "Please," I whisper when everyone turns to me. "Can we...can you...not do this right now? Not right here? I just...I need you not to shout."

Orrin clenches his fists, takes a breath. "I'm sorry, Rhi," he whispers.

"Me too," Hugh says. He rubs a fond hand over my arm. "I will try not to let worry overcome good sense." He smiles wanly. Marguerite rolls her eyes a little.

"I'll do it. For Rhi. For a way to help her. I'll...contact the Cardinal. Send to him," Orrin says, his voice wavering.

"Ah...why don't we talk more outside," Hugh says. "Maybe we can come up with a way you won't have to."

Marguerite sighs and takes each of them by the arm. "Then the two of you go." She escorts them to the door. When she's shoved both of them out, she turns back.

"My dear, I do want you to think about all of this— but when you're better. You need to rest and recover. You are very strong, but even strong young women need help and time to heal." She crosses to my side and takes my hand in hers.

"When I convince my stubborn son that I'm right, you will travel to Corat, and maybe a change in location will lift some of this burden from your shoulders." She smirks a little. "And Connor is there, of course," she says in a teasing tone. "I'd trust that young man with any life. Especially yours."

I try not to either blush or grimace. "I will think about it, Your Grace."

She cups my face, smiling gently. "You needn't hide your feelings from me. I don't judge you for having them." She smooths my wild tangle of hair back and kisses my forehead, which makes me teary again. "I'll speak more with you later. For now, have some breakfast and then have a nap."

I watch her leave, blinking. I try to move the tray off my lap so I can lie down.

"You're not eating," Linnet says, adjusting the tray back in my lap. "It's all cold now, probably. At least have the bread."

"Did you eat?" I ask.

"I will."

I sigh at her and pick up the bread, trying to get a more critical look at her. "Did you eat yesterday?" She just rolls her eyes. "Little bird..." I start, and she bristles, folding her arms.

"You're not Mum," she snaps.

"And you're not an actual bird, but you still have to eat food," I snap back.

Linnet huffs at me. "I will! I am! Stop nagging!"

"If I don't nag, you don't eat."

She rolls her eyes again. "Don't be so dramatic. I eat plenty."

"I worry about you, Linnet. That's all." I offer her my bread.

"That's yours. Don't worry about me. I'm not the one getting kidnapped and disappearing and everything. I'm just fine."

"I'm not—Linnet, I'm not disappearing."

She glowers, and I eat the bread. When I'm done, and I drink the lukewarm, bitter tea, she takes the tray and leaves the room without speaking again.

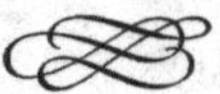

CHAPTER 7

It's the one-year anniversary of my family's death. Murder. Hanging.

It's a beautiful spring day, sunny and pleasant, with chirping birds and buzzing insects, flowers everywhere. The kind of spring day that makes one rejoice in new leaves.

Linnet, Orrin, and I are huddled up in Orrin's room, sitting on the floor under the windows, leaning on each other. I'd shut the window against the birdsong, but that would mean leaving our pile. None of us has said anything, either aloud or through a sending, for some time.

There's a tap on the door, then it opens, even though we stay silent.

"Hello, you three," Hugh says quietly as his head pokes in.

"That wasn't a real knock," I say creakily. He smiles a little.

"How about some lunch?" he asks. Kindly, but it scrapes along my nerves anyway. We all stare at him in silence. "How about a picnic?" We stare some more, Linnet somewhat glaring. "Not outside, obviously— that's a terrible idea. But right here—on the floor. A floor picnic is just a grand idea." He comes all the way in, bearing a large basket and blankets. "I brought something to sit on. And enough food to tempt a sea dragon, so I hope you're all hungry."

Orrin stirs on Linnet's other side. "I'm not sure pirate ships and squid were on anyone's dietary agenda for today," he says drily. Hugh grins beatifically at him, as though offered praise.

"Perhaps not, but would you like some scones? I know you're fond of them. Oh, and clotted cream, of course." He spreads one of the blankets out and sits down opposite us, just next to the bed. "I have some nice ham in here as well, always interesting to dragons and non-dragons alike—if they like ham. And fresh bread, cheese, cider, and some lovely early berries. Small but so sweet." He smiles again, tentatively this time. "I thought, if you wanted, you all could tell me some stories. About —about whatever you like. Happy times, childhood. If you think it might help."

Linnet glares her usual glare. Orrin sighs and picks out one of the scones Hugh pulls from the basket. I don't really feel like eating. My mouth feels glued shut and my stomach is a fist. Hugh rummages through the basket again and comes out with bread and cheese and ham and puts them on a serviette; I take some ham and try to nibble.

"I used to have picnics like this with Juli and Connor and Alex, when we were younger," Hugh says. "We'd nick food from the palace kitchens and hide up in our rooms. Alex was always in trouble with his tutors or someone, so we were always smuggling him food when he wasn't supposed to have any supper. He was always particularly fond of fresh bread." He smiles, reaching in to help himself.

For a little while, there's only the sound of chewing, and the birds outside. Linnet finally takes a scone and holds it, then hands another still-warm one to me.

"Mum loved scones," she blurts, staring at the scone. "And cream. She used to say that cream was one of life's pleasures, and that I was to enjoy pure pleasures with my whole heart, to accept their blessing."

Hugh dollops clotted cream on a plate and hands it to her. Tears drip down her face, off her nose, and he hands her a serviette, too.

"I remember Da teasing Mum over the scones and cream," I say suddenly, caught by a memory of his mischievous grin and him tickling her as he walked past, a quick kiss to her hair. "He used to say a scone a day kept age at bay—it must, because she was still a spring chicken. He'd always kiss her before he went off to weave or to the guildhall. Every time. And he'd steal some cream." I wipe at my face.

Hugh watches and listens with wet eyes and a soft, sympathetic mouth. He hands serviettes around and pours us cider.

Orrin stirs a little. "When I first came to the monastery, I was so homesick I could hardly eat. Keenan was so kind—he brought me homemade scones and coaxed me into sharing them. He talked to me about his family, teased me into talking about mine. My mum's scones are better," he says with a wry shrug as he looks over at me. "Butter from our herd is the best that ever was made. Cream, too. Keenan laughed when I told him that, and asked about our farm, the land, my sisters."

He falls silent, looking at the scone. "He was one of the kindest people I ever knew. He never hurt anyone. I miss him so much sometimes."

"I miss him, too. He was the best brother." Linnet just sniffles. I grip her hand a little tighter. All of us are watery.

"He sent to me about you," I say to Orrin. "Just a little. My Sight was pretty weak, so it was just images, short messages, and a joke or two. I didn't understand it then, but when I think of what he sent—he loved you, too. So much."

Orrin wipes his eyes with his hand, takes a deep breath. "He sent me some memories of you, too. Just some little moments—your family laughing and bickering, gathering to talk or eat...it reminded me of home. It used to make me feel a little better when I was down. He helped me with my studies, too. Well, we helped each other. He was always stronger than I was in magic, but he was rubbish when it came to languages. We –"

Orrin cuts off as the buzzing starts, low in my bones, in my head. Linnet yelps and shoves out from between us, rubbing at her elbows like they itch. Hugh reaches out to steady her.

"What? What is it?" he asks, breaking his silence. "Oh, stars above us, I feel it too," he exclaims, helping Linnet scoot further away. Orrin and I push away from each other, try to contain the magic. A vision clamps down on us both.

The monastery, the woods beyond. The grounds near the gardens. A vortex forms in the air, spitting out a large wooden structure. It wavers and crumples.

Soldiers in Fanthas attire appear with it, are crushed as it falls. Bodies, wood, metal, all twisted and wrong.

Linnet yanks me further from Orrin and shoves a scone in my mouth. I choke a little, spit it into my hands, coughing. The vision recedes while I wheeze.

When I look over at Orrin, Hugh has him pulled half into his lap, his arms wrapped tight around his shoulders.

"Monastery," Orrin gasps out.

"Soldiers," I rasp. "Soldiers and weapons—or something, but it's all gone wrong. Now—or very soon." I cough up crumbs.

"Now? Show me," Hugh demands. I let Orrin send him the vision.

"It's coming soon," Orrin says, wincing as he pulls away from Hugh. Hugh winces, too.

"We need to get there," I say and struggle to my knees.

"I'll go, but you all stay here," Hugh commands, standing and striding from the room. I can hear him barking orders as he hurries down the stairs and out the front hall. Mounts, an advance scout, a unit of guards.

"I don't see why we should stay here," Linnet says sourly.

"We're not guards," I shrug, but I want to go, too.

"It's not that far from here—we can walk," Orrin says. "We'd be far enough behind that we could keep out of the way."

Linnet and I look at each other and shrug. "A walk sounds delightful," I say. It's rather a long walk, but at least it's a nice day. And it's something distracting to do.

"The guards are busy," Orrin says. "We don't want to steal anyone away from an important duty just to trail us. It should be perfectly safe." I nod. We don't tell anyone we're leaving, instead surreptitiously walking out in the hubbub of guards departing and everyone else running around to other duties. No one seems to notice.

The road away from the castle winds along the cliff for a bit before descending toward either town or away from it. I haven't been to town often recently. Nor do I walk much of anywhere anymore, outside of castle grounds or the beach under the battlements when the tide is low. I don't want to see anyone from town. After the guild settled money on us for my family, they made it quite clear that we would not be welcomed back. It isn't an experience I'm eager to repeat.

A walk away from town on the road toward the monastery feels a bit like we're getting away with something. Hugh and the guards are well ahead of us, horses being faster than feet. No one follows us or tells us we should be somewhere else. Linnet takes Orrin's hand, while I swing my arms as we walk and let the sunlight warm my face. We tramp our slow way toward the monastery to just peek at what's going on. I don't want us to be in the way, but it would be nice to find out if our vision came early enough to change things. Or if it was right at all.

I feel compelled to point out that if enemy soldiers have shown up to invade, we should probably not go, Orrin sends.

It doesn't feel like an invasion, I send back, which causes both of them to roll their eyes. But it doesn't. The soldiers we Saw didn't seem capable of invading anyone. If they're there like in the vision, they'll need help—they didn't seem in any shape to fight.

Hugh brought his sword. He's prepared to fight, Linnet sends. Orrin looks worried.

We've walked halfway when the rattle of wheels on the road disturbs our otherwise silent conversation. We step to the side to let the carriage pass.

Instead, it slows as it passes us. It's the ducal carriage. A footman steps to open the door, and Duchess Marguerite leans out, peering back at us.

"What are you doing out here, children? And without your guard detail," she calls to us. "Are you honestly going to walk all that way?"

We guiltily look around us before we approach the carriage.

"All what way, Your Grace?" I ask cautiously.

"Don't be ridiculous. Get in, all of you. If you think you're fooling anyone for even an instant..." She sighs. "For Dorei's sake."

We glance at each other, but when she disappears into the carriage interior, we climb in after. The footman closes the door, and the carriage rumbles forward a moment later.

"Tell me what's happening," she says shortly.

I exchange a look with the other two. "We don't know, Your Grace," I say.

"I know perfectly well all of you can send to Hugh and find out." She glares at us. "Well? I'm waiting."

I clear my throat. "I don't think he wanted us to come," I say, just loud enough to be heard over the rumbling wheels.

"If Fanthas has penetrated this far, we will turn around right now and begin preparing for a siege. Which is why I need to know. Immediately, Rhiannon. Or Orrin—I don't care which. Although he's less likely to yell at you, Orrin. Send now and find out."

"Your Grace," Orrin starts, but she raises her eyebrow at him, waiting, so he takes a breath and sends to Hugh.

What did you find, he sends, including Linnet and me. *Your mother wants to know.*

I feel a moment of confusion from Hugh, then weary outrage. *Do not come out here. Do not let her come out here. No, we are not invaded. But it's...something odd. I will tell you all about it. Later. At the castle. Please, all of you go home. I'm busy and I can't spare the people.*

Hugh's mental voice is exasperated and worried. What I sense around him seems busy but not desperate. Which is better than I feared.

"He says not to come out, but that we're not invaded. He specifically said not to let you go there," Orrin says carefully.

She snorts. "Just who lets me do anything, I ask you," but it seems a rhetorical question, and even Linnet doesn't answer it, although I can tell she's biting her tongue. "Don't look at me like that. I am duchess here, and I work very hard to keep all of my people safe. I need to know what's happened."

The rest of the ride to the monastery is mostly silent. Marguerite has us repeat what we Saw in our vision, and she sighs heavily, settling back into her seat. She puts her arm around Linnet and squeezes her absently but doesn't press further.

The carriage slows near the gate to the monastery. A castle guard on horseback approaches, the horses restless and whickering to his. The guard salutes and rides away after speaking with the driver, and the footman comes to the door and opens it.

"Your Grace, the guard asks that you and your party

wait here while they check with the duke regarding your presence."

"I will not," she says shortly and pushes past him out of the carriage. We file out after, the footman wisely giving way.

"Your Grace," a soldier wearing kirche colors says as we make for the knot of people just past the gate. "Your Grace, please stay back."

"Don't be ridiculous. If there isn't any danger, and clearly there isn't, I will see what's happened for myself. Move aside," she says and simply walks past him. Even though she's a small woman and he could easily stop her, he does not. He glares at all of us, but Marguerite gestures imperiously and we meekly follow her. Linnet takes my hand and, looking at Orrin's set and grim face, I take his.

I don't suppose he really wants to see the monastery, for all we came here on purpose.

We walk past the gate and into the open garden and court before the monastery. Off to the side is a smashed area, with broken wood and metal and churned up ground. The frame of what appears to have been a siege engine is twisted—not as high as the castle wall, perhaps, when it was upright, but now there's only a mess half again as tall as Hugh, maybe three times as long. No Fanthan soldiers lie injured or dead on the ground. A knot of Haverston guards and some acolytes gather around the structure, gesturing and talking loudly. Hugh turns back toward us, his hair shining in the sunlight. He blinks when he sees us, takes a deep breath and blows his cheeks out, closing his eyes.

He walks over to us. "I asked you not to come," he says in a low voice, frowning at Marguerite. "Mother, there's no need for you to be here. I'll report to you later."

"If you'd simply told me what I asked when Orrin contacted you, I might not have had to. But here I am, so report to me now," she snaps. "If there's no imminent danger then here is where I'm going to be. You do not get to order me about like one of the guards, Hugh Theroux."

Hugh runs his hand through his hair, grimacing, faint lines around his mouth appearing as he clenches his jaw. "We don't know exactly what happened. Apparently, this pile of broken wood and metal appeared in the yard just before I arrived, but no one saw how it got here. There was a magical disturbance, the monks say, but it's...odd."

That means the vision was earlier than the event, but not early enough for Hugh to get here on horseback to witness or stop it. We walk closer. It is odd. The pile looks like a siege engine turned upside down—or inside out—and then smashed. There are a few dark patches on it and the ground around it.

"Is that blood?" Linnet asks, getting right to the point.

Hugh grimaces. "Really, Linnet," he says.

"Is it, though?" I ask.

"I wish you wouldn't," he mutters.

"Really Hugh, answer the question. It certainly looks like blood." Marguerite bends down to look closer at a patch.

"Dorei preserve us," he sighs. "Yes, we think it is. We haven't found any people anywhere bleeding all over, so we're not sure where it came from. Are you happy now?"

"Of course I'm not happy, Hugh," Marguerite snaps. "Please don't be obtuse."

"Your Grace!" A voice shouts over the general noise of people talking in low voices, and Orrin stiffens beside me.

Hugh rolls his eyes when he turns to find the prior of the monastery striding toward us, dark robes flapping around him in his own breeze. "What now," he mutters.

"Your Grace," the prior calls out. "All these soldiers of yours, I really must..." he stops in his tracks when he sees Orrin. And then me.

"Unacceptable," he barks. "We cannot have blasphemers on holy grounds. I protest most strongly!"

Hugh's chin comes up and his eyes narrow. He doesn't like that we're here, but he likes the prior's insults even less. Before he can speak, Marguerite's hand on his shoulder stays him.

"What I find unacceptable, Prior," Marguerite snaps at the man, "is the manner in which you are speaking to us. I will not have my wards and guest treated so. I remind you that I have some say in who is named prior in this monastery and who I will accept rents from. And I remind you of your manners, which you seem to have abandoned."

"Your Grace," he sputters. "I hardly think–"

"That much is completely obvious. Stop speaking immediately until you do."

"Your Grace," the prior wheezes.

Hugh steps forward. "Enough. You may leave us. Someone will inform you when you may have access to this area again. For now, it is off limits to everyone without my direct permission. Take your people and go inside." He gestures to several of his guards, who start forward to escort the prior away.

The prior stands agape for a few moments. My glare matches Linnet's and Orrin's. He turns with a snarl and stalks away, shaking off the guards and shouting for someone.

Hugh sighs and turns to us. "Since you're apparently staying, come closer and maybe help figure out how this came to be here. I'd like to know what happened and why." He looks around at his guards. "But let's see if we can manage less of an audience while you do. This situation is volatile enough."

Hugh orders them further from us while we shuffle nearer to the broken pile of wood and metal, feeling conspicuous. They glance warily at us out of the corners of their eyes. Further away, kirche guards, monastery acolytes, and priests are less circumspect. The weight of their stares makes me tired. Hugh clears the area as best he can, glancing at us to make sure we're mostly alone.

He wants us to use the Sight, I send to Orrin, but this time I'm not narrow enough in the sending, and Linnet hears it too.

Obviously. She snorts.

We did come here against his wishes. I suppose it's only polite to try to help out, Orrin Sends back.

Linnet sniffs. *He can be polite first, then. I don't like how he talks to any of us.*

"Don't send in company, children. It's rude," Marguerite admonishes. "Or at least tell me what you're saying. I hate to be left out of gossip."

"Just arguing, Your Grace," I murmur.

"Ah, then feel free to keep it to yourself," she smiles softly.

Hugh comes back, meeting Linnet's scowl with a brighter smile. "All right, let's try this. I know it's been a difficult day. I appreciate everyone's help." He turns his charm on Orrin and me next. "How would you like to proceed?"

He shines a little in the sunlight—unfairly, I feel. I sigh at him and shake my head.

Orrin blinks at Hugh a few times, his mouth slightly open. With a shake of his head and a wince, he turns to look at the broken siege engine. After a moment's contemplation he says, "I think Rhi and I should try separately."

I exchange a glance with him, and he gestures me forward. Gingerly, I bend forward to touch the blood. Hugh sucks in a breath but doesn't stop me. I want to know what happened. But I'm afraid I won't like the answer.

I'm right.

The magic reaches up for me as I stretch a finger toward the blood—before I've had a chance to call it, before I do more than think, it surrounds me. Faces, voices, screams cut off in terror and pain. Soldiers in the vortex, with the siege engine, something going wrong with the spell. It is a spell, and they knew it was dangerous, and now—now they are dead. They were meant to come through together with the engine, but the spell failed. What came out instead is the broken siege engine and blood, but not the people—not the bodies, anyway. The person the soldiers see before they step into the spell is Montmoore—cold, calculating, chanting as they walk toward him. He opens the air and they step into it and then it twists them and the engine they entered with.

The magic clings a little as I push it away, let it go. I stand up, feeling breathless and sick. "It is a siege engine," I rasp past bile in my throat. "I Saw Montmoore chanting a spell to open a vortex, like in our vision. He sent them through it, sent people pulling the engine through the vortex on purpose, and then it went wrong. The people, they're...still in there. Not alive, but..." I shudder, feeling their deaths, a wrongness up my spine.

Hugh steadies me by the elbow for a moment. "Share it with me, please Rhia. If you can." I nod shakily, and do as he asks.

He winces as I send it, sucking in a breath. "Thank you. I know that was hard." He pats my arm, turns to Orrin. "Orrin, will you try as well?" He gestures at the engine.

Orrin purses his lips, nods. He steps forward, avoiding the blood and touching a twisted, splintery piece of wood. I feel the magic reach for him and I step back. He tenses, his eyes going wide, and clutches at the siege engine.

"Not enough," he rasps, stumbling back a few moments later. Hugh steadies him, hand on his back, stepping closer.

"Not enough what?" he asks softly.

"Not enough power, magic, not enough to finish. The engine was too big, or there were too many people, or— he calculated wrong. The vortex closed on his side and trapped them all, twisted everything. And it took...time. Days. It took days."

"What do you mean?" Marguerite asks. "What took days?"

"They sent this days ago. The spell failed on their

end, but the end of it came out here, today. It was a test, but it was supposed to end up somewhere else."

"Where was it to go?" Hugh asks grimly.

"I—to the castle? I think outside Haverston castle. It wasn't clear—the minds of the people were too crazed. They were—they were in there alive all that time, lost and terrified, getting crushed as the vortex twisted the siege engine."

We all shudder in horror.

"What do we do now?" Linnet asks.

"Hugh will make arrangements to remove this from the monastery, and we shall return to the castle. Hugh, please meet us there and we will discuss what comes next."

Marguerite turns Linnet's shoulders toward the carriage and urges her toward it.

"Make sure to find me when you return," she orders Hugh, taking Orrin's arm, firmly leading him away. I follow meekly behind.

Hugh snaps orders as we depart the monastery, the birds still singing, the day still pleasant and warm. I shiver against remembered visions and sink gratefully into the carriage seat.

CHAPTER 8

When Hugh and the castle guard return with a wagonload of mangled siege engine, Marguerite summons him to attend her in the library. She's dismissed her ladies, so it's just the three of us and one of the castle dogs with her when he arrives.I sit on the hearth, petting the dog's soft ears. He's older, a small rodent hunter retired now from anything save keeping Marguerite company and he likes a warm hearth. He is quiet and sweet and likes his ears scratched. He'll leave when he's had enough, but for now he seems content in my company and I'm grateful.

Hugh joins us with a rush of air and voices, tossing a dismissal over his shoulder. He closes the door behind him and crosses to Marguerite, sighing.

"Hello, Mother. Orrin, Rhia, Linnet. May I sit?" he asks, as he bends to kiss his mother's cheek.

"Certainly you may sit, ridiculous boy. I have food for you. Eat," she says, proffering a plate of sandwiches.

"Dorei bless you, Mother. I'm famished." Pushing a

stack of books aside, he takes the plate and sits at the table close to Orrin.

"What more occurred after we left?" Marguerite says, pouring him a glass of cider after he's made an inroad on the food.

"I learned the prior is even more of an ass than I'd supposed. And that a siege engine in twisted pieces is harder to move than one whole."

"I see," she says.

"Is that all?" Linnet snaps. "I could have told you that." She turns to glare out the window. I keep petting the dog, my mouth pressed thin.

"Any more visions?" Hugh asks Orrin. He turns to me as well. "Anything strange at all since?"

Orrin shakes his head. I shrug, concentrating on the small, fuzzy space between the dog's ears.

"They've been twitchy," Linnet offers, keeping her gaze out the window.

"You would be, too," I mutter.

"Twitchy? How?"

Linnet sighs and looks back at us. "I don't know. Just —they both jump at the smallest noise. And they're crabby."

I snort. "You're one to talk," I say.

"I don't think it's unusual to be affected by a disturbing vision," Marguerite says quietly. "They're behaving as anyone might in similar circumstances. I've been keeping an eye on them, and they seem otherwise fine."

Linnet shrugs, looking back out the window. She's not wrong that we're twitchy, but she is, too. I think she feels left out somehow.

Hugh purses his lips, looking sidelong at Orrin, who picks at his own sleeve.

"What are you going to do with the...it?" I ask.

"We moved the pieces to the guards' courtyard for now," Hugh says, "but there isn't really a good place to store them. We took it apart, as best we can. I'd like to find some proof of what happened beyond..." he indicates Orrin and me "...just the vision. We need to figure out how to keep it from happening again." Hugh gulps some cider, stands abruptly.

"Rhia, please try to contact Cardinal Robere for me tonight. I've sent a bird, but I should alert the king immediately. I'd like to get on top of this before the Butcher's people get involved."

Marguerite taps his arm. "And I think we'll need to send these children to Corat sooner rather than later, Hugh dear. This is the third incident where someone has tried to get through to Haverston—twice where they were specifically after Rhiannon and Orrin. I don't think we can keep them safe here. Or the rest of the duchy." She levels a serious look at her son.

Hugh rubs his face, smearing a bit of butter across his stubble.

"I'll discuss it with the king." He strides from the room, shaking his head.

CHAPTER 9

Hugh is impatient to get through tonight's lessons so I can send to Cardinal Robere. Even with all my magic, hours of preparation and coaching, it's difficult for me to send all the way to Corat, and as far as we're aware no one other than Orrin and I can do it. Discovering it was possible at all was a shock the first time. But now that Hugh knows we can, he wants instant gratification every time.

But the magic is difficult to control at this distance—like trying to do complex equations while stitching and pushing in icy slurry through my bones. It requires all my concentration, and I'm worn out and shaky after.

The information I get for Hugh tonight had better be worth it.

When we're able to reach him, Robere will ask questions and convey messages from the king. Sometimes they're in code, and I don't know what they mean. I try not to be resentful—the king has no reason to entrust me with his secrets.

Sometimes I can sense the other people around the

cardinal–usually the king, or sometimes Connor. My stomach flutters when I know he's there, and it's harder to concentrate.

I wish he would write. He hasn't in weeks, and I'm too nervous to write and ask why. I know I should anyway, but I'm too embarrassed. He might just be busy. But maybe I've been wrong about his feelings this whole time. Maybe he regrets kissing me that night before he left. Everything was so fraught—after Gantry's death, and the Wasting, and Archbishop Montmoore escaping —maybe he was just relieved we all lived. Maybe I just didn't understand, and his letters were just him being kind.

I thought he wanted...me. But he's a taciturn, dour, unreadable man whose mind is opaque even to my wild Sight. If he doesn't think of me as anything more than a companion—or more likely a burden —he might not say. He might not want to hurt my feelings. All those thoughts revolve in my mind when I send to Robere and he's there with the cardinal.

He might be there tonight when I send. But before I do, we have magical practice to get through. Hugh wants to find out why my magic keeps linking with Linnet's. Despite our best efforts, my magic attaches to her whenever I'm not paying attention. Hugh says we should only link our power on purpose—that uncon- scious linking could cause one of us to harm the other without meaning to. We've been working on linking and unlinking, both of us cinching the magic down and cutting the link off, then linking again, over and over.

A vision rackets against my awareness. Orrin feels it, too, sends to me about it. It's been building for hours, and Hugh wants us to wait, try to See it at the same time. Sometimes we can push them back, fight them off for a while. This one is growing insistent. It won't be hard to let it in.

But meanwhile I'm unlinking my magic from Linnet, staring at nothing, pulling in the threads of magic. Or at least that's what I'm trying to do.

Linnet scowls. "Quit reaching for me," she snaps.

"I'm not!" I insist, but she's right, I See the pale green tendril of my power trying to latch onto her. I ruthlessly clamp down on myself, and it disappears.

"All right, now I want you to relax, but stay unlinked," Hugh says quietly. I nod, and let the magic flow through me, but only through me.

"Stop it," Linnet hisses. The tendril is back.

"Try to pull back gently, Rhiannon. Just stay inside your skin."

I grimace, picturing my runes and the magic flowing inside me. The tendril fades on one side, sprouting back from another angle.

I look at Hugh. "I can't concentrate with this vision pushing at me," I say, feeling defeated. I wipe my sweaty hands on my pale green day dress, feeling gritty and tired.

Hugh sighs, and Linnet throws her hands in the air. "I told you it wasn't my fault," she grumbles.

"Let's find out about this vision, then. Orrin, are you ready?"

Orrin stands from the bed and walks to stand facing me. "I'm ready when you are, Rhi." His voice is steady, but after last time I'm not so sure I am. Hugh looks calm, but Linnet seems ready to jump on either of us if anything strange happens.

I nod at Orrin and let the magic rise again, allowing

the vision through. A rush of power like falling, like howling wind, and I See. The battle again, the palace overrun, Fanthas soldiers in the courtyard. It's all hazy like a dream this time, but I See us—Orrin and me, fighting. Not winning.

But the demons—I See them clearly as they flow out of the vortex, trailing destruction as they pass by, writhing, killing people. I shout in horror.

One of them turns and looks at me—Sees me. It starts toward me. I back up a step, two, start to fall...

The roaring wind of the vortex surrounds me, and I'm falling, the gale and the voices of demons spinning around me. There's little light, just swirling colors and shadow. I reach out my hands for balance but I'm still just stumbling on nothing. Everything is charcoal-green and purple and misty, a twilight gloaming and storm smell. A flash of light stutters somewhere ahead.

Connor stumbles out of the fog and storm. His face drips blood from a cut on his head and he holds a sword in one hand, his other arm pressed to his side. I shout his name, but I can't hear myself over the rushing wind.

He looks up. He looks at me, and then glances behind him, seeing something, someone else. What is this vision? Or is this happening now? Did I somehow bring him here? I don't know and I'm terrified. Connor looks back at me, his face drawn and frightened, and then someone pulls me from the vortex into daylight and I trip and fall into a heap, panting, tears still pouring down my cheeks.

Linnet lies on me, her arms around me like a vise, still yelling. I look around the room, panting. Hugh holds Orrin upright in a tight grip. "We have to—we have to find out if he's all right," I say.

"If who? Who's all right?" Hugh asks.

"Connor—Connor was in the vortex with us. He was lost. He was hurt. We have to make sure," I croak, my voice going hoarse.

Orrin just looks at me, his face waxy with exhaustion. *Are you sure it was Connor?* he sends.

I'm sure. "I need to send to—send to Corat. To someone who can find out," I rasp.

"What are you talking about?" Linnet demands, letting go of me and staggering to her feet. "You were disappearing again. Don't you care about that?"

"I care," Hugh says. "Very much. I don't think—that is, you two shouldn't try visions together anymore. Not—not ever, maybe." His voice is ragged.

"But we might have to get him out!" I shout, and Linnet shoves away from me and stands up.

"What are you talking about?" she shouts back.

"Connor! He saw me. He saw me, Linnet. It wasn't just—I think he was really in there." I feel the tears pouring down my face. "He was lost."

I just have to be sure, I have to find out. I have to find him.

"Like those soldiers from Fanthas, you mean? You think someone sent him into a vortex somehow?" Orrin asks.

"I don't know—I don't know, but what if he's stuck in there? You said it killed them..." I gasp.

"Not right away," he insists.

"Not good enough."

I start to reach out toward Corat, the way I have before. It hurts; the vision we just shared took more than it should have, as short as it was. Orrin links to me to shore me up. Hugh and Linnet are still protesting as I send to Cardinal Robere. I know I'm earlier than we had planned. I don't care.

Cardinal, please, are you there? I send. *I need you to find Connor FitzWellan for me, please. Cardinal?*

My goodness, Rhiannon, this is a strong sending. Please pull back—you're hurting me.

I'm so sorry, Cardinal, I send, reining in the magic and trying to mellow it. Orrin moderates the power he's linking, moderates the magic that I'm pulling up from the power well. I ignore the blooming ache in my temples. *Can you find the earl for me? It's very important.*

Nothing back for a moment, but a puzzled feeling. *He's right here, child. I am with him and the king. Has something happened?*

He's there? He's...he's not hurt or missing? I'm aware of Linnet shouting at me, Hugh trying to calm her, to be calm, to keep out of this. I'm aware of Orrin standing by my side, feeding me magic in a thin stream. I'm aware of the magic gathering around us in a sluggish molten pool, and that is what catches Robere's attention.

What are you doing? Yes, Lord fitzWellan has been here. He's fine. You are using too much magic, Rhiannon. The both of you. Stop this sending and deal with the magic now, before something happens!

He throws me out of the sending, and I reel backward into the wall behind me. Orrin fights with the magic, trying to direct it down, back to its well under the cliffs and away from us. It doesn't want to go. I can feel the runes on both of our bodies fighting us, and I look into his eyes. *We have to unlink,* I send.

What do you think I'm trying to do? He asks, and I can feel him, in my head, in my runes, my runes reaching for his. His runes reaching for me.

Hugh steps between us and drags Orrin physically from the tower room, while Linnet knocks me over onto the bed and just sits on me.

"Stop it!" she screams in my face.

Reducing our proximity helps, but I still have to fight the magic back. I see her get ready to hit me, and I hold up my arm.

"Don't!" I yell. "I'm trying, I'm trying Linnet. Just give me a moment."

"Try. Better." She grimaces as the magic tries to pull at her, too. I ruthlessly cut off any link to her, which leaves us both gasping. The magic finally sluggishly slumps back away under the castle, and I just lie under Linnet, both of us panting and teary.

"Why are you like this?" she asks, but not as if she expects an answer. I just shake my head.

Hugh comes back into the room and helps Linnet off me. He sends her to check on Orrin. She goes willingly enough, if scowling. I sit up on the bed and wipe my forehead with my sleeve.

"So Connor is not stuck in the vortex, it seems," Hugh says quietly.

"Not according to the cardinal," I say.

"I know. I heard. Everyone in the room heard. It's possible everyone in the castle heard. Rhiannon, you—you need to exert more control. You can't be so impulsive with this magic or draw that much power at once. It's dangerous. None of it behaves in normal ways for you and Orrin."

"I know," I mutter.

"I'm not telling you not to be worried or afraid when odd things happen, but please take a breath and think. Let us help you. It's not necessary to respond to every problem as an emergency."

"He was in there, Hugh. I saw him—it felt like it was happening right then. I Saw him. And I didn't reopen the vortex—I didn't plan to try until I verified if anyone knew where he was. I was trying to be responsible!"

Hugh sighs and sits next to me. "I believe you. But you had other choices. You could have explained what you Saw in the vision more, first, so we could discuss it. If we had time to assess, we probably would have sent to Robere to ask, in a more controlled way, and avoided you drawing so much power. I worry you'll do some real damage doing that."

"I was tired, and I miscalculated," I mutter.

"I understand. Please know I'm not angry, just worried. You are powerful—and you and Orrin together are...a dangerous combination. The two of you feed off of each other in ways I can't predict, and you often use too much power for me to control. If I need to help you, I'm not sure I could do it." He sighs, closing his eyes for a moment.

"I just want you to be safe. I want you both to be safe. Now that you know Connor's not in any danger, let's take a breath. We'll work out what it was you Saw. If it's part of the future, perhaps we can prevent it."

I nod listlessly, and he pulls me into his side for a hug. "We'll figure it out," he says quietly. I try to believe him.

CHAPTER 10

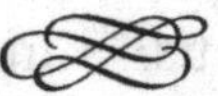

Several weeks go by in a haze of lessons and work to keep our magic unlinked. Visions come and go, but Orrin and I make sure to have them as far from each other as we can manage. When we're together, we run to another room to shake and See future palace battles, each one slightly changed but still terrible.

This need for distance makes going anywhere other than our rooms awkward, and I feel caged. Duchess Marguerite makes sure to take Orrin and I on separate walks in the garden or along the castle wall when the weather allows. Linnet throws herself into weaving. The magic etches itself along our nerves, reaching out even when we're not near one another.

On a rainy spring evening, Hugh asks us to his rooms for dinner. "I've received a bird today," he says over the soup course, holding a missive. "The king summons Rhia and Orrin to Corat as soon as possible. I'll make the arrangements. Connor will meet us partway there, and we'll travel with several guards. The king means to take no chances with your safety."

Orrin snorts but doesn't comment. Hugh waits with a raised eyebrow, but continues when Orrin just eats his soup quietly. "We leave in four days, if I can get everything prepared."

"You're coming with us?" Linnet asks.

"I'm going—you're not," he replies.

"What? I am too!" she insists.

Hugh grimaces. "I think it's too dangerous as it is, Linnet. You can stay here with my mother. Surely you have some friends to keep you busy."

I wince, anticipating what is next.

Linnet slaps her hands against the table, surging to her feet. "As if I have any friends left after last year. You're not taking my only family away from me. I'm not staying behind! You can't make me!"

"It's for the best, Linnet," Hugh tries, but she snarls at him.

"Best for who? Not me!"

"Rhiannon and Orrin's magic is out of control. No one wants you to get hurt. You and Rhia keep linking despite our best efforts to stop you. What if something terrible happens?"

"What if something happens to them and I'm not there? You can't keep me from my sister," she snaps, but her voice breaks. "You can't leave me behind."

Hugh covers his eyes and I stand up and pull my baby sister into a hug. "I don't want to leave her, Hugh," I say.

Orrin hesitantly touches Hugh's hand with his. "I don't think you can separate us at this point," he says gently. Hugh looks at Orrin's hand on his, swallows.

"All right. All right. You're all coming, Dorei help us. I'll make the arrangements. And we'll need to work together, Linnet, to keep your magic separate from your sister's. And Orrin too."

Linnet subsides into her chair, shrugging me off. "You're in charge," she mutters sarcastically, but her expression shows relief.

"As if that were ever true," Hugh mutters back.

CHAPTER 11

Despite all our work, when I go to chapel the next day, I still feel Orrin in my runes. I sit in a star chamber by myself and try to pray, but I don't know what for. I still believe in Dorei and the Lord of Stars. I still believe my parents and my brother are part of a constellation of light; new stars in the heavens, lighting our path. I just don't understand what that path is, or how to follow it. I don't know how to listen for wisdom or grace. I don't know what to do about this magic, how to control it. I decide to pray for cleverness, but that feels futile too.

Orrin can feel me in his runes, too. And chafes against my presence in chapel.

Later we chance a walk together on the barbican. "I wasn't trying to make you come with me, Orrin. I was just trying to...find some peace. Some answers."

"You won't find them there."

"But I might, for me. Why can't you just..." I trail off. I know why he can't, and I don't have any answers yet, so what argument do I have? "I don't understand why you're mad I went for me."

He stares out over the water. We keep coming back to the west barbican, even after the kidnap attempt. It seems as safe as anywhere else. Hugh and Captain Nerishe station guards at all times along the wall and the harbor gate, on frequent rotation. They keep a wary eye on both of us and past the wall, but at least no one is sneaking up the harbor steps on anyone else.

Orrin scowls, tossing a small rock in his hand. "I feel deep betrayal in my heart, Rhi. The Kirche. Every time I look at Sonnenist symbols or texts, or think about any of the miracles, all I see is another party to demons. To a darkness with no stars in it at all."

"But," I start, but he cuts me off with a sharp gesture.

"How do you still go to chapel? How do you listen to them when we're surrounded by people who know what Gantry did and yet still whisper that we must have deserved it somehow? That the demons chose us for a reason—I know you can hear them. Calling us 'touched'—a heartbeat from calling us 'tainted' to our faces—because of the things that man did to us. And all those in the Inquisitor's building or the monastery, telling us to have faith—as if they ever did anything for their faith other than look down on people."

He spits on the ground and flings his rock the wall into the harbor far below. "Those cowards let Gantry just tell them what to do, even when they knew he was doing something awful. About the hospice and people dying. But because they were poor, those useless priests and monks and acolytes kept their mouths shut and let them die."

I think about arguing, but he doesn't want to hear

about too-little-too-late complaints to the duchess. They didn't try to stop Gantry, anyway. To hell with them. He's right about that.

"We will carry his scars forever," he snaps, "and this power—do they think we wanted it? In exchange for what? The deaths of our loved ones? To never know peace again? To share such hateful, cruel thoughts with small-minded, blinkered idiots? Who would want that?"

He slaps his hands on the top of the wall, gaze fixed on the horizon. "I can't ever be a priest. I can't ever be part of the kirche again. I know too much about people —I do not want to save them. Cardinal Robere will tell me it's my duty, that I should not give up my calling. But that calling is gone."

I reach out my hand, grasp his. "I will never tell you to do anything you don't want to," I promise. He looks sidelong at me. "Not without a really good reason," I hedge.

He grimaces at the ocean. "And?" he asks.

"Because Cardinal Robere thinks we're fascinating is not a really good reason. I don't want to be an acolyte, either."

"Robere can go to hell."

"Only maybe we could just tell him no thanks?" I say. It almost gets a laugh from him.

"Rhi, you are going to end up doing what he wants if you go all wishy-washy."

"It's not wishy-washy to say no thanks. It's just...more polite."

"Polite will be ridden down like rabbits before a cavalry charge."

"I'll just pretend to be Duchess Marguerite. There's sharp steel under her polite."

He snorts. "You need another thirty years before you can be Duchess Marguerite or anything like."

"Then I have something to aspire to," I say, my nose in the air.

"Rhi, this is important. And if he ropes you in, he will blackmail me."

I shake my head. "I don't think he'd do that."

Orrin glances sideways at me, an evening breeze playing with his hair. "Have you been paying attention to this country at all in the past year? Why wouldn't he do that?"

I shrug, although I have no evidence he wouldn't do that, and plenty of evidence anyone in the kirche hierarchy might do much worse. But deep down I don't feel like he would.

"If he were going to, he would have already."

Orrin shakes his head. "He just hasn't had to yet. When he does have to, he will. He'll make that call, or the king will, or someone will force them to. This country is Sonnenist at its core, now. None of the Lunastris—or even Doreians—have any sway. If your magic isn't under kirche control, then the kirche doesn't want you to have it. And we have more magic than any seven of them combined, each of us alone.

"They'll want to control us. They'll have to. If we can't make ourselves invaluable to the crown without the kirche, we'll be forced to join or flee. The king doesn't want us, or he'd have sent for us before this. I don't know what's coming, Rhi, but we have to be prepared. The kidnappers were only the beginning. We're in trouble. We have to count on each other."

He's trembling. I'm trembling. I can feel fear and anger rolling off of him in waves—I feel it in my head, in my heart, through our shared scars. And I know he's right. But—

"We aren't friendless," I say.

"What can Hugh do, or Connor or Julianna, against the king and the kirche? What can any of them do if the entire court wants us dead or gone? Why would they defend us if we are more dangerous alive? We have to find ways to be invaluable, or places to run. What we're doing now is something, but it isn't enough. I'm looking for...I'm looking for somewhere to go. If I have to."

I shudder, fighting back tears. "Where?"

He shakes his head, looks back out to sea. "I don't know yet. Maybe the empire. Maybe Zarha. But we have to control our magic first. I'd ha-," he swallows, starts again. "We'd have to be anonymous. We'd have to pretend to be less than we are. Or we'd be in the same trouble all over again. And I don't know how to control the magic yet."

"Maybe we do need the cardinal, then," I whisper, a roiling nausea in my belly.

His eyes narrow as he cuts a glance at me. "Maybe. I won't unless I absolutely have to. I'm going to look for other ways out of here, Rhiannon. If you don't—if you don't want to come with me when I go, I understand."

"What about...what about your family?"

"They would understand. They'd probably help." He reaches for my hand. "I know what you're thinking. I can feel what you're thinking. We don't have to go tomorrow. But we might—we might have to go. Think about it, Rhiannon. Help me plan. Let's be ready to run if we have to, to live."

"Hugh will keep us safe," I say, unsure.

"Hugh will try. But I'm not waiting around for 'try,' if

I can get out and have a life somewhere else. I'm not getting caught again, Rhiannon. Never again."

I nod miserably. He leans in and kisses my forehead.

"Don't let them bully you. Don't let me bully you. You're strong. You're tremendous. I know you'll fight for me, and I will fight for you. I'll fight for us both," he says, one hand on my shoulder, the other cupping my cheek. He wipes a tear away with his thumb. "And Linnet, too."

"She'll fight for herself," I say, a smile creeping sideways onto my mouth.

"I'm counting on it," he says. "Let's go inside. You're shivering." Orrin squeezes my shoulder again, then steps away.

I wonder if it's easier for him to contemplate leaving because he has left before. He left his family to become an acolyte, which was his dream. Then it became a nightmare. My nightmare took place here, in my own home. I should want to go. I should want to jump into the sea to become a sea dragon and never return. But the thought of leaving Haverston, even travelling to Corat, makes me wheezy.

I follow Orrin into the castle, trying to plan for all the futures we hope to stave off.

CHAPTER 12

I knock on Linnet's door and wait for her grunt to come in. She's half-spread across the loom in the corner, muttering to herself.

"You can't take the loom with you, Linnet. It's not practical."

She turns to glare at me. "I know that. I'm just trying to figure out dimensions. I might need to redo all of this," she says, gesturing to the work partly finished.

"I'm sure Her Grace would be happy to leave this room as-is until we return," I say, not sure if it's true.

"I'm sure she would too," Linnet says, taking measurements and counting under her breath. "But I might have a better idea when I get back and I want to remember the pattern I had planned. Now hush, I'm counting." She scribbles a note on a piece of paper and waves me away.

I turn toward her bed to find a few gowns and some colorful skeins of thread strewn on it but not much else. I sigh and lay out underthings and stockings, her hair brush, and a selection of things I retrieve from the bathing room. She turns around and growls at me. "I'm getting to it!" I shrug elaborately, because her getting to it means leaving half of it behind, but she makes a rude gesture back at me.

"Crow brain," I snap, and throw a handful of shifts at her.

"Nag!" She throws them back. We're laughing and slapping each other with stockings when the duchess walks in.

"Oh, Your Grace," I gasp, out of breath.

"Hello girls," she says, smiling indulgently. "I see you're...packing."

"*I* was packing, but Rhiannon has to be in charge of everything," Linnet says, sticking her tongue out.

"You weren't packing, you were puttering," I say, sticking my tongue out right back.

"Sibling squabbles are all well and good, but I need to speak with you both," Marguerite breaks in, laying a hand on Linnet's shoulder. "Why don't we sit down." She gestures to a small table in the other corner of the room.

We sit, Marguerite taking the chair most in sunlight. Linnet scoots in next to me. "I have something to discuss with you," she says, laying two jingling leather purses on the table. "I have negotiated a further settlement with the guilds and the kirche on your behalf. I insisted they pay a higher death-geld for your family and write more comprehensive statements of their innocence. I can't bring your family back, but I can make sure they aren't vilified in the official records."

I swallow sudden tears. "Thank you, Your Grace," I say. Linnet plays with the edge of the ornate table and stays silent.

"I have most of the money for you in a trust, but you can ask for it at any time. This is just a portion for you to take to Corat, so you have some independence."

I take a deep breath and reach for the purses. Marguerite puts her hand over mine, looking gravely at the both of us.

"Which brings me to my other reason for speaking to you now—Corat. I do think it will be physically safer for you there, but the political environment in the palace is...precarious, and I think you should be prepared.

"There are many volatile factions in the capital, most of them hostile to any new players. The King's spymaster , Marchioness Boucher, most of all. She is a dangerous woman, who plays very deep political games. She supports the king, but has her own agenda. And as I told you, she has a hatred toward me and mine. That will include you now, too."

"Why does she hate you?" Linnet asks.

"Oh, that is a very old, very long story," Marguerite says, waving the question away airily. "Suffice it to say that in her opinion I was a jumped-up Cit who married a duke, and she thinks my children's influence on King Peter is too great. We were never friendly, but I put her in her place one too many times long ago.

"She holds a grudge, and has the king's ear. I want you to be wary; she will likely be antagonistic toward you, and is a dangerous woman to have as an enemy. She thinks she wants what's best for Talaria. But she only wants that if it's also what's best for herself. Because you are allied with me, and with Connor, whom she also dislikes, she will think the worst of you. Keep clear of her if you can."

"Why does she dislike Connor?" I ask quietly.

Marguerite hums, a little sad sound. "I don't know all of the reasons there. It has to do with her brother's death, and that of the crown prince Maxime. You can ask Connor or Hugh for background, but I doubt they'll tell you. It was years ago, but I know Yvonne. She blames Connor, and she does not forgive. She will look to discredit you with the king because of Connor and because of me. And also, because you have a power she will want to either eliminate or use. Be wary," she repeats.

I bite my lip—just what I wanted, another enemy. I nod grimly.

Marguerite sighs and stands up, patting my hand. "You are both welcome to come here—come home to me, if needed. I want you to be safe, and I think Corat is better placed to keep you that way. But I will always welcome you, as will my son. You do not go friendless into the great, wide world." She smiles at us, chucks me under my chin, and leaves.

I sigh, too. "We need to finish packing," I say. "We are leaving tomorrow."

"I know that," Linnet says, sullenly, shifting away to go back to the loom.

"Hugh says he'll buy us new gowns when we get to Corat," I tell her, which seems to cheer her up.

"And we have money now," she says, and I can see her thinking how much the best cloth will cost, what traders might be in Corat, and what fashion might be on display there. I stand and leave her to it, hoping she'll remember tooth powder. I'll pack extra, just in case.

"What do you think you're doing?" Captain Nerishe's voice cuts the morning air around me, and I startle, turn around guiltily with the bag I'm carrying, but she's not speaking to me. The guard she barks at salutes and stands at attention.

"I've been assigned to oversee the packing of these supplies, Captain."

Nerishe eyes him quietly. The courtyard bustles with people getting the coaches ready and the horses we're to ride. The coach is painted in ducal colors but isn't as fancy as the one we rode in with the duchess.

"Where is Corporal Watson? I believe he was assigned to this duty."

"Watson was called to the gate, Captain. He asked me to take over." The guard isn't someone I recognize, but then I don't know all of them on sight.

"I see," Nerishe answers him. She eyes the guard. "Watson asked you personally?"

"Yes, Captain."

"Go back to your other duties, Allard. I'll take over here." She dismisses him with a gesture. He looks taken aback, but after a moment of confusion, he salutes and leaves.

When the captain sees me watching her, she walks over and takes the bag from my arms. "It's best to be cautious. I don't want anyone I haven't vetted personally touching these supplies. Allard is new, and I don't trust anyone new right now."

I look over my shoulder at the retreating figure of Allard. "You think he's...a spy?"

"It's best to be cautious," she says. I look back at her. She smiles at my expression. "He's probably not. But caution and control are the key to security." She pats my arm. "Is this yours? You don't have a trunk?"

"Oh," I say, "we're not to bring trunks. Hugh just told us. He said we would need new clothes, anyway, and best to get them once we've arrived in Corat."

Nerishe raises her eyebrows. "Traveling light, are we? That will make things easier. I'll get everything settled here. Are you and the others about ready?"

"Very soon, Captain." I smile and offer my own salute.

She looks over her shoulder as corporal Watson joins us. Her smile fades, and she looks him over quietly as he begins to help load the coach. He looks up at her and nods once.

"We should get going," Nerishe says, pursing her lips. "We'll want to make the first stop before dark."

My stomach lurches at the thought of leaving, but I force myself to smile again. "I'll make sure to hurry everyone along." I turn and flee back to Linnet.

Linnet is of course not ready, but deep down, neither am I. I busy myself with chivvying her along, much to her annoyance, but we tumble out to the courtyard not too much later than I had planned.

Orrin waits for us with Captain Nerishe and the horses, wearing dark brown and gray traveling clothes and a neutral expression, but he smiles slightly when he sees us. The horses look bored, flicking their tails and chewing at nothing.

Our mounts are a compromise between our inexperience and our need to be swift. We won't be riding the whole time, but Hugh says it's a useful skill and wants us to get used to it. And coaches can lose wheels or become mired. We're to switch between riding on the horses and in one of the coaches.

Linnet and I don't know much about riding. Guild families ride in caravans or in coaches or ships, and ours was well enough off to keep a coach at home. Horses just for riding; that's for the nobility. Or farmers. I used to try to befriend our coach horses, but Mum didn't like me to spend time in the carriage house.

Not even when I was pretending to nobility did I ride a horse. I have only been on one a few times. I find them beautiful and alarming. Today, mine is named Blackie, because she's mostly black with a white blaze on her nose. I've decided that's too prosaic. I'm calling her Storm.

"She isn't a pet, Rhi," Linnet scowls. But I see her petting the nose of her own pretty bay.

"You never had pets, did you?" Orrin says. Orrin rides like a farmer—because his family are farmers. He can stay on the back of a horse, but he isn't used to long rides anymore.

"No pets around the cloth—the dirt and hair—Da would never allow it. Gran, when she was alive, she always had dogs and cats at her farmhouse—we went to see her sometimes. But she died when Linnet was just a baby. Oh, and the fuss Da would make when we'd come home dirty."

"Animal hair is impossible to keep off cloth," Linnet sniffs.

"Some of the cloth is made of animal hair, Li." Orrin wrinkles his nose at her.

Her head snaps up at the baby name—Keenan used to call her that. Da used to use rhyming pet names—Kee,

Rhi, and Li. But Linnet made me stop ages ago, after Keenan went for a priest. That Orrin uses it now...I watch her face as it drains of color but for two bright, red splotches on her cheeks.

"With carefully cleaned and culled hair," she mutters, but otherwise lets the pet name slide.

Captain Nerishe shakes her head, laughing at us. "A horse is not a dog or a cat, but they'll take to kindness just the same. You'll all be much better riders for making friends. I can't speak to the problems of horsehair and fancy weaving, but that isn't our concern today."

Nerishe turns at the sound of footsteps. "Ah, Your Grace, there you are."

I turn to find Hugh walking toward us, a strained smile on his face and his mother on his arm.

"Hello, Anouk, how is the expedition shaping up?" Marguerite asks.

"Just fine, Your Grace. You're looking well."

"Why thank you, Anouk. Always nice to hear from such a lovely friend. How are the children these days?"

"Mischievous devils, every one. Just like their mother," Captain Nerishe laughs.

Marguerite grins at her. "And how is your Lauren? I haven't seen her in months, it seems."

"Busy with the printing press, as always, Your Grace. If she didn't have the littles to distract her, she'd be at it every moment of the day, would my girl."

I didn't know the captain had children—or a wife. But...Lauren Nerishe, yes, I do know Lauren now I think of it. A small spark of a woman—dark hair and eyes, four or five children, and a biting wit—who runs the press. I just didn't know her "handsome guard captain" was the same as ours.

"Mother, it's kind of you to see us off, but it's really not necessary. I'm sure you have other things to do." Hugh's patience has worn out.

"Don't be ridiculous, Hugh. I need to say goodbye to these youngsters before they go. Linnet, come here, child."

Hugh rolls his eyes but kisses his mother's head and walks to his own mount, a tall gray.

Duchess Marguerite takes Linnet's hands in hers, kisses her cheeks, and speaks low to her for a few minutes. Linnet lets out a low sob and throws herself into the duchess' arms.

Her Grace murmurs a low sound and holds her close. I realize I'm staring when the duchess looks over at me and smiles an understanding sort of smile.

"Don't stand on ceremony, my dear. Come and say goodbye." I feel myself tearing up as well, and I let her pull me into her embrace. "It won't be so bad. The king is a good man, and you'll have Hugh and Connor and Julianna with you. And remember," she says, pulling back. "Remember that you can come to me at any time. Rely on Captain Nerishe. She will see you safe." She looks in our eyes, cups each of our cheeks for a moment. Then steps back. "Orrin, my dear, come and say goodbye."

Hugh watches Orrin walk towards Marguerite. He catches me looking and blushes, then busily checks his mount over.

Orrin bows to Marguerite when he stands before her, but she makes him straighten up. "Give me a proper farewell, young man," she says and hugs him, as well. "You will be missed, Orrin. I know you don't feel it to be true, but I will miss you, and so will many others. Keep yourself safe, dear. Keep my son safe, as well." She smiles at him, and Orrin's cheeks darken as he looks away. I raise my eyebrows and grin at him, but he won't meet my eyes.

"Time to go, Mother," Hugh says, a blush reddening his face. Orrin pointedly doesn't look at Hugh, either.

We head for our mounts as Hugh embraces his mum and kisses her cheek. "Love you," he murmurs.

"Take care, Hugh. Take very good care of yourself and these children. And tell Julianna to write me more often. I want word of my granddaughter."

"Yes, Mum," he says.

Captain Nerishe nods to Marguerite, who nods back, very slowly.

"I know you're in good hands with Anouk," the duchess says to Hugh. "She's one of the best women I know. Keep that in mind, dear."

"Yes, Mum." She kisses his cheek and steps back to let him mount up.

"I'll send a bird as soon as I can. Take care of Haverston for me."

"I always do." We start to move out as she waves goodbye.

This is my first time leaving the duchy. I was supposed to travel when I married, but I've been in Haverston and surrounds my whole life. My heart pounds as we ride out of the gate, down the road and away from the coast. Linnet and Orrin talk quietly, and the coaches rattle and rumble. The creak of leather saddles and jingling of bits and stirrups fill my ears at every step, Storm's muscles bunching and stretching and shifting under me. The salt breeze ruffles my curls. The sea birds cry and wheel. I am leaving home. Every step is a step further away than I've ever been before. I send a quick prayer to Keenan to watch over us. I have a feeling we'll need it.

CHAPTER 13

Getting used to riding is harder than I thought —after only an hour Hugh tells us to get in the coach. My posterior is grateful. I try not to rub it too obviously. Linnet leans on my shoulder as I nestle in the corner and Orrin stretches out on the opposite bench.

We pull off the road to let troops pass by us going the opposite way. The soldiers look exhausted and dirty, their bandages and missing limbs a stark reminder that there's a war on, miles away at the border. Most of them don't even look at us, and I try to decide if it's best to not stare out the window so as not to seem rude or to look and remember them so that they know someone is paying attention. Neither seems like an adequate response. Our party continues somberly for the much of the afternoon.

The first inn we stay at knows His Grace well, and we are well-cared for by the staff. Our aching muscles get to soak in wooden tubs in the bathing room, and we only have to double-up in the rooms. Hugh says we won't always have such nice accommodations this journey, so we should enjoy it while we have it. I'm not sure I enjoy a strange bed and a strange bathing room, but the food tastes delicious.

The late spring days continue bright and warm. After four days of following the road and staying at inns, Hugh sends the coaches on without us, and seven of us —Hugh, Orrin, Linnet, Captain Nerishe, the guards Watson and Gengler, and me—head cross country to meet Connor. No more inns. Camping, Hugh says. Nerishe hides a smile at the grimace Hugh makes at his own plans.

"I don't enjoy the idea any more than you do," he says to our raised eyebrows. "But I want to keep us a little more hidden than every traveler's inn between here and Corat." He wrinkles his nose. "No matter how much I dislike it."

"Where are we meeting Connor, Your Grace?" Orrin asks.

"I'm going to keep that to myself for the time being," Hugh answers.

"Do you think we're surrounded by spies right this minute?" Linnet asks sarcastically, looking around her at the trees.

"Indulge me," is all Hugh says. Linnet rolls her eyes. Orrin snorts but gives Hugh an innocent look when he glares.

Captain Nerishe keeps her mouth shut and her eyes forward. I pat Storm's neck and try to settle into the feel of a horse beneath me. I'm worried about spies, too, although not necessarily from the people with us here. Would it be hard to follow a group this size? Without a road, we'll be seven people and horses leaving tracks. I can't help but remember the last time I tried to hide in the woods. I keep listening for baying hounds. Linnet hisses at me to stop twitching several times, but I think I'm mostly keeping my nervousness to myself.

No one else seems concerned, at least that I can tell. Linnet is having an adventure, Orrin somber but not obviously worried, and Hugh tries to inject cheer into everything. Captain Nerishe seems amused and competent, and Gerard Watson and Mirelle Gengler are...hard for me to read. Which is unusual—mostly I have to try not to read people anymore. But the two of them have very good natural barriers. Or someone is helping them.

It makes me nervous. I haven't had any visions that they are spies—at least not yet. And Orrin hasn't said anything. But then we haven't had many visions since we left Haverston and the power well behind us. The only vision of any strength was about that battle again, and we kept that to ourselves. Magic is much thinner on the ground here, in trickles or small pools. I feel more myself than I have in months. Orrin seems more comfortable as well. We don't have to be so careful about not touching, about our feelings. It's easier to keep inside our own heads without leaking. Linnet hasn't had to work so hard to keep from linking to me, either.

I still feel the magic, though. I think it feels me, too. I sense it questing toward us if we stay for long in one spot. But it doesn't insist or push its way in.

When we make camp for the evening —our first, Hugh lets Nerishe hand out chores for everyone. Hugh to water and settle the horses with Orrin. Linnet helps Watson prepare dinner, and Gengler and I head off to gather wood. Nerishe sets up several small tents.

I think Nerishe sent Orrin and Hugh off together on

purpose. The tension growing between them—all the blushing and sideways glances and staring when they don't think the other is looking—it's more depressing than funny. I don't know how either of them can stand it.

Right now they're having a private discussion several trees away from me, while letting the horses drink from a stream. I was looking for somewhere quiet to dig a latrine and also to use it. This might not be the best spot, after all, I think drily.

I'm trying not to eavesdrop, but there isn't anywhere to go that won't make me obvious, and I'm not sure flailing around loudly is a good idea. So far they haven't seen me, and I don't want to make this more embarrassing for either of them. Or for me. I keep still.

"My parents want me to come home," Orrin says. "They think if I'm not to go on in the kirche, then I should come back to the farm. And they don't understand why I can't. I don't know how to explain it to them." He pats the side of the horse he's standing by, not looking at Hugh.

"Have you lost your calling, then?" Hugh asks. "I mean, utterly? I understand you have your reasons, but maybe it's not lost. Just redirected."

"Redirected to what? The god I worshipped took the man I loved, and tortured and killed other good people. What calling could survive that?"

"The god didn't hurt them. The Star Lord wasn't with the people who tortured and killed and –"

"They thought he was. I was in Gantry's mind for a long time. He was convinced of his right to do what he was doing. And he was sure the Star Lord would support him—was supporting him—that he alone could handle the demons and their power, if only everyone would just cooperate. The Lord of Stars didn't stop him —Rhiannon and everyone else did. I did. I worked to stop him, and Rhiannon risked her life, and there wasn't a god to be found anywhere. If he even exists, why didn't he intervene? That wasn't just evil done in his name. That was evil pretending to be the god itself."

Hugh reaches out, caresses Orrin's shoulder. "I can't tell you to keep your faith, Orrin. I won't tell you not to be angry. But I don't think the Star Lord—or any god— was helping Bishop Gantry. Nor do I think the Lord of Stars is helping Stephen and Archbishop Montmoore now. They're on their own," Hugh says.

"We're all on our own," Orrin mutters.

I bite my lips, wryly thinking that's not strictly true. I really should try to leave, but any move I make will make noise. And I really have to pee.

"You're not on your own, Orrin," Hugh says. "We're here with you—your friends. We can't replace what you lost, we can't fix it, but we care about you and support you. I...care about you."

I risk a look up, and see Hugh take one of Orrin's elegant brown hands in both of his, chafing it gently, caressing the knuckles. I hold my breath and look down. I desperately don't want to ruin the moment. As long as Hugh isn't just flirting. But I don't think he is. Not just. I keep my thoughts clamped down tight in my head and try to stay very still.

The horses end the moment for them, frothing the water of the stream as they step back from their drink, tired and wanting supper. I stay where I am, crouched behind a tree, until they walk back for the next couple of horses. I look for a latrine spot a little further from the water.

It's stew for dinner, with some rabbit that Captain Nerishe killed while we rode. Hugh makes grumpy faces at his bowl, but it is the easiest thing to make with a pot and meat and some well-traveled vegetables. This was his idea, anyway. Linnet snaps at him when he starts to complain, since she helped cook it, and he sighs and shuts up.

After dinner I stare at the fire, throwing twigs in. I've been feeling tense since accidentally spying on Orrin and Hugh. Unsettled and restless. Orrin stands nearby, staring off into the woods. Linnet sings to herself as she combs her hair out, and Nerishe hums along, gathering the dishes.

Magic crawls in tiny tendrils up my runes, into my bones. It's a trickle, just a tickle, so I don't stop it. It feels friendly, warm.

It's a mistake. The vision pushes its way through my runes, a rush of magic I wasn't ready for. I stand up in alarm, try to get away from the fire.

I should stay away from Orrin, but the magic makes me dizzy, and his arm is there, just reflex, just self-preservation.

But self-preservation should mean we stay clear of each other when visions take us, even far from the Seely Magan cliffs, it seems.

The vision rips through us both—Orrin cries out from the pain of it. Pain, this time, heaving through my runes, and I See.

It's the battle in the courtyard again, and I See myself standing in front of the vortex, screaming for Orrin to help me. Demons swirl through the air, try to latch onto people, onto me. I can hear them speaking to me, calling to me.

And I can almost understand what they're saying.

Orrin from the future looks up at me. I can't See his now self. He's trying to tell me something, but I can't understand him. The demons notice the me here in this vision. They start to circle closer.

The magic reaches out—to me now, to me in the future, to Orrin, connecting us in the vortex, and I can almost hear my own sending to myself, to all of us. Panicking, I watch everything turn to disaster. All the death, all the awful spells. Power swirls through the air, heavy and burning. Part of me, somewhere, wants that power so much I can taste it. My stomach heaves.

A stinging slap brings me back to the present, to the fire, out of the vision. I stumble away from Linnet and almost retch into the leaf litter on the ground. I look over at Linnet yelling at Hugh to slap Orrin. Orrin's body fades in and out of solidity in front of Hugh, still caught in the spell. I can see trees through him, and then I can't—and Hugh's hands seem to be the only thing holding him here. Barely. The shaking isn't working.

Linnet takes matters into her own hands and punches Orrin in the stomach the next time he's solid. Orrin doubles over, hacking, then drops to all fours and vomits. Hugh glares at Linnet, but she just shrugs, although her face is pale and her eyes wide with fear.

"Well, it worked," she says.

I sit on the ground, put my head between my knees, and gasp, stomach still roiling.

"What did you See," Captain Nerishe asks quietly. I look up. She and Watson and Gengler stare at our tableau, the latter two with horrified expressions. Captain Nerishe just looks concerned.

"Battle," I say. "The ex-duke's forces attacking. And...and demons." I shudder. "And the magic was...not normal."

"What do you mean, not normal?" she asks sharply.

"Demon-ridden," Orrin says, his voice just short of a sob. "Those soldiers—those people—the demons were attacking them. Attacking us. I don't know what the bishop thinks he can–" he breaks off. "And there was so much power there, just calling to us." He shivers, panting.

I crawl over the rocky ground to his side, but I don't touch him yet. It might still be too dangerous for us to touch. The magic still courses through us both.

Hugh gathers Orrin back into his arms and holds him. "Are you all right?" he asks me.

"I...I don't know," I wheeze. "I guess so. This was just, it seemed...stronger. I don't know how."

"It shouldn't be, way out here. There isn't much magic to draw on."

"It's finding us," Orrin says, pushing Hugh away to stand, brushing himself off. "It's seeking us out."

Hugh looks at Nerishe and jerks his chin at Gengler and Watson. Captain Nerishe stands up. "Right. Let's get everything cleaned up and set the watches. Watson, you're up first with me. Gengler, bank the fire. Time for bed."

Still shaky, I take Linnet's hand and head for the saddlebags and our tent. Washing up in a stream is strange but the running water is soothing. Orrin and I keep away from each other. When I crawl into the small tent, I curl up with Linnet and clamp my eyes and mouth shut. I don't know what to think about myself right now. The demon power should repulse me, shouldn't it? But I wanted to reach for it like nothing else. And future me was saying that was exactly what I should do.

CHAPTER 14

Trail riding on forest paths, following whatever path Hugh has mapped out to wherever we're going, feels like I've entered a dream world, one filled with saddle sores and aching muscles. I don't think we get as far each day as Hugh would like, but Orrin, Linnet, and I have to rest as we get used to the horses. We're not naturals.

To further wear us out, each afternoon when we stop Captain Nerishe instructs us on the finer points of defending ourselves against people who want to kidnap or harm us. We're not naturals at that, either. Watson and Gengler make it clear they will not spar with witches, although not in so many words. I tell Captain Nerishe not to force them. I don't want to work with them, either. They look at us with such distrust.

Captain Nerishe or Hugh take the lead for sparring, or we go against one another. Linnet hits hard, surprising no one. Orrin and I are afraid to touch one another, so we keep to other partners. Since they don't join in the sparring Nerishe assigns Gengler and Watson longer watches at night.

We do manage to get the drop on Captain Nerishe once during sparring—all three of us. But it's only because we can send to one another. Hugh laughs on the sidelines when we knock her feet out from under her. She laughs at us and tells us good work, but I think she let us win.

Each night in our tents, Linnet, Orrin and I sleep sore and weary—deeply but not enough. One benefit to all this activity is that it does keep our visions to a mini-mum, and the magic isn't gathering as strongly where we've been. I suspect Hugh of taking paths where he knows wild magic is weak.

On our tenth day of camping, we follow a road past a small village and toward a rough keep on a hill above a river. Hugh tells us its name is Dorward, where we're finally meeting Connor. I'm certain Captain Nerishe and the guards suspected where we were going far sooner, but if Hugh thinks we might have foiled spies in keeping that to himself, it at least makes him feel better.

The keep has dark, ruddy sandstone walls and a square tower that doesn't look as though it's been updated in several centuries. The more modern manor to the south seems less substantial, but I lay bets on it being far less drafty.

When we reach the gate, I see guards along the crenellations, a few of whom look familiar. They must be the guard Connor traveled with to Corat when he left Haverston last fall. They seem as competent as always, watching without staring, bowing to Hugh when we arrive, tired and sore form an almost full day of riding.

The courtyard is smaller than Haverston castle's, in

part because the manor takes up much of the old yard. I look around for Connor, but don't see him. I desperately look forward to dismounting. My stomach dances with butterflies, but my thighs and rear are glad to see the end of this day's ride. Despite special ointments from Captain Nerishe, I ache and chafe, and I'm certain that I won't be comfortable sitting for weeks.

When the captain halts her mount, all our horses shuffle to a stop. Everyone starts to dismount. Linnet and Orrin do so without help this time. I scowl at them, determined to do as well as they. I lean forward, grasping the pommel and the reins, and try to lift my right leg. I swear I can hear my bones creaking. I've been assured I'm too young for that, but I feel it nonetheless.

Easing my leg up and over the saddle takes concentration, as I try to keep my split skirt from tangling on the gear. I let out an involuntary soft groan.

Hands grasp my waist and help me finish dismounting. I startle, look over my shoulder. Connor's face, his mouth crooked in a tiny smile, looks at me.

"Oh," I say stupidly, my heart kicking into a flutter, and I lean a little on him as my feet try out the ground. "Con...my lord, how good to see you," I stammer, not sure how to start with him now, after not seeing him for so long. He takes a breath, his smile tightening, and nods, quickly whisking his hands from my waist when Hugh laughs.

"Connor!" Hugh calls. "Well met indeed, my friend. I am so very glad to get here and have a rest in a proper bed."

I stand, unsure, the reins still in my grip until a stable hand clears her throat, and I blush and give them to her. Blush more.

"I have no doubt," Connor says to Hugh, smiling. "I'm sure everyone is tired of your complaining by now."

"I don't know what you're talking about," Hugh sniffs. Orrin smirks and looks away.

"My lord fitzWellan," Nerishe says with a bow when he turns to her.

"Captain," he returns. "I trust things are under control."

"Yes, my lord."

Watson and Gengler head off with the horses, and Connor smiles at everyone with a genial look that isn't really like him. "Welcome to Dorward. It isn't much, but it makes a decent profit in hardwoods and small farms—enough to keep everyone here fed and housed." He makes a sweeping motion to include the keep and yard. "Let's go inside. You'll have a few days to relax before we move on. Take some time to rest now before dinner. There are several rooms prepared." He motions toward the manor, not the keep, thank goodness, and we start to walk.

He keeps his back to me, falling into step with Hugh and clapping him on the back, the rough banter of old friends between them. I glance at Orrin. He shrugs and follows along.

I trail behind, uncertain if his reaction to me was about me or if I just imagined his sudden withdrawal. Connor is usually brusque, I remind myself. At best, I add. And we are in...well, not a hurry. Yet. But there's probably a lot to do. There's no reason for him to linger with me.

He turns his head to give me a speculative glance but keeps talking to Hugh. I'm not sure how I'm supposed to act. We never had any kind of...understanding. But I thought he understood, anyway. Now I'm not sure.

Linnet walks beside me, scowling. That's not unusual, so I don't know if it's Connor, me, the weather, her sore rear, or any combination of these things. But she does seem to be directing most of her scowl at Connor.

"He could have taken time to greet you properly," she mutters.

"He did help her down from the horse," Orrin says, falling in on my other side.

"Will you two hush," I whisper, embarrassed.

"I wasn't loud. And anyway, I hope he does hear me," Linnet says. "He should feel bad."

"Maybe he wants to talk to her in private first, to see what kind of public displays she wants. It could be he's trying to be considerate."

"Or he's a jerk, like I always thought," Linnet says.

"Both of you. Shut. Up." I grind out between clenched teeth. Hugh looks around, his face full of questions, and I beam brilliantly at him. It does nothing to diminish his questions.

What's the matter, he sends to us.

Absolutely nothing. Please ignore us, I send back.

Connor is rude, Linnet breaks in, and I grab her arm and smile at everyone as we enter the manor. Linnet winces.

"Ow!"

Hugh looks between us all in confusion, glancing at Connor.

Not rude. Ignore her. Ignore all of us, I send firmly, which makes everyone wince, including Orrin, who I didn't mean to include. I wince back in apology.

"I think a rest would be a very good idea," I say too brightly as we gather in the entry hall. Connor gives me a wry look. He can tell when conversations are happening without him. I just hope he can't tell what they're about. "Where are those rooms?"

How was Connor rude? Hugh sends.

Never mind, I send firmly to everyone. Except Connor. I take a deep breath and hold it, smiling with determination.

Connor nods to the stairs. "Third door on the left, second floor. It should be aired and ready. Someone will wake you in plenty of time for dinner."

"Thank you," I say. Curtseying in my best manners, I turn and drag Linnet and Orrin with me up the stairs.

"Orrin, you and Hugh take the second door," Connor calls after us.

"You didn't wait to hear his news," Orrin says.

"I don't trust either one of you, and we're all going to take a nice nap right now and hear the news later. It won't change between now and then."

"Quit pinching me," Linnet complains.

"Quit being a pain," I say. She kicks at my foot, but I drag her up the stairs and down the hall anyway.

"I don't know why you're mad at me," she sulks. "He's the one who was rude."

I drag us into the third door. The room is well-furnished, but the fabrics are old and just barely north of shabby. I think Connor's coffers might not be up to managing this estate—at least one he says he sees so seldom.

"He wasn't being rude, Linnet. He just wasn't effusive. And—and we haven't had a chance to...to talk about anything."

"He's a crummy correspondent, too, then," she harrumphs.

"I'm sure he's been busy." I don't know why I'm defending him. She won't listen, and I we never wrote down anything specific. I mean about us.

We did write letters, at first. He wrote me specifically about Julianna, the baby, the kirche's decision about Gantry, about how they'd mostly left my powers—and Orrin's—out of the story. Although rumors got out, and the Indrani Empire will be sending a new ambassador to court, likely to find out more, and many people want to inspect us. Some threatened to travel to Haverston, but with the army sending new troops forward and wounded back through the town, the duchess asked the king to keep courtiers away.

He wrote me some about those things. But never specifically about us. And so I didn't, either. The letters stopped a few months ago. Three months ago...and two weeks. But travel days don't count.

I sit down on the bed. The bedding is clean and dust-free, at least, so some effort has been made to air and clean the room.

"I'm tired, Linnet, and I ache. I really don't want to talk about it."

"Fine. Do you have the ointment the captain gave you?"

"It's—it's in the pack." I groan and stand up. "I'll go find it."

The hallway is striped in shadow and the fading daylight. Voices carry along the hall from downstairs.

"I don't trust that he didn't have anyone following you," Connor says.

"We did our best to confuse matters, my lord, but I

can't be entirely certain," Nerishe answers. "Our party is not completely inconspicuous, but we stayed off the main roads and camped. Which took us longer than I liked, but considering the youngsters' inexperience, we made good enough time."

"How was it?" Connor asks. I lean on the wall, waiting to hear her answers.

"Unsettling," Hugh says. "We need to discuss what's happening with Orrin and Rhiannon. The magic is getting stronger, and the visions are...taking them somehow. I think they're in some sort of loop that's twisting on itself. We need to consider all help that might be...offered." He sounds grim. I bite my lips and hunch over a little. It's been days, but yes, that strong vision was disturbing.

"Then it's still happening? Even away from Haverston?"

"It happened once on the trip here—the vision pulling them into it. They had one other vision of a battle, but not nearly as strong. Orrin and Rhiannon can't touch one another when the magic is moving in them. And it does move in them. I've consulted with Nerishe on how to handle them in the future. They need something physical to hold onto when they're fading. It helps to end the vision. But it's getting harder to do. Linnet has turned to punching and slapping to get them back."

Honestly I don't think Connor is surprised to hear that. I hear him snort, then sigh.

"But the trip over was otherwise uneventful? No sign of anyone following?"

"Not that any of us could tell, sir," Captain Nerishe answers.

"And what is your view of Orrin and Rhiannon and Linnet?"

"They're good young people. They learn fast and don't try to pretend they know things they don't...most of the time."

I wince. I really did think I could cook over a fire. I was just wrong, that's all.

"And you trust Gengler and Watson? I looked into their backgrounds, but you've known them longer."

"I can confirm your assessment," the captain says quietly.

"How are they taking the magic portion of the assignment?"

"They knew some of it going in, of course. I don't think they're happy about it, but they haven't said anything out loud."

"And you've seen nothing suspicious from either of them?"

"I saw nothing amiss," Hugh says. Nerishe says nothing.

"Do we continue with the same travel plan then?" Hugh asks after a moment.

"I think it best. Staying off the roads as much as possible seems to have kept them safe so far."

"How likely do you think it is we'll be attacked in small inns now? Surely we could at least take the hill route. It's less traveled."

"How likely was an attack in Haverston? I think two days rest, then continuing on horseback off road is the smartest plan."

"I think you want to do it just to torment me," Hugh says, his voice peevish.

"Don't be ridiculous," Connor laughs. "You're just grumpy because you hate to camp."

"I don't hate to camp. I hate to forage. And I hate stew."

"My lords, I could let you continue this conversation in private," Captain Nerishe says. I pull further back into the hall, not wanting to be discovered.

"Go get some rest, Hugh," Connor says. "You're cranky."

"Pot calling kettle," Hugh grumps back, and starts to stomp up the stairs toward me. I backtrack to my door and pretend I just came out of it as he turns the corner.

"What is it, Rhiannon?" he asks me.

"I've forgotten something I need from the packs," I mumble.

"Well, make sure you get some rest, wouldn't want anyone to think you're grumpy," he mutters to the corridor in general, and lets himself into his room. I head downstairs, where Captain Nerishe is taking her leave of Connor and heading up the stairs herself. She smiles at me as she passes, and then I'm face to face with Connor.

"Hello," I say, trying to be cheerful as I pass by. I can feel my cheeks burning.

"Rhiannon—is there something wrong with the room?" Connor asks.

"Oh, no, I just forgot something in my pack," I say, and try to edge past.

"I have someone bringing your bags in now," Connor says. "I can have them brought to you. You don't have to get them yourself."

"Oh." I bite my lip, and gesture back to the stairs. "I'll just, um, go back then."

He reaches toward me, then lets his hand drop. "Wait. Can you stay back a moment? I want..." he hesitates. "I think we need to talk."

Talk. Yes. My cheeks get hotter, and the little moths in my stomach flutter harder. "Of course," I say, and follow him through a door off the hall. His library, or maybe a study. It's small, with a desk and bookshelves and a short couch, a comfy chair. He watches me look around.

"I know it's not very large, but it's comfortable," he says. He gestures to the couch, and I sit. He fidgets a moment, then sits next to me. I raise my eyebrows. Fidgeting is not like him.

"What's wrong?" I ask.

He sighs and looks at his knuckles. "I wanted to tell you...in person that..."

The door pushes farther open and a young man enters. "My lord, the stablemaster is asking for you. There seems to be a problem with one of the mares."

"Thank you, Percy." Connor says, sighing again. He closes his eyes as the man exits. "Rhiannon, I...I don't wish to, that is, I regret..." My stomach plummets. He seems at a loss, so I finish for him.

"Your feelings for me have changed," I say woodenly. "I understand."

He looks dismayed but not surprised. My heart sinks along with my stomach. "That isn't what I was going to say, exactly. They haven't changed, per se..."

I stand up. "But you regret them. You regret me."

"No, I don't. Please understand."

"I understand," I say and turn blindly to the door, my headache much worse. "You should really go out to the stables. You're needed to deal with a problem."

"Rhiannon, stop," he says sharply.

"No," I say, but his hand is on my arm. "Let me go." I don't want to look at him. I don't want to start crying.

He turns me, his hands on my shoulders. "I will, but please look at me first." Reluctantly I raise my eyes, blinking. "Will you let me actually say what I mean?" he asks.

"Fine."

"I have...certain responsibilities. To my king, to my country. To my family. They are oaths I took a long time ago, but they are oaths. I take them seriously. Which means that I..." he closes his eyes, presses his lips together.

"Just say it."

"I'm constrained in what I can do, Rhiannon."

"You can't court me because your oaths won't allow it?"

"I'm trying to-"

"You're trying to be kind about something that isn't kind at all," I say, clenching my teeth. "You're trying to tell me you don't like me. I understand." My breath is fast and my eyes sting. My heart gallops and my treacherous skin tingles where he's touching me. He glares into my eyes, and I glare back. "Fine. I don't like you, either."

He takes a deep breath, lowering his chin. "Well, that's disappointing," he says. "Because I like you every bit as much as I ever did."

"Oh," I say. Stupidly.

"I am still attracted to you, Rhiannon. I shouldn't be. I'm too old for you. It would be taking advantage. I have responsibilities that mean I shouldn't—but I do. I care for you far too much." He cups my cheek, his palm warm on my skin. "I'm sorry, Rhiannon. I'm sorry for everything." He leans in a little but doesn't kiss me.

I lean up to kiss him instead. He leans back, away from me. I cringe away, embarrassed.

"I really am sorry," he says. "You have every right to be upset with me. But I can't...pursue a romance with you."

I step back. "That doesn't make any sense," I say, my voice thick.

"I know."

"What does your age have to do with anything? I never said you were taking advantage. And what responsibilities? Can't you tell me more than that?" I feel my voice go wobbly with tears. I am so angry.

He sighs and looks down. "Maybe I should let you get some rest. You might find you agree with me after you have a chance to calm down."

"Calm down?" I sputter. "Are you trying to be patronizing right now?"

He winces. "I apologize. I apologize for everything." He spreads his hands wide, looking sad but immovable. I feel the tears starting, so I spin around and head back for the room with Linnet, wiping furiously at my eyes. He doesn't want any part of me. I am too young, he is too oathbound, and he is constrained from courting me. Fine. He is a fathead. I stalk back to the bedroom and throw open the door and slam it behind me.

Linnet jumps, muffling a squeak, standing in front of the window. When she sees it's me, she glares. "They brought the bags up while you were gone. Where did you go?"

"Nowhere."

"Are you—are you crying?"

"No. Shut up. I'm tired, and I need a nap," I say. "Apparently, I'm cranky, too. Let's just rest and not talk."

"Connor was a jerk again, wasn't he?"

"I'm not talking now, I'm sleeping." I snarl and crawl onto the creaky old bed after stripping out of my traveling clothes down to my shift.

Linnet climbs up next to me without saying another word and pets my head while I snuffle into a wadded handkerchief, the one with Connor's initials on it, until Orrin knocks later. Linnet answers the door, but she tells him we'll take a tray in the room and to let us rest. I can feel them sending to each other in the back of my mind, but I shut them out and curl up tighter, until I fall asleep.

CHAPTER 15

I wake with a gasp, energy zinging through me, jerking me out of sleep. The room is dark—it feels late, or early. An unsettling restlessness crawls through my limbs, while Linnet snores lightly beside me.

I hear voices murmuring to each other down the hall. I stare at the ceiling, making out dim shapes in the waning moonlight through the window. The drapes are open a crack, just enough for unfamiliar shapes to look ominous.

The zinging gets stronger. Magic, stirring and moving under my skin. A vision wants in: that's what woke me.

I throw back the covers and stand. Linnet stirs but doesn't wake. I grab my dress from the foot of the bed and toss it over my shift. Magic pushes at my boundaries. I can feel it building again. I don't want a vision right now. I don't know what's causing this one, but I think I'll need help if it gets stronger.

I could stay here, but I'm too restless. I don't want to

wake Linnet—she'll only punch me or something. Maybe I can fight it back if I distract myself. I think about waking Orrin, or Hugh, but Orrin and I feed off each other too much, and Hugh—well, Hugh might be downstairs. Maybe I'll go downstairs. Connor might be downstairs.

I don't let myself think much past that. Opening the door, I pad down the dark hall. The voices are somewhere nearby. I recognize Nerishe but not the other.

A door opens down the hall, an arc of light spills out onto the floor. "Don't do anything yet," I hear her say, angry and harsh. "And don't let anyone see you, for pity's sake."

A surge of fear jolts through me. Why would she say that? To whom? I feel the magic jump in my skin, in my bones, and I scuttle behind a wall hanging, waiting for the person to step fully out the door and hoping they don't look down to see my toes sticking out.

I hold my breath; listening to booted footsteps quietly and quickly heading for the back stairs. I peek out and peer down the hall, but all I see is a dark shape disappearing around a corner.

The captain's door is closed now. The only light is pale moonlight from the windows, slowly giving way to dawn. My hands shake with uncertain fear and gathering magic. I watch them tremble, watch the world go transparent.

I brush at the hanging but it's so heavy. The vision pushes at me from the inside out.

Through it, I See the walls of the keep in early morning light, ruddy and tall and imposing. Running people, a man, an explosion, blood—so much blood, always blood...

I fight this vision. I'm not ready for it, and it's coming at me in waves, in bits and pieces, trying to draw me through the yawning vortex that blows through my mind, pulling me closer, calling to me.

Wheezing, I yank myself back to now, to here, in this hall, fallen on my hands and knees, no screaming, no explosions, no vortex. I scramble to my feet and run down the hall. Which one is Connor's door? Connor, I need Connor. I can feel him downstairs, can feel his heartbeat when I search for it, his quiet, closed mind giving nothing away.

I cling to the banister as I rush to him, tripping, fading, concentrating on the feel of wood and stone, the single lamp in the entrance hall. I stumble down the last few steps—the sting and slap of stone under my hands when I fall.

Explosions—again—screaming horses, running people, blood on the grass. The grass under my hands—no, no—stone.

I scramble my way to the library, weeping. The room flickers in front of me, and I sway, leaning against the open door as Connor jolts to standing from the chair in front of the fire.

"Rhiannon, what is it? What's wrong?"

I can feel myself fading, the magic coursing through me to bring me to the vision, to bring me to the vortex, all of the magic crawling through me and trying to tell me—what? The door clicks shut behind me as I let it take my weight.

"Help me. I'm lost...I'm—the vision..." I gasp, reaching one hand to him. His horrified face fades, becomes the broken wall of the keep, the blood on the grass, his own body lying limp and covered in rubble. I shake my head, try to back away from it. I pull up short, pulled back to the present by the strong grasp of Connor's hand.

"Stay here. Stay here with me. What's the vision? What does it want you to know?"

"An explosion," I say, panting. "Here, the keep wall—someone is trying to—you're hurt, the keep falls," I cry. His hands pull me close, his arms around me.

"Rhiannon, stay here. Do not let this pull you away. Stay here," he commands, and I try to do as he says, try to direct the flow of the magic away.

He grasps my face in both hands and looks in my eyes. "Where are you going?" he rasps.

"I don't know, I'm lost, I'm lost," I whimper, as his eyes show me the explosions again. My body shudders as too much magic rushes through me.

"You're not lost. Come back. Come find me," he says, and then his lips are fierce on mine, desperate, and I kiss him back. The hot course of something other than magic through my veins—the power finding another path as the kiss grounds me in the here and now.

A low sound escapes me, and Connor groans back, his hands tightening, arms surrounding me, his chest warm and solid under my hands. I slide my palms up to his shoulders, pull myself closer. My knees grow weak, my head spinning.

There's a pounding in my head, in my chest, and also, I realize after a moment, on the door. Connor breaks the kiss off, panting, stares at me as I stare back, my arms still around his neck. He gently tugs my hands down, holding them as he backs up a step.

"What is it?" he says aloud. I look at him in confusion, and then understand that he's asking whoever is knocking. The door bangs open, Linnet throwing it wide in haste, Hugh carrying Orrin behind her.

"Thank Dorei, here you are. Orrin almost disappeared this time, the vision was so strong. And when we couldn't find Rhiannon, or reach her anywhere, we were..." Hugh trails off, out of breath.

"Why didn't you respond when I was sending to you?" Linnet accuses, taking in Connor and I, disheveled and holding hands.

"Is Orrin hurt?" I demand, dropping Connor's hands. "He fainted?" The vision was strong, but we weren't close to one another this time. I didn't See him in the vision. "He's never fainted before. What happened?"

"Tackled him," Linnet says. "Hugh was shaking him, and it wasn't working, so I threw him to the ground."

"Linnet! Did you knock him out?"

"Well, it worked. The magic let him go."

Orrin's eyes flutter, and he winces. Hugh takes him to the couch and sets him down, his face grim with concern. "I don't know if it was Linnet or the magic, but he's been out cold." Orrin's eyes open at that, and he looks up at Hugh, his eyes blinking and confused.

"No, I haven't," he rasps.

Hugh shakes his head at him and brushes his hand over his forehead. "No? Then where are we, and how did we get here?"

Orrin frowns, his face going red under the brown of his skin. "All right, maybe I wasn't entirely here for a moment," he mutters.

I stay back, remembering not to touch him. Although the magic seems to be waning for the moment. Still there, but it's...simmering. We could end up in another vision if we touch now, even with it backing down. I want to sit beside my friend and hug him. I settle on sending to him instead.

Are you all right now? Did you See the explosion?

I'm fine. And yes—but I didn't See you.

"What did you See," Connor asks, and I turn to him, my own cheeks still hot, going warmer again as I realize how close he is. He backs up a step, and so do I. Taking a deep breath, I look back at everyone else.

"It was here," Orrin says. "The stables. On fire. There was a...we are betrayed..." he breaks off to start to sit up, groans and grabs his head. "I Saw Lieutenant Watson. He's a spy. I saw him set a flame, saw him run from the blast and head toward the keep wall. And I saw you, Your Grace," he says to Hugh. "You ran toward the fire and then...Gods. Don't run toward the fire."

"Watson," Hugh hisses. "Are you sure?"

"It's a vision," Orrin grumbles. "I can't be sure of anything. I don't know why he set that explosion, only that he's going to. Or is probably going to. But the feeling through the vision is that he is determined in his course, and it isn't a kind one."

"Was your vision the same, Rhiannon?"

"You had one, too?" Hugh asks.

"I told you. I felt the pull," Linnet says.

"I thought that leak was shut down," Hugh frowns at her.

"It was! Until it wasn't," Linnet mutters. "It's not my fault."

"Then whose fault is it?" he asks, but his attention isn't on her, he's fussing over Orrin, putting a blanket over his shoulders. Linnet glares at me.

"Rhiannon's. Probably."

I shake my head at her, shrug. "We'll keep working on it," I mumble.

"What was your vision, Rhiannon?" Connor asks.

I can only look at him out of the corner of my eyes. I don't know how to react to anything. "Similar, but from another angle. I Saw a man, but I couldn't tell who it was. There's another explosion at the keep, or part of the wall, and..." I stammer, clear my throat. "There was a lot of blood. Connor—the wall collapsed on you, and I was being dragged away, or I was running, or...I don't know, it was...disjointed."

"Disjointed how?" Hugh asks.

"I was fighting it. I didn't want it. I didn't want the magic to pull me in. It felt...dangerous."

Hugh stops his fussing, his hand on Orrin's shoulder, but everyone looks at me.

"It's been dangerous, Rhiannon," Hugh says gently.

"More dangerous."

"When you–"

"Can we figure out when this is happening?" Connor asks. "Did you See anything that lets us know the timeframe? It happens here—soon—because we aren't going to stay here more than a day or two. Has the charge already been set?"

"It was morning," I say.

"It is morning," Linnet snaps. "So is it now?"

The ground shakes, a sudden explosion cracking across the yard. Everyone ducks or crouches as the building rattles and shudders.

"I guess that answers that question," Connor snarls,

pulling me further away from the windows. "Hugh, with me. Everyone else stay here."

He strides out of the library, Hugh on his heels, and I look at Orrin and Linnet, in shock.

"If he thinks we're staying here just on his say-so, he's going to be sadly disappointed," I say, and Linnet stands from her crouch.

"Where are you going?"

"To stop Connor from getting crushed by a wall. He didn't even check where he shouldn't stand, that fathead. You and Orrin stay together, get Captain Nerishe—or—no. Don't," I say, a feeling of dread creeping over me.

"What? Why?"

"I don't know."

Orrin looks at me, nods. Magic swells again between us. He can feel it, too. The dread.

"'I don't know' isn't a good answer," Linnet snaps.

"It's all I have. Just—go get our things, be ready to make a run for it if Connor or Hugh say so."

"Don't you get crushed by a wall," she demands. "Why don't I go with you?"

"Because someone needs to be with Orrin, too, and Connor will keep me safe," I say.

"Not if he's dead," she snaps and I shove her toward the door.

"No one is dying. I won't let them. Get our things. Stay away from—oh, everyone. Just in case." I hug her from behind fiercely, and she turns and grabs onto me. I don't reach for Orrin, but he nods at me.

"Stay safe," he says to me. "Don't let Hugh run into the fire. Stay away from Watson if you can."

"You two keep each other safe. I'll get Connor and Hugh," I say.

We file out of the library carefully. Shouting people rush past, out the door to the courtyard. We let ourselves get caught up in the movements of panicked people. No one pays any attention to us.

I make my way outside. The stables are on fire. Through the smoke I can see people leading horses out across the courtyard, vague shapes against the morning light. Dawn broke while we were in the library. The flames look strange against the brightening sky. Don't let Hugh run toward the fire, Orrin said.

Hugh helps a water bucket brigade but isn't running toward the fire—good. Now I just have to stop Connor from getting crushed.

I find him stalking someone near the keep wall. He's flattened against the stones, edging toward a corner. No one seems to see him but me. No one pays attention to anything but the fire.

Magic licks along my scars like flames, like lightning. Like balefire. I run to Connor.

I See...me. Me standing by the wall, the wall that is about to explode, and I know I am Seeing myself having my vision.

"No. No no no no," I yell, and reach Connor's side to yank him away from the danger.

"Rhi—what—stop it," he sputters.

"Get away from the wall," I shout, watching myself flicker and fade over his shoulder. He blinks and then lets me pull at him. It all looks so familiar—the light, the air, the smell of magic and something caustic, and fire, and then another explosion as we run from the keep.

It knocks me sideways and Connor with me. My head rings like a bell as I hit the ground, stones raining down around us and everything moving in slow motion.

I struggle to my hands and knees, shaking my head, trying to make my ears and eyes work together. I look around for Connor, find him unconscious beside me. Patting his face doesn't wake him up, but I don't see any blood, which is a relief. He sports a rising lump on the back of his head, maybe a scrape. Nothing obviously broken.

Ringing fills my ears, and I squint against blossoming pain in my neck and head, looking around for help. I try to send to Linnet but wince against the ache.

Where are you? Are you hurt? Hugh, Linnet, Orrin—all of them clamoring in my head. I clap my hands over my ears in a useless gesture against all the sendings in my mind.

Connor was knocked out, I send with difficulty. *We're near the keep.* I look up to find two men prowling toward us, one of them Lieutenant Watson, and I panic. I can't leave Connor. I try to drag him by his arms, but he's too heavy. *Watson is coming. I need help—Hurry!*

Watson and the other man look grim and determined. I stand in front of Connor with my feet apart, trying to remember all the lessons Captain Nerishe taught us these past days. I promised Linnet I'd stay safe. I don't know how to fight—not really.

But I'm not helpless. I call up magic—less than I'd have at Haverston, but still plenty—and work a spell Hugh's been teaching me. It makes a physical barrier that can repel people. My power runs hot again as I push the barrier into place. The grass in front of me starts to crackle and smoke.

The guards stop, glancing at each other. They must know they don't have much time before help reaches me. I only have to hold out for a little while.

My ringing head and ears make it hard to handle the magic, though. I can feel it starting to overheat. There are tiny flames licking the grass now, too.

Watson lunges at the barrier. It pushes back, and he screams as it burns him. I drop the spell in horror as he falls to the ground, rolling and yelling. The other man charges and knocks me down in a bruising heap over Connor, who groans. I groan, too.

Then it is my turn to scream as the man yanks my arms forward and snaps manacles on my wrists. It hurts, it burns so much—all I can do is scream with it.

Connor surges up from under us, knife flashing. He and the guard fight above me for less time than it takes me to scream myself out of breath.

The guard is messily dead, his blood on the grass all around me. Connor kneels over the still living Lieutenant Watson, dripping knife in one hand, the other gripping the man's shirt.

"Remove the restraints or die," he says, his voice gravelly and dangerous. Watson shakes his head, but his eyes are wide with fear.

I try to breathe through the pain, but it takes all my strength. Magic streams through me into the manacles, dragging along my scars, along my bones, scraping me from the inside. I whimper with each breath, as softly as I can manage. Captain Nerishe runs up, her sword drawn, panting. Half of her dark face reflects the morning sunlight, painting the rest in shadow.

Watson remains silent at Connor's threat. "The restraints," Connor repeats. "Remove them or I'll kill you."

Nerishe looks at them, then at me, and squats down beside me. She reaches out for my arms but I wince away, crying out. Everything hurts. Touching will only make it worse, I'm sure of it. I feel magic draining from me in great draughts and I don't know how to stop it.

I slump forward. "Get them off, please get them off," I gasp.

Nerishe glances at Connor, then stands and yanks Watson away from him and off the ground. He's burned and charred in places but mostly in one piece. He spits, glaring as she shakes him to standing. I don't know if he's making a statement or just getting blood out of his mouth.

"I don't think the ex-duke wanted these two harmed at all. Your delivery methods are flawed," she says, then slashes his throat with a quick slice of her sword.

"Why did you—Captain!" Connor flinches back from the blood spatter, shock on his face. Then anger. "You're with them," he snarls.

"I am not, my lord, or I wouldn't have killed him. We have to get everyone to the horses," she says calmly, then shakes her head. "If any of them are rideable now."

Connor puts up his guard. I writhe away from both of them, painfully pushing myself along the ground.

"You're not taking us anywhere," he says.

"No, I'm not." She agrees. Connor narrows his eyes.

"What are you playing at, Nerishe?"

Hugh and Orrin and Linnet come barreling around the corner, Hugh's blade is out, Linnet leaning on Orrin, limping but furious and ready to jump in. But Anouk Nerishe taught us all the fighting moves we have, and only in the last several days. I don't think anyone but Hugh will be any help in this situation. I curl on my side around my hands and try to keep myself together.

Nerishe slowly puts her sword down, carefully away

from the blood and the two dead men. "I'm not playing at anything right now, my lord. He was going to send to his master, and we needed him not to do it."

"I needed him to get those damn things off of her!"

Whatever spell drives the restraints, it's pulling magic through me, drawing it from the ground and into me and then the metal, like I am a spindle and the yarn both and spinning out thinner and thinner.

"What happened?" Hugh demands as they approach.

"She's with them—with Watson," Connor snarls.

"No, I'm not. I was working against them," Nerishe says, sweat dripping down her temple. "I know how to remove the manacles, but you'll have to do it. The little magic I have—I can't touch them."

Connor kneels beside me on the bloody ground. I feel his hands on mine as I gasp, too tired to cry out anymore. "What do I do," he snaps, his face fierce and close.

"Between the wrists is a clasp. Using this key, you have to push in and twist," she says, and a key appears in her hand. Connor rips it away from her and fumbles at my wrists for a moment. I try to say something pithy, but I'm grinding my teeth together too hard to open my mouth.

"I've got you," Connor murmurs, his voice harsh. A click, and the sensation of my spirit being pulled from my skin turns off like a water spigot. Connor rips the manacles off and flings them away. I sag to my back, and he grasps my head gently between his hands, looks in my eyes.

"Rhiannon, how are you hurt? What do you need?"

I feel the tears cooling on my cheeks, the grass tickling my neck, my calves where my skirt has rucked up. I take deep, gulping breaths, the relief from the pain almost euphoric. I smile shakily. "I...I feel a lot better," I say. "Just let me...let me breathe a bit."

"You swore you wouldn't get hurt!" Linnet yells, limping toward me. Orrin helps her, keeping a wary eye on the messy corpses that are too close, too upsetting. I swallow back bile and keep breathing.

Hugh flanks the captain, keeping between her and the rest of us. She stands with her hands out to her sides, palms up, unarmed.

"I offer you no harm," she says.

"You've already done the harm," Connor growls. "Hugh, what's the damage?"

"Stables are a loss, but most of the horses were saved. A few burns, some cuts and broken limbs on people. These are the only two dead, I believe. Your people are taking control, and the fire's almost out. You were the only ones near this explosion."

"Good."

"My lord, Your Grace, we should leave immediately. The horses–" Nerishe starts, but Hugh cuts her off.

"No. Not on horseback. Connor—backup plan."

"Yes," Connor says, his face grim.

"We'll need to find Percy. We'll have him take six— no, five people on horses and set out toward the capital in an hour. I'll make sure they look plausible." Hugh turns to Orrin and Linnet. "Orrin, I'm going to need you to get the packs together, and we'll leave another way."

"First secure this...Nerishe," Connor says. He looks up over Hugh's head. "Over here," he calls past us to the courtyard.

"Do you know who you can trust?" Nerishe asks.

"Do you?" Connor snarls back at her.

"Some of them."

"But we can't trust you, can we?" Hugh asks quietly, looking disappointed and grave, smudges of ash on his pale face.

"Look in my vest pocket, Your Grace. You'll find a letter from your mother."

"My m-, what has my mother to do with any of this?" Hugh hisses.

"Perhaps the letter will explain that," Linnet mutters, trying to help me to stand.

"I had no choice," Nerishe says. "They threatened my family. The duchess advised this course of action to keep my children and wife safe. I fed the spies misleading information and did my best to stop them from harming anyone. The letter will tell you that."

"You didn't keep them from harming anyone," Connor snarls. He sheathes his sword and takes over from Linnet, hauling me up in his arms.

"I can walk," I say, but my voice is weak, and I'm not sure of it.

"All the same," he says to me. He turns to the soldiers who've run over at his call, gestures to Nerishe. "Bring her to the hall and keep her under guard. I need a full damage report—injuries, all of it. I need Quentin and Raoul to ready the river barge. And go to the village for the fisicus. Quickly."

My limbs and head are heavy and the world swirls around me. It's just as well Connor picked me up after all. I look up at him, at his fierce expression, and feel a bit like laughing. He frowns at me, striding toward the manor.

"What are you smiling about?"

"I don't know. We're alive—that seems nice."

He looks concerned rather than pleased, but I'm glad we're alive. He holds me a little closer. "It was too close. You should have run," he growls.

"Don't yell at her, you big oaf." Linnet snaps at him, jogging unevenly at his side.

"How did you get hurt," I ask her. "Why are you limping?"

She glares at the general surroundings. "I tripped when I felt the magic draining from you—because you keep linking to me. Orrin was helping me stop it. It was hard, but we did it, the both of us. And then we came to find you. But we fixed that stupid link for good, I think. I don't feel it at all, now."

Connor sweeps in through the front doors of the manor with me in his arms, and then into the library to put me down on a couch.

"Stay here," he orders. He shouts for someone to attend him as he strides away again.

Orrin and Hugh duck in the doorway. Hugh comes to look at me, examines my wrists. They aren't burned this time, although they do ache. "Is it like before?" He asks.

"I don't know. Maybe," I say, but I'm so tired.

"All right. Rest now. If anything—anything else—happens, just send for me. Orrin, will you come with me? I might need you," he says, and the two of them disappear after Connor. Linnet slumps down beside me on the couch.

"Not the best day," she mutters. I lay my head back and close my eyes. No, it's not.

CHAPTER 16

The sense of panic and fear in the manor changes as Connor takes charge. Linnet arrives, moving to a chair to deposit a bundle of coats and other things and stares out the library's window at the courtyard, where some people tend to frightened and injured horses while others ascertain the stability of what's left of the keep wall.

Connor and Hugh organize the hall outside into a makeshift infirmary for the seriously injured. Hugh sends for a fisicus from the nearby village—there's no full Healer close by—and everyone tries to settle their shattered nerves.

Connor comes in to check on Linnet and me, with his steward a step behind. "Will your guests need the fisicus as well, my lord?"

Connor looks at me. I don't think a fisicus will be able to help—whatever else those manacles are, they're magic, and a village fisicus probably won't know what to do with me. I don't want to be examined by a stranger. I shake my head. He closes his eyes for a moment, and sighs. "No time. We must leave immediately. The manor will be safer after we've gone."

"As you wish, my lord," the steward intones. I crane my neck a little to see out the door as he leaves, but I'm too tired to try very hard. Linnet finds a blanket in the bundle and offers it to me. I protest that I'm warm, but it makes her feel better, so I take it. She returns to the chair, dumps the rest of the bundle on the floor, and slumps back with a sigh of her own.

The morning passes, and after a while Orrin wanders in, followed by someone with a tray.

"I thought you might want breakfast," he says, lowering himself next to me on the couch with a wince.

I startle a little out of a daze when he speaks. I realize that I didn't feel him coming in my head, along my runes.

In fact, I think now, I don't feel anything—except sore. I'm not feeling any twinges from being so close to Orrin, and usually I would. I try to send to him, just asking him if he hears me. He pats my foot but doesn't respond.

The server arranges the tray on a low table and pours tea for us, then leaves. Linnet descends on the food like a starving goat, and Orrin rescues several muffins from her ravening horde impression. He offers me one.

"Quick, before they're all gone," he smiles and I'm distracted for a moment by the gratifying sight of my sister eating with appetite and my friend smiling. Even if it is a tentative, worried sort of smile.

The sort of smile you offer your injured friend after they've been attacked—again—and rescued—again—and you wonder if they want comfort or distraction. I take the distraction.

"She might devour the tray as well," I say softly, but Linnet hears me and makes a rude gesture.

"These are really good muffins," she mumbles around a mouthful. Orrin hands her another and takes more for himself.

Hugh walks into the room. "Here you are. Where are your bags?"

"Front hall," Orrin answers around his own muffin.

"Good," Hugh says. "Get ready to leave."

"No more horses," Linnet groans.

"No. Not horses. Boats. Come on."

"What?" I ask, trying to sit up and finding it ridiculously hard.

"Barge, actually," Connor says, coming into the room. He looks around at us—dirty, me splattered with blood, scratched, disheveled. "Did no one bring you anything to clean up with?"

"They might have been a little busy," I murmur, but Connor just shakes his head. A bruise rises above his eye, another on his cheek. Either the rocks or the spies, or both. He looks nearly as disreputable as we do, but at least he washed his face.

"There's no time now. You'll have to clean up on the barge. We leave as soon as everyone's aboard. I don't think Stephen will have anyone ready quickly enough to follow us that way. We'll just have to hope he won't have anyone on the river docks in Corat."

"Barge?" Orrin asks. "A river barge down the Dorward?"

"Corat has plenty of canals and a lot of traffic. We'll be just another delivery of hardwood," Hugh says. His face is a picture of cheer that I know is false, but he does it very well. "It'll be an adventure."

"I hate adventure," I mutter.

"Very sensible of you," Orrin agrees.

"What did the letter say?" I ask, and Hugh and Connor both glance sidelong at each other, keeping their eyes from mine.

"What letter?" Connor says in a distracted tone I don't believe for a moment.

"The letter from Duchess Marguerite that Captain Nerishe said she had, obviously," Linnet drawls.

"Don't be ridiculous. That letter is not from the duchess," Connor snaps. "You don't need to see it."

"Yes I do," I insist. Hugh glowers out the window but says nothing. "Yes, I do. Your Grace, did you even look at it? Does it sound like something she'd say?"

Reluctantly, he turns around. "It does have a code phrase that lets me know it's authentic," he says quietly. "But she might have been fooled by someone much more skilled than she is at subterfuge."

"We don't have time to discuss this now. Let's get going," Connor glowers at us, but I'm not going to budge on this.

"I want to see it," I insist.

Connor glares harder at me. "I don't have it."

"I don't believe you. Let me see it."

"Rhiannon—"

"Let me read it, Connor. What harm can I do?"

I watch as he struggles with his desire to be quick, his desire to be done with this subject, and his desire to be fair. Fairness wins, and he sighs and fishes the letter out of his pocket and walks it over to me.

"Read it quickly," he says flatly. "We're leaving as soon as I get everyone aboard."

"I want to read it, too," Linnet says. Orrin just shifts to look over my shoulder. Connor throws his hands up in the air and stalks away.

"Get them ready to leave," he snaps at Hugh. Hugh rolls his eyes.

I open the letter. It's on heavy paper, folded precisely, a little wrinkled from various pockets. I wait to feel something from it, some zing from the magic, a vision telling me something about who wrote it. But the magic is...just gone. The constant draw and movement along my runes, in my bones, has been replaced with silence and a dull, blunt ache. I suppress a shiver and concentrate on the words.

Marguerite has a lovely, even script, but the words seem benign. I know it's in code, but all the letter looks to say is that Anouk's family misses her and meanwhile spring is lovely in Haverston.

I remember last night—this morning, hearing Nerishe warn someone not to be seen. Shivering, I look up at Hugh. "How can you tell there's a code? It just looks like an ordinary letter. Does it really say Captain Nerishe is working for her and not the ex-duke? Is it enough for you to believe her?"

"The code is right. I'll show it to you sometime. It's pretty sparse in content, but it says to trust Nerishe and that she vouches for her. I'm just not certain that she wrote it of her own will. And I don't like that she had to write it at all."

Orrin looks at me, and I think he's trying to send to me, but I get...nothing. He stares a moment longer, then reaches over and takes the letter from my hands.

His face goes stiff, and I can almost feel the magic working in him. In him, but not in me. "She wrote it. She is—was—unhappy to have to, because she's so upset with Stephen. She's angry about Nerishe's children and wife. It's...she most definitely wrote it of her own free will."

"You're certain," Hugh says and nods at Orrin's sharp look. "All right. We'll discuss it further once we're on our way. Rhiannon, do you think you can walk?"

I assess myself, lowering my legs to the floor. The room spins lazily and the idea of standing seems like a bad one. "I don't think so," I say. "Not yet."

Hugh leans in and scoops me up. "Let's get you settled on the barge then. Everything else will work out. It won't be luxurious, but we've two small cabins with cots. The sooner we leave, the sooner we can get to Corat and have Julianna look at you."

He strides through the manor and the grounds as though he's familiar and comfortable here. We end up at a small dock, through a heavy gate in the manor walls hard by the river.

Hugh's breath is a little harsh as he maneuvers his way up the gangway and onto the barge. I'm tall and not a lightweight, and I start to feel self-conscious about being hauled about like so much freight. "You can put me down. I can make it," I say once we're on board.

"Nonsense. I don't want you falling," Hugh grunts at me. Linnet, trailing behind, snorts.

"Well don't drop her."

Hugh looks offended. "I'm not going to drop her. Open this door—this is one of ours."

It's a smallish cabin with two cots stacked bunk style along each side wall. A narrow table sits against the outside wall under the window, everything made of middling brown or painted gray wood. Hugh settles me into one of the bottom cots and straightens, tugging his shirt into place.

"I'm going to check on Connor," he says, panting a little. "I'm worried that he has a head injury, and no one's made him sit down yet. You, young lady, need to rest. We have several days journey to Corat. You should be able to just lie here decadently and let us take care of you until you're recovered." He smiles and brushes my hair back. "I'll check back in once we're underway."

He glances at Orrin, and I can tell they're sending to one another. But I get nothing. I stare at them, and Hugh looks back, a frown he can't erase sitting behind his reassuring smile. When he leaves, Linnet follows him, after a worried glance at me.

Orrin sits next to me on the cot, folding himself a little to be under the upper bed. "Rhi, I've been trying to send to you—is—it's like your magic is just—I can't feel it anymore." He rubs my shoulder, but I can't look at him.

I pick at the thin gray blanket under me. "I think it's gone," I whisper. He looks at me, eyes wide, takes my hand in his.

"I'll get Hugh," he says, and he's sending again.

"Don't bother them now," I start, but soon everyone is in the cabin, including Connor and Captain Nerishe.

"Why's she here?" Linnet demands.

"It's my duty to bring her to the king," Connor says shortly and glares at everyone in general. "What's wrong with Rhiannon?"

"Nothing, that is, I just..." I look helplessly up at everyone. From a bed. Again. I hate this. "I think the manacles took my magic, at least for now. I can't feel...anything." Except exhausted and unhappy. But honestly, that's pretty normal anymore.

Hugh takes a deep breath. "Are you sure it's gone? Could it be over-extended? Or suppressed due to injury?"

I feel myself shrinking smaller. "It's—there's nothing there. Those—those manacles broke me. Or...I don't know what they did."

Connor shoves Captain Nerishe against the wall with sudden violence that takes all our breath away— especially Nerishe's.

"What did those things do to her?"

Nerishe shakes her head to clear it, or in answer. "I don't know, my lord. I only knew how to remove them."

"How do you reverse it?"

"I don't know."

Connor's arm starts to cut off her airflow, but other than choking she doesn't fight him off.

"Tell me!"

"Connor, that's enough! That won't help anything." Hugh pulls at Connor, shoves his way between them. "I'll take her to the other room. Just—just stay here," he says, and pushes Connor away from Nerishe.

She looks at me. "I'm sorry, Rhiannon. I did not know they had the manacles ready. I would've stopped them sooner." Hugh leads her out of the cabin, Connor glowering after them even as the door closes.

Orrin stands up, letting go of my hand with a squeeze. "I'll come check on you later," he says and grabs Linnet to steer her out.

"What?" she squeaks. "Why am I leaving? I'm going to stay here and–" but Orrin pushes her out the door, past Connor. Who does not look at me. He stands, hands on his hips, still staring at the door. Not even out the tiny window.

I feel stupid. I sit up and look down at my hands, pick at my cuticles. Everything hurts, my head most of all. Connor angry with someone is nothing new. So why do I feel like it's aimed at me?

"You did it again," he growls. Oh, he is angry at me, then. "You put yourself in danger and got hurt. What am I going to do with you?"

"What was I supposed to do? Let them skewer you? He was going to try the manacle thing anyway. At least I didn't just stand there—"

"You're not a fighter! Just standing there would have been more logical. Or running away!"

"I've been learning to defend myself! And I was doing all right for a moment there."

"What do you mean, you've been learning...Captain Nerishe has been coaching you while you traveled," he deduces.

I shrug. "Yes."

"Who is a traitor."

"Hugh was teaching us too—I was using his spell. And anyway, there's that letter from the duchess. Nerishe is not necessarily a traitor."

He brushes that away with an abrupt gesture. "That could be forged or coerced—at this point I don't trust Anouk Nerishe at all. Or anything she taught you."

"Orrin says the letter is genuine. And besides, it's not as though she'd be able to teach us how to fight incorrectly without Hugh noticing," I scoff, rolling my eyes. "Honestly, Connor. Besides, you're mad at me for trying to keep you alive, and I refuse to feel badly about that."

"They weren't going to kill me," Connor dismisses with a wave.

"They would have if I didn't drag you away from that wall—did you forget my vision already? Even if they weren't supposed to hurt you, why would you trust in that? Lord of Stars, Connor—they blew up your keep! They weren't all that careful with you!"

He sighs and steps toward me, then sits on the cot. Leaning forward, he brushes a lock of hair from my face. "Your hair is getting long," he says.

I shake my head. "You can't tell me not to be who I am, Connor."

"I know," he sighs.

"Then stop yelling at me," I snap.

He smiles crookedly. "I have. You should catch up."

"You should apologize," I say, glaring through my headache.

"I'm sorry. Thank you for being who you are. Thank you for trying to help me." He caresses my face. "Please stop getting hurt."

I indicate his own bruised face, the bloody scratch on his neck from the fight with the dead man. One of the dead men. "You, too."

"We are a pair, aren't we?" He smiles sadly, leans over and kisses my forehead. "You should rest."

"Everyone keeps saying that. You should rest, too."

"I can't, yet." He looks away. "I have things I need to see to. But I'll send the others in, if you don't want to be alone."

He leaves before I answer, but I know he'll tell them.

I huddle into the scratchy blanket. I desperately do not want to be alone—alone in my head as I haven't been in more than a year—longer—even before this spell on my body. I'd always had Keenan in my head and some magic in my veins. And for a year and more I've had a lot of power swirling through my blood and bones, so much that now my bones ache with emptiness. I can't feel anyone else past the pounding of my own temples, and I won't. Not without the magic that now seems to be gone. Perhaps gone forever. If we can't figure out what those manacles did, what the spell is, I may be without magic always. And isn't that what I sometimes wanted?

But now I don't know. I push the tears away. I hurt too much to cry. I don't even know what I'd be crying about.

Night comes, bringing more frustrations than revelations. My magic is still gone, and Hugh can't resist poking at it. He at least waits until I've cleaned up and eaten dinner to start questioning me again.

"Are you getting anything? Anything at all?" He sits next to me, while Orrin rests on the other cot. Connor and Linnet crowd the entrance into the cabin.

All I'm getting is another splitting headache and a sharp dose of temper. "I already told you, no." I can't feel anything from Hugh. I can't even feel Orrin, whose magic is much stronger anyway. And if me linking to Linnet is any indication then I'm magicless, because her magic can't find me, either.

Hugh bites his lip. "I've looked at the manacles, but I haven't touched them. I'm reluctant, honestly, to try any spells on them without more knowledge." I nod, because I wouldn't touch them, either. He sighs and pats my hand. "I don't know exactly what they did to you. Nerishe says she was told only that they would keep you from using your magic, not that they would drain you or harm you in any way. She didn't trust that, especially after what happened in Haverston, but she doesn't have any real information about them. She was going to try to prevent them from using them at all."

"She would say that, now," Connor mutters.

"She's saying the right things, Connor, and Orrin says my mother wrote that letter."

"That doesn't mean Nerishe is trustworthy, only that your mother trusts her."

"Connor, could you please not let your–" Hugh starts, but snaps his mouth shut and shakes his head. "There's an excellent chance she's telling the truth."

"There's an excellent chance–"

"Shut. Up." I say, quietly but with force.

"Rhiannon," Connor starts, but I hold up my hand.

"Just go argue somewhere else. I'm tired of all of you."

"I'm not arguing," Linnet protests. I glare at her, because of course, now she is.

"I would like some rest, as everyone keeps saying I need, so please leave," I say to the room at large. I'm quite ready to be alone after all if this is what being with everyone means. I look significantly at Hugh. I catch a look between him and Orrin. I think I'm hurt that Orrin is sending to him now, when he mostly refused before. But that's selfish. I feel selfish. I glare around generally. "Everyone just go," I say. I'm tired of arguments over my sick bed. I'm tired of having a sick bed. I'm tired of everything.

Hugh stands up and grabs Connor by the shoulders

and propels him out of the cabin. Orrin kisses my forehead. "We'll let you have your sulk, then," he says.

"You shut up, too," I mutter. He just smiles and asks Linnet to join him on the deck. I glower at everyone, and then at the empty cabin, then slump back into the cot blankets to mope my way to sleep.

CHAPTER 17

I get out of bed the next morning determined to act as normal as possible, against Hugh's wishes. But I can't sit in the cell-like cabin any longer. I go out on the deck with the mid-morning clouds to stare at the water.

The barge is wide and flat, with a structure in the middle like a fat loaf of bread, containing our cabins and one for the captain. A mast with a square sail rises toward the front of the barge—nothing like the fancy rigging of ocean vessels, but we can sail with the wind.

Below decks is a hold for more delicate cargo than the logs stacked behind us and casks of what I'm told is wine. Connor says this barge was going downriver anyway, he just delayed it by a few days. The cargo is his, so I suppose they were willing to let him pay for the delay.

And for the added crew—I think some of them are Connor's people, but I can't be sure. It seems like more people than a barge needs, but I know little enough about barges or how they run. No matter who's paying them, they all ignore us and go about their work, poling or steering or cleaning or sleeping on the deck off shift. We are just that much more cargo.

Leaning on the rail, I stare out at the water. A breeze picks up, snapping the sail. I'm restless—I can't stand my own silence anymore. I'm tired of everything.

Standing in the brisk wind, I wish the sound of the river would relax me, but it doesn't. It will take at least three days to float to Corat, and watching the clouds and water go by just makes me itch. Captain Nerishe has answers to some of my questions. I decide to ask them.

The rocking of the barge is heavier under sail than in full current, chivvying us along. Captain Nerishe looks up a little when I open the door to the other passenger cabin, but otherwise doesn't move. She sits slumped on the floor, hands tied together in front of her, the rope fastened to a ring set into the floor.

I close the door behind me. "Why did you do it?"

She looks at me from under dark eyebrows, her hair disheveled for the first time since I've known her. It pulls in fuzzy tufts from her braids.

"Why did I agree to help the ex-duke of Clarence?"

"Yes."

"I already told the duke. I had little choice."

"Your children—your wife. Yes, but you could have told that to Hu-, to the duke right away. You didn't have to go through Duchess Marguerite and hide it from him."

"I trust Duchess Marguerite above all people outside my family. I don't know her son nearly so well. And she is the one who advised me not to tell him right away—to go along just long enough to catch the spies. Why should I doubt her advice? Why would I tell His Grace if it would endanger my family?"

"But the duke advises the king," I start, and she snorts derisively.

"King Peter? And why should I trust him? He slaughtered hundreds in his own bid for the throne twenty-five years ago. His hands are not clean. My parents died just for being in the wrong place at the wrong time. I barely survived, myself. We were loyal to King Edouard —but being loyal to a king shouldn't get you killed when you're just a common soldier or villager. We don't have a wide choice in kings. It's not as though Peter has been such a great king after all—his own court and kirche conspiring against him. If he were a good ruler would that happen?"

"But—"

"And his son! That lout should never get anywhere near the throne. The only reason he was named the heir is because Prince Maxime died. Alexander was never supposed to rule. They let him run wild for too long, and the king won't check him even now. Do you think the nobility will follow him willingly as king? I don't."

It's true that, according to rumor, people haven't approved of Prince Alexander's leadership, except in battle. And I know something of how he treats Julianna, which makes me predisposed not to like him. But our alternatives are worse—Fanthas over-running the country and installing Stephen Valcourt as ruler. "So you do support Stephen, then," I say.

"No. I do not. Gerald was no better than his brother,

just greedier. Stephen follows in his father's footsteps. That whole family is–"

"Watch your tongue," I warn her.

She takes a deep breath. "Apologies. It isn't the whole family. Princess Eleanore is a sensible child, by reports. And the earl seems a man I could follow as a soldier. I do not want Stephen for a king. But I see no reason to let my family die just so Alexander can take the throne."

"Prince Alexander is the king's choice for heir, and you have pledged your life to the kingdom through your service to Haverston." I jump at Connor's voice. I spin around to see him standing in the open doorway. "But I would not see your family die for any reason, Anouk Nerishe."

Nerishe looks steadily at him. "I meant what I said."

"So did I." He jerks his head at me to tell me to leave, which I find rude. "Your sister is looking for you."

"You just want me to go so you can talk to her without me here."

"That, too." He points out the door, and I glare at him. The bruise on his forehead has begun to give him a black eye, the purple and green pooling into deep shadows, giving him a lopsided, piratical look.

"I think I have a right to talk to Captain Nerishe," I insist.

"Not a captain anymore. And no." Connor gestures to the door, his face stern. But he interrupted me, and even if he does have more experience than I do, that doesn't mean he gets to boss me around.

"Then make me leave, if you want to, Connor. I have questions. I'm staying."

He throws his hands up in the air, rolling his eyes. "Rhiannon, for once in your life just do what you're asked. For pity's sake. I'm not going to torture her. But you don't get to be involved in—"

"I'm already involved!" I sit on the cot nearest to Nerishe. "I'm staying. You can always question her later without me, anyway."

Nerishe laughs, her voice scratchy. "You may as well, my lord. My story will stay the same with her here or without. There's no reason to make her leave. You both already know the bulk of it."

"You betrayed your companions," Connor starts, but Nerishe cuts him off.

"I protected my companions as best I could while working for Her Grace as a spy."

"An unsanctioned spy," he snaps.

"I was sanctioned, just not by you. You saw the letter."

"What sort of spy carries a letter like that? You most likely wrote it yourself."

"I knew I was going to need it—and I planned on giving it to His Grace before we reached Corat. I kept it on my person. My personal dislike of King Peter doesn't mean I would willingly lead his enemies to his door. I have that much honor."

"So you claim," Connor says, his voice flat.

I shake my head. "Connor—Orrin is sure the letter is genuine. And Hugh said the code was real, and Nerishe is—"

He spins to me "You don't know anything about her, or spies, for that matter."

"I know when you're angrier because you were left out of the loop than because of what happened."

Nerishe laughs. "He's angry because you got hurt. He's angry I let it happen. So am I."

"You said you didn't know they planned to use the...the manacles."

"I didn't. I told them not to go forward with the attack yet, that it was a bad idea with Dorward's soldiers around us. I told them we weren't ready, and I hoped they would wait. I didn't catch on soon enough that they were going ahead." She sighs.

"I don't understand how you can be angry with yourselves, when both Orrin and I, who both have visions of the future...well, I used to." I take a breath. "And we didn't know about it. We just knew—I just knew that the wall was going to fall, maybe. And when I Saw...I Saw..." I start to realize that when I Saw myself, I knew to push Connor out of the way. He didn't get crushed by that wall, because I Saw myself Seeing the explosion, and I changed it. Somehow.

"Rhiannon, what is it?" Connor turns fully to me. "What did you See?"

"Connor, I...I Saw myself. I Saw myself having the vision, and I did something different. And it changed it. I changed what happened because I knew what I wanted to change." I open my hands like they can show him, but I have no magic to make any illusions or to send to him. Not that he could receive a sending.

Connor looks hard at me, at Nerishe, then takes my arm, draws me out of the room. I look back at Nerishe, tied up, shaking her head and staring after us. He shuts the door and cuts off anything she might have said. "Let's not discuss this here," he says firmly and pulls me along back to the other cabin.

"I'm sorry," I say quietly, but I'm not. Not really. I don't have any room left in my head for sorry. I'm full only of this realization. The reality happened, and I saw myself having the vision of it at the same time. I've been on both sides of a vision before, but this is the first time I've had a vision and then the vision happened, and I beheld the vision me and knew what to do about it.

We enter the other cabin. "Where's Hugh?" Connor asks Orrin, who's lying on one of the cots.

"How should I know?" he asks sullenly, and I wonder if they've argued. Connor raises his eyebrow, and Orrin grimaces, sends to Hugh. "He's with the barge captain. He says he'll be here soon."

"Good. Rhiannon, I think you all need to discuss what you just realized. It sounds important, but I'm not sure of the implications. Hugh knows far more about magic than I do."

Linnet walks in the door. "Everyone knows more about magic than you do," she scoffs.

"Linnet, that's not true, and it was rude," I admonish her, but Connor just sighs.

"You three discuss this with Hugh. I'll talk to him later," Connor says, and leaves. He's going back to interrogate Captain Nerishe without me there, I know. I'm tempted to run after him, but he's not wrong that I need to tell Orrin and Hugh and Linnet what I've realized.

Hugh and Orrin ask the expected questions, and Linnet wants to know why I didn't do something useful like tell past me to tell past the rest of us what was going to happen. I just shake my head at her. There wasn't exactly time to tell past me anything. I Saw me, I knew the wall was coming down, and I saved Connor from getting crushed. I kept the vision from happening while I was having it.

After we've exhausted our ideas about what it means, when—if ever—my magic might return, and what we can try to do the next time one of us has a vision, it's time for lunch. And a nap. There isn't much else for us to do. I still feel exhausted down to my bones. It's only been a day, I remind myself.

I spend what's left of the afternoon staring at the water out on the deck, playing with the dice Hugh thought to bring, and trying to figure out Connor.

He said he couldn't court me but then I had the vision, and we kissed...All of his behavior since then tells me he still cares about me. But he also said he didn't want to. I'm angry with him. We've had a very trying couple of days, however. I'm trying to decide how I feel.

So I decide to figure out Captain Nerishe. By going to see her again, obviously.

"I'm back," I say, as I close the door.

"I see that," she says wearily, sitting on one of the cots, rope stretched to it's full length. "I'm fairly certain you're not supposed to be in here."

"You're probably right," I say, and I sit gingerly on the cot opposite her. "I'm not sure I care right now. I wanted to know what you know about Connor's brother and Archb-, Montmoore. Did you meet either of them?"

"No, I never met them. I was blackmailed by proxy," she says bitterly. "I was given proof that my family would be in danger if I didn't help his people infiltrate the castle and get close to you all. I only know it was the ex-duke and Montmoore because of the symbol on the letter I was shown and the image in the seer stone. I have no proof, of course. I went to the duchess in hopes she could help me.

"I worked very hard for my position as captain. But I love my family far more. There is nothing I wouldn't do for them," she says fiercely.

"Of course," I say, but that's when Connor enters the cabin.

He stops in the doorway, glares at us both. "That's it. Rhiannon, come with me."

"Connor..."

"We need to talk. Now." He gestures out the door, his face carved from granite. Growling in frustration, I push past him heading away from the cabins to the rear of the barge—aft, I think they call it. If he's going to lecture me, I'm going to watch the water go by in the fading light. I walk to the rail and lean on it, clenching my jaw.

I feel him come up behind me. "You can't just keep me away from her, from everything, Connor. How can I help, how can I figure out what all of the different visions might mean if I'm not..." But I trail off, because I don't have the visions anymore.

He joins me at the railing. "I can't tell you everything, Rhiannon. Whether I want to or not, whether you should know or not, there are some things I simply cannot tell you about. It is the nature of what I do. And you cannot just interrogate prisoners at your own whim."

"It's not a whim! I need information."

"Then I will get it for you. Trust me to do my job, Rhiannon. Trust me to take care of you."

"I can take care of myself," I mutter.

"Not like that. Not without help. Please don't put yourself in more danger than you must. It's exhausting. For me, personally."

I look at him sidelong. He's frowning like he has a headache.

"You should be resting," I tell him.

"So should you."

I shrug. There is nothing seriously wrong with me—I'm just tired, and I don't have any magic anymore. It is an ache on my spine, a missing thought, some cog gone from my apparatus, but I am not injured. And anyway, isn't this what I wanted?

It seems a terrible trade to lose the magic and still not get my family back.

"I'm not the one with a head injury," I say instead of all that, and he just looks at me, puts his hand over mine on the railing. We stand silently, watching the water go by.

"We'll see what happens when we reach Corat. Maybe the Cardinal, or Julianna, or someone else will know what those manacles are and how to reverse the spell. They didn't come from nowhere."

I feel tears in my eyes, which is stupid. I didn't even want this power. Or the scars. The scars I still have that now are just scars, making me ugly to no purpose.

But I am alive, and so is Connor, and we know what the enemy is after. And now they can't have it—me, anyway. We still must shield Orrin.

Connor turns me by my shoulders, lifts my chin up with a finger. "It won't be this way forever," he says gently. "We'll figure it out."

"What if there's nothing to figure out?" I ask miserably. "I wasn't special before. I'm not special now."

"Don't say that. You were always and you will always be special." He shakes his head as if shaking away flies, or bad thoughts. "I can't–" he starts. "I am not...I'm not able to..." he squeezes my shoulders, his eyes shut. "I am not free, Rhiannon, to offer you what I'd like. But you should know how I feel about you. You are—you are remarkable. With or without astounding amounts of magical power."

"Offer me what you'd like? You already told me you have obligations that mean you can't court me. What are you saying now?"

He drops his hands from me, blows out a sigh. "I wanted to explain. I was...instructed..." He curses and looks away. "I'm not free to be with you, because the Indrani ambassador informed King Peter that I'm to be married only at Indranah's discretion, as grandson of the empress. And that only specifically suitable parties would be...considered. I was ordered to stay away from you. Specifically." He shakes his head, reaches to tuck a strand of hair behind my ear. "I was not careful enough with our correspondence, and Marchioness Boucher dropped a word in the ambassador's ear. She would like to see me wed outside of Talaria entirely so she can be rid of me. The king says he's considering it, but he's stalling, as he wants me here, working for him. He doesn't want me courting anyone at all, for various reasons."

A stone falls in my stomach. And then more stones fall. I think it is my heart. "Oh." My voice is very small.

"I did not want to tell you like this. I tried to tell you before, but everything seemed so...I wanted—I did not want to hurt you. But the king is trying to avert a war and gather allies—still, and I am......"

"His nephew. And a grandson of the empress," I say, the impossibility of me being with him—a guild daughter with a grandson of an empress—hitting me with finality.

"A pawn." He scowls. "I am sorry, Rhiannon. I don't...I wish..."

"It's fine," I say, mumbling, my body, my face, my hands are ice water and I turn like a golem, clumsy, away from him, away from this conversation.

"Rhiannon..."

"I think I'd like to try to rest now. Good night." I can feel the sobs shaking my lungs, but I keep them down, until I reach the cabin and let myself in. Linnet looks up from the pallet at me, and doesn't speak, just moves over to make room. I crawl in beside her and sob silently into her shoulder as she holds me, not asking me questions.

She likely already knows. Orrin was still on the other side of the cabins. He probably eavesdropped. I'm just as glad not to speak.

"How much are you accomplishing bringing her to the palace in chains, really?" Orrin argues, again, with Connor. "And you," he turns to Hugh. "Are you really going to disbelieve your own mother?"

Connor glares at him. "How can you be utterly certain that letter is from the duchess? There are ways to fake such things. Until I know for sure..."

Hugh interrupts him. "It's from her, Connor. We established this." He sounds defeated. "I don't know what she was about, doing it this way, but she obviously felt it was best. The code is true. The code is mine, Connor. And I know my mother's handwriting and style. One or two could maybe be faked, but all three? Very unlikely."

"We live in a world of unlikely," Connor says mulishly.

"Try being reasonable, Connor," I snap back at him, glaring.

"It's Nerishe's fault you were hurt in the first place," he snarls. "At least you could be a little cautious for once in your life."

"Don't you dare," I warn him, well aware I am raising my voice. "Before we left, Her Grace told me I could trust Captain Nerishe with my life. And now she's told us again—so I'm choosing to trust. Don't make that seem like I'm endangering everyone because of it."

"Doesn't it occur to you that you might be? It's my duty to see to your safety, and I take my duty very seriously." He jabs his finger toward me to make his point, and I have to work not to slap at it.

"Oh, we all know how very seriously you take your duty, Connor fitzWellan," I growl back at him, furious. "But maybe this time you could try having a duty to not be a giant ass."

Linnet snorts. Hugh and Orrin both bite their lips and look away.

"If I'm the one who's an ass for keeping everyone safe, then I will take it. Don't be so childish."

There is no continuing an argument with such a bully. If I try, then I'm still childish. I turn to Hugh. "You talk sense into him. I think it's dangerous to walk Captain Nerishe into the palace in chains—for her and for her family. I think she deserves more consideration than that, especially if she has been trying to avert worse damage from Stephen and Montmoore." I look sideways at Connor. "I don't want anyone hurt through carelessness."

"Do you really think I'm careless? For pity's sake, Rhiannon." Connor scowls at all of us.

"Well, we are having this conversation without checking for other spies," Linnet points out. I realize we've been getting louder. The barge's walls are not that thick.

"This ship is fully staffed by my people," Connor points out. "They have all worked for me before. I do not take chances with the safety of my people."

Hugh raises his eyebrows at Connor. I just sigh and lean my head back on the wall, rolling my eyes.

"All right, fine," Connor snarls. "I will do as you ask. We will all walk into the palace together, free of bonds. But Nerishe will be with me at all times. Hugh will report to the king while I keep her far away from anyone who might harm her or be harmed by her. Will that suffice? Or must I outfit her with weapons and give her a detailed map of the palace as well?"

Orrin smiles. "I think that your guard should be sufficient, my lord," he says quietly. I nod once at the room at large and let myself out into the morning air. I very carefully do not slam the door.

CHAPTER 18

The city of Corat is a river city, a port city, and a plains city all at once. The Dorward runs into the larger river Arquelle, which runs into the sea. Just as it does, it creates a large delta, and the city is built half on canals; this I know from maps and geography.

But seeing the shining river in the cloud-filtered sun, the bridges everywhere, the feats of human-built miracles like the broad walls around the heart of the town, is fascinating. I've seen those walls in my visions, in my dreams. Here in person those walls seem impossibly tall. Huge smooth stones, flaring out thicker at the base, they seem impenetrable. Atop an atoll in the center of the town, along a tributary of the river, the palace stands inside its own thick walls of bluish stone—a glittering, new-polished jewel. The old palace has been overbuilt bit by bit, some of the older, square towers only half-undone into round towers and pillared facades.

"It's so...sprawling," Linnet says, looking over the city. She stares out at it with me, her eyes wide with anticipation and some anxiety, too. So many buildings—it's overwhelming.

"It's the oldest city in Talaria," Orrin says from behind me. Connor stands further down the rail, a dark cipher against the backdrop of passing buildings as we pass into the city proper. He says nothing to any of us. As per usual, the last few days. I feel a flare of temper and tamp it down. Now is not the time for temper.

The one good thing about the magic being gone is that I can lean into a hug from Orrin without worry that we'll set each other off. He squeezes me back as we watch the city go by. Linnet glares out into it, palpably willing herself fierce. I would tell her she's already fierce, but I'm pretty sure she'd kick me.

One of the deck hands brushes past us, and Orrin gasps, his hand clamping onto my shoulder. A sharp flare of buzzing rushes through me and away again—a vision. I almost See something, but it's gone again as soon as it starts, leaving me sick to my stomach. Orrin's face goes slack along with his legs, and he slumps half onto me as I shift to grab him.

"Linnet, help me!" I cry. "Catch him!" She fumbles for his shoulders so we can keep him from hitting his head on the railing. Hugh hurries to Orrin's side.

"What is it? A vision? Here?" Hugh asks while I struggle with Orrin's weight. He takes him from me and slips under his shoulder. Connor strides to us as Orrin moans. My skin buzzes with stings and zaps, as if bugs are biting me. When I let go of Orrin it settles a little. I bite back a whimper of my own.

Orrin shakes his head. "They're waiting for us," he says, and Connor's gaze snaps up to his.

"Who?" asks Hugh, but he looks up and around to the front of the boat. To the docks.

And indeed, it seems as though an entire regiment of soldiers waits for us on the street next to the riverboat docks. Shining and precise in royal tabards, armed and ready. Connor swears viciously, his mouth a grim slash across his face.

"How do you suppose they..." I start, but Connor gives a sharp shake of his head.

"The Butcher is good at her job," he says. "And I was wrong about someone." He turns to Nerishe, who has sat quiet and still on the bench all this while. "I don't know if I'll be able to deliver on my promise right away. But if I have a say in anything, you'll speak directly to the king. I apologize, Captain."

It's the first time he's called her captain since Dorward. She looks up at us all, her face just as grim. "Can't have everything," she says in a flat voice.

My bones still vibrate at a low pitch. I look at Orrin, who leans against Hugh like the effort of standing is too much. His face is blank, and I realize he's doing what Hugh wanted all along—contacting the cardinal. He shakes his head and looks up at Hugh. "Send someone to Julianna, if you can. I've—I've sent to Robere. He doesn't think he'll make it to us in time."

Linnet grabs Connor's arm. "Send me. No one will even look at me. I'll go."

I want to tell her she doesn't even know where she's going, but I don't want her in the clutches of someone called "The Butcher" even more, so I just take a breath, nod at her.

Connor shakes his head at all of us. "You should all three of you go. I'll have Raoul take you—you're safer if you wait until we're gone. Hugh and I can handle the soldiers. Wait in the cabins until we've left. Get to the castle, find the princess. She'll get the king." He motions to a deckhand who must be one of his spies. They all are, of course. He told us these were all his people.

We hurry toward the cabins as the boat comes into dock. But we never get the chance to carry out the plan. "Take everyone from the ship," I hear as footsteps thud on the deck. Connor's and Hugh's voices raise in anger, insisting they are in charge, but it doesn't sound like they're winning any arguments. The door to the cabin slams open and a burly soldier barges in.

"Everyone out! Up with you," he shouts, and we follow, because what are we going to do about it now?

There are too many soldiers on deck, everywhere. Connor spits words at a soldier and Hugh, haughty and pale, threatens them with punishment for laying hands on a duke, but it's to no avail. "We have our orders, and everyone on this boat is coming with us," the captain insists, and gestures to the soldiers around everyone.

They have rope. The trembling from my bones becomes a trembling in my skin, in my muscles, in my breath. My stomach lurches as one woman reaches for me, grabs my arms. I don't plan to fight, but I jerk away, skitter backward into Linnet.

"You're coming now," the soldier says, and I grit my teeth and try to stand still, not make it worse. Connor looks over and strides away from the soldiers surrounding him, sending one crashing to the ground.

"Stop him," the guard captain shouts, but Connor turns and glares, command in the line of his body.

"Don't you dare try, Captain," he snarls. "And stop

menacing my people." The captain glares back, but signals to her soldiers.

Connor snatches the rope away from the soldier binding me. "No one needs to be tied. We are coming with you. But if you put any kind of rope on any of these people at all, I will see you court martialed. Is that clear?" he shouts loud enough to be heard throughout the docks. "No one is to be bound." He takes my hand. "We are coming now." He puts my hand on his arm and starts to walk down the gangway. "We will go peacefully, everyone. But this explanation had better be good."

The carts are rough jail wagons, closed with no windows, and we're herded into them, accompanied by grumbles and shoves from soldiers. I can't stop shaking, but I'm working on breathing.

We duck in one by one. It has a low ceiling and a splintery wooden bench running along each side. Connor sits on one side of me, Linnet on the other. Hugh helps Orrin and Nerishe in, then steps in himself. The door slams behind him. He sits gingerly, grimacing.

"That could have gone better. I hope none of the rest of your people will be hurt."

The air in the cart quickly grows stuffy and sticky. I lean on Linnet and she holds my hand. Sweat trickles down my stomach and back, through my hair, and I shudder. I'm too hot, but I can't let her go.

I look sidelong at Connor. His face is a study of worry and rage. "I'm sorry," I whisper. "I-I don't know –"

"You were surrounded by soldiers and they were trying to tie you up. I remember what happened to you last year, not to mention just a few days ago. So do you. Your body reacted. Just try to breathe. It's all right. I'll make it all right."

I look at Orrin and Hugh. Hugh holds Orrin's arm, and Orrin leans into him just a little. Orrin grimaces at me. I wish I could send to him right now.

"Do...do they know who you are?" I ask Hugh.

"They know. They have orders," Connor snaps. I knew this "Butcher" was a political enemy of Connor's, but still, this seems a risky move, if he is at all in the king's graces. Why arrest us all? Surely she can't mean to truly keep even Hugh in custody.

I try to breathe more evenly, but it's so stuffy and close in the cart. My heart beats in frantic pulse points all over my skin, prickling into sweat on my scalp. A residual sting of magic sings along my bones, in my scars.

Orrin trembles, holding back a vision I think. Maybe that's the stinging—is it my magic coming back? At least it isn't spurring his on right now. I'm not sure our sort of vision will help us at the moment. I can only imagine what the soldiers would think of him fading in and out.

The cart comes to a jolting stop. "Let me do the talking," Hugh says. I nod, although he's really speaking to Connor. If a duke can't convince them to listen, there's little I can do about it. Connor grimaces but nods his agreement.

The door to the cart yanks open and a soldier peers in. "Everyone out."

"You meant to say 'If you please, Your Grace,' I believe," Hugh says with cold hauteur.

"So you say," the soldier mutters.

"I do say. And as I am the Duke of Haverston, I am right." His tone is as ducal as I've ever heard it. He gracefully steps through the door, his face as forbidding as his voice. The rest of us exit less gracefully, although only Linnet and I are truly clumsy. We step one by one out of the cart into what must be the palace barracks yard. The high stone walls around us and the long two-story buildings on two sides, plus a large stable and all of the soldiers surrounding us, seem evidence of that.

Two other carts discharge the people who were on the boat with us—deckhands and the captain. Connor flicks his gaze over them but otherwise keeps his eyes on the tall and stately woman making her way to us from the gateway, her silver braided hair striking against olive brown skin. Her gown is practical but looks expensive. It flows around her legs as she makes her way, a heavy fabric in dark blue and bronze.

"Ah. Lord Valcourt," she addresses Connor. "And Your Grace. It is so disappointing to find you mixed up in this plot," she intones in a plummy alto as she nears.

"My lady Boucher, greetings," Hugh says, with a shallow bow. "I do not know to what plot you are referring. We are bringing our guests to His Majesty, as requested. We are under orders to do so. Never tell me you aren't aware of them."

I try not to be noticeable at all. Linnet's hand is glued to mine with our combined sweat, and I can feel her glaring, but she seems to be keeping it at the ground. I glance out of the corner of my eye at Connor. His glaring is more noticeable, but he is an earl, and the marchioness already knows him.

"I'm aware of a great many things, Your Grace. Including your involvement in a plot to get an assassin into the palace."

All of us wrinkle our brows at that. Hugh shakes his head. "That's one I didn't know myself. How can I plot to bring an assassin into the palace without knowing about it? Your informant is mistaken."

"Then who is this woman," the marchioness asks, gesturing to Nerishe, who shifts slightly away from us. I think she's trying to distance herself for our sake.

"This is Captain Nerishe of Haverston guard. She is one of my guard captains, and I have to speak to the king about her," Hugh says, his voice even. "There was no need to drag us here in a prisoner cart."

"There is if you think you can bring an assassin to the palace. I will stop any and all threats to the crown, even if they come from you, Your Grace." Her voice gets lower, harder, and her golden-brown eyes narrow. "I expected this kind of double-cross from Valcourt, but I had hoped for better from the brother to the princess."

"My surname is fitzWellan, and no one here is plotting against the crown, my lady Boucher. You are mistaken." Connor's voice is a low burr, but I can feel the anger in it.

"You can take other names if you like, traitor. But I remember your father and brother too well."

"This is all very tiresome, my lady. We have orders directly from the king," Hugh says, picking idly at dirt on his sleeve. "I am—"

"And I have orders from the king to keep this palace and this country safe from traitors!" Her voice goes hoarse, and her jaw looks hard as granite. She turns—all of us do—at the clang of soldiers shifting.

A page comes running from the arch that probably leads to the palace. Behind the page hurries a man in swaying dark robes—Cardinal Robere, I think. I haven't seen him in months, and my heart beats so hard that my eyes blur. As he comes closer I see nods of respect among the soldiers, but not from all of them.

The page reaches the marchioness first but hesitates, unsure to whom he should deliver his message. "Give it to me," Boucher snaps, and holds out her hand. The page looks around, and Hugh nods regally. The page hesitantly hands the paper to Lady Boucher, who snatches it from his fingers. I'm not sure the marchioness wouldn't have stabbed the child herself if he'd disobeyed her.

Unfolding the note, she reads it and then crumples it in a fist as Robere nears. "Ah, good, you've received the king's message," he says, a little winded.

"Why should you bring the king's message, Cardinal Robere? Why should you be here at all? No one called for you." The marchioness' voice could cut the ground we stand on. I shiver from the chill. Linnet leans into me.

"I am not the bearer of the message, my lady. I am merely here to see my dear friend the duke. Your Grace," he says, bowing.

"Your Eminence," Hugh says back.

"Oh, for pity's sake. Bring them all," the marchioness snaps, and we're rounded up behind her as her skirt snaps in the wind of her passage.

The palace starts grand and continues grander, marble and carpets and statues—and I know we are not the richest country in the world, but the kingdom is old and we have traded our hardwoods well, I guess, since there are Indrani carpets and Shovahn ceramics, and I can see Linnet staring at the hangings with some longing and professional assessment.

Connor and Hugh stay slightly ahead of us all, Nerishe closely guarded behind them, with us and the minor horde of Connor's people from the boat following. And guards, alongside us, every step. I have no doubt of their abilities with weapons, so I keep hold of Linnet and Orrin and hope to stay as unnoticed as possible.

We all march into a hall of some sort, guards stationed at the doors. Heavy curtains of dark russet velvet surround windows of very clear glass. The wallpaper is a pretty and luxurious gold-red stripe, and the furniture, of which there is little, is plush or made of dark wood or both.

In front of a curtained alcove near the end of the hall stands a man. Julianna stands next to him, and I've never been so glad to see her. They turn as we approach, all of us in our grubby numbers. Julianna wears a polite smile along with her navy day gown, but the king—I think it is the king—stays expressionless.

He is not a tall man, with light brown hair fading to iron gray and a bit of a paunch. He wears an understated coat in very fine gray and blue summer weight wool, with cool ivory linen underneath. His olive skin sags around his eyes and jowls, and he commands the room because everyone here waits for him to do it.

Hugh and Connor stop behind Boucher. Both bow, I presume the appropriate amount and the appropriate distance away. Linnet, Orrin and I stagger a bit into our bows, but we bow lower. Nerishe's bow is a bit stilted by guards. My heart pounds in my throat.

The marchioness waits a heartbeat, then bows very low, but very close to the king. "Your Majesty, I have come as you asked, and brought..." she gestures to us. "Well, all of them. Although I feel I must voice an objection to bringing them directly to you."

"Noted," the king says in a mild baritone.

I keep hold of Linnet's and Orrin's hands, Orrin gripping me tightly. I can feel him trying to ground himself, not give into the magic that is trying to well up in him. I'm uncertain how I'm feeling it, but I try to help. I try to reach for it, to bring some into me, but it's all broken—fizzy and sputtering and lost—and it hurts, suddenly. A lot. I bite back a whimper, but some escapes, anyway.

I can feel people looking. The marchioness, the king. I keep my eyes on the ground, let the sweat drip down my temples without wiping at it. Hugh shifts forward a step and bows again.

"My king," he says, and I let go of Orrin's hand. He shifts to the other side of Linnet.

"Hugh, dearest," Julianna says brightly and strides forward to grab her brother's hands. "I have missed you so much." She leans up to kiss his cheek, then turns and does the same for Connor. "And you, my lord. You've both been gone for far too long. We've all missed you."

The light from the windows gleams on her blond hair, her kind smile, her shining eyes, and I'm struck again at her beauty. It's something she's doing, I think—making us all look at her for a moment, relieving the tension. She's using her energy to calm everyone.

And it works a little. Everyone smiles at her, breathes easier. Except for Boucher.

"Touching. Or it would be, were it true," Boucher says drily.

"Don't be jealous, dear," Julianna says sweetly. "We'd miss you too, if you ever went away."

Boucher's face darkens, but the king looks amused.

As Marchioness Boucher glares at Julianna, the door behind the king opens and a guard lets a tall blond man wearing the royal silver and blue into the room. His beauty is striking at once, like a blow, and I blink under the strength of it, even as I start to recognize him. He looks around at the tableau before him.

"Good morning, Father. I came as soon as I..."

"Yes, yes, thank you, Alexander," the king waves away his words. "We don't need you right now."

Lady Boucher raises an eyebrow as Prince Alexander flushes an angry red. She bows deeply to the prince. "Your Highness."

Everyone bows. I bow too, but I keep my eyes up. The prince's face twists in a sneer as he takes in the room.

"I see my wife is deploying her singular diplomacy again. Perhaps you should leave it to your brother. He's usually much better at it—as at so many other things," the prince says in a meaner voice than he began.

"Alexander," the king says, warning.

"Why, here is Hugh now. And, of course, my dear cousin Connor. How good to see you again, Cousin. I see you've brought guests."

"Now isn't the time, dearest," Julianna murmurs, but Alexander ignores her.

"What interesting companions have you brought with you today?" he smirks.

"Your Highness, as I was saying," the marchioness breaks in. "Your Majesty, I think it rash to bring plotters and assassins directly to you. But I have done as you requested. I have several suggestions as to what should be done with them."

"Plotters? Assassins? Surely you're mistaken, my lady," interrupts Cardinal Robere.

"I am not. I have direct confirmation that this

woman is a traitor and has plotted with Stephen Valcourt against this country." She indicates Nerishe, who keeps edging away from us, I think so we're not too close to her if things go badly. "Furthermore, I believe Connor Valcourt–"

"fitzWellan," Connor interrupts.

"...to be in direct contact with his brother the traitor."

"All of these statements are incorrect, Your Majesty," Connor says.

"He would say that!" Lady Boucher scoffs.

"Connor is not a traitor," Julianna says, trying to sound reasonable. "And neither is Hugh. You have received mistaken information."

I have never wished so hard for my magic. I can tell Hugh and Linnet and Orrin and Robere are all subtly sending to one another, but I have no idea what they're saying or what they're planning. What I should do. I haven't stopped trembling since we docked, and I'm getting so tired.

"Lady Boucher, kindly desist," the king says. "In fact, everyone desist. Connor, Hugh, explain."

Connor subtly nods to Hugh, who takes the lead. "This is delicate, Your Majesty, and all precautions must be taken. Stephen Valcourt has threatened Captain Nerishe's family. I have evidence that despite this she's been acting in Talaria's best interests, and I trust the source."

"Your mother is not a source, Haverston," Boucher derides.

"The Duchess of Haverston vouches for this person? Despite what you told me in your earlier dispatch, Hugh?"

Boucher looks a bit startled, but she hides it well. "I was not told of a dispatch," she says.

"No, you were not," the king says quietly, and Boucher bows, but not before I see her eyes narrow for a moment, and I wonder what that cold expression means. Nothing good.

"My king," Hugh says, "I do recognize that Captain Nerishe has a...complicated story. As I mentioned to you in my dispatch, which is why we planned to report to you immediately upon our arrival. I don't think it was necessary to intercept and arrest us before we could do so."

"I did not order any arrest," the king says quietly. Boucher stiffens but bows slightly.

"I thought it best, Majesty. The information I had gave me ample reason for concern."

"Concern, perhaps. But not theatrics, Yvonne. Please bring me such concerns in the future. I have faith in Connor fitzWellan, and Marguerite and Hugh Theroux."

Boucher bows, her face a blank mask.

"Why should we take their word without investigating, Father?" Alexander asks. "How can we be sure any of them are telling the truth?"

King Peter turns his head and raises one eyebrow at his son. "I am not incompetent, Alexander," he says mildly.

Alexander flushes. "Of course not, Father," he says, but his right hand balls into a fist, his jaw rigid and pale.

"May I see the letter, Hugh?"

"Of course, my king." Hugh fishes in his breast pocket and draws out the letter, handing it to the king with a slight bow. "I am certain it is genuine, but I also sent her a missive immediately. I expect her confirmation very soon."

The king reads the letter and folds it again, raises his eyebrows. "Captain Anouk Nerishe," he says. Nerishe raises her eyes to his, her braids still fuzzy and her face grave. "What do you have to say about all of this?" the king asks.

"Father, really," Alexander mutters with scorn.

"Alexander, really," Julianna hisses.

"I'm speaking with the captain at the moment," King Peter says mildly. "Captain?"

"Your Majesty," Nerishe croaks. "I did what I could to keep the situation from deteriorating further. Any injuries or mistakes I take responsibility for. I have no intention of assassinating anyone."

"Something any half-competent assassin would say under the circumstances, Father. Why should we trust her when our own informants tell a different story?" Alexander's voice is dark and sardonic.

"Do they? Do they indeed," the king says.

"Majesty," Nerishe says, "I can only tell you what I've told the earl and duke—I may not be the best soldier, but I am loyal to Her Grace, and I would not place her or any person in her entourage in any danger if I could help it." Her voice rasps quietly over the rustle of clothes and whispers in the hall.

There are too many people. I tremble with stress and exhaustion. Orrin's face is slick with sweat. I'm sure mine looks no better. Linnet grips my hand still, her other arm around Orrin's waist as he leans on her. I hope the king comes to a decision soon. A good decision. I bite my lips, waiting.

"And were there injuries due to your mistakes, Captain?" the king asks.

Connor, Hugh, and Nerishe all pointedly do not look my way.

"Yes, Your Majesty."

"And you take full responsibility?"

"Yes, Your Majesty."

"Connor? What do you have to say?"

Connor takes a deep breath. "While I could wish she had come to me with all of this, I have no reason to disbelieve her, or the letter, at this time. Nor do I expect to find one. She did what she thought best to save people from material harm. I believe she acted in good faith toward our party, as well as she could under the circumstances. I think we will find that Duchess Marguerite will say the same."

"Your Majesty, I feel that..." Boucher begins.

"Yes, I know," the king says sharply. He considers us all, his eyes flicking briefly over everyone. My jaw tightens to a sharp ache with anxiety. I look at the king in snatches, sidelong glances, and he catches my eye for a moment. I freeze. He raises his eyebrow a fraction, then moves on to studying the rest of us. His mild expression turns wry.

"Very well. I have considered all sides. Captain Nerishe, while we are confirming your story, we must place you under arrest." He gestures to Connor and Hugh. "While you are detained, we will consult with Duchess Marguerite on how best to keep your family safe." He studies her for a moment. "A room in the east tower will suffice for now, under guard. I expect her to be treated fairly while under our supervision. Alex, see to it."

Alexander blinks. "Father, we should..."

"Now."

He raises his chin and smiles angrily at everyone. "Of course, my king. At your service." He jerks his head at two guards, who come forward for Nerishe. She flinches the tiniest bit—I think I see it only because she's right in front of me, but she keeps her expression flat as they take her from the hall.

"My king, I would like to speak to you further about..."

"Yes, Yvonne, I know very well what you would like to speak on. I will not hear you now." He turns away from her to speak to Hugh. Boucher's cheeks turn ruddy, but her face retains its flat regard. She bows deeply before stepping back to confer with a guard.

Hugh nods as the king murmurs to him. Julianna looks us all over, her face tight with sympathy. She curtseys in a way that makes eyes turn to her.

"Majesty, perhaps we could show our other guests to their rooms now? I'm sure they're all quite fatigued. You'll meet them all formally later, of course."

The king looks at Hugh and Connor. "I will keep Hugh with me for a moment. Connor?"

"By your leave, Your Majesty, I will take my people and settle them appropriately," Connor says, bowing.

The king eyes us all dispassionately, his face a polite mask. "By all means. You may go."

Connor turns to us and with a few nods, all are bowing and turning to leave. His people surround us, but with a hand on a shoulder he stops one man, a deckhand from the ship, youngish, who looks at Connor with despair in his eyes. "This one is not mine," he says quietly, and the man lowers his head, his face miserable.

"Not his fault," Orrin gasps a little, but Connor shakes his head.

"I know whose fault it is. But he made his choice." He looks hard at the man for a moment, then exits. The young man looks a bit lost as the others file out. Hugh nods to another guard, who pulls the young man aside and escorts him out. Yvonne Boucher looks on from her corner, expressionless.

Julianna turns to us. "Oh, my dears, you must be exhausted," she says soothingly. "Come with me—we'll set you all to rights." We bow in our turns to the king and follow her from the room.

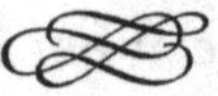

The palace continues to impress—hangings and statues and lovely carvings on the arches that lead from hallway to hallway. I'm completely turned around by now and can't tell which way the stables were. We three follow Julianna with weary bodies and minds—or at least, I presume Orrin and Linnet are as weary as I am.

The princess cheerfully narrates the way, but I'm too fuzzy to follow any of what she's saying. It's enough that it's her voice, and that we aren't in any immediate danger now. I find myself staring at the sumptuous carpets and pretty marble floors and just making sure I'm not falling behind, Linnet's hand still in mine.

"Here we are, this will do for you girls—it's a lovely suite. You each get your own chamber off this one." We follow her into a sumptuous sitting room of various pale blues, with a window seat and nice breeze coming in from the open window. "Orrin, you're just across the hall. Connor isn't far from here, either. I'll get the three of you settled in, and then we'll worry about when your things will get here and what you'll need in the meantime. Hugh wrote that you'll need court clothes for all occasions, including your formal introduction to the court, and of course the presentation of your new titles and lands in a few months, so..." Juliana turns, voice trailing off as we all stare at her in stunned silence.

"Our what?" Orrin's voice breaks upward.

"You...didn't Connor tell you?"

We look at one another, consternated. "No," I say. "Tell us what, exactly?"

"Oh, for pity's sake. This is really a conversation he should have had with you, but it's too late now," Julianna says, hands on hips. "Rhiannon, your family—but really you—are to be given the Wolff barony, with all titles and lands and the manor house that attends it. And Orrin, your family is being granted unclaimed land surrounding their farm and the means to build a new manor house, as well as the currently unclaimed barony of Estienne. Your parents been invited for the investiture."

Orrin freezes. "What?"

I myself feel pretty frozen right now. Linnet is the only one of us who seems capable of rationality.

"Where are these lands? How big a manor house? What must we do to prepare?" she asks.

Orrin raises his hands to stop her. "Wait—you informed my family before me? You invited them here— here? You're putting them in danger?"

"Orrin, the king sent the notices weeks ago. You must have left before they reached Haverston," Julianna tries to soothe him.

"They needn't have waited for a notice, though, right? We have other means of communication," he gestures to us, then grimaces as he realizes that I don't have that means anymore.

"You have made it clear that you don't welcome direct communication from the Cardinal, dear. And Robere would never presume to intrude when you didn't want it. Hugh or Connor really should have mentioned it. Connor knew before he left to meet you."

"I see," Orrin says.

Julianna looks at all of us. "I'm sorry to spring this on you. But it's happy news, really, it is. You're much better protected with a noble title, even a minor one. It gives you more options, more authority, and it protects your families as well."

"What do they want from us in return?" Orrin says flatly.

"What all nobility does, of course. Honor the realm, serve the king."

"What kind of service? No—don't answer. What if I don't accept?"

Julianna blinks. She looks at me. "I think we'll have to discuss–"

"I want it," Linnet says quickly. "We deserve it. After everything we've been through, we should be rewarded in some way." She looks defiantly at me, at Orrin, and crosses her arms over her chest. "We should. We will accept."

"You aren't the one who'll be yoked to the kirche one way or the other," Orrin says darkly.

Julianna tries to placate him, saying "That's not what it means."

"Doesn't it? They want us bound, they want us controlled. They will wrap us up in dogma or in bonds to the kingdom, and then they will find a way to say we have broken some law, and then we are doomed."

"That's not true, Orrin," Connor says as he enters. We all turn to him, most of us angry. "I did knock."

"Isn't it true, though? What has the king decided to do with us if we don't want this?" Orrin demands.

"It...was not brought up as a possibility," Julianna temporizes. "Cardinal Robere was of the opinion you would not want anything to do with the kirche–"

"I do not," Orrin snaps, almost spitting his words.

"Why didn't you tell us about this before?" I ask Connor sharply, my own anger rising.

Connor raises his hands. "It seemed...wrong after the attack. I didn't want to complicate matters further. I thought it would be better to explain once we arrived here."

I glare at him, and he shakes his head. "I see you disagree."

"It would have been nice to be prepared."

"Oh, you will be prepared. You have time yet, and we'll get everything squared away beforehand," Julianna says.

"I don't mean...I don't want to be a baroness," I say, throwing my hands up. "It's so...it's too much!"

"It isn't anything," Connor says, trying to sound soothing. "It's just a barony that's been in my care."

"I remember the Wolff barony, my lord," I mutter darkly. "I pretended a claim to it last year, if you'll recall." It was his distant cousin's misfortune that gave me cover as his ward and Julianna's handmaid. I took that name as a disguise during a time of turmoil and grief, mainly to keep from being executed. I'm not sure I want to wear it again.

"But this time it will be real," he says. "The land is north of Haverston, toward Fanthas. There's a manor house, and a farm. With some funds and the sheep for income, you both could be quite comfortable. And it's a way to...a way to start over. If you want it. Even if you don't want to live there, a good land manager can be found. It's...it's really a small thing. You won't be bound, and your responsibilities are minor. If the king wanted more from you, he could have done much better."

"Not easily," Julianna mutters, and I turn to glare at her. She sighs. "This way the barony isn't languishing," she says, sounding exasperated. "You and Orrin both need the protection that nobility can bring, so why not use it? It's a better option than becoming Boucher's wards, which is what Alexander suggested. You're of age now, and Linnet isn't far behind. I know the guilds do this sort of thing. Creating wardships or betrothals and marrying young to keep land and money in family hands. Dorei knows the nobility aren't any better. But there's no reason the two of you can't be in charge of yourselves. Linnet has you, and you can always apply to me or Hugh for guidance on how to manage an estate."

"And what about Orrin," I insist. "He's not even—it's his family farm, but you want him here? You're forcing us to choose a barony or the kirche."

Connor throws up his hands. "No one is forcing either of you to choose the kirche. Yes, the kirche is part of the monetary recompense for all of you—Duchess Marguerite made certain of that. The death-geld and recompense for the injury they caused—directly and indirectly. A recompense you deserve to receive, and they deserve to pay. It will help you settle into your new titles."

"What are they asking in return?" Orrin growls.

"The king is asking Cardinal Robere to look into your magic," Connor admits.

"So the kirche pays money to the king for access to us because we're too dangerous. Because of our magic."

"Your magic is dangerous, but if you want someone else to look into it, there are magic schools that can help that aren't part of the kirche," Connor says. "I'm sure something can be arranged."

"Not easily," Julianna says again. Connor glares at her, but she waves him away. "Look, both of you—the magic you carry is more powerful than most magicians ever even witness, much less reach. The Healing school isn't the right place for you, and most other schools in Talaria are kirche-run. Those that aren't have either been shuttered or transitioned. You'd have to go out of the country to go to a school that isn't kirche-run. And that's a fine proposition—for another time, just not now. Not while we're at war with Fanthas and we don't know enough about either your magic or how to keep you safe.

"So no, we're not forcing either of you to be a Sonnenian acolyte. But you might have to work with the cardinal right now, because we're short of people who can help us."

"What about the Indrani?" Orrin asks.

Connor heaves a sigh. "There are a lot of political considerations to be made regarding the Indrani Empire. The compromises we'd be forced to make are...unfavorable to Talaria."

"But what about Asa?" I ask.

"She is loyal to the empress before all else. Indranah would like nothing better than a foothold this far north. They'll swallow Talaria whole if they get the chance."

"Aren't you the grandson of –"

"The empress is my grandmother, yes," Connor says. "And Asa is my aunt, sort of. They're still Indrani, and they consider me their...never mind. They might help us, but I doubt you'd appreciate their help any more than Cardinal Robere's. Likely a lot less."

"But I can't accept that title from you!" I burst out. Connor takes a step back. I realize I'm near tears—somehow the idea of being Rhia Wolff again, having a title attached to his family, makes me weepy. It was a disguise I wore when I was weak, not who I am. I find myself shaking with unshed tears.

"Rhiannon," Julianna hesitates. "It will be from the king. it's a reward from the king. Connor is just holding it in abeyance for now, it doesn't belong to him. And it's...this is the best way to keep you all safe, don't you see?"

I look at the floor. Linnet growls, "I'm picking this room," and stomps off through the door closest to her.

"I think we're all very tired," Orrin says at last.

"Yes, of course you are. I'm sorry, why don't you all take some time to rest? I'll have someone bring wash water and food." Julianna slips out of the sitting room before I can bring myself to remember to curtsey. Connor follows, with a last brooding look at me before he turns away.

Orrin hugs me once we're alone. "My family are coming here," he says, the both of us trembling with tension and all the emotions of the day so far.

"Maybe it will be good to see them?" I offer, wiping

at my eyes. He lets me go. "They're your family, though. You know better than I do." I fight fresh tears. "I would want to see mine."

Orrin shakes his head. "That's not fair," he says.

"No," I agree, hugging him again. Then I push him away. "Go wash up. Sleep. Cry. That's what I'm going to do."

When he's gone I enter the room opposite Linnet's. It's more opulent than any I've had before, but the high bed with fluffy white bedding is all I'm focused on. It's soft and, despite feeling grubby and grimy, I take off everything but my shift and crawl into it gratefully without waiting for the wash water.

I wake sometime later to a buzzing in my body, my scars, and my bones. My face feels grubby. Rubbing at it with one hand, I shudder off the not-quite pain. Streaming light from the window tells me it's the same day—or maybe it's daytime again. I can't tell how long I've been asleep, but it feels like some time. A clean, perfectly pressed blue dress I've never seen before hangs on the door of the wardrobe. The clothes I took off before crawling into bed are gone, and I climb out of bed with a groan.

There's a water pitcher on a side table with tepid water. If it was warm when it arrived, that was some time ago. Still, it's enough to wash my face and hands for now. I search for a water closet, and finding one inside an attached bathing room, I use it gratefully. Someone anticipated this need as well, as there is lovely, soft-scented soap and some clean underthings laid out for me.

My bones still buzz, a feeling like far away magic crawling under my skin, like earthworms, like oceans I can't reach. Nausea seeps through my middle. Sometimes that means I haven't eaten. Maybe I should eat.

I put on the blue dress and enter the main suite. The sitting room is empty, and Linnet doesn't seem to be in her room. I cross the hall to Orrin's rooms and knock.

"Who is it?" I hear Hugh say, his voice strained.

"It's Rhiannon," I say, and Hugh yanks open the door.

"Good, come help me," he says, breathless, and I rush after him into the room.

Orrin stands hunched over a chair, caught deep in the magic that fizzes and reverberates in the air. He looks up at me, his body going fuzzy around the edges. The curtains behind him show through his fading outline. I reach for him, but with the buzzing in my bones—just a brush of whatever vision has Orrin in its grip—I don't know what my touching him will do.

"For pity's sake, Hugh, grab him," I shout, in a panic to keep Orrin from fading all together. If he's pulled fully into the vortex—I remember what happened to those soldiers with the siege engine.

"I've been trying," he snaps. He reaches for Orrin in a moment of semi-solidity. Hugh's hands almost push him over, almost grasp nothing.

"He's still fading," Hugh says roughly, trying to shake Orrin. But it's like shaking air. "He needs to be brought back. This isn't working!"

Orrin needs physical sensation to ground him here, and I'm afraid he'll just ignore pain. But...

"Kiss him," I shout. Hugh looks at me, startled wariness in his face. "Do it now!" I yell, watching as Orrin starts to fade in again.

Hugh grabs for Orrin's face and hauls the sputtering pieces of him in for a kiss. The first meeting of faces is rough and looks teeth-bumpy. But Orrin's eyes snap open and focus on Hugh in surprise, and his form stops fading. Then they are both present, both kissing, and the kiss turns both gentle and urgent.

I press my lips together and turn away, feeling fluttery and shaky. I brush away tears, not knowing why I'm crying, but when I hear a passionate moan from one or the other of them, I wipe my face again and clear my throat gently.

"I'm, uh, just going to go," I murmur, thinking I'll slip away and they won't really notice. But I hear startled gasps and stumbling behind me.

When I turn around, Hugh has backed up and looks at the ground, and Orrin's hand is over his mouth.

"What, ah, what did you...that is, what was the vision?" Hugh asks, his gaze flitting from one architectural feature to another, but staying away from either Orrin or myself.

Orrin looks lost, looks bereft, looks like he can't use words.

"Are you all right?" I ask him, still afraid to touch, afraid of what little magic I feel stuttering about me might do to him. He shakes his head, covers his face with his hands.

"There...there was some sort of elaborate spell, something Montmoore was working on," he says into his palms.

"What do you mean?" Hugh asks, looking at him now.

"I don't know what I mean. I don't know enough

about spells—I didn't recognize the runes or the diagrams." Orrin sinks to the floor, starting to shiver.

Hugh looks at me in alarm. I raise my eyebrows and gesture—go to him, you idiot. Hugh takes one hesitant step to him, then another, then kneels in front of Orrin and reaches his arms around him.

"Maybe now you'll let me bring you to the Cardinal," Hugh says in a voice he means to be soothing. I don't even have time to finish rolling my eyes before Orrin shoves him away and scrambles to his feet.

"If I wanted to speak with Cardinal Robere, I would. I don't need you to bring me before anyone," he spits, and stalks out of the room. Hugh's face is a study in frustration. He sighs and stands, turns to me.

"I don't know how else to help him."

"He doesn't want to talk to the Cardinal, Hugh," I say.

"I know that! But there isn't anyone else here who can help him. Not since the dogmatics started driving out anyone not kirche trained. There aren't even any Doreian acolytes left near the court. I can't find anyone to help who isn't part of the Sonnenian kirche anywhere in Talaria right now. I can't ask anyone else, not even in secret, or we risk an ugly fight."

"Hugh,"

"I am trying, Rhiannon. But there is only so much I can do. Your magic—yours and Orrin's—is remarkable, and dangerous, and unknown. What happened to you two is unheard of, and we don't understand it. All the same, we really don't want that knowledge spread around, so you become even more of a target. And the only capable person we can consult with about any of it —the only trustworthy person, here and available to us

—is Cardinal Robere. I don't know what Orrin expects me to do."

I try to keep my own temper in the face of his unraveling one. "He expects you to show him you care. He expects you to—I don't know—not push the kirche at him! Don't be stupid. You know what he expects." I stare him down when he spins to face me. "Go find him and tell him you're on his side. That he gets to decide what he does. The kirche betrayed him. They all betrayed both of us—my whole family! Even if it wasn't every priest, every acolyte, it was enough. You said you can't trust the kirche yourself right now. How are we—how is Orrin—supposed to trust any of them? Even someone you say you do?"

"I would never let anyone hurt him," Hugh protests, pacing.

Frustrated and tired or arguing, I throw my hands out. "What if you can't stop it? What if you're not in charge, like yesterday?" I grit out through my rising anger. "Orrin trusted the kirche before—can you blame him if he can't anymore? If we don't? You're a duke, but you're not the king. What if Cardinal Robere and the king decide we're too dangerous? What if they decide to imprison us for the good of Talaria? What will you do then?"

"The king will listen to me," Hugh starts, but I wave that away.

"Are you so sure? What about the marchioness? What if she convinces him not to? What if he decides we're too much trouble? He's done it before. His own brother, remember? And Captain Nerishe..."

"Captain Nerishe is being well-treated for a suspected traitor."

"Do you think she's a traitor?"

He grabs his hair, tugs at it. "We can't be sure until I hear from my mother."

"I don't think she is."

"You don't have the Sight right now, and Orrin says her mind is closed to him."

I don't have the Sight right now. It twists something in my chest to hear him say it. I wave it away, grimacing. "She's as hard to read as Connor. Harder."

"Spies often are, or they don't live long. Which doesn't help me trust her any better."

"None of that tells me why I should trust the king to keep Orrin and me safe. He's practically selling us to the kirche as it is."

"No, that's not what—Rhia, he is the king!"

I scowl at him. "You said yourself King Peter has done questionable things in the past. You warned me—"

"Keep your voice down! That is not what I said. Don't be absurd. The king won't harm you or Orrin. And while he and I do not always agree, he is my king. I am his subject as well as a relation by marriage—a vassal and a peer of the realm. Do not be so casual about insults to the king in this palace, Rhiannon."

"Indeed," a voice purrs. "That would be gauche."

Both Hugh and I spin to see who has crept up and entered the room without us knowing. To my dismay, it's Prince Alexander.

"Alex," Hugh breathes a nervous laugh, "What a start you gave me."

"Whatever are the two of you arguing about? You are so serious, brother dear."

Brother. The way Hugh winces, I don't think he likes when Alexander calls him that. I watch Hugh devolve into a caricature of himself, while I hold myself ready for any and all violence. I do not trust this man.

"Oh, you," Hugh laughs breathlessly. "You know I'm seldom serious."

Standing next to each other, the two men are a pair of young, blond gods, all strong jaws and blue eyes and wavy hair. I feel smudgy just being near them. But Hugh's eyes are kinder, and he stands a little straighter to emphasize the height he has on Alexander. I wonder if he realizes he's done it.

"We were speaking only in relative terms, of course," Hugh says as though he's never uttered a cross word in his life. "Dear Rhiannon is so young, and is new to all our courtly ways. I'm only trying to help keep her from the pitfalls, you know."

"Ah yes, so many pitfalls for a young miss—what is it Father is trying to land on you—a barony? For 'services rendered?' And such services, my dear. Such extraordinary services. You should be more grateful. Do you know how to be grateful, Lady almost-Baroness?"

The prince circles me as he speaks, cutting me off from Hugh in a subtle but very effective maneuver. I turn with him, refusing to let him get behind me. It might be more politic to look down, to curtsey, but I keep my eyes on his face. He looks me up and down like saleable cattle. I will not allow him to get behind me with that look in his eyes.

"Really, Alex. Don't be crude." Hugh's admonishment has the sound of habit. I entirely understand Nerishe's dislike of the prince.

"Have you nothing to say for yourself, my dear?" Alexander asks me.

"What would you like to hear, Your Highness?" I do not promise to say it.

"I would like to hear about this amazing ability of yours that I've heard so much...or no, rather, that I have heard almost nothing about. Not even from my darling bride, who dotes so upon me. Nor my father, nor my dearest, oldest friend Hugh, here. Why even my favorite cousin is all but silent. Although, to be fair, we don't talk much anymore, not after all our battles together. Certainly not since I stole his first—and second—loves." Alexander grins a nasty grin and aims a sidelong look at Hugh. Hugh's disappointment and distress only seems to delight Alexander.

"Alex, stop this. This behavior is beneath you."

"Do not dare to lecture me, brother dearest," he snaps, and Hugh's eyes go wide. "You and Julianna and my own father have been keeping secrets. And such delectable secrets they are." His voice changes back to a threatening purr. "Tell me, young Rhiannon, what am I thinking right now? Can you? Can you read my mind? Can you reach into people's thoughts and pluck them out?"

From the corner of my eye, Hugh shakes his head just slightly, warning me. I don't need the warning. Even with only a small amount of power brushing along my skin like a breeze, I can tell Prince Alexander is furious —and dangerous with it. As for what he's thinking, I wouldn't want to be in his head even if he weren't ready to slaughter everyone in front of him on a whim. He is mesmerizingly beautiful and as dangerous as a poised landslide. I must not provoke him, but I want to punch his smug face as hard as I can.

I'm sure he'd be able to block it easily if I tried.

"My apologies, Your Highness. I don't know what you've been told, but I have no wish to read anyone's mind," I say, perfectly truthfully. In my head I add the words *You giant jackass.*

Hugh's gaze jerks to mine, and I can't be sure he didn't catch that. He raises his eyebrow at me as Prince Alexander begins to grin, his eyes livid.

"That was almost diplomatic, my dear. You have nearly perfected the courtier's art of not quite lying whilst also not quite telling me to go to hell. I see no reason at all for Hugh to tutor you in arts you already know."

"It was not my intention to offend you, Highness," I say, while he laughs.

"Merely a side benefit, I take it. And yet you haven't told me anything, really. All these secrets. What other secrets have you been keeping to yourself up in the wilds of the north, Hugh?"

Alexander steps too close and I don't know how to draw away without making everything worse. Hugh seems rather at a loss, which isn't how I'm used to viewing him. I am at a loss, as well, and if he's trying to send to my mind, I can't hear him any better now than I could yesterday when we last tried. I very much do not want to end up imprisoned for offering violence to the crown prince. A crown prince who seems very intent on creating violence out of thin air.

"Perhaps I should pay attention to what Lady Boucher has been saying about you all along," he says, speaking to Hugh but still glaring at me. Anger floods into his voice. "My past affection for you won't stop me from getting to the bottom of all of this. Don't think to endanger my kingdom for one of your little strays."

Hugh lays his hand on Alexander's arm, trying to placate him, murmuring something about of course not, what are you talking about, you misunderstand. Alexander shakes him off, rounding on him, his hand snapping around Hugh's wrist like a vise.

We are in so much trouble.

CHAPTER 20

"Oh, Alexander, there you are," trills a voice from the hall, and we all turn toward the door. We really must remember to shut doors from now on, but I'm glad someone has come to rescue us.

A young woman walks into the room, leaning on a cane. She is small with light brown skin and dark eyes and hair, dressed in a lovely gown of bright peach. Princess Eleanore, I realize. She's relatively ordinary looking compared to her older half-brother, until she smiles. We all smile back.

A tickle of magic plays along my skin as the tension in the room fades at her presence. I think it's coming from her, but everything has been so fraught, I can't be certain. I take a careful breath and step slightly back from Alexander when he turns to face his sister.

"Papa has been looking for you. He sent Faris for you," she says with a light scold, "but I see he hasn't found you yet. And here you are with Hugh—and our new guest! It's perfect, as Papa wants to see Hugh, too."

She beams a sunlight smile at us, and I blink as all the viciousness seems to bleed out of Alexander.

"Hullo, darling. Did Papa say where he wanted us?" Alexander steps forward to grasp Eleanore on both arms and kiss her cheek.

"Oh, he's in the map room, of course. Where else is he when it isn't court these days? In any case, I think you'd better hurry. He's got a terrible lot of somebodies with him, and they all want an accounting of something or other." She leans on her brother to turn toward us and laughs and swats him on the shoulder when he picks her up and twirls her around.

"Alex," she laughs, "let me say hello properly."

He sets her carefully on her feet, his arm around her shoulder, his mood seemingly completely changed to cheerful bonhomie.

"Hello, Hugh. It's so good to see you," the princess beams as Hugh sweeps a deep bow.

"Your Highness, your beauty and kindness are a wonder to behold, as always," he says, grinning as she steps forward to hug him. He glances at me, his expression cheerful, a warning in his eyes. I change my expression to polite and smiling to match.

"You're my favorite brother-in-law," she laughs.

"I'm your only brother-in-law, but I'd be your favorite, anyway," he says. "This lovely lady is Rhiannon Owen. She and her sister are guests here," Hugh says carefully.

"Your Highness," I say quietly and curtsey.

"It's lovely to meet you, Rhiannon Owen. Alex," she turns to her brother, "you really should hurry to find Papa. It's probably important."

"We'll go, then." He smiles indulgently. "I'll escort you back to your rooms on the way."

"Oh no," Eleanore smiles. "I came all this way to meet our guests. You go ahead, Alex. I'm paying a visit."

"I'm sure she would prefer some time to rest after her arrival. Why don't you take a turn in the gardens?" he says. His gaze, when he turns it on me, holds a warning, but I'm not sure what he's warning me about—or against. Eleanore simply smiles at him, and he relaxes and smiles back.

Hugh leans in for a kiss on Eleanore's cheek as they leave, and he gives me a warning look, too. If only I could read minds—but I'll just have to muddle through without. I presume Hugh wants me to watch my tongue. I presume Alexander wants me to disappear down a deep, dark hole. Or at least he wants me to stay away from his sister. If only I knew why he's so angry.

Princess Eleanore looks at me expectantly as they leave, so I guess she actually does want to visit. I curtsey again and smile a little.

"Highness," I say, but I don't know what to add, so I leave it at that.

"Shall I show you around the palace? Or would you like me to go find your friend?" Eleanore asks me. "He was pretty angry, but I saw where he stalked off to."

I blink at her. "Were you...near us the whole time?"

She grins at me. "Are you asking if I was eavesdropping?"

"Of course not, Highness," I say carefully. "I would never suggest such a thing." I keep my tone neutral, but she grins even more.

"Well, that's silly, because I eavesdrop all the time. It's the only way to learn anything around here. Well, not the only way, but it is the easiest." She laughs at my expression.

I take a careful breath. I'm not sure what to say to that. Is she going to be trouble for me? Or Orrin? How much, exactly, did she witness or hear? Will she blackmail us? All I know about her is that she's Linnet's age, maybe a year older, and she's the king's daughter. In this moment I wish fervently for the Sight back, if only I could know what she's thinking.

She cocks her head to the side, considering me. "I don't think you're quite the menace that my brother is sure you are. And you're not the innocent bumpkin you're playing at, either."

I smile and shrug my shoulders. "You'd be surprised at how bumpkin-like I'm feeling, then."

She laughs, letting her cane take her weight and grabbing my hand "Oh, I do like you. I thought so, the way you and your sister are, and how you've treated Hugh, and well, Julianna said I would."

I think carefully about the last day or so. "When did you see me with my sister?"

Eleanore grins at me. "Well, that would be telling, wouldn't it? But we have so much to do to show you around. Let's start with the most practical and then go to something really exciting, like the dungeons." I blink back several things I shouldn't say and let her lead the way.

Eleanore leads me to the back stairs. "They have better railings, so it's easier for me. Father made them put in bannisters in the new wings, but they're all these grand marble monstrosities and hard to hold onto. These servant's stairs with wooden rails are much better. But don't tell Father; he'd be crushed." She seems easy on the stairs using the rail with her cane on the other side. I follow without a word.

We go through a few back corridors full of passing servants who bow low, but they seem accustomed to the princess making her way there. She leads me out an unprepossessing door, emerging into a warm, sunny day. It's mid-afternoon—later than I thought. We're in the kitchen gardens, I'm guessing, surrounded by high walls somewhere in the middle of the palace grounds. The smell of growing herbs and vegetables reminds me that I haven't eaten yet.

"There are really nice paths here leading all the way into the formal gardens that we can walk around. Or I can show you some of my best eavesdropping places—but of course you'd never want to use those." She grins over her shoulder at me, and I smile back without thinking about it.

I can feel myself pulled along by the sheer force of her personality. Faint tingles along my skin make me wary—there is definitely magic coming from her. Is she using it to charm me? I didn't think the royal family had any magic.

They're not supposed to—King Peter vowed he would keep everything but Healing magic out of the succession to placate the clergy, and Eleanore is currently next in line after Alexander. Baby Atarah can't be declared heir to the throne until after she's past her first year, so for now ...

Eleanore chats at me and I barely register her words, trying to follow the wriggle of runes under my skin. "I'm sorry, Your Highness. I didn't hear you," I say, and she stops in front of a large lavender bush.

"Oh," she says as she leans on her cane and tucks a

hair behind her ear with her free hand. "I'm just wondering if you've been to see Captain Nerishe yet."

I feel an unaccountable urge to smile at her—she's so disarming. But I've spent too much time with Julianna and Hugh to be easy with charm offensives. They talked me into all the plots of last year with no magic at all. What is it Eleanore wants? I shake my head slowly and answer her. "Not since she was placed under arrest, no."

"Of course not, how silly of me. Let's go now."

"What?" I ask, but she's walking, faster than I expect, and I hurry to follow.

"You can see the palace is still being built on, and we're importing rugs as we can—did you know many of the floors used to be covered in those awful old rush mats? As if it were a century ago! Obviously, my mother made them get rid of that mess, even before I needed to walk. Can you imagine? So dirty, always needing to be replaced. And the vermin! Or at least that's what my mother sa-, I mean, used to say." She pauses, takes a deep breath as we enter the palace through a different unassuming door.

"Your Highness," I start, but she cuts me off.

"I'm so glad we have such lovely carpets in so many areas of the palace now. Some of them came from the Indrani empire ages ago, of course. I think the empress gifted some of them when Connor's mother arrived. They're so pretty and colorful, and make everything seem much cleaner."

I nod helplessly when she looks at me. The faint tickle on my skin grows stronger the more time I spend with her. It's making me nervous, because it seems to want me to relax.

"Anyway, we're ever so much more sophisticated

now than we used to be, as a country. That new Indrani ambassador likes to tell us how backward we are all the time, but he's such an old stick. He probably is right, but who can stand to listen to him? If Indranah is so wonderful, he was probably sent here as a punishment. And as a punishment for us. At least his scribe is an interesting person. She has some of the best stories.

"I'll bet you have wonderful stories, Rhiannon Owen." She stops in the hallway and looks me in the face. "Wouldn't you like to tell me some? I'd love to hear all about how you fought that Bishop Gantry."

I choke a moment, startled and caught off-guard. "I didn't—that is—it's not...It wasn't, um, all that great of a story, really," I stammer.

A flash of wary irritation shows on her face. "I'm sure that's not true," she says lightly enough. "But as you like."

I follow her along corridors that go from utilitarian to grander with carpeting and back to utilitarian again. She chatters happily through all of them, and I'm about to ask her where we're going when we turn a corner to find guards standing outside of a door.

"Here we are," Eleanore says brightly. "Hello Carmina. I've brought a visitor for Captain Nerishe." Her smile looks the same as Julianna's expectant one, and I think I know where she learned it. The tingling on my arms and legs worsens, itching like a sunburn.

The guards blink and slide looks at one another, but their faces relax into half-smiles. "We weren't told about any visitors, Highness. This is very irregular."

"It's only irregular if you look at it the wrong way," Eleanore says with a smile that almost matches the guards', brighter by just a little. "Surely you can see what I mean."

The guards smile a bit more to match her, and the burning feeling sinks a little into my bones. I try not to groan with the ache of it. Eleanore shoots a look at my grimace and then doesn't look at me again, although she does grab my arm with her free hand.

With very little more than happy nods, the guards open the door, and Eleanore moves forward, towing me along. It closes behind us and we find ourselves in a smallish room with a narrow bed and a chair. Captain Nerishe stands in a ready stance between them, staring at us.

"Rhiannon Owen and Princess Eleanore." Nerishe looks us both up and down with grave concern, ignoring the gamine smile on Eleanore's face. "Forgive me for not bowing, Highness. I tend toward informal when I feel there might be danger. Is there danger?"

"No danger at all, Captain," Eleanore says, her magic, for I'm sure it is magic, pushing at the air to make Nerishe compliant or whatever she's aiming for. I bite my lip and gesture with my head to the princess.

"I don't know," I say at the same time.

"Nonsense." Eleanore turns to me, graceful but growing sharp in her movements. I feel the magic trying to burrow into my skin. Or trying to get out. I'm not sure which.

"Please stop whatever you're doing," I plead through clenched teeth. "It's not working the way you want, and it's really uncomfortable for me."

The burning stops like a spigot turning off, and I wheeze in relief. "So you do have magic. You don't feel like your friend, the acolyte man," Eleanore says. She turns to Nerishe. "And you're, what, immune?"

Nerishe snorts. "I'm not sure being wary of bright

happy feelings whilst I'm currently a prisoner, no matter how well I might be treated, counts as anything but good sense."

"Are you immune to any magic?" Eleanore asks, her voice sweet but still demanding.

"Are you using some mind-bending magic on people in this palace?" Nerishe asks back, her voice a lot less sweet.

Eleanore lifts her chin and considers both of us. "I'm not doing anything to anyone's mind. I have a few spells that I know that make some things a little...easier."

"Spells like that are risky," Nerishe says, and she's right. Except ...

"No, Highness. You weren't just using spells someone taught you. You were using raw magic of your own to manipulate people's feelings. And on your own brother, too." I take a deep breath. "Your Highness, that is...a very dangerous game."

"A game you were grateful enough for when it calmed him down," Eleanore sniffs.

Nerishe sits very carefully down on the bed, as if her bones ache. "Magic is not a game," she says quietly.

Eleanore stands as tall as she can. "I know that! She called it a game—I merely said it back. And you aren't in any position to judge me, Captain Nerishe."

"I wouldn't dream of it," Nerishe says drily.

"Why did you bring me here?" I ask her. "What is it you're after?"

Eleanore's face is set, determined, and very different from the one she showed me earlier. "I'm just trying to uncover what kind of people you are, what kind of danger you're bringing to my home. I'm only looking for information."

"And what your father the king tells you isn't enough? You needed to see for yourself. And you needed to use magic—magic you aren't supposed to have, as far as anyone knows—to get close to Rhiannon. You needed it to manage your brother, as well, I gather. Are you using it on him often? Because I'm not sure you're being as stealthy as you think you are. People are going to notice, and they are going to be very unhappy." Nerishe shakes her head. "I'm unhappy knowing this. I can't imagine others will take it well."

"You can't tell anyone. I order you not to tell anyone," Eleanore says, her hands clenched in fists. I feel the magic ramping up, and I wince, glare at her.

"Stop it," I hiss.

Nerishe just shakes her head. "I'm afraid we'll need more assurance than that, Princess. And it's no good ordering us not to tell people who could in turn order the truth from us about anything we know and who have more power than you. If you wanted to keep this secret, you should have kept your magic to yourself."

"That's unreasonable," Eleanore snaps. "I have to use it sometimes. To practice. To keep from going crazy here. And it ..." she trails off.

"It's fun," I say. She looks at me, then down at her feet. "It's fun for you to manipulate people sometimes, isn't it? Everyone does what you want, and you can just smile and be loved. It makes everything easy for you, and you can get away with anything you like."

She glares back at me. "What do you know about it? How easy or hard anything is for me? And anyway, I'm the royal princess. Everyone has to do what I say, no matter what."

Nerishe snorts. "Oh now, that's not true. You have

privilege and influence—and power, in a very select sphere—but all your power comes from your father and place in court. You're too young, and without any money or appointments to have any real power. But here is your magic—magic no one even knows you have—and you can play all you like. It must be a great game."

"I'm not the one calling it a game!" Eleanore grits out.

"Then what is it?" I ask.

"Safety," she snaps back. "Information. And sometimes...sometimes it's me saving everyone's tailfeathers from the fire."

Nerishe raises her eyebrows. "Is it?"

Eleanore leans back against the wall and crosses her arms over her chest, cane dangling. "Yes. I'm not lying."

"Did I accuse you of lying?"

"You implied."

Nerishe just shakes her head. "Then tell me what saving everyone's tailfeathers looks like," she says evenly. "How is it you're saving them, when no one knows?"

Eleanore shrugs, a little uncertain, since she's not using her magic on us to make us like her, I think.

"I just...diffuse things sometimes. And I know who to use magic around and who not to. I'm not stupid."

"I don't think you're stupid," I say, and mean it. She's definitely reckless, though I keep that thought to myself for now. "But I'm surprised Duke Haverston hasn't noticed before now."

"I don't normally have to use it in front of Hugh. Alex is usually a lot happier with him," she mutters.

"What sorts of things do you diffuse?" Nerishe asks.

Eleanore puts her cane back down and shifts her weight, scowling at the captain. "Why do you get to know that? You're imprisoned by my father while he decides what to do with you."

"Why did you come here at all? As you say, I am a prisoner—now a prisoner with information you don't want bandied about, so I have a bargaining chip. If what you wanted was information from me, you've gone about it backwards."

Eleanore continues to scowl, but her face turns ruddy with embarrassment, and I can almost feel frustration radiating off her. "You can't tell anyone. It's dangerous for you, too. If the court thinks you're conspiring with magic they don't trust, they won't like you any better. And anyway, who will believe you over me?"

I shake my head. "I have people who will believe me."

"I wouldn't count on people not believing us, Your Highness." Nerishe shakes her head. "We have our allies, as well."

"How can I convince you?" she asks a bit desperately, and I can feel the magic in the air, hovering around her. She wants to use it. I take a deep breath.

"You have to stop manipulating people with magic. I can feel it around you now, you can't force people to do what you want. That's, that's evil."

"I'm not forcing anyone!" she protests.

"What would those guards outside think? If you had just shown up with Rhiannon and asked to come in here and not used magic, what would they have done? And if someone comes to check on us now, what happens to them? How will they be punished? You must think of the consequences for other people. What of your brother? What will he think when he finds out you've been changing his mind for him? And what happens if he doesn't, but other people do?" Nerishe covers her eyes for a moment, scrubs her hands over her face. "You are very young—you are both so very young, and too much is given to you, and you understand so little."

I feel a bit stung. "I'm not manipulating anyone," I mutter, but she just shakes her head.

"Honestly, I don't have to do much magic to get most people to do what I want," Eleanore says, and Nerishe shakes her head some more.

"That doesn't really make me feel better, Highness," she mutters.

"Who trained you, Highness? Are you working with Cardinal Robere?" I ask.

Eleanore narrows her eyes at me. "The thing about a secret is that you don't tell people about it. I know better than to use my power in front of Cardinal Robere."

"But who taught you? How did you learn to do what you're doing?" She hesitates.

Nerishe blows out a breath. "It was your mother, wasn't it? I remember people were so surprised that King Peter chose her for his second wife. She didn't seem like the right type at all for a Queen. But she had this ability, too, didn't she? Even though he was deliberately looking for an alliance with Kantir, someone of quiet lineage, with no magic abilities to upset the kirche hierarchy. Your mother's father is a third grandson of a Kantiri noble, but no one heard about her having any magic at all. How did she manage that, I wonder? And how did she keep you a secret?"

Eleanore's face growns pale with a greenish sheen. "I don't know what you mean. My mother loved my father."

"Maybe she did. But you having power goes against

some pretty stringent requirements the king had in place for a queen."

"Those are stupid rules. And it's not the law, just a way to placate spiteful kirche bishops."

"Spiteful kirche bishops get people killed in Talaria these days."

I flinch, and Nerishe winces, shaking her head.

"With tensions as they are, you having magic that can influence people's minds is a raging fire just waiting for a spark. What do you think people will do if they find out?"

"Oh for...please, don't tell," she begs, frustration on her face. She stares at us for a moment, then looks crafty and eager at the same time. "I can help you. I can tell you all of the court secrets and gossip and work on Papa so that he goes easy on you and I can—"

"No!" Nerishe puts her hands up to stop her. "Do not —for the love of all Dorei shines upon—do not manipulate the king for any reason. Certainly not on my behalf," she says, squeezing her eyes shut.

"I only meant I would talk to him."

"Don't do that either, Princess. I will take care of myself. Do not intercede."

"Fine. Whatever you want. But I can tell you both so much that you might need to know! I know the best eavesdropping spots, all the good gossip. Even without magic, people tell me all sorts of things. And I know how to listen where people aren't always careful about how loud they are."

"What do you know about Marchioness Boucher?" I ask.

Eleanore smiles triumphantly and makes her way

over to the chair. "What do you want to know?" She sits down and rests her cane across her lap.

"Rhiannon –" Nerishe starts, but I focus on the princess.

"I want to know what she's pushing the king to do about Captain Nerishe. I want to know why she's so intent on harming Lord fitzWellan. I want to know as much as you can tell me about her."

"I know I'm not the only person at court with secret magic abilities," she says.

Nerishe and I stare at her in shock.

"You're certain?" Nerishe asks.

"It might be someone working for her," Eleanore answers. "But someone else is pushing people, and I think it's her." She scowls. "She's been pushing my brother for some time."

"How can you tell?"

"I know what people act like when they've been pushed. I know the signs. She's careful, but I can tell."

"If you can tell, why can't anyone else?"

"You don't think very much of me, do you Captain Nerishe?" Eleanore puts her cane on the floor and leans into it. "People who have been pushed are often a little confused for a short time after and easier to lead. Alex has been pushed too hard. I never push him anymore, I only try to keep him on an even keel. I do have training, and I know what I'm talking about."

"I would question anyone who made the claims you have. I don't have your magic, but I know some of how it works. From what I have learned of you just this visit, Highness, I find you both very impressive and very troubling. You say Lady Boucher is using illicit magic, and I guess I believe you, although that's a terrifying thought. Are you certain of what you say?"

"I'm certain. My mother was very thorough. She was smart and she knew what she was doing." Eleanore grips her cane with whitening fingers, her voice terse, her eyes wide with sudden unshed tears.

"I'm sure she did. I'm sorry about her death," Nerishe says quietly.

Eleanore turns to me. "I want you to tell me how Gantry died," she speaks quietly, every word sharp. "I want to know his expression, what happened, every moment of it. I want to know that he paid for what he did."

I flounder for words. I know Gantry killed Queen Esther with his demon Wasting spell, but I hadn't considered that she would want information about his death. I swallow. "I—of course. If you wish, Highness." I don't want to talk about him. But if anyone deserves to know, I guess she does. And the king, should he ask it. "I'm sorry. It's awful what happened," I say, my voice rough. I don't wake up weeping as often as I used to, and I reach for Keenan less—but I miss them, and I am angry, still. Forever.

She must be, as well.

She stares at me, her eyes blazing. "I want to stop Stephen Valcourt, too. I want them to pay for hurting my...hurting people."

"I'm sorry for your loss, Highness," Nerishe says again. "But your being here is...you need to leave this room as soon as possible before someone else comes. Especially if the Butcher is doing what you say. It puts us all in even more danger, and I am already in plenty as it is. Please..."

"I can help you," Eleanore blurts. "I can help you both. I know all the best eavesdropping spots. I told you that. We could find out..."

"No," Nerishe says with finality.

"It might be a good idea to just check out," I say, considering. "We might need to...pay attention."

"Rhiannon," Nerishe shakes her head. "Please, don't."

"You still have to ask for help," I say to Eleanore. "Princess Julianna can help you. Or Hugh. We can trust them. And they have some practice in these kinds of secrets," I continue, but Nerishe drops her head in her hands.

"Children, both of you, get out. I don't want to know anything. I know nothing about either of you. You were never here. Just go, now."

"Why did you work for Valcourt, only to betray him?" Eleanore asks.

"Highness, I have children. I have a wife. And I don't have to speak to you any longer. Get out before you're caught."

I help Eleanore to her feet. "She's right, we should leave. Captain Nerishe, I promise I'll talk to Duchess Marguerite about what's happened with you."

"Get out, children. Please do not help in any way. I refuse to be a part of any of your plans," she mutters, lying down on her bed and covering her head with her pillow. "What have we come to," I think she says, but it's muffled by her pillow. I urge the princess out the door.

Eleanore turns on her charm—and magic—to get us past the guards again, who look dazed but otherwise unhurt. But it's disconcerting to see and feel her magic at work. I can't be sure she knows what she's doing. Or the possible consequences. I don't know them, either.

I'm beginning to understand Hugh's obsession with bringing in Cardinal Robere. I feel like we need an adult, someone with much more magical training and knowledge. I just wish everyone with those qualifications weren't part of the kirche.

"What is it you're doing to them, when you push?" I ask.

"Me? I'm not doing a thing. You're the great and terrible magician," she says sweetly, her face full of charm. I snort, exasperated, but I know I won't get any information out of her right now.

"You'll have to speak to Julianna very soon," I say.

"I already promised I would," Eleanore says, the sweetness still there, but thinly covering a sharp irritation.

"You didn't promise, exactly, and I'm not so sure your idea of soon is the same as mine."

"I'm not so sure you won't be found out for clandestinely visiting a prisoner."

"Are you going to turn this around on me?"

She smiles. "I won't have to do a thing. I haven't so far. I'm just here, in my own palace, minding my own business."

I narrow my eyes at her. "You have to speak to Julianna."

"Of course, Baroness. What must you think of me?"

"Stop it," I say firmly, and she grins at me.

Eleanore leaves me at the corridor to our rooms—she has a schedule she interrupted to save me from her brother. Or to spy on us. For all I know she's left to spy on us some more.

I open the door to find my sister lying on the lush carpet in the center of a sunny patch, a child in a frilly short gown crawling on her and babbling.

Linnet looks up as I come in. "I got to meet a princess today, too," she says, and holds the child up by her armpits, grinning at her. "Didn't I, Your Highness," she coos in a baby voice. The baby—the Princess Atarah Kieran—laughs and waves her arms.

"We've met her before," I say.

Linnet sticks her tongue out at me, then grins at the baby.

"She doesn't remember that."

Julianna steps in from Linnet's side of the suite. "There you are, Rhia. Did you have a nice visit with Princess Eleanore?"

I blink a few times, then remember that everyone

else still has access to magic and can send to one another whenever they like. "Hugh said something to you?" I venture.

"Well, yes, but there are servants to tell us things, as well." She smiles at me. "I heard from several that Eleanore was escorting you around the palace."

Linnet keeps playing with the baby. "Hugh said that Orrin had a vision and then went out, and afterward Prince Alexander came to bring Hugh to King Peter, so Eleanore offered to keep you company. I don't suppose it occurred to you to come and get me." She shoots me a grumpy look. "I might have liked a tour of the palace, as well."

I shoot her one right back. "As a matter of fact, no, it didn't. Because she didn't offer so much as insist. I didn't really have a lot of input on the proceedings at all," I retort. "You'll meet her eventually, anyway." Part of me winces at the thought of the damage the two of them could do if they get along.

Julianna puts a placating hand on my arm. "You'll meet Princess Eleanore soon. She's a dear child," she says, but she hesitates as she says it. "She can be a bit impetuous. And so much energy. But no one has slighted you on purpose, Linnet. And in any case, there aren't many people I would allow to crawl around with my daughter. You should be feeling pretty special yourself right now."

Linnet makes a face. "So special." But the baby squeals and grabs for her face, and Linnet grins again.

Atarah is so much bigger than last I saw her. Of course, she's nearly a year old now, crawling and smiling and obviously as smitten with her mother as everyone else. Julianna evidently returns the favor, taking her baby from Linnet and bouncing her in her arms, smiling at her in delight.

"Did you meet Prince Alexander as well?" Linnet asks—not so innocently, as she gets up to sit on the couch. I wonder what Hugh told her. I bite my lips.

"Um, briefly." I cast a wary look at Julianna.

Julianna shifts Atarah, who is beginning to fuss, into a more comfortable hold, swaying gently. She looks up at me, raises her eyebrows. "What is it?" she asks.

"We just had...an introduction," I say non-commitally. "But I spent much more time with Princess Eleanore." I take a breath. "She has some weighty matters on her mind. She mentioned she was going to speak to you about them," I say, raising my eyebrows.

"Well just tell us what they are then," Linnet says. "Don't dance your face about like we're supposed to know already when we don't."

Julianna chuckles. "If Eleanore spoke in confidence, of course Rhiannon cannot tell. But I do wonder if I should speak with her," she says smoothly, glancing up at me, then going back to making faces at the baby.

"I think that would be...wise," I say. "But I never told you that."

"Of course not, dear. I'm very good at getting people to tell me things. They needn't think the idea came from anyone but me."

"I'm aware," I mutter.

She laughs. "I suppose you are." She smiles at me and pats my shoulder.

A brisk knock at the suite door startles all of us. Connor walks in after barely a moment—his version of polite. But then I see his scowl, and I realize courtesy is not on his mind. I roll my eyes, ready to reprimand him for his bad manners, but he starts in with his own reprimand before I can.

"What were you thinking?" he barks, glaring at me.

"You'll have to be more specific," I spit back, my heart suddenly pounding. "I've done any number of questionable things since this morning, so I can't possibly be sure of whichever one you're referencing." I try to sound arch, but I think it probably just sounds snotty.

"Specifically, I'm referring to you breaking into a guarded room and interrogating a royal prisoner without permission," he growls. Julianna and Linnet both gasp, mouths dropping open.

"That," I grind out, "was not my idea. And I think I did a pretty good job of keeping it from escalating further. Which, if you got your information from Captain Nerishe, you should know. And I didn't interrogate anyone. Well," I amend, "maybe Princess Eleanore."

"Not escalating further? Your plans to go spying with the crown princess isn't escalating? Not to mention she apparently has a secret magic power she's been hiding—even from the king?"

Linnet gapes even further. Julianna's mouth snaps shut and she takes a deep breath, her brows furrowing in anger or hurt.

"Magic," she says quietly. "Are you sure?"

Linnet stands up and punches me in the arm, hard.

"Ow!" I say, swatting her back.

"That's for not coming to get me!" she snaps.

"It wasn't exactly a fun afternoon, Linnet," I snap back.

"Oh, I'm sure it was a lark, suborning those guards," Connor says flatly.

"I didn't do that, either," I say, temper rising hot, a

prickle along my skin. "And good job keeping all of this quiet, by the way. Why not just shout it out one of these windows? Can you be sure we're not being watched right now?"

Connor tugs at his hair in frustration. "I know exactly who is and is not watching these rooms right now—I am not completely incompetent. But those guards are people I've worked hard to personally make sure of, and now they're compromised. How can I keep Captain Nerishe safe if I can't trust the guards I've set at her door? You and the princess trotted in there without any consideration for how that would affect them, or Nerishe. Rhiannon, you can't just make these kinds of decisions without telling other people. You should have sent for Hugh immediately."

A furious pulse runs the length of my spine. "Sent for Hugh? And how precisely was I to do that? With my *magic?*"

Connor winces, and out of the corner of my eye I see Linnet roll her eyes, cross her arms over her chest and stomp back to the couch, throwing herself onto it. Connor sighs and runs his hands through his hair again, and I grit my teeth, breathing hard.

Julianna steps between us, baby on her hip. "That's enough, Connor," she scolds, arching her eyebrow at him.

"I'm sorry, Rhiannon. I should not have said that," Connor mutters. Julianna glares at him a moment longer. "And perhaps I over-reacted," he adds grudgingly. "Why don't you tell us about what happened this morning."

"Start with Orrin's vision. What did he See?" Linnet barks.

I glare over at her. "Not. Helping." I mouth. She just shrugs, slouching further.

"I think I'd best let Orrin and Hugh tell you about that," I say.

"And Prince Alexander?"

I turn fully to scowl at Linnet. "I think I'd best let Hugh tell you about that, too." I roll my eyes at Linnet rolling her eyes, turn back to face Julianna. "I can tell you that Princess Eleanore is able to use her magic to manipulate people into feeling almost whatever she'd like them to. Apparently, she's been doing it unsupervised ever since her mother died. And she's angry and scared and mistrustful. And I wasn't supposed to tell you any of that because she promised to tell you herself! Which I promised to allow." I release a shuddery sigh. It's probably better they know, I tell myself. But I still feel like I betrayed her trust.

"She isn't supposed to have any magic at all," Julianna frets. "The main reason so many nobles have hated my marriage to Alexander all these years is that I have healing magic, and my brother is a magician. However did Cecily hide it all that time?"

"I can't answer that," I say truthfully. "You'll have to speak with Eleanore.

"Obviously I will," she says. "And much more urgently than I had thought. I will try to keep her from knowing you told us. I can encourage her to think it was her own idea." She smiles at me, but it's ruined by Connor.

"Likely too late for that. I saw her already in the hall and told her she will not be visiting any more prisoners or suborning any more guards," he says, but at least he looks a little sheepish.

"Oh, Connor," she sighs.

"I wish you hadn't," I grumble.

"I can't let that kind of behavior go unremarked," he insists. "She cannot manipulate people in such a fashion."

"It rather sounds like she can," Linnet says drily. I glare at her again because she's still not helping. And the fact that she looks intrigued, not appalled, is worrying.

"I told her so myself. Please stop yelling at me for things that aren't my fault."

"I –" he sighs. "I apologize. Again. Ad nauseum, it seems."

Atarah chooses to let out a loud wail and burrows her head in her mother's shoulder.

"Well, it's nap time for some of us. Maybe for all of us. Rhiannon, have you eaten? Perhaps you should—I'll have a tray sent up. Linnet, would you like to help me put Atarah down for a nap? And then we can talk about the fabrics you were interested in." She smiles and pats Connor on the cheek, then reaches her hand out for Linnet.

Linnet looks from Julianna to Connor and me. "Anything to get away from these two," she mutters and follows Julianna out of the room. This time I remember to curtsey, but Julianna isn't looking, anyway.

"I think Juli was trying to be subtle," Connor says wryly.

"No, she wasn't," I snap. "She was trying to give you a chance to stop being an ass."

"I may have jumped to the wrong conclusion about your involvement, but I was not wrong to be concerned about this situation. I apologize for losing my temper with you."

"Again," I say.

"You should talk, speaking of losing one's temper."

I clench my hands into fists. "If you're speaking of yesterday, my lord, and the surprise barony, then I think I was perfectly reasonable in being upset, as was Orrin. We are not pawns. It's not fair to keep things like that from us."

"What is it you want from me, Rhiannon?" Connor snaps.

"Nothing at all, my lord. I don't want anything from you." I grit my teeth and turn to stalk into my bedroom, but he grabs my arm.

"Rhiannon," he starts, then sighs and lets go. "Forgive me. I'll not detain you if you wish to go." I raise my eyebrow, looking at him over my shoulder.

"But?"

"Will you let me explain?"

"You already explained, quite fully. I am not an idiot."

"I never said—"

"Then why is it you treat me like one? You barge in here, ready for a fight, and you don't give me a chance to explain. You shout at me for things that I didn't start. All right, maybe I could have handled Eleanore differently, but in that moment, I did what I thought was the right thing. I didn't want to call out her magic—that everyone thinks she doesn't have—in front of a palace full of people. And meanwhile her magic was hurting me –"

"Hurting you? How are you hurt? Did she do something on purpose? Are you in pain now?" he interrupts, putting his hands on my shoulders and looking me over.

"Connor, stop. Please. I'm not hurt now." He lets his arms drop as I pull away. I resist the urge to step forward into his embrace again. "She didn't do anything to me on purpose, other than try to manipulate me. But I guess my magic was able to work at least that much. I could feel her trying, but it just stung me."

He takes a deep breath, nods. "I'm concerned about you, Rhiannon. I want you to be safe."

"Who is safe right now, Connor? Because it isn't anyone in this country."

"That's what I'm trying to fix. That's what I've been working on—and that's why I think you and Linnet and Orrin will be better off once we've had the investiture..."

I drop my head back and groan. "Connor. Stop. I don't want it."

He tries to touch my arm again, but I step further away. "No, I said. You've made yourself very clear, but here you are, making things muddy again. You are not free to, how did you put it, 'pursue a romance,' with me, but you'd like me to accept this perfectly normal gift of a title and property and one of your family names and your constant, never-ending oversight as though I needed a keeper."

"You are in danger! And yes, you do need a keeper! For pity's sake, Rhiannon. I care about you, beyond romance. I want you to be safe and well cared-for."

"I am perfectly capable of caring for myself, my Lord. And my sister. I have...I have..."

"You have no family, no guild connections, no land, and no title. And in this political climate, no say in what happens to you without those things. I just—I want you to have options, Rhiannon. I don't want you to be pressured into...I don't want you to be pressured."

I feel my lips pressing together against my teeth, against all the yelling that I want to do. But Connor is right. Without Hugh and Duchess Marguerite's protection, we would be in dire straits, since the guilds will not claim us now.

"I do not think it's right to accept this title. It—it isn't seemly. We aren't family, no matter what we had to pretend last year." I spit the words out instead of what I want to say, which is that if we aren't going to court one another then I don't want anything to do with him. It isn't true, anyway. It just feels true. It feels very true. I'd like to kick him.

"It won't come from me. It will look as though the king stripped it from me. I won't protest, but if we aren't —it won't look improper, if that's what you're worried about."

"I'm not worried about it looking improper, Connor!" I yell. "I'm worried—oh, I'm not worried about anything. Fine. I'll take your stupid title. I'll be some benighted baroness if it will just make you go away!"

His face may turn to a stoic mask, but I can see the flinch of his body. "Of course, my lady. I am your servant."

I snap at him as he bows and walks away. "That's never been true. Not even once!" But at least I don't cry.

CHAPTER 22

The next morning, Julianna arrives in our suite with a set of seamsters and more bolts of cloth than I've seen outside of a guild house.

"We're going to need to outfit you all better than what you brought in your saddlebags. Don't look so panicked, Rhia," she says to me as I stand gaping.

Linnet claps her hands in glee. "Oh, I am looking forward to this. Look at these silks!" Her happy face almost looks like old times, and I make my shoulders drop. Strangers aren't always a threat, I tell myself.

"Lovely," I say about the silks.

"Not that one," she says to a yellow that's beautiful, but not a good match for either of us.

There's a lot of standing and pins and measuring that goes into properly attiring a courtier. Linnet is more relaxed and cheerful than she's been since...well, since. I'm glad she's happy, but I feel awkward and strange. The wary sidelong glances from the seamsters grate on me, and I glare at a few of them to keep them from

Linnet, since she doesn't seem to notice. They're more focused on me, anyway.

I can't hide my scars during a fitting. And though no one says anything that I overhear, their reluctance to touch me is palpable. Not all of them manage to contain their stares. The master seamster raps one girl on the head to get her to come near me at all. I keep my gaze mostly vague, a mask of pleasantry on my face.

"No, the green, I think," Linnet says to the master about me. "Blue for me. But Rhiannon looks better in that jewel green."

I let her take point. She is the artist, after all.

Julianna supervises a bit haphazardly, leaving us for a while and then returning to help finalize details. The workers gather up their drawings and partially pinned patterns and samples and quietly leave.

"We'll need the presentation gowns within two weeks," she tells the woman taking notes. "A few day dresses and dinner outfits, and they'll each need a riding habit."

"Oh, but –" I start, but Julianna cuts me off before I can tell her that our only real riding experience was in getting here—was it only a week ago we were on horseback?

"We'll worry about the rest later," she says firmly. She smiles but I know she wants no protests from me about her directions. She's likely keeping me from blabbing about our inability to ride or do anything courtier-like. Why advertise our shortcomings?

"I'm going to help with the design of those presentation gowns," Linnet says, following them out. I think she might be imposing, but Julianna waves her along.

"Your artist's eye will be appreciated. Your taste is always impeccable."

I'm not sure how she knows that, since other than some of her weaving work, Julianna has never seen Linnet's real taste. But perhaps that was for the benefit of the master seamster, who looks about to be offended. She subsides at Julianna's commendation but doesn't look happy about it.

Julianna turns to me when everyone is gone.

"Maybe now we can have a chat, Rhiannon. Come sit with me."

I feel that she's hinting at something, that this conversation might be uncomfortable, but honestly, I'm longing to talk to someone. I don't have many friends anymore, and Julianna feels like extended family. I follow her to the couch and sit.

"I spoke with Alexander," she says. "It seems you made quite an impression on him yesterday."

I stiffen. "We barely spoke," I say carefully. "I'm not sure I had enough time to make any impression at all."

I'm not certain how I should tell her that her husband seems awful, and also dangerous.

"Is that so?" she says casually. "He seemed quite interested in you after your discussion." I bite my lips and shrug, looking away. "Oh dear. Was he entirely terrible?" She takes a deep breath. "All right. Tell me."

I look at the determined set of her mouth. "He seems...dangerous. And awful," I say, giving in. "I—I'm sorry. He was cruel to Hugh, and he made me extremely uncomfortable."

Julianna taps her fingers on her lap. "That's not very specific. What made you uncomfortable?"

"He made comments about me, about my magic. And Hugh. He was...aggressive. Insulting."

She shakes her head. "I know he's often brusque, and he can be insensitive. Maybe you misunderstood."

"It's hard to misunderstand someone who is circling you like a wolf. He wanted me to be uncomfortable. And he wanted to hurt Hugh."

She sighs. "Damn." She starts, stops, starts again. "He's trying to step into a role he should have stepped into years ago, after his brother died. He's trying to finally..." She looks out the window. "He's spent a very long time bucking responsibility. Now that he's trying to shoulder it, he's furious that no one takes him seriously. And he's taking it out on...everyone."

I try to look sympathetic, but it sounds kind of childish for someone who is at least a decade older than I am.

"There is a good person in there, but he isn't—he hasn't been himself for years. At first I thought it was grief, after his brother was killed. That he'd work through it. But...I am worried," she says, turning to look at me. "I am worried that he's getting twisted, somehow. And I don't know how that is."

I think of what Eleanore said. "The Princess might have some idea," I say. Julianna tilts her head.

"I will speak to her about it. Maybe she can help me...do something. Although I'm at a loss as to what." She sighs, shakes her head.

"Enough about that. I want to know what's going on with your magic. Hugh filled me in some, but I really want to talk to you about it. Maybe I can help."

I shrug my shoulders a little. "It's not...entirely gone. Maybe blocked somehow? I'm not sure. The spell on the manacles hurt a lot, and after it seemed like my magic was completely gone. But now...everything feels different, and the ways I used to use my magic don't work. Ever since the morning we got here, I can feel magic happening, even if I can't use it. I feel when Orrin's having a vision if I'm close enough, and I could feel when the princess was using her magic."

"Why don't you let me take a look?" she asks. She reaches for me with both her magic and her hands, and I sit still. She closes her eyes to concentrate. I can just slightly feel the cool touch of her magic sliding through me. I study her face as she works. There are new lines around her mouth, her eyes. Subtle, tiny wrinkles that weren't there before she left Haverston last autumn. She seems more tired than usual, a little quieter.

Her magic withdraws, and I watch her open her eyes, frowning at me. "The flow of power in you seems tangled up, somehow. It's not something I've encountered before. Is that how it feels to you? Tangled?"

I nod, blinking back the sting of tears. It's not like I expected her to be able to fix it. Except, I did, I realize. A little bit, I did.

"I'll look into it some more. Maybe the cardinal has ideas." I shift uncomfortably. The Cardinal again. I'm not as against it as Orrin is, but the kirche still makes me nervous, the cardinal included. I'm worried about speaking with him. I'm worried about going to chapel here, how we'll be perceived. I'm worried that we'll be vilified as much or more than in Haverston. I'm worried that my magic will be twisted forever and I'll never understand it, but spending time with anyone from the kirche makes my teeth ache from clenching.

"I just wish..."

"What is it?"

Shrugging, I stare at my hands. "I'm not sure how I feel about the magic being gone, or tangled, I suppose," I say, avoiding talking to her about the cardinal.

"What do you mean, dear?"

"I just feel...there wasn't ever much special about me, before. Before all of this happened. I was content enough, but I wasn't important. I did what my parents expected because that's how I thought I was going to get what I wanted—a household of my own, time to read and study, a budget to travel. At least, I thought I wanted that. I followed the rules mostly, because not following them didn't get me anywhere. But then everything bad happened anyway. It didn't help me, being good and obedient.

"And then there was everything that came after, and I got...used to being important. Or at least a little needed —someone who can do things. But I thought I didn't want it. It's so hard, all that magic running through me, the awful visions, not knowing what I'm doing most of the time. People always being afraid of me whether I mean any harm or not. I thought if it would go away...I wanted it to never have happened. But not having magic is harder than I thought it would be."

"Oh, Rhiannon," Julianna says, shaking her head.

"It's just—it's gone, now. And I'm nothing special without it."

"That's not true. There's a lot to be said for who you are. You have many wonderful qualities, and you always have. You're smart, and kind, and pretty –"

I cut her off. "I've never been pretty, Your Highness."

Julianna tilts her head to look at me, purses her lips. "All right, you aren't a conventional beauty, but your features are even, you have nice hair, and your eyes are really lovely."

"No one is going to write passionate poetry about my even features," I say to possibly the loveliest woman I have ever met.

"Those poems are almost uniformly terrible, my dear. I do not recommend receiving them. Then the author would insist on reading them to you, and believe you me, there's nothing more awkward or tedious."

"Even the poetry from someone...special?"

She raises her eyebrows. "There is someone you wish would write you dreadful poetry?"

"No." I scowl. "I just wish I were pretty enough, or interesting enough, to catch...someone's attention."

"Oh, my dearest girl. No one can claim you aren't interesting. And as for attention, you have more than you want, already. If you want...ah." She smiles a little playful smile at me. "You were speaking of a specific someone. Who isn't paying the right kind of attention."

I look at my hands, clenched in my lap. I don't say anything.

"Well, beauty is mostly fashion and confidence, anyway. If you want to appear beautiful, Rhiannon, that is easy enough to achieve. But if this someone, who shall remain nameless, isn't more than a little in love with you already, I'll eat this seat cushion."

"How would you –"

"I've known Con—pardon, certain people—a long time. Noticing you and loving you isn't the problem. You are already enormously interesting, beautiful, and loveable in any estimation. But he is too honorable to trifle with you when he knows he...cannot follow through."

I glare out the window, and she takes my hands in hers.

"I've been friends with Connor for years," she says, giving up any pretense of not knowing who I mean. "I can tell when he cares about someone."

I turn back to her, throwing caution to the wind.

"Prince Alexander said...he said something about how he stole Connor's first and second loves from him. He said it in front of Hugh, and I'm pretty sure he was talking about Hugh. I think he meant to be hurtful, and I think it worked."

Julianna lets go of my hands to massage her temples. "Oh, Alexander." She sighs deeply. "Hugh's relationship with Alex is...complicated."

"And with Connor," I add hesitantly.

"Hugh's relationships are complicated with a lot of people," she mutters.

"And Connor's...with you?" I venture. I'm not sure quite how to say it.

Julianna blinks a few times. "You mean—oh." She smiles ruefully. "I suppose you could look at it as complicated. He's certainly been close to our family for a long time. Connor loves deeply, when he loves. But Connor is not in love with Hugh. Or with me." She shakes her head.

"Not anymore, you mean," I say, and she pushes her lips together.

"I'm not sure he ever really was. Maybe puppy love. We've always been close, but he hasn't been in any kind of love with me since we were much younger, anyway," she insists.

Not so much younger, I think, knowing how he felt about her just last year.

"No, Rhiannon. I know where his heart lies now. It isn't easy for him because he's a deeply honorable person who takes his duties seriously. His loyalty to the king is strong, and he's pulled in different directions by his various relations. But I think he's hopelessly falling for you. I don't know what he's going to do about it, but he loves you."

I feel myself go hot and cold in waves. She grabs my hands. "I think you return the feeling, and I'm glad. He needs someone like you," she says.

"A mess always in need of rescuing?" My mouth twists as I speak, trying to hold back bitterness.

"No, Rhia. No. A strong, passionate person who sees him clearly and wants him for who he is. Someone who doesn't run away from trouble."

"Instead, I bring it with me."

She brushes my hair behind my ear. "Maybe. But you aren't boring."

I laugh a little desperately.

"And anyway, no one else in his life has any less trouble, so you're in his usual wheelhouse."

I roll my eyes and she chuckles at me.

"I think Connor has given up too much for both countries that claim him for too long," Julianna says. "There's no reason besides orneriness and the need to control everyone that the empress wants to hold Connor's potential betrothal as a bargaining chip. She knows very well his marriage won't bring her any political allies—he's tied himself too firmly to us. And Peter can't keep him isolated from everyone forever, even if he thinks it helps him. No, it's high time he defied them all."

"I don't know that I'm worth defying royalty over," I mutter.

"Of course you are! In fact, you should insist on it. He should defy everyone for you. Alexander defied king and kirche to marry me because he loved me. Connor should at least find a way to court you. The king and Empress Heroha can bluster all they like, but he has every right. We'll just convince him he can beg pardon after. He is a grown man, not a political toy."

"It doesn't matter, really. Connor doesn't want to fight for a chance or...be willing to take a stand, over me. I am...I'm just not what he wants. I'm too young, and I'm not important enough," I mutter.

"He isn't backing away because you aren't important. He's backing away because he's afraid to hurt you in any way. You are younger than he is, and he doesn't want to take advantage of that. And this kingdom keeps asking him to sacrifice his entire life to a cause, which gets in the way as well. But I'll work on that part. You just need..." She trails off.

"A different face?" I offer.

"Oh Rhiannon, no. Your face is just fine. You are just fine. But perhaps," she looks me over. "Perhaps we could make you sparkle. Just a little."

CHAPTER 23

The throne room is lovely, full of light and color and sound—and it is utterly intimidating. I salute the architects of the palace. The soaring marble buttresses and carvings, the sheer size of the room, the high windows and elegant chandeliers, all keep one feeling very small in comparison.

I step forward with Linnet and Orrin, as Connor and Hugh lead us to the throne. They're here to sponsor us to the court and present us to the king. It's been twelve days since our eventful arrival, so hopefully the scandal of our arrest at the docks has died down some. I glance at the faces of the people gathered for court today. They are not uniformly unfriendly, but I don't see many welcoming faces, either. Mostly I see curiosity or disdain. It does not make me feel any better.

We approach the dais, where King Peter sits on a lovely carved throne of golden wood, adorned with velvet and some actual gold, three shallow steps up from the main floor. Julianna and Alexander stand to his left. Eleanore sits in a chair to his right, her cane in a stand beside her. She catches my eye as we come closer, quirks an eyebrow at me. I can't tell if she's angry with me or not. Julianna must have spoken to her by now. I haven't seen her since our adventure.

Connor and Hugh stop before the bottom step and bow, and Linnet and I drop into deep curtseys beside Orrin's bow.

"My King, may I present to you Rhiannon and Linnet Owen, late of Haverston, late of the weaver's guild," Hugh says. "And Orrin Beaudreau, of Haverston and Jervaulx."

Both Connor and Hugh step aside while Linnet, Orrin, and I stay in our obeisance, which isn't as easy as it looks. I feel myself start to wobble before the king finally speaks.

"You may rise." We do, relief that I didn't fall likely showing in my face, and I look up. The king looks amused. I'm not sure I'm happy about that. "We understand the three of you were most helpful to us this past year. We are grateful for your generous service to the crown."

We all bow our heads, murmur, "Of course, Your Majesty," and wait.

"We would like to reward each of you for that service. We will hold an investiture for your new titles a season hence, near the equinox."

I suppress a grimace. But we've been coached, and we curtsey low again. My knees crack. I hear a titter from the crowd behind us.

"We thank you, Your Majesty," I say with as steady a voice as I can muster, alongside murmurs from Linnet and Orrin. I think again that I don't want this, but Linnet and Julianna convinced me not to protest. Orrin has decided it will help his family, even if he's concerned about his own situation. Linnet is pleased with the idea of being Lady Linnet. I'm not so sanguine.

King Peter dismisses us with a pleasant smile and wave, and we're ushered away by Hugh, Connor, and a footman, who bring us to the lesser ballroom for the reception to follow. Everything runs efficiently. Everyone knows their place. King Peter always receives formal presentations at the beginning of the week, hears audiences the next day, and has decisions and rulings at week's end. The reception is normal court procedure, and we shouldn't be that interesting.

But the stares and glares and murmurs—all extremely pointed with a courtly, sneering civility which I fear takes years to master—that we receive as we stand in our little group tell me that something is being said about us.

"We seem to be unpopular," Hugh remarks drolly to Connor, as he motions for a man with a tray of goblets to come closer. "Have I forgotten to wash?"

"Never fear, my friend," Connor drawls. "Unpopularity remains my job—you may rest assured any offense to these good people comes from my existence. Although you should wash," he adds.

"It might be Rhiannon," Linnet says. "She's been sweating since we started getting ready."

I smack her arm. "It might be your face, you little snipe!" Orrin snickers, which is the first smile I've seen from him all day. I hit his arm too, but not as hard. "You're no help," I say.

"You're doing so stellar on your own," he laughs.

"I should sell you both to pirates," I mutter.

"Children, don't bicker," Hugh says indulgently, but he's grinning at us.

Orrin rolls his eyes. "Perhaps it is your smell, Your Grace. How many bottles of perfume did you roll in today?"

Hugh colors, but grins gamely on. "So it is my scent that offends? Perhaps I overdid it a bit, but I wanted to overwhelm everyone's senses so they couldn't hear your knees knocking," he teases Orrin. Orrin chuckles but looks anywhere other than at Hugh.

"Here you are," Julianna says, strolling up to us. We were one of the last presentations today, so the reception is filling rapidly with courtiers. She holds up her goblet to us. "You all did well. I'm proud of you," she says.

"We genuflected and said yes and thank you. I should hope we managed at least that much," I say, rolling my eyes.

"Praises where praises are due, dearest. You look well tonight. Doesn't she?" Julianna asks everyone, and I feel my face flame with a blush. "Such a lovely color for you. Linnet picked perfect shades for both your gowns. Wouldn't you agree?" She turns to Hugh.

Hugh raises one eyebrow at her but smiles benevolently at us. "Yes, very lovely, the both of you. You, all of you, look quite stunning all cleaned up," he continues, gesturing to include Orrin as well. "Breathtaking, the lot of you."

Orrin's color deepens, and he looks down into his drink. Linnet lifts her chin. "I never miss with colors."

"I love my dress," I say to her, trying not to look directly at Connor. "Thank you, little bird."

She smiles at me. "You're welcome. Try not to hunch your shoulders. You're ruining the lines."

Julianna puts her arm through Hugh's. "Dance with me, brother dear. They're starting up the music, and I need a partner." She tugs him toward the dance floor in the center of the soaring space.

The first notes start from the strings in the orchestra, and I chance a glance at Connor. When his gaze meets mine over his drink, I think he's going to ask me to dance, and my stomach swoops for a moment. Something catches his attention over Linnet's shoulder, halting his smile at me. His expression freezes, but when I look, I can't tell what's caught his eye. It's people all around, and I know almost no one.

Connor turns his gaze back to us with a falsely jovial expression. I know it is false, because Connor is almost never jovial. But if you didn't know him, you might be fooled. "Orrin, can I steal you away for a moment? Ladies, please excuse us for just a little while. I'll return him to you shortly." He bows slightly, and Orrin, looking bemused, follows him toward the side of the ballroom, away from us. And away from where he was looking.

"What was that about?" Linnet asks.

"I have no idea," I say, bewildered. I look around, feeling a little abandoned. I've never done well at parties. I always feel like an imposter, and this one is more like that than ever.

Movement at odds with the pattern of dancers and murmuring wanderers catches my eye, and I turn toward it. Princess Eleanore heads toward Linnet and me, her cane a distinctive tump-tumping noise amid all these soft shoes. She raises both of her eyebrows at me, as we curtsey.

"Princess Eleanore, may I present to you my sister, Linnet Owen," I say, a little breathless with heat and anxiety. Too many people, too much noise.

"Hello, Linnet. You look like sisters," she says. Linnet and I both make a face, and Eleanore laughs. "So much alike."

"Perhaps not as alike as we look, Highness," I say.

"Maybe I should get to know Linnet better, then. Perhaps she's better at keeping her own counsel," Eleanore shoots back.

Ah, she is upset after all. "I didn't really have a choice in counsel-keeping, Highness," I say, trying not to be bitter.

"What choices do any of us have," she replies pleasantly. "After you so blithely took mine away."

Linnet glares at her. "Rhiannon didn't betray any confidence. That was Captain Nerishe. If you're going to be snotty, do it right." I grab Linnet's arm, gasping, my eyes wide.

Eleanore blinks a few times, then smiles wide. "'Do it right, Your Highness,' you meant to say."

I think I'm about to reprimand Linnet or make apologies, but instead I blink for a moment. "Did you—did you just defend me?" I squeak at Linnet.

She shrugs off my hand, looking uncomfortable. "She's wrong, though. She can yell at you all she wants about stuff you actually do. But you weren't the one who betrayed someone. This time."

I shake my head at her, trying not to smile.

"Touching," Eleanore says. I stiffen, and she laughs. "No, it is. Quite touching. But I'm still angry at you."

I take a deep breath, ready to apologize further, but

she forestalls me. "I know how you can make it up to me," she says, a dangerous gleam in her eye.

"Your Highness," I start, but she's already walking away. I look at Linnet, who shrugs. Eleanore turns her head and gestures for us to follow her out of the reception.

"What could go wrong?" Linnet asks. I roll my eyes and let her drag me in her wake after Eleanore. "Besides, at least this time I'm with you."

Eleanore moves relatively fast through the halls. "Keep up," she calls softly. The corridors begin to empty of people, who all stop to bow to Eleanore, but she waves negligently at them as she continues.

Linnet and I catch up. "Where are we going?" I ask

"Shh. You'll see."

I'm beginning to get a bad feeling about it. She leads us into an unoccupied back corridor. Looking around, she motions us closer to a wall hanging. She lifts it and steps through into the darker hall behind it. "Come on," she whispers, "but keep quiet."

Linnet steps through immediately, and I take a deep breath and step in right behind her. Hidden passages are not historically my best memories. But this seems perfectly safe so far, I tell myself.

Glowsand lamps light the passage, and I realize it's a servant's hallway. We follow Eleanore to a little cutout alcove with some chairs and music stands, with a low railing and curtains at the back. Or front—this is a musician's gallery, I realize. The curtains are mostly closed, a dash of light falling across the floor where panels don't quite touch. Voices murmur in the room beyond.

Eleanore quietly eases into the gallery and sits in the

chair closest to the curtains. Linnet tiptoes in after her, crouching on the floor to peer through just behind her. Holding my breath, I step behind them both, trying to see over their heads and stay out of the light.

Through the gap I can see King Peter, standing in the receiving hall where we first encountered him. It appears he uses this room for less formal conversations, as well.

"... the reports I've heard of them since they've arrived are much less fraught than that," the king is saying.

"But what of these dangerous powers we've heard tell of, my king?"

I recognize Marchioness Boucher's voice. My stomach clenches, a chill shooting up my spine. This was a bad idea.

"How can we be certain they're under control?" she asks. "I don't know how we can trust these unknown magicians with such power. Should they have some check, some authority keeping them from harming others? The archbishop of Serramonte has expressed some concern that they are so close to you and not under kirche authority."

"Yes, Father. The reports I've had from Haverston and others indicate that they are both volatile and untrained. Surely the kirche magicians should have charge of them while they're here. Otherwise what assurances do we have of people's safety?"

Prince Alexander takes Boucher's part against us. My shoulders hunch and I grit my teeth. I cannot like that man. And here his sister sits with us. Spying on him. Nothing about this is good, but I want to know what they say next.

"Cardinal Robere will stay informed of any magical activities. Is that not enough kirche oversight? And don't you trust Hugh and Julianna, Alexander? It's their word I'm taking about these youngsters." King Peter sounds mild, preoccupied. But his gaze is sharp, turning toward Alexander as he passes into view, pacing with agitation.

"His Grace of Haverston doesn't always keep everyone strictly informed, my king," Boucher says. "Can you be sure he's being entirely truthful with you?" Her low voice carries easily in the hall, smooth and cold and confident. Her comment was to the king, but it's Alexander who reacts, turning to gape at her with consternation.

The king's gaze sharpens further, his features hardening into a determinedly pleasant mask, which is somehow very frightening. "Hugh Theroux's reports to me are thorough and concrete, Yvonne. He is not under your purview to manage. Your concerns have been heard and addressed."

Alexander huffs in frustration. "But Father —"

"Enough, Alexander. I have all the information I need at the moment. You may rest easy that Cardinal Robere and Hugh have the situation well in hand. Now, I am going to the reception, should you care to attend. I'm sure we can arrange for you to speak with our new guests and gauge them for yourselves."

The king strides out of our sight, the sound of a door shutting ringing across the otherwise silent room.

"I did tell you we didn't have enough evidence of their perfidy to sway your father," Boucher says to Alexander. I suppose she means Hugh and Connor, but she may mean Orrin and me, as well. Perfidy seems a strong word for us.

"You're the one who told me to take your warnings seriously. I had a look at the little witch girl. She doesn't seem like much at first glance, but there's something off-putting about her. That acolyte doesn't look like anything much, either, but if they're as powerful as we've been told, I think they should be confined to their rooms, not praised and paraded about," Alexander says waspishly.

I knew he didn't like me either. Linnet looks over her shoulder at me, and I shrug.

"We'll have to work subtly, my prince. Any overt moves against Valcourt's pets might cause the king to look favorably on them. You know how he dotes on your cousin."

"You began the overt moves when you tried to arrest them all," he accuses. "If you'd waited as I asked and confronted them later, we might have had time to convince him. Your obsession with imprisoning my cousin clouds your judgement."

Alexander glares at her as he paces, then pauses, his face going slack suddenly. I feel a flare of something along my skin. A pain in my head. I stifle a whimper, heart pounding harder, eyes watering as magic writhes along my scars.

"I had my reasons," Boucher says, her voice a little deeper.

"Yes," Alexander says, seeming mollified.

"You should listen to my counsel, Your Highness. There are better ways to approach this—" she cuts off abruptly.

Eleanore stands and waves me back, and I realize I've touched the curtain. It's swaying a little. We must be too quick for silence as we scramble back, our slippers making noise and Eleanore's cane skidding.

Eleanore grabs my arm and I grab Linnet. We start to hurry back the way we came, but she stops and yanks us around, loudly saying, "And this servant's passage is a short cut through the—oh! Well, they left in a hurry, didn't they?"

We hear the curtain snap back and light floods the hall near the alcove.

"Hello?" Eleanore calls. "Oh, hello Alex, Lady Boucher. Was that person here for you?" She looks innocently at them, leaning heavily on her cane, not looking at me or Linnet at all.

"What are you playing at?" snaps Boucher. She glares at us all. "Who was here?"

Some internal nudge has me point down the hall away from us, Linnet doing the same. We hear a clatter down further, and I feel a light tug along my senses. I think Linnet has used her magic to knock something over further down the hall. I try to send a thought to her, to Orrin, anyone, but of course I can't.

Stupidly my arm is still raised.

"A man just ran down the passage from here. Perhaps we startled him," Eleanore says with such blinking confusion I almost believe her.

Boucher continues to glower, but Alexander yells for guards and opens the railing to the alcove to come in.

"Come away from there! What are you doing in there anyway?" he scolds his sister. He peers down the hall, growls in frustration. "Guards!" He pulls Eleanore out into the room, and Linnet and I follow meekly, holding hands.

Several guards rush through the door at the other

end of the hall, hands on swords, and he instructs them to follow the "man," whom we are only able to describe as "dark. Maybe tall?" I take all my cues from Eleanore. She knows better what will be believed. I try not to flinch from the guards.

"Well, they're likely long gone by now," Alexander mutters as he storms after them.

"Do you think so?" asks Boucher archly, eyeing the three of us. "And what precisely were you doing in the servant's passage, Your Highness? With these new companions of yours."

"Why, I was merely showing them a short-cut back to their rooms," Eleanore says. "This is the quickest way from the reception hall."

"Linnet tore her hem," I blurt, then bite my lip. Well, she did, but it was when I stepped on it just now stumbling, and I only noticed it just this second, but it could be a reason to go back to our rooms. "We need to mend it," I finish, a little shaky. Both Eleanore and Linnet look at me as though I've lost my mind, but they nod slowly. "My lady," I add belatedly.

"And why didn't you just send for a servant to help, instead of going all that way yourself?"

I blink, but Linnet shakes her head. "I need the matching thread, and it will be a better hem if I take care of it myself, my lady."

"Linnet's very good with a needle," I say, a little breathless.

"I thought your family was Weaver's guild," Boucher says, her eyes narrowing at us.

"It's important to be skillful with all manner of cloth, at all stages, my lady," Linnet answers with a quiet dignity.

"And are you?"

"Yes, my lady." Linnet's chin lifts. No false modesty, as it's just true. Linnet's talent is well known.

"I've heard your work is exquisite, of course," Eleanore breaks in. "I do hope you'll let me see some while you're here." She beams brilliantly at Yvonne Boucher. "Should we continue to your rooms? We must take the long way now, but I can still show you," she offers.

"Don't be ridiculous, Your Highness. You shouldn't need to hobble after them on such an errand."

Eleanore stiffens at that, offended, but makes no outward protest.

"I'll make sure someone shows them where they need to go. Why don't you head back to the reception? I'm sure the king is looking for you." Boucher smiles with enough sincerity that it's hard to catch the malevolence, but I feel it.

"I'm sure we can find our way, thanks ever so," I say, edging for the door with Linnet's hand in mine. I try not to sound desperate.

"No trouble. I'll see to it myself, in fact," Boucher says, implacable.

I try not to look panicked. I'm certain being alone with Boucher is a terrible idea right now. Linnet glances between me and at the door. I hope I'm interpreting that as she's sending to someone. If only someone would get here.

"But Lady Boucher, aren't you heading to the reception? I'm sure Papa expects you there."

Boucher stops her slow walk toward the door and pivots a hair toward the princess. "I've already spoken to your father. And he would want to be certain two of his esteemed guests were able to find their rooms and return unmolested, yes? I will bring them with me to the reception once we've repaired young Linnet's hem, of course."

"We needn't all return to the room," Linnet says. "Rhiannon, why don't you go to the reception with Her Highness? I'm perfectly able to repair my hem without supervision."

Of course she is, but I don't want her alone with Boucher any more than I want me to be. I raise an eyebrow, but she just raises hers back.

"Do I hear voices in here," a man says, and the door to the main corridor opens further, letting in Cardinal Robere. "I do. And here you are, my lady. And Your Highness, ladies."

I smile brightly. "Your Eminence," I say, and Linnet and I both curtsey. "Were you looking for us?"

"No, my apologies. I've been looking for Lady Boucher. My lady, the king is asking for you. He told me to look for you here."

"Of course, Cardinal. I was just going to escort the Misses Owen to their rooms. Was it urgent?"

"I'm afraid I don't know. He did say he was hoping you would join him soon."

"Errand boy again, Your Eminence? Surely your time is too valuable for that," Boucher says with poisoned ice in her voice.

Alexander's voice echoes out from behind us. "They got away, whomever they were. Oh, Cardinal. I didn't see you," he says as he steps out of the musician's gallery.

As they exchange bows and false pleasantries, I grab Linnet's hand and start to edge toward the door, gesturing with my chin to Eleanore.

"Who got away?" Robere asks.

"We're not sure. Eleanore and these two saw him—it was a man, yes?" Alexander asks, and we freeze.

"Oh, well," I hesitate, and Linnet says, "It was dark."

"They were wearing trousers," Eleanore says, which is quicker thinking than I've been doing. "Servant's clothes, it looked like, but it was hard to see for certain."

Robere looks at us gravely but otherwise makes no comment. Boucher looks as though she'd like to make a great many comments. Alexander just looks frustrated.

"We'll just have to tell Father," he says to Eleanore and Boucher. He gestures to the door, expecting everyone to follow his lead. Well, he is the crown prince.

Boucher gestures to us. "Leaving these two without escort? I couldn't hear of it—not with someone roaming the halls who might be bent on mischief," she says.

"Oh, I can escort them," Robere offers. "You must report to the king, of course. I'll see to the Misses Owen. Where is it you need to go, my ladies?" he says smoothly.

"Just to our rooms," Linnet says. "Thank you so much, Your Eminence."

Boucher opens her mouth to object, but looks at Alexander's frustrated, strangely confused face and acquiesces with only a raised eyebrow. "Of course. I'll see you all back at the reception soon, I am sure."

Alexander takes his sister's arm, opening the door and starting off at a relatively brisk pace. Boucher merely shoots me a cold glance as she follows them.

I wait until they've turned a corner, the three of us stepping softly into the hall, before I let go of a relieved breath.

"That may have been a tactical error," I whisper.

"Many who have gone against the Butcher have felt

the same," Robere murmurs. "So far you are alive and not under arrest. Let's mark that in the good column. Shall we head to your rooms then? We should do what we said we were going to."

He gestures for us to precede him, and we head down the corridor. I try to surreptitiously study him as we walk. He has short white hair, dark skin, a round-ish face, and kind eyes. But I don't know him well—a few short conversations when he was in Haverston, a brush of his highly-ordered mind during a sending—but we've never spoken for long, and I don't feel comfortable with him. I wish I knew him better.

I know that Hugh and Connor and Julianna all trust him. But he belongs to the kirche. The same kirche that shelters people who hate me for existing at all, even before the scars and all they bring. They hate anything they can't control. That is the kirche I'm familiar with now. It's not how Keenan felt. But it's the kirche I've known since this power was forced on me, and before, when my Sight was smaller and more contained. My own parents warned me to keep my magic quiet from the kirche, even after Keenan went for a priest. The kirche controls or it destroys—at least it does in this country.

What is it like for Robere, who is a part of it, who calls the faithful to pray and worship? How does he reconcile the harm the kirche does with the good he claims it can do? Who will he back if it comes down to a choice—the kirche or us?

He catches my eye as I look sidelong at him again. "Do I have something on my face, child?" he inquires, his eyebrows quirked in amusement.

"What? Oh, no. S-, sorry, Your Eminence," I stammer.

"Then ask me the question. That you have one is obvious," he adds, when I blink, startled.

"She wants to know if we can trust you," Linnet says, ever-so-helpful. "So do I."

"Ah," he replies, gesturing us around a corner into a hall that looks familiar. "It would behoove me to say yes, wouldn't it? But how could you be sure from that answer? For all you know, I'd be lying. I suppose the only answer to that question is that I hope you can trust me. Because I think you're going to need me. I know that I need you—all of you. I believe much about this war is going to get worse before it gets better."

"That's not comforting," I mutter.

"No, it isn't," he agrees, as we reach one door. "I will wait here for you both and escort you back," he says.

"Surely come into the sitting room, and er, sit," I say.

"Thank you dear, but no. I can stand for the time it will take you to mend a hem. And talk about me where I can't hear you," he smiles.

"Don't be stupid. Come in here," Linnet snarls, and stomps into the room. "As if we're done questioning you."

"We can always talk about you behind your back later," I add.

He laughs, surprised, I think, and follows us into the sitting room. Linnet disappears into her room to sew her hem.

"What other questions do you have, my dear?" he asks me diffidently.

I can feel my mind freeze—of course when he says it like that, I can't think of any. And it's been a long day already. I don't feel I'm at my best and brightest at the moment.

I try to smile, but it comes out a grimace—I can feel it. "If you'll just give me a moment, Cardinal. I just need something from my chamber." I rush out like my tail is on fire, and close the door to my room, cross to the bathing chamber, and use the garderobe to take a moment to think.

I do have other questions, but how to ask them? Is he going to betray us? Turn Orrin and me over to torturers to find out if we're demon tainted? Did he have any idea what Gantry was doing? How could he not save us?

If I start howling that, I'll never stop. I know exactly why Orrin doesn't trust him. I feel it too when I let myself.

I gather my wits together, wash my hands, pat at my sweaty face with the toweling. I take a deep breath and return to the sitting room. Where Linnet stands in the middle of the room, pointing an accusing finger at the cardinal and growling.

"You could have stopped him once you knew! You could have used your influence or your magic to keep him from hurting people!"

"No, I'm sorry. I'm sorry I didn't get there faster, but from where I was, I could not stop him. And I didn't know exactly what he was doing until it was far too late."

"You knew he was doing harm! You knew because you saw my sister! You knew because His Grace told you!"

"After it had happened. We made the mistake of thinking the torture was the point, not anything else. Once he thought she was dead, I presumed the immediate danger was over. That was my error. I did not comprehend that he was summoning demons. And from afar—my magic is not powerful enough to halt a man from half a country away, nor so powerful that it could halt a man at all. It does not work the way Orrin's and Rhiannon's does—or did," he says, nodding at me. Which hurts more than I'd like.

"I am a learned magician, no more. I cannot stop things before they happen. Mine is not the power of the Sight. I had no foreknowledge of his plans."

"You knew they weren't good," I mutter.

He takes a deep breath and turns to me. "Yes. I did know that. But I am one cardinal out of six. I don't have ruling authority over all in the kirche. The holy Seer at Shovahn has that honor in our sect. And I am on the outs with him.

"No, what political power I hold is more secular—tied to the king. King Peter trusts me, and so I have influence here in Talaria. But I cannot run rough-shod over all the clergy, even if I'm right. I must give a reason for my actions. While I helped where I could, my duties were here in Corat," he explains.

"I've done my best to keep witch hunters from our country, with help from the king. There are more than a few who want to bring that evil here—it's rampant in Kantir and Fanthas as well. I don't know how long we can keep such from spreading throughout Talaria, to be honest. There are many who believe that any magic not cleansed by kirche control is evil. You are all in danger now, just for existing. You have been since Bishop Gantry started his foul spells and involved you in them, and the danger is greater the more people know about your magic and want it for themselves. I can only do so much to help. But I do mean to help. I hope you will let me."

I take a few deep breaths, trying to stay calm. Linnet balls her hands into fists and turns away.

"And what will you do to help us now?" I ask.

"Whatever I can. I'm researching runes to find any like those you bear and trying to keep the rhetoric of my more extreme compatriots from spreading. But I have to be careful. The political climate is primed for violence. There are those who oppose me as Cardinal. Those who oppose the king himself. Some honestly see you—or anyone with magic outside kirche governance—as abominations. You've been spared some ugliness so far because Duchess Marguerite, and now the king, seem to favor you. But that likely won't last."

Linnet and I look at each other, grimace, look away.

"All right," she says and turns to go. "Let's go back. I fixed the hem." She barrels out the door in a rush of blue silk and flickering bright hair.

"She makes her decisions quickly, doesn't she?" Robere asks, amusement in his voice.

For once, I don't feel like laughing at my sister's expense. I don't know what I feel. I just nod and quietly follow my sister out, waiting for Robere to join us. She may have made a decision, but it's more likely she's waiting to see if he's telling the truth. I suppose I am, too.

CHAPTER 24

When we return to the reception, the dancing is fully underway. I feel we've been gone forever but it doesn't look like anyone has particularly missed us. Cardinal Robere stays with us, and chats amiably about the weather. It is, indeed, a warm spring. The flowers have been quite bursting from the ground. I look over my shoulder when I hear Connor's voice.

"Here you are, finally," he says. "Where did you disappear to for so long?"

Linnet blinks innocently up at him. "We had to repair my hem. Rhi stepped on it."

"I see," he says quietly. "Interesting. Is that why I've had three people tell me you've done something rash since I've seen you last?"

"I wonder who that could be, since everyone we've spoken with knows about Linnet's hem and Cardinal Robere's kind escort to our rooms," I remark, trying to calmly remove lint from my sleeve.

"Orrin had something interesting to say," Connor remarks, his voice mild.

"Oh?" I say. "I haven't seen Orrin since before we left. To fix Linnet's hem." I look sideways at him, then deliberately over to Linnet. "I haven't spoken to him at all."

Linnet laughs, and I smile. Cardinal Robere quirks an eyebrow at Connor. "It's only the truth, of course," he says drily.

"Oh, I'm aware," Connor replies. "It's what's behind the truth that always comes back to bite us all."

"If anyone is to be doing any biting, dear Connor, it's to be me, of course," Hugh says, coming up behind him. "It's my usual job." He smiles at us all. "Let's enjoy the party until it comes up, shall we? Your Eminence, I hate to interrupt, but do you have a few moments? There's someone who would like to meet you."

Cardinal Robere nods and follows Hugh, and Linnet abandons me for the refreshments table. I think about following her, but Connor puts his hand lightly on my wrist.

"I wonder if," he starts, then stops. His face darkens a bit along his cheekbones. He clears his throat. "Perhaps you'd care to dance," he says. It isn't quite a question, but I know he's wary considering our tone toward each other lately. I draw a breath and nod, keeping my face neutral. My heartbeat is less neutral, but I try to ignore it. I'm still angry with his high-handedness. I'm still hurt. But I do really, really want to dance tonight. With Connor.

"Of course, my lord," I say a little shakily, and he leads me to the floor with a light touch on elbow and back.

The orchestra begins music for a monde, and I try to

remember the steps. Connor seems self-assured. I hope I can rely on him for how it goes.

"So as I understand it, Princess Eleanore and Linnet and you..." he says slowly.

"Yes?" I say innocently.

"... went for a bit of a stroll together, and disturbed a —what was it? A burglar? Or was it a spy? Or a servant? It just wasn't clear what it is you three saw in the servant's hall."

"No, it wasn't," I say. "Not clear in any way, what was seen or heard."

"Hmm, and what did you hear?" he asks in a low voice as he bows over my hand.

"Conversations that mean we're in deep trouble," I say quietly. I shrug a bit as he quirks an eyebrow at me and pulls me into the dance.

"Not exactly a revelation, then," he says. "So was there a good reason for the walk?"

"The hem," I remind him, and he does an excellent job of not rolling his eyes. I smile as winsomely as I can manage, which makes his face soften as he looks at me.

"You look lovely," he says.

"Her Highness and Linnet helped with the gown," I reply, blushing, looking away.

"It's not the gown," he says quietly, and I'm startled into looking in his eyes. He smiles tightly. "You always look lovely."

"Don't be absurd" I scoff. "I know perfectly well that's not true. And I know you've seen me looking terrible."

He considers for a moment. "Perhaps 'look' is the wrong word. You always are lovely. Whatever you look like."

My heart pounds harder and my legs get weak.

Connor smiles softly and pulls me a bit tighter, whirling me through a turn. I open my mouth, but I can't think of any words.

"I...it's nice to dance with you," I manage to stammer.

He raises a brow. "But we've danced before," he replies, his voice flirting with irony.

"I'm afraid I just wasn't myself the last time we danced." I smile back at him as innocently as I can. I remember when we last danced, too—when we were enspelled to look like other people.

Connor bursts out laughing. I drop my eyes and smile. It's an amazing laugh. It does something fluttery to my stomach. I concentrate on the steps and try not to tremble.

"You were entirely yourself, as usual—even wearing someone else's face. And you always dance very well."

"I do enjoy dancing," I say, trying not to grin foolishly.

"I remember."

His gaze catches on something over my shoulder, and his arms tense up under my hands. When he looks back at me, his eyes aren't as warm, but they are fierce. "Whatever happens next, Rhiannon, you know I have your back. Even if I can't act like it, I am your friend. Keep your guard up."

His voice rumbles low under the ending musical chords and he releases me to bow. I curtsey low, catch movement out of the corner of my eye through the other dancers, and ready myself for something unpleasant. Connor's blandly polite face warns me when I straighten.

"Good evening, Dorward," a tenor voice says, and

Connor deftly turns me into his side as if to escort me from the dance floor.

Prince Alexander examines us both with a devil-may-care grin and maliciously gleaming eyes. "I'm surprised to find you dancing with our latest celebrity. Such notoriety usually does not suit you. Or perhaps you cannot resist such a luminous creature." He looks me up and down critically, and I feel my face turn fiery. "Have you quite recovered from your earlier adventures, little almost-Baroness? And are everyone's hemlines safe and secure?"

I curtsey, for lack of anything better to do. "I'm quite well, thank you Your Highness," I murmur. I'm sure my glare only amuses him. The music begins again, along with the increased susurrus of people murmuring, moving. They eye us warily, edging away, leaving a circle of space around us.

"Is there something I may help you with, Your Highness," Connor says in a bored monotone.

"Why yes, Cousin. You can entertain my wife. She's positively longing for you, hoping for a dance. You remember how to dance with her, don't you? You used to partner her so well," he drawls. Connor's face, gone cold and remote, stays bland. Only the slightest clench of his hand on my elbow tells me he's angry.

"I shall find her in just a moment, Highness," he says. "Let me escort my partner off the dance floor."

"Oh, no need. I shall dance with the young lady. You run along and find my wife. She'll be quite put out if you don't, you know."

Connor's look of disdain as he bows perfunctorily over my hand startles me, even though he warned me.

"Thank you for the dance, my lady." His eyes stay as cold as his voice.

I curtsey, but he drops my hand as if I were nothing and stalks away. I keep his words about being my friend close, try not to feel hurt. I can't keep my gaze from following his form from the dance floor.

Prince Alexander chuckles. "Oh dear. You mustn't judge cousin Connor too harshly for his bad manners. He's been a stick for just ages. But come, little Baroness. I shall dance with you." Alexander's expression of gleeful malice does nothing for my mood, but I curtsey again and let him lead me in the next dance. I try for a pleasant expression.

He smiles down at me and I try not to shiver. He is gorgeous, I note again, but there's none of Hugh's warmth in it. It makes me feel small and cold.

"I have been wondering about your little adventure earlier, with my sister. It comes to me that it's such a coincidence you were there at that time."

"I suppose it is, Highness," I murmur, keeping my eyes over his shoulder.

"And I ask myself, why should she be showing you around the palace, in any case? Why would you ask her to do it? We do have servants for such tasks. And many, many guards."

"Her Highness is kind and generous, indeed," I answer. I flick my eyes around the room, trying to see if there's any help to hand. But who will do anything to save me from dancing with the crown prince? In a crowded ballroom?

He pivots me inexorably to the side of the room, away from other dancers. We end up just past a large potted plant in a quiet corner, where he stops dancing but does not let me go. I pull a bit at my hands, but he brings them together between us, gripping my wrists in one hand. I could pull harder, but then it will be a real struggle, and not just a moment in a dance. I'm not sure if that will make this worse or not.

"You present me with something of a quandary, Baroness," Alexander says to me in a conversational tone. But he's backed me into this corner, and I can't get away without making a scene. This doesn't feel like a conversation to me.

"What kind of quandary, Your Highness," I ask, "can I present? I'm not so important."

He laughs and leans over to tug at one of my curls with his free hand. I pull my head back. "Oh, that's not true, is it? You are important to so many people, but you are also very dangerous, aren't you?" He reaches for my hair again, but I lean away, scowling at him.

He lets his hand drop, but continues to loom, smirking.

"I'm not dangerous," I mutter, thinking I could do something about this situation if I were.

"Oh, but you are. And your power is such an unknown factor. Everyone who's anyone is simply abuzz about it. You and that kirche acolyte."

"Orrin's not an acolyte."

Alexander waves this away as of no importance. "So I find I must learn as much as I can about you. My father, the king, would like me to get to know you." He reaches toward me again. My back is against the wall; I can't retreat any further.

"I doubt he meant 'get to know' as in 'trap young women in corners and try to touch them,'" I snap, temper lost. My voice is too loud.

"Indeed not," a voice says from over Alexander's shoulder. Julianna's voice.

Alex flinches, dropping my hands like hot irons. He gathers himself, turning to smile at his wife.

"My dear, here you are. I was just telling young Rhiannon here that I must get to know her better, as she is such a good friend to you."

Julianna looks gravely into his eyes. "Of course, Alex," she says evenly, brushing past her husband's looming presence to hold her hand out to me. "Come with me, Rhiannon. I need you."

I allow her to pull me out of the corner, very aware of how I'm sweating. I don't look at the prince again, but I can feel his gaze on me as I walk across the room, towed by Julianna. She doesn't look back, either. Everyone is staring.

She pulls my hand through her arm and leans into my shoulder, her head close to mine.

"Keep your chin up. Smile," she says to me, her own smile radiant and somehow easy. "We are enjoying this party. Look, Hugh and Orrin are right over here."

I take a shuddering breath as we approach our friends, moisten my dry lips and smile tremulously. I'm still furious, and so is Julianna. I can feel it. But you wouldn't know it to look at her.

"Are we having fraught times at this party?" Hugh asks as we join them. Orrin looks uncomfortable and unhappy. Despite his own jovial expression, Hugh seems almost as furious as Julianna.

"Oh, fraught is an understatement. How is it we are managing to be so very fraught, brother mine? It's only one party."

"We have talent and beauty, my dearest sister. How is your husband this evening?"

"He is in fine form. Something has set him off."

I think I know what. I'm wondering if I should say it here, but Hugh shoots me a warning glance. I keep my smile pasted on and my mouth shut.

"It's about to get more fraught," Orrin says, and Hugh turns smoothly to greet an approaching figure.

"Good evening, Your Majesty," he says, his face a delighted smile of welcome. I try not to jolt in surprise. All of us bow or curtsey, smiling, and the king is not fooled for a moment, I am sure.

"Good evening. How is everyone enjoying the party?"

"It's a lovely party, sire," Julianna says, coming up from her curtsey. "The musicians are very good, and the food is exquisite."

"You haven't had a moment to try the food, as I am well aware, daughter. Hugh, perhaps you could fix your sister a plate? Julianna, go with your brother."

Hugh smiles cheerfully at his king and says he would like nothing more, bowing and offering Julianna his arm. She takes it with a curtsey to the king and a bright smile for Orrin and me. Orrin looks like he'd like to scurry away with them. I would, too.

"And how are you enjoying yourself since our chat, young man?" King Peter focuses on Orrin like a hawk sighting a rabbit, and Orrin visibly flinches.

"Quite well, Majesty," he says, bowing. "I am happy to be here."

"I appreciate your saying so," the king says, his face pleasant. "Have you eaten?"

"Not yet, Majesty." Orrin and I look at each other

sidelong, hoping for some way out of this encounter without giving offense.

"Then you should hurry along after His Grace. He knows which dishes are best at these things. He won't steer you wrong," King Peter adds, his voice sharp.

Orrin bows deeply. "Thank you, Your Majesty," he says, and backs away for the three steps required before walking away, looking back at me with worried eyes.

I'm worried, too.

"Walk with me, young lady," King Peter says. He takes my arm and links it through his, begins to stroll around the edges of the ballroom. Everyone else falls back a respectful distance; far enough that if we keep our voices hushed, we can pretend no one can hear us. But the bodyguards are close enough that they could intervene should I try anything treasonous. Unless I were a trained assassin, I suppose. I presume the king has signals for such contingencies.

I glance up to see Connor as he steps out of our path. He bows to the king but sends a warning look at me. If only I knew what he wanted to warn me about.

"I've been told so many things about you. Details full of contradictions," King Peter says.

"I'd be happy to help you decipher which are accurate, Your Majesty."

"That is gratifying to hear. Accuracy isn't necessarily the issue, young Rhiannon. People are often full of contradictions. The issue is deciphering which contradictions have meaning. Are you a good person? Do you mean well?"

"Oh, I...that is...I can only try my best, Your Majesty. Trying hard is important, my mother always said."

"Ah yes, your mother. A guildwoman from a fine

family, I understand. Quite proud. Originally from the metalworkers guild, married your father quite young, although that is normal in the guilds. All of eighteen when she wed, wasn't she?"

I feel taken aback. I'm not prepared to talk about my family. "Yes, I believe so."

"You're not certain?"

"I was not there, Your Majesty."

He harrumphs a laugh. "That is true enough. Very well, likely eighteen, as that is what the records tell us. Your father showed skill as a weaver early, which was his family's guild, and also was a keen businessman. But his political ambitions landed your family into trouble."

"It was other guildmembers taking advantage of my father's politics, and the greed of Bishop Gantry—that's what killed my family, Your Majesty. That's more than trouble. My parents and brother died for it." My voice breaks only a little—I feel proud of myself for that.

"Yes, that was unjust and terrible. My condolences." He considers me as we stroll. "You have some backbone, don't you? At least that hasn't been misconstrued."

I take a deep breath and try not to shrug. Shrugging at the king is probably rude. "I am my parents' daughter, Your Majesty. Our family, as you said, is proud."

"Pride has its place. And a backbone is important to have, considering your travails."

I don't know what to say to that, so I press my lips together, keep my eyes downcast.

"I understand you've been harmed by some magical means," he says. The room is crowded and murmuring, but we are in our own little bubble of silence. I still look around, and he chuckles at me.

"You needn't worry about anyone listening in. I know exactly who is and who is not eavesdropping."

I'm sure. "Yes, Majesty," I say. "I was injured, yes. But we don't know exactly what the...consequences are."

"Hmm. Are you in pain?"

"Sometimes, Majesty."

"That is unfortunate. Can you still access your power?"

"Not so far, Majesty."

He nods, pats my hand. "I suppose then," he says quietly, "I need only decide what to do with one overly powerful magician, rather than two."

My heart stutters with alarm. "Orrin Beaudreau is a good person, sire. He is not—he wouldn't hurt anyone. I would...beg you treat him kindly." I end my sentence with trepidation. One should not reprimand one's king.

His arch look of disapproval says I may have gone too far. "Why would you think I meant to do otherwise? Have you been told I would harm him in some manner?"

I feel caught in his sharp gaze. I don't dare tell him the telling came from Orrin himself—and my own fear. "I—I only meant...it just seems that we are, we might be...politically difficult," I stutter.

The king chuckles, his face a happy smile, but his voice is bitter. "Everything is politically difficult. Don't let anyone tell you otherwise. But why would you go from that to a fear that I would harm your friend? Or you? I am not a monster."

But we are, I think—we are the monsters to everyone. I swallow hard. "Of course not, Majesty. But..." and I stop myself. Now is not the time to be stupid.

"But what, Rhiannon Owen?"

"It is nothing, Majesty," I murmur.

"I insist." His voice is pleasant, but I don't know how liberal he is. I know so little about him, except...

"You are the king, Majesty. You rule all of Talaria."

He looks at me from under his brows, under the crown on his head—a marvel of jewels and metal, but I bet it's heavy, uncomfortable. I wonder if he must wear it for occasions like this or if he chooses to.

"Yes, I do," he says. His nod tells me he understands that I mean my statement as answer to his question. He is the king. His decisions affect the entire country—he cannot rule only for the well-being of a single subject or group. He must decide what is best for the whole country. Or what he thinks is best.

It seems to me that I'm in dangerous territory in my thoughts. I'm no longer sure I believe kings and queens are good for countries—or at least not the people in them. I cannot say that aloud to my sworn monarch. The courtiers and the council aren't guaranteed to be good for the people, either. But if this king—my king—wants to kill my friend, what can I do about it? More things not to say to my monarch.

"You are soon to be a baroness," he says, and it feels like it's in answer to my thoughts. I look at him, startled, and my confusion must show on my face. "You'll have some responsibilities to this country as a baroness that are more involved than that of a guild member. You must think of the good of the whole of your people, as well as your own family. Your deeds cannot all be what is best for you and yours, because 'yours' now encompasses much more than family. You have to think of everyone under your banner and of Talaria as a whole."

I clench my jaw as my temper rises in response to his patronizing tone. Talaria has undergone much that wasn't good for any people, and this king and these nobles didn't stop any of it. Decades ago he took the crown from King Edouard because he thought he'd be better at it, but is he? Captain Nerishe has a point about that. I try to say something neutral.

"Sometimes the best thing for the individual is also the best for the country, Your Majesty. And sometimes what seems like a good thing for the country to one person seems like ruin to others."

"A valid point, Rhiannon Owen. It is a happy ruler who has varied and intelligent advisors to help them decide which is which. Well," he amends, "perhaps not happy. But I have many advisors, and a council, and I work quite hard to ensure the safety and security of my entire realm. As a ruler must."

I try to rein in my anger. What good will it do me now? Rather, what harm? "Of course, Majesty," I say. Because he is a king, and I am not, and Julianna and Hugh can talk to him much more safely than I about these things. I press my mouth shut.

"Let me return you to your friends. You should enjoy the party. Dance with someone who will bring back your smile. Have some refreshments. Go on walks with my daughter."

I flinch and blink up at him, feeling my heart stutter. He smiles humorlessly. "She does enjoy a good walk."

"Yes, Your Majesty," I murmur. "So I've noticed." I should not be surprised. Obviously he would hear about what happened earlier tonight. But what does he know? And does he know about before, with Captain Nerishe?"

"Although I might suggest walks along more suitable pathways. Perhaps the gardens."

"Her Highness has been very kind to show me around," I say carefully.

"She is kind like that. As for showing you around, you might also spend more time with Cardinal Robere. He's another who enjoys a walk, and he knows his way around the palace and court. He could be a good source of information—for you and your young friend Orrin particularly. It might be best if you stayed close to him. I may have to insist on it. You young people could learn much from such an elder of the kirche."

"Yes, Your Majesty," I choke out. "Of course."

"Let us find Lord fitzWellan. He's a fine fellow. I am fond of him," the king says. "He's a fine dancer, as well. I saw him partnering you earlier. You looked well out there together. But don't get too attached to him staying close to court, of course. He has many duties." I hear a warning from him in the words. I don't have anything to say.

Connor is suddenly by my side, bowing. "My king," he says quietly.

"Yes, very well, Connor," King Peter answers Connor's unspoken question. "I return your young friend to you. I expect I will speak to you before the night is through," he says, and he nods as we bow and curtsey and I sweat more, again, dripping down the inside of my bodice, and the back of my neck, and wait for his presence to leave us.

The crowd seems to thin a little as he walks away.

"You look like you could use some air," Connor says, and I gasp a little and grip his arm.

"Please," I whimper.

CHAPTER 25

Connor leads me out wide doors framed by heavy dark blue curtains to a broad stone balcony. Shallow stairs lead down into a garden, shifting soft shadows and darkness beyond the lamplight. Cooler air makes it easier to breathe, which suddenly I desperately need. I'm all but letting him drag me as we get into fresh air. Panting and overheated, I let go of him and grasp gratefully onto the cool, smooth railing, lean over, and press my hot forehead onto it.

"Oh, Dorei," I moan as I rub my skin back and forth against silky stone. "This night will never end."

"It is, as you say, endless," Connor intones. He props his arms on the balustrade beside me and sighs. "I shouldn't have led you out here alone. Now there'll be more talk and suspicion."

"There won't be less," I mutter. "Even if you didn't, it's not as though your knowing me is a surprise. Can you just be here for one moment without making me feel worse? Please?"

"Rhiannon, the appearance of a dalliance with me could be harmful to you. There are those who want me to—there are many factors to take into consideration."

"I know! Just shut up, Connor," I plead, feeling tears threaten. "Just for once, no lecture."

"Rhi," he says, but I look pathetically up at him from where I've pressed my face into the rail. He relents, looking over my sweating face and pained expression. "All right." He takes my hand and leads me to a bench in the shadows away from the light. "Come and sit. The air is cooler over here."

I let him guide me, tug his hand until he sits next to me. It's too easy to lean on his shoulder and let out a shuddering breath. He puts his arm around me and rests his chin on the crown of my head, and I let him comfort me. I feel entirely used up. After a few moments, I feel him brush his lips against my temple.

"Good evening, Lord fitzWellan," says an accented voice I don't recognize. I didn't hear anyone walking out here, and I flinch. Connor stiffens, breathing in sharply, but here we are, his arm around me, his cheek against my hair, me plastered to his side. Too late for decorum, my lord.

"Good evening, Lord Ambassador," Connor says, and pulls away from me to stand and bow. "It is good to see you. Did you just arrive today?"

"Indeed, I arrived only this afternoon," says the man. He is older, perhaps in his fifth decade, but I can't be sure. His face is a shade lighter than Connor's, his hair peppered with gray, his eyes deeper set. His sharp gaze pins us in the half dark. "I had hoped to be introduced to your friends," he says, and indicates me. "Is this not one of the young people about whom I have heard so much?"

He has a buzzing baritone voice, droning along my skin like so many insects. I straighten my spine against the back of the bench, hoping the stone will bolster me.

"May I present Rhiannon Owen, late of Haverston. Rhiannon, this is Lord Nasesh Acarla, the current ambassador from Indranah. He has returned from the Imperial Court only today."

"A pleasure to meet you," I murmur, deciding not to stand.

"A very great pleasure," he says smoothly, but his voice stings, and I shiver. His gaze narrows at me. "I beg your pardon—are you chilled?"

"I, I suppose I am a little," I falter, trying to figure out what's happening. It dawns on me that it isn't his voice— it's magic, crawling along my bones. I shift to the edge of the bench and blink at the ambassador, trying to look bland and normal. I grab Connor's wrist tightly, and he turns, ostensibly to help me stand. I widen my eyes at him, try to let him know something is wrong. He merely turns smoothly with my arm in his as he pulls me up.

"Perhaps we might continue to converse inside, then," the ambassador says, his gaze tight on me. I feel a deeper lash of magic, but I don't know if he's doing it or if it's something happening with Orrin.

If it's the ambassador, I don't want him to know he's affected me. I feel certain of that. Something about him makes me wary. I lean into Connor.

"It is getting a bit late," I say, trying to think of a reason to leave. "I do beg your pardon, Ambassador. It has been quite a tiring day. I find I am not used to so much excitement."

"Indeed? That is not what I understood," he says, as a sharp, cramping pain sweeps through me. I clutch

Connor's arm and it's all I can do to stay upright. He takes my weight with aplomb, his expression not shifting.

"Miss Owen is right—it has been quite a long day for everyone. I'm afraid we were about to find Her Highness so Miss Owen might make her farewells."

"I am sorry, Lord Ambassador," I murmur. "I'm afraid I really am quite exhausted. But I'm sure we will meet again." My voice is wobbly and my vision goes blurry— the pain is taking a lot of my concentration. I don't want to vomit at the party.

"My lord, please excuse us," Connor says hastily, puts his hand on my back to lead me back through the ball-room. "I must see to Miss Owen's escort."

"By all means," I hear the ambassador say, his voice a lathe on my skin, and I flinch and stumble despite my best efforts. Connor grabs me more firmly and hauls me almost indecorously back into the ballroom.

"What is it?" he hisses in my ear.

"Not sure. Maybe him? But magic," I hiss back. "Hurts," I add, as I lean into him.

Connor curses and looks around, taking me around the edge of the room. I see Orrin in a corner with Hugh, Hugh's arms almost all the way around him, hauling him similarly to the doors, Linnet following behind.

I hear a bright laugh and the music starts up loudly— a valz. Through my watering eyes, I look up and see Julianna in the center of the ballroom, spinning with Alexander, drawing the attention of most of the room. Away from us. I'm not certain Alexander knows he's being used this way right now, but I'm positive Julianna pulls focus on purpose. She keeps everyone looking at her so Hugh can rescue Orrin—which means I can escape as well.

"What is wrong?" Connor asks as we get close to Hugh.

"Vision," Hugh mutters as we get into the hall, where there are fewer people around. "Let's get them to their rooms, quickly."

Orrin's skin looks pinched around his mouth, and he's shivering. Hugh laughs a little and says, "That will teach you to over-imbibe, my young friend. The wine is never watered at my table," his voice just loud enough to be overheard by the few people in the hall.

"Magic," Orrin whispers. "There was someone else." He grimaces in Hugh's grip as his form flickers a bit, and Hugh grips him tighter.

"We need to hurry," Hugh grits out.

Linnet slips ahead of all of us. "Then through the servant's hall, right? I remember." She flits down the hall as Connor and Hugh lug us along, me feeling better the further we get from the ballroom. Orrin looks dreadful.

"That ambassador," he wheezes.

"Not yet," Connor snaps. Linnet looks back, but he gestures her onward. "We'll have you back to your rooms soon, not to worry," he says soothingly, which is unlike him. It's for the servants who are scurrying back and forth, I realize.

Linnet flings back the tapestry in the right place, gestures us through. The corridor is deserted—the servants are busy in the ballroom right now, and not using this hallway at all. Hugh scoops Orrin up in his arms and strides ahead. Connor looks at me, and I take a breath.

"I'm better," I say and hurry beside him. He takes me at my word but keeps a hand on my back.

The five of us exit the servant's hall in a rush when Hugh ducks through a tapestry with us following, and I recognize where we are. A few more turns and Hugh all but kicks Orrin's door down, until Connor reaches the handle and opens it for him.

"My thanks," Hugh pants.

We tumble into Orrin's rooms, and Hugh takes a controlled fall backward onto the couch with his arms full of Orrin. Orrin shivers and tries to climb off him, but Hugh just rearranges them both until he's cradling him in his lap. "I'm not letting you go until I'm sure you're not going to fade out on me. Just settle," he says.

"What happened?" Connor asks as he closes the door. "Rhiannon was hit with some kind of...magic backlash, and we came in to find you...like this. Do you know why?"

Orrin begins to laugh. "Why? Do I know why?" His laughter starts to sound more like sobs and Hugh holds him tighter.

Connor takes a deep breath. "All right. Rhiannon, do you have any idea what happened? Linnet? Hugh?"

Linnet folds her arms over her chest. "That ambassador was talking to Orrin for a while before Hugh could interrupt. Julianna told me who he was. He didn't look friendly," she says.

Orrin laughs harder at that, tears running down his face.

"Did Orrin send anything to you about it?"

"No, he wasn't sending to me," Linnet says. "Not since we came back to the ballroom."

Orrin takes a deep breath. "Of course not," he whispers. "How was it safe, in this palace, with that ambassador around, to use magic so profligately? Why would I take such a chance?" He shudders and pulls away from Hugh, who lets him go reluctantly. He huddles into the other end of the couch. "I was cornered into a conversation by the king, the marchioness, and Ambassador Acarla by turns. Conversations, hah. They were all of them interrogations. The last one was the worst."

"Who is this ambassador?" Linnet asks. "Why is he so awful?"

"He's new to the court since last year," Hugh says slowly. "He replaced Ambassador Dahren after they were recalled. I don't know why."

We all look at Connor, who grimaces. "It's...complicated," he mutters. "And the new ambassador is mostly unknown to me. But he knows my family very well. He made sure to notify me when he arrived at court this last winter. He has made it his mission to inform me how disappointed the empress is with me." He runs his hand over his face. "What happened with the magic, Orrin? Do you know?"

"No. I don't know anything. I felt some...sharp magic come at me while I was speaking with him, before Hugh intervened. I don't know where it came from, only that it was...seeking. Like hands reaching, or needles. It felt sharp, cutting. I closed my barriers as tightly as I could. And when I retreated with Hugh, the vision struck."

He stands and paces unsteadily to the window to lean on the sill.

"What did you See?" I ask.

"Death," he whispers. "It's always death."

I walk over to him. "The same death, or new?"

He turns to face us and lets his head fall back against

the window, staring up at the ceiling. "I didn't get a good grounding in it—Hugh stopped it before I Saw more than the blood on the floor."

"Floor? So this blood was inside, then?" Connor asks.

"I—yes. It was a floor. A stone floor in a room with few furnishings. That's all I saw before Hugh...interrupted."

"That's a little new, then," I say. He just folds his arms more tightly around his middle.

"I'm very tired. Can we talk about this later?"

"I think we should talk to Cardinal Robere," Linnet says.

Orrin snaps his head up and glares at her. She glares back. "We talked to him tonight, Rhi and I did. He seemed better than I thought he'd be. He seemed like he might help. And you—we need help."

"I cannot trust him," Orrin hisses. "He is part of the kirche. He's a cardinal! He had the power to help us last year, and he did not. He left me with that—that demon-" he breaks off, chest heaving.

Hugh stands up. "I won't let him hurt you," he says quietly. "But Linnet is right. We do need help. And Cardinal Robere is the only person in this entire city we can trust at all to give it. Perhaps he failed you last year, but some of that fault is mine. I did not understand the true danger you were in, and I'm sorry for that. I will always, always be sorry for that, Orrin."

Orrin turns his face away, his lips pressed tight together.

"I share that blame, Orrin," Connor says quietly. "Rhiannon tried to warn us of the danger but we didn't comprehend the extent. I should never have let you go with him. I'm sorry, too."

Orrin shudders. "The true fault is in that man, and the kirche that allowed him to flourish."

Hugh closes his eyes, rubs his hands through his hair. His shirt is half untucked from his sash and his collar is askew, which is extremely mussed for him. He takes a deep breath and blows it out again. "The kirche has its failings. I agree. But Cardinal Robere has access to a lot more information about the runes, about what might be happening, than I do. And I have known him for years. If he can't help, I am certain he won't hurt. Will you please, for your own health, speak to him? I beg of you."

"I will not be a part of the kirche ever again," Orrin snaps.

"I know. He knows. You owe the kirche nothing."

I brush Orrin's shoulder with mine, look sidelong at him. "We can speak to him together—you and Linnet and me. But only if you agree."

He drops his head into his hands and breathes for a few moments. When he lets his hands fall, he doesn't look at anyone.

"Fine. Yes. I'll do it. I'm going to bed now," he says, and walks abruptly out of the sitting room, shutting the door to his bedroom firmly behind him.

Connor lets out a breath. "Hugh, I'll leave the arrangements to you. I have to get back before the king asks for me." He turns, glancing sidelong at me. Before I can do more than blink, he lets himself out of the room.

Hugh stares at Orrin's bedroom door, biting his lip, looking uncertain. Shaking my head, I take Hugh's arm, lead him out after Connor, beckoning Linnet to follow.

"It's time to say good night, Your Grace," I say quietly.

"Yes, good night," he says after a bemused moment. "I'll come find you tomorrow."

"Not if I find you first," Linnet says, and he smiles slightly.

"Even then," he says. "I'm pretty good at finding."

He turns and walks away down the hall, and Linnet and I head into our rooms and to bed with few other words between us.

CHAPTER 26

The next day finds me exhausted and low—dare I say cranky. Linnet refuses to come out for breakfast. I think she feels the same way. A tray waits on the table in the sitting room, with several covered dishes and some cooling tea. Coddled eggs and toast and porridge—very light compared to previous days.

Julianna sends a note via a servant bearing compliments from last night, but it is a bland, nothing note that merely tells me that she is offering expected social niceties. I suppose that could mean I'm to write thank you notes as well, but I don't know if it's only to social equals, or betters, or the host. My mother would have said write a note to the host as guests and to everyone else as esteemed friends. But the guild world is different from the noble one, and I don't know the customs. Is it proper to write a thank you note to a king? I take a nap rather than think harder about it.

Orrin stays holed up in his room as well, with a curt "I'm fine go away" when I try to talk to him. The door to his bedroom stays firmly shut, and I tell him to come find us when he wants to.

Two lunch trays wait in the hall outside our rooms. I bring Orrin's into his sitting room, then retreat across the hall to my own. Linnet comes out for lunch long enough to eat soup and grumble, but mostly wants the same as Orrin. I don't hear from Connor at all. My runes, for a relief, stay quiescent.

Hugh comes by to see us in the afternoon. He smiles his charming-you-into-something smile, and I wait for whatever unpleasant thing he has to tell us. He gestures for us to sit down, putting himself next to me so he can overwhelm me with how sorry and pretty he is. I let him. He is pretty, and if he needs to be sorry I want to see it.

"I'm glad you've stayed in your rooms today. In fact, I'd like you to stay here for several more. The cardinal and I are working on a theory about you and Orrin and your magic. I think it would be safer for now if you stay away from court and the gossips. I've put it about that Rhia and Orrin both have caught cold, and you, Linnet, are helping to take care of them."

Linnet rolls her eyes. "That sounds like a lot of fun," she mutters. "Am I supposed to wipe their noses, too?"

"The servants have been instructed to keep away and let you rest. In the meantime," Hugh speaks over her loudly, "I will need you to use your artistic skills. I need," he breaks off, looks at me. "Rhiannon, we need a current drawing of your scars. Will you let Linnet sketch them for us?"

A pit yawns in my stomach. I hate it when anyone looks at my scars. I hate looking at them myself. Biting the inside of my cheek, I turn my face away. I stare at the rich carpeting—the delicate pattern, the colors, the plush nap. It probably cost a lot of money. I follow the pattern with my eyes, think about what kind of loom might have been used.

Hugh clears his throat. "I know it's a hard thing to ask, Rhia. I'm going to ask Orrin, too. But we do need it, to confirm our theory."

"I thought you had...drawings already," I manage to say.

"We do," he says, touching my arm lightly. "But we need to do them again. They might not be accurate. Will you let us do this?"

I take a deep breath and nod, still not looking at him. He rises and gently lays his hand on my shoulder.

"I appreciate it. I really do. I'm going to speak with Orrin now. If he—if he needs you, I'll come to get you."

I nod, but Orrin might not want to see us, either. He's been retreating since we got to Corat. I want to retreat, myself. All the way to Haverston and back before last year.

When he leaves, Linnet rises to go into her room. She turns to look back at me. "When do you want to..." She stops and waits.

My bones ache with the weight of my skin. I shrug a shoulder. "Today, I guess," I whisper. She nods and looks at the window.

"Soon, then. Before we lose the light. Or I can do it in the morning."

Suppressing a shudder, I nod. "Morning, then," I say. I don't want to do it right now.

Later, Hugh lets himself back into our rooms quietly. Finding me curled on the couch, he moves his head to indicate Orrin's rooms. "He'll need to talk to someone.

Not me," he says, and looks away. He sighs quietly as he leaves.

I slide myself to standing and go to Orrin's rooms, my feet clumsy, all my limbs numb and heavy. I knock on the door to his bedroom.

"It's me," I say quietly, although he hasn't answered the knock. "Do you still want me to go away?"

After a moment the door opens a crack, and he looks at me through it.

"I hate this," he whispers.

"Me too," I whisper back. He opens the door wider and then goes back to his bed, crawling into it and pulling the blankets around his neck. I creak my bones up beside him and rest my head on his shoulder. We sit for a long time, until Connor knocks on the door carrying a sheaf of papers.

"Orrin, Hugh asked me to..." he stops when he sees me. "Ah. Should I come back later?"

Orrin shrugs. I sit up and look at him, asking without saying anything. He shrugs again. "No. No, let's just, let's just finish it."

I kiss Orrin's cheek and get up to leave. When I pass Connor, he touches the back of my hand. I look up at him, and he cups my face, caressing my ear. His hand is warm and more comforting than I want it to be. "Chin up," he says softly. Smiling a polite fiction, I draw away and head back to my room. Time to pull the covers up around my own neck.

———

The next morning brings Linnet and Julianna to my door long before I'm ready to face the task ahead. I've spent the last year not looking at my skin if I can help it. I wear my sleeves long and my necklines high to hide my scars, even more modest than a guildwoman is brought up to be. I don't like to be reminded how they look—white ruched and pink and gray, carved into me like a cursed plaster wall. Instead, they remind me of their existence with stinging pain whenever magic flows anywhere near me.

Julianna knocks and enters my room without waiting for me to answer. "Good morning, Rhia dear. Come on, get up. It's time to get this over with."

I glare at her. She's stunning in a simple, pale green day dress, the sun through the window shining through gauzy curtains on her golden hair as she draws back heavy drapes. She turns and smiles gently at me. "It's no use scowling. Orrin's done his part. It's your turn. Linnet's ready. And while she draws, I'll work more with you on what's going on with your magic. All right?"

I collapse down on my back and shudder. "Fine," I say, already fighting tears. What's one more indignity, when all's said and done? I let my legs slide out of bed, get up and use the garderobe, wash my hands, and stand grimly in the center of the bedroom.

Linnet comes in quietly, carrying her sketchbook and pencils. She sits down on the bed and waits for me to stand where Julianna directs.

Julianna pulls me into place, undresses me as if she were my lady's maid. The nightgown slips off, then the underthings, and I stand in the gauzy light, revealed, trying not to fold my arms over my body and hunch to hide it. Neither Linnet nor Julianna so much as blink. Linnet begins to draw, and Julianna stands at my side, holding my hand, going deep into her magic and letting her magic go into me. I close my eyes and pretend I'm somewhere else, somewhere quiet and calm with waves lapping the shore and no one else nearby.

Faintly I feel Julianna's magic move in me. The blue thread of it dances a little, darts and flows and pokes here and there, tugging lightly at knots of energy in my body.

Linnet asks me to turn, move my arms. Julianna guides me so Linnet can complete the drawings. I keep my eyes shut and let my body be led. When a shudder runs through me, Julianna takes my face in her hands, gently pulling me down to kiss my forehead, then hugs me softly. I stay there, head on her soft shoulder, while Linnet finishes.

"You're safe, you're fine," Julianna whispers, strokes my hair and shoulders. "Everything is going to be fine."

"I'm done," Linnet says from behind me. She comes to us and hands me my robe. "I'll go draw you a bath, if you want," she offers, her face grave. I nod as I pull the robe on. When she leaves, I crawl back into bed, pulling up the blankets and huddling under them. Julianna clucks at me and tucks me in.

"I know, dearest. I'll let Linnet get you for your bath. I'll take the drawings out of here, and we'll talk about everything later."

When Linnet tells me the bath is ready, I'm tempted to pull the covers over my head and ignore it. But I want to wash the day off, too. I let guilt at having a bath drawn and wasted pull me out of bed. Linnet picks out my clothes after, brings me food. She offers to brush my hair. We don't talk a lot.

Hugh comes to us later - Julianna, Connor, and Orrin with him. We have dinner and conversation in our sitting room. Or rather, conversation happens with Julianna, Hugh, and Connor. Sometimes Linnet. Orrin and I push our food around and try to seem interested.

A vision grips Orrin suddenly, magic rippling from him in waves, burning across my skin. Hugh scoops him from his chair before he can more than stiffen his spine. Hugging him close as he shudders, Hugh whispers "stay here with me" to him until the vision lets him go. Everyone else surges to their feet. I stay where I am, skin vibrating, buzzing, and a feeling that I know what Orrin is going to say.

"Demons" he whispers, and I whisper along with him, even though I didn't have a vision. "Ships in the harbor."

"The city on fire," we say together, and I shudder along with him.

"The city on fire? Demons?" Connor asks sharply. "What do you mean?"

Orrin can't speak anymore, the power pulsing through him has taken all his energy, and he slumps in Hugh's arms. Connor looks to me. "Did you see it? Did you have the vision too?"

Shaking my head, I sit back in my seat slowly. "No, I only...I only knew what he was going to say. I...have a picture, maybe. In my head. But not like a vision comes. Like...like I imagined it, after someone told me about it." Shimmery, a frost on the glass of my memory—too many ships in the harbor, soldiers emerging out of nothing, a rip in the air, demons chittering, magic weaving around everyone in storm colors, blood pooling on stone. I describe it, but I don't know if that's what Orrin means.

I look at him, cradled now in Hugh's lap. Orrin keeps

his eyes closed, lets Hugh hold him. But he nods slightly. "Yes, more or less. It's a demon magic—they're going to use the vortex like they tried to in Haverston, but the demons...they're trying to get free. If it works at all, it will be worse than we've imagined. Worse than the visions were before."

"You think Montmoore is using demons to strengthen the vortex? They'll successfully send soldiers through it? Did you get a sense of when?"

Orrin opens his eyes, shadowed and fathomless, and stares at Connor. "I don't know. Soon."

"We'd better set up that meeting with Robere. Immediately," Connor says to Hugh.

"You'd better put Orrin to bed. That vision drained him," Julianna says with some asperity. "And you'd better find out if Robere's theory about their magic has any merit. We need to get to the bottom of all of this quickly —for Orrin and Rhiannon's sake, if nothing else. The way the power moves through them...none of this is normal."

We all look at her. "I realize you know it's not normal. But I spent time with Rhia today, really looking at what's going on underneath. Her magic has substantially changed. It's even stronger than it was when I saw them last, and that strength is hard on her bones, pulling at them through her muscles and nerves. Even if she can't access it at the moment, the capacity is still there, and it's still frighteningly enormous. Orrin's body isn't fighting it as hard, but he wasn't harmed with those manacles you showed me. They're supposed to suppress magic, you said. I think they harmed Rhiannon in a fundamental way, and her body is trying to find ways around it. So far it hasn't hurt her permanently, but I can't be sure it won't."

My stomach clenches around what little I managed to eat. "Is there something I can do? You can do?"

She shakes her head. "I'm afraid of making it worse. I'm afraid of harming you. I think it's best we study it more, first. But if you find yourself in terrible pain, or if something worse happens, I will do everything I know how to do to help," she says. Her face is solemn. "I won't take drastic action if it isn't necessary. You might not recover."

I take a deep breath and rise from the table. "Thank you for dinner, Your Grace, Your Highness. Please excuse me," I say. I make my way toward my bedroom.

"Rhiannon," Connor says, and I turn. He stands near me, though I didn't hear him move. I just look into his dark eyes, and he takes my hand. "We'll figure something out," he says quietly. "I promise."

I squeeze his hand once, then draw away. "Don't make promises you can't keep," I whisper, smiling a little to take the sting away. I walk into my room and shut the door quietly. Crawling into bed is really the only answer to the day.

CHAPTER 27

Hugh sets up a meeting with Robere the next afternoon, a few hours before dinner. Sooner than I'd like, but still plenty of time to let nerves roil my stomach. Linnet catches me chewing on my lip often enough to start tapping me hard on the cheek when she sees it.

"Stop it," she grumps at me. "You'll get all chapped."

"Who's going to care?" I snap at her.

"Connor might," she says sweetly and skips lightly away when I swipe at her.

"Shut your mouth," I grump.

"Don't chew on yours!" she snaps back, but she smiles as she does.

Otherwise, our day passes uneventfully, and when Linnet and I finally arrive at Hugh's rooms, he opens the door with cheerful aplomb. "Come in, come in. We haven't started yet." His hair falls jauntily over his eyes and he smiles winningly, the charm offensive already begun. I shake my head and enter behind Linnet.

Hugh's sumptuous rooms are in the family wing of the palace, well-appointed and flatteringly near to the royal suites. The deep pile of the woven carpet in the sitting room is luxurious. From Kantir, I think. Or Indranah. That, along with the dark, polished wood of the furnishings, the delicate cream upholstery and touches of burgundy, gives the room a rich, warm feeling.

Eleanore arrives just after we do. "Good evening, Princess Eleanore," Hugh says as he ushers her in.

"Don't 'good evening' me. I'm here under duress," she sulks at him.

"Duress is a good word for it," Orrin mutters, slouched in a chair by the windows. He looks even less happy today than he did last night. The strain of the past months shows on his face, and in his tendency to hold himself tense, vigilant. It's a tendency I recognize from my own shoulders and neck, tired and aching.

As far as I can tell, Hugh keeps his cheerful smile in place through sheer determination against all our sullenness. Although I bet it costs him.

"Duress is not a good word for it," he says through a blistering smile. "Necessity is the word I would use."

Neither Orrin nor Eleanore deigns to answer that. Linnet makes a face but keeps silent, too. I aim for a smile, just to help Hugh look a little less manic.

"You're looking well," I say to him. It's only true—he nearly always looks well. Orrin rolls his eyes, and I can't resist teasing the both of them. "That's a very nice color on you, Your Grace. It complements Orrin's shirt—like a matched set." Orrin is wearing a paler blue than Hugh, but the colors are equally lovely on two very pretty men.

Two very pretty men who might also look well together, if they'd only stop bickering.

Hugh blushes a bit, and Orrin raises an eyebrow at me grumpily. But he does glance at Hugh, who is very nearly preening for him as he brushes his hand down his front.

"In fact, it is a very flattering color for the both of you," I say, smiling at them. "Don't you think?"

Hugh clears his throat, his cheeks high in color as he refuses to look at Orrin. "Oh, well, blue is almost universally flattering," he says, then flinches. "I mean, Orrin does look wonderfully well in...so many colors," he adds haltingly, as if even he can't quite believe how incredibly clumsy he sounds right now. Where is the smooth, playboy duke? I shake my head at him, rolling my eyes, and he winces.

"Oh, for pity's sake," Eleanore mutters, but Linnet laughs, so that's something, anyway.

A knock on the door, and Hugh hurries to open it and end this conversation.

Cardinal Robere follows him back into the room, and they both smile genially at the assembled, grouchy party. "Good evening to you all," Robere says. He isn't wearing kirche robes tonight, which is likely a good choice. Instead, he has on a pale yellow embroidered shirt, dark trousers and soft house boots. He looks comfortable and easy, like a favorite uncle. I'm not sure how much it will change anyone's mind, but it does mean we aren't all glaring at his robes.

"I'm so glad to spend some time with you today. I've been going over the drawings and notes you were so kind as to provide me, and I have some thoughts. Shall we begin?" he says as he sits down on the couch near me.

At our blank nods, he opens the book he brought, takes out his pencil, and makes a few marks on a sheet of tiny, neat writing.

"Good. Let's start with the idea of lessons for you all. I know you've all had some instruction in your magic, but it has been piecemeal or designed for magic that may function drastically different now, yes? I propose we make time for some basics and figure out where each of you stand. You can work with either His Grace or myself on finesse and control. My availability is limited, of course, as is the duke's, so we'll have to figure out some scheduling, but I think an hour or two a week with each of you will be manageable. Are we agreed?"

Eleanore huffs. "My time is important, too, you know."

"I agree that it is, Your Highness. But we must work to keep you safe, and you do need oversight. Your magic is a very delicate matter, and you'll require a good deal of control before you use it without supervision. Your father insists."

King Peter knowing about his daughter's magic is obviously a sore subject. Eleanore's pale face tells me she isn't happy about it. I can only assume he spoke to her, but I doubt it was a happy discussion.

Robere looks around at all of us. "I have some idea of what you all are experiencing, although later I will want some more specifics. Right now, let's establish that while I do not know everything about every kind of magic or magician, I have many years of learning under my belt, and I have access to a rather impressive library for reference. So please do ask any questions and voice any concerns. I am here to help. And also to decide what kind of training and control regimen might be the most beneficial for each of you."

Orrin huffs but doesn't say anything. Eleanore merely scowls. I...am not sure how I feel right now. Linnet leans forward, actually interested and maybe a little hopeful. She has had to deal with a lot of magical backlash that wasn't specifically hers, so I can't say I blame her. I do find her non-sullenness for once in the face of the rest of us a tad ironic.

"Does anyone have anything they'd like to ask before we begin?"

No one speaks up. I look around at everyone else. Of course, now that he's asked, I can't think of anything coherent. I chew on my lips. All I can think of is "Why is magic doing this, and how can we stop it," which seems too broad. Orrin looks out the window, and Eleanore inspects her hands. Linnet looks at all of us and rolls her eyes.

"I have a question," she says.

"Yes?" Cardinal Robere turns his attention to her, and she straightens her shoulders.

"How do we stop Orrin and Rhiannon from fading out of existence when the magic hits them?"

"I'm not fading anymore," I say, a bit too pedantic, but I can't help myself.

"But you could again, and I want to stop it," Linnet snaps.

"It is a good question," Robere says in his mellow baritone, and I keep my mouth shut to listen to him. "It's something I'm hoping we can work out together—both what's causing it to happen and how to curtail the phenomenon."

Orrin rolls his eyes and huffs again. Eleanore leans back in her seat but doesn't comment. Hugh sits next to Robere on the couch and tries to look supportive of everyone. No mean feat.

Robere looks at me meaningfully. "Since it's only the two of you who have been affected this way, and were used in that terrible spell, we can assume that the fact that you are power wells has something to do with it. Our knowledge of human power wells is limited, mainly because the lore surrounding them has been destroyed or sequestered to keep people from doing this horrible thing.

"But now that you have this power, we need to learn about it and how to control it. I've worked with each of you long distance on that, and we've discovered a few things. I have some guesses at some others. But we should all work together to find solutions to these problems.

"One of the mysteries I would like to figure out is about your runes. The drawings given me today show patterns that are noticeably different from what they looked like just after the banishment of the demons last autumn. The runes you bear are changing, without doubt. I do not recognize all of them."

Changing. On their own. Under our skin. I shudder and look at Orrin. He looks back at me, his eyes deep and haunted. "Changed how? Are they going to keep changing?" I ask in a small voice.

"I cannot say how much they will continue to change, nor do I know when they began to diverge from each of your origins. Orrin, you and Rhiannon used to have matching runes, for the most part. And Rhiannon's spell—that tremendous burst of will and power that she bore upon you both—changed the runes to something less anathematic to your lives but still powerful and dangerous," Robere answers.

"But how..." I start, and trail off.

The cardinal nods slowly. "It's my theory that the change in your powers over these last months, the visions, the vortices, all of these are mapped out in your runes. I think the runes react to what you're going through. But I don't recognize many of the rune figures or know their meanings. I'm not certain if you are changing them subconsciously yourselves or if the power is changing itself to suit some unknown pattern."

Cold dread pools in my stomach. "Could—could demons be...be controlling..." I can't finish the sentence. I don't feel as though I'm a demon puppet. But who ever does?

Cardinal Robere shakes his head. "I don't think so, no."

"But you aren't certain," Orrin says, his lips a grim slash on his face.

Robere sighs. "I don't know how I can be certain of something so very beyond my, or anyone in my sphere's, experience. But neither of you are raving mad, and you haven't tried to slaughter everyone in their beds, nor thrown yourselves from a cliff, so I'm as certain as I can be about demons."

"Is that...usual for demon possession?" Eleanore asks.

"Yes," Robere says shortly. "It is absolutely usual for people possessed by demons to become homicidal and destructive. We have been keeping watch on the two of you, and none of your behaviors match those of people tainted by demons."

"I'll let you know if she tries to stab me," Linnet says drily.

"I could have a good reason," I mutter.

"Sororicide isn't defensible just because you're crabby," she says, and I stick out my tongue.

"Ladies," Hugh says, "please."

"I think we're getting off topic," Robere jumps in. "The point is that though your magic is powerful and potentially dangerous, I do not think you demon tainted. The demons themselves—we don't know enough about them. Those who summon demons to use their magic take deathly risks. We only know that they are other-planar creatures of magic, that they can boost a spell or a magician's power to an immense degree, and that they will eventually drive the magician to insanity and death. That their power is unpredictable and changeable and often causes destruction and devastation, no matter the intentions. And left on our plane of existence, they are a seething mass of death magic. It is extremely rare that anyone tries to work with them. Gantry was an isolated case. Most people won't risk the damage demons could do."

"There's that distressing habit the summoners have of going stark raving mad," Hugh murmurs.

"Yes, it is a downside," Robere comments drily.

"Why did Gantry pick Rhiannon and Orrin for his spells, anyway?" Linnet asks.

"Because they have the Sight," Robere answers. "We know that those with the Sight are better at receiving demon magic and at using it. We know that the Sight is a little like traveling to other planes already—planes in time and place, if nothing else. Because to See the future or to comprehend the thoughts and minds of others, you must be able to sense that other plane in ways most people cannot. But how that makes you better able to translate the magic of demons—or more susceptible to it—no one has figured out yet."

"Are people trying to?" Linnet asks.

"Not that I have heard of—no sensible or sane magician would risk it. But with you two, we might have to. Without resorting to summoning any more demons."

"So then, demons aren't evil?" asks Eleanore.

"They are...bad for us. Whether or not they're bad in and of themselves is a theological question that we could debate forever with no resolution, and we don't have that kind of time."

"What am I supposed to do with that?" Orrin snarls viciously. Robere blinks at him. "You come in here with notes and schedules and scholarly horseshit about theological questions, but this magic is trying to kill me and possibly take everyone else here with me. And you tell me you don't know what to make of it? Maybe demons aren't evil? Are you serious?" He explodes from the chair he's sitting in, yelling. "I have visions that leave me weak and sick every day! I almost disappear into a vortex that no one can explain or even see. I hurt, my bones hurt, my scars hurt, my soul hurts. And Rhiannon was attacked, she's been injured, she's in pain all the time, and we are just—the scars are changing? They might be part of this? That's all you have?"

"Orrin Beaudreau," Robere says quietly. "I promise you, I am doing everything I can. I will do everything in my power to help you."

"And I'm just supposed to trust you?" Orrin's voice scrapes out.

Robere takes a deep breath. "I understand why you

can't. But I wish you would. Because I really don't see that any of us have a better choice."

Connor chooses this moment to walk into the room. "Your Eminence, Your Highness, Your Grace. Hello everyone. I'm sorry to interrupt, but the king requests his Eminence's presence. He wishes you to meet him in the map room. The Indrani ambassador is with him."

Cardinal Robere stands. "Please think about what I've said. I will not force anyone to work with me, but matters are dire for our little corner of the world right now. And each of you could help us or harm us. Please come to me if you need anything."

"Thank you, Cardinal," Hugh says. "I'll walk you out." He follows Robere from the room, and Connor looks at us all for a moment.

"Chins up. We'll figure out this magic," he says in an uncharacteristic show of joviality. I blink at him, and he smiles grimly. "We have to, or we won't survive," he adds, and leaves. There he is, I think to myself. Our own ray of sunshine. But that he tried to cheer us up at all, we must look desperately distressed.

I take a deep breath. "The Cardinal is right about one thing—we don't have many choices. Not good ones. Orrin. Can you—will you be able to work with him?"

Orrin stares at the ceiling, refusing to look at any of us. "I'll do what needs doing. But I don't trust him. I'm going to eat in my rooms. Please convey my apologies to Princess Julianna for missing dinner, will you?" He bows shallowly to all of us and exits quickly, brushing past Hugh as he returns.

"Orrin," Hugh starts, but Orrin leaves without looking back.

"I think you should let him go," Eleanore says, standing. "And I think we should not talk about these things anymore tonight." She walks to Hugh's side and embraces him fondly. I look out the window. Linnet holds my hand until it's time for dinner.

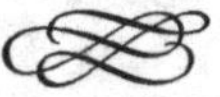

Dinner with Julianna and Hugh is a tense, quiet affair. Mostly we pick at our food, but Connor glares at Linnet and me until we finish our roast servings and insists on dishing out more potatoes. I roll my eyes, catch Linnet doing the same, but we both eat more than we would have. Connor's glares tend to be effective.

Eleanore grins at him and avoids potatoes, instead filling up on bread.

"I want you to meet with me tomorrow, Rhia," Hugh says. "I have some things I want to try with the magic. Juli, can you help me?"

"What time tomorrow? I have several appointments in the afternoon," Julianna says.

"We could meet after breakfast."

"I can manage that." They consult one another but I haven't said yes, yet. I don't think I get to say no, but that feels too much like it was before.

"I'll let you know if I can," I say quietly and excuse myself. "I think I'll check on Orrin."

"Rhia," Hugh starts, but Connor glares at him, too, and stands as I leave. He nods at me. Linnet glares only at the table. I make my way back to Orrin's rooms in our wing.

"Orrin, can I come in?" I call as I knock. The halls are empty of servants, although a few glowsand lamps light the hall in elegant golds.

Orrin opens the door for me, stands back to let me in. He's changed into an old gray shirt, and he looks like he's been napping. Or weeping.

"Hi," I say. "Hard day."

"Hard season," he answers.

"Hard year," we both say, and he smiles weakly at me. We settle on his couch in his sitting room. The colors here are dark and cool, grays and deep greens. He lays his head on the back of the couch and stares up at the ceiling. I pull his arm over me and lean into his side.

"I'm not sure what to do," I say.

"Do any of us know what to do?" he asks. "They're all just guessing, too. We're just the ones who must bear the brunt of it. We're the ones with out-of-control power of unknown origins."

"We know the origins," I say darkly.

"Not really. Not enough to do anything with it."

"I don't trust this magic, Orrin. I don't trust myself," I whisper. "I can feel it in me, still, even if I can't use it right. It's using me. Or I'm somehow using it without knowing it. How can I trust it? How can I trust me?"

"I don't know what to do. I don't trust myself, either," he says, still staring at the ceiling.

"I trust you," I tell him. "I trust you to tell me if I'm doing the right thing or the wrong thing. I trust you to help me figure out what to do."

"I trust you, too. But I don't trust Robere. I don't trust the kirche."

I nod against his shoulder. "I know. I don't blame you. But I don't think he's lying to us."

"He's not telling us the whole truth, either."

"Likely not."

"He has an angle."

I think about it. "Yes," I say. "Probably."

"I want to know what that angle is before we go any further." He looks sidelong at me. "We should ask Connor to find out what it is."

"What?" I sit up abruptly, startled. "That seems...pushy. We should—we can ask Hugh ..."

"Hugh trusts Robere too much. Connor is suspicious of everyone."

"He is not," I say, oddly defensive.

"I am, though," Connor says from the doorway as he pushes inside. I jump and let out a breathy shriek, stand to glare at him.

"Don't do that," I snarl.

"I did knock," he says.

"No you didn't! Knocking and opening the door at the same time is not knocking!"

He shrugs and comes further into the room. "It isn't? Hmm. Who am I suspicious of this time?" he asks Orrin.

"Cardinal Robere," Orrin says darkly.

Connor rocks back on his heels a little. "Ah. That's not entirely true, as I mostly trust him."

"Mostly?" I say, raising my eyebrow.

"He does have his own agenda, as anyone who works that hard to come to power does," Connor replies, going to the window to look out at the gathering dark. "He's a complex person. But a good one, in the main. I trust him to do as he says he will and to try to do good in the world."

"What is his agenda?" Orrin growls.

Connor leans his shoulder against the wall by the window, looks at us speculatively. "He wants to bridge the gap between the different religious schisms, and he wants to be the leader he thinks the kirche in this country needs. He thinks he can do a better job than anyone else. He might even be right. But he is at heart an ethical man, from what I have observed."

"Kirche leaders are not high on my list of people I think of as ethical at the moment," Orrin mutters.

Connor nods, looks away. "You have good reason to feel that way. I'm not here to tell you what to do."

"Then why are you here?" I ask. Rudely. I feel so off-balance with Connor and it makes me surly. He's cold one moment, affectionate the next. He hasn't said anything to me about holding me at the reception party. I don't know what to think of him. But I want to kiss him, and I want to punch him for making me want that if he doesn't want that, too.

Connor looks at me as if he knows what I'm think-ing. Which is silly, since he doesn't have that sort of magic.

But Orrin does. I doubt my barriers are working any better than the rest of my magic. I blush and look away. Poor Orrin.

"I'm here to talk to you—both of you—about what you want to do and how I can help. We do need to be discrete, no matter what you decide to do. But you should know, King Peter wants you to work with the cardinal. And you can still choose to not do that, but it would put everyone in...a difficult position."

"Especially you," I mutter.

"Especially you, Rhiannon. Especially your sister. Kings give orders expecting them to be obeyed. He expects loyalty."

"What about his loyalty to us?" Orrin says. "We're citizens of Talaria—we're his people. He should want to protect us."

"He has to protect everyone. You two are weapons that can be pointed at his throat if you aren't contained."

And after the king so much as told me that he would never harm us. I bite back furious tears. "So now we have to be contained? How? In a prison?" I ask, my voice shaking.

"Rhiannon, no." Connor pulls his hands through his hair. "But you must realize, you aren't just citizens. You're full of magic we don't understand, and you might be the key to defeating this country's enemies before they can harm us further. King Peter needs stability, and you need to know how your magic works. Both of you do.

"Can you trust me to keep you safe, to keep you in the king's good graces as best I can? Can you trust me to take care of you? I will not let him harm you. I will not let you harm anyone if I can help it. Especially not yourselves. If you can't trust anyone else, can you please trust me?"

It's hard. My chest shakes with suppressed sobs, denial on my tongue, but it's nonsensical. I take a shaky breath and try to come up with words. Connor just waits.

"All right," Orrin says. "All right. I'll—we'll trust you."

Connor nods, his own breath unsteady. "And you, Rhiannon?"

I swallow hard and nod, but I still can't find my voice.

Connor takes a deep breath, runs his hands through his hair again. "Very well. I'll..." he clears his throat. "I'll tell Hugh to find you after breakfast tomorrow, then. And Hugh will want to make a schedule for you as well, Orrin.

Orrin gives a tight nod. "Yes, fine."

Connor looks into my eyes, grimaces at whatever he sees there. "Yes. Fine. I'll go tell him," he says, and leaves.

Orrin lets out a deep gusty sigh. "I guess we do this, then. For now."

"For now," I say.

"And you should talk to him," he says, nodding at the door Connor just left through. "You should talk to each other."

"What? I just did."

"Rhi," he says softly, and I remember again that he can sometimes hear people's thoughts. And probably can't help it when their feelings are strong. I flush hot and cold. "He has things he should say to you, too," Orrin murmurs.

"I'll talk to Connor when you talk to Hugh," I retort. Orrin grimaces, and I feel vindicated. "You both have a lot of things you should say to one another, too."

"I know what he has to say," he says flatly.

I snort, turn to leave. "If you can't come up with something better than that, then I have no reason to listen to you about Connor."

Orrin throws an embroidered cushion at me as I leave, but it misses and hits the door. I stick my tongue out at him and shut the door firmly behind me.

CHAPTER 29

"I'm telling you, this will work," I say. Linnet rolls her eyes, but Orrin nods at me. After several weeks of lessons with Hugh or Robere and conversations with Julianna, both of us are itchy. The magic moves under my skin. We think it's trying to link to Orrin and Linnet, but all that happens is pain and a buzzing echo of Orrin's visions. I'm tired of dark looks from the priests in the chapel when we meet with Robere there. It doesn't help me concentrate. I want to try something else.

Orrin agreed to try my idea—to try to link while he has a vision. The magic in our bodies is not the same as it was before Stephen's spies hurt me. It should be safe enough for us to be in the same room, trying for a vision. Rather, Orrin trying for a vision. I doubt I'll See anything more than an echo, like the last few times. But I think if I can just feel my way around it, I might figure out why or be able to link to either Linnet or Orrin.

Linnet doesn't think this is a good plan. But Orrin can't stop the visions coming anyway, and what else does she have to do with her morning? She agreed to be here in case something goes wrong, but she's ready to send for Hugh. I hate feeling like an experiment gone wrong, which is how I feel whenever we work with Hugh and Cardinal Robere. I'm determined this time will be different.

The magic around the palace is more dilute than in Haverston, but it's around if you know how to feel for it. It seeks us out—Orrin much more than me. It scurries around me more as if it's a kitten trying to play. But I can feel it: its little sharp claws itch and burn across my flesh. The runes ache with it from time to time, deep in my muscles and bones.

We stand in Orrin's rooms, Linnet curled in a corner of the couch, arms crossed, glowering. Orrin takes a breath and reaches for the magic. I feel a weird tug in my mind, like voices muted but echoing. Linnet yelps suddenly and jumps up, staring.

"How are you doing that? How are you both here and there?"

"What do you mean?" I ask. A buzzing starts low in my bones, shifting under my skin. Orrin's face goes blank with an oncoming vision, sharp and sudden. I can feel him falling.

"No!" I shout as he blinks out of sight, and I reach—

My hand finds his and we fall together. I hear Linnet shriek, but it's cut off. The dark storm of the vortex roils around us.

The vision bubbles into place—the courtyard, the fighting, the demons. A huge vortex with soldiers staggering through, Montmoore chanting that awful spell. Magic reaches for me from all sides—my own magic, reaching from myself, Orrin's magic, reaching from

Orrin, to me, to every version of me, every version of Orrin, all of us looking at each other from different visions and times. It stings and burns along all the runes, realigns me—my skin crawls like snakes. I See myself in the vision—blood slicks my hands and I reach out for more magic, desperate to flood the spell I'm chanting with enough power to stop Montmoore.

Orrin staggers, his hand pulling me, and we lurch back into the vortex, falling through the storm colors and gray and rushing sound. I stumble as a floor rises up beneath us. Orrin's sweaty hand slips from mine as we trip out of the vortex, spill onto stone and fall in a heap. We're not back with Linnet, though. We've fallen out somewhere else.

It's a long hallway somewhere in what looks like the palace, but it has no carpet or decorations or carvings along the ceiling, no plaster work. I crawl to my hands and knees, trying to get breath and bearing. Orrin wheezes and works to right himself.

"Wh-, where, where are we?" he stammers. Shaking my head, I start to say I don't know, but it's familiar.

Because it's the hallway up at the top of the palace, where they've placed Anouk Nerishe under guard. Only when I turn toward her door, a guard lies bleeding on the hall floor, and the door is open.

I lurch to my feet, hearing a choking sound, a thud and a grunt. "Nerishe," I gasp and rush past the guard with Orrin close behind me. When I push it open, two people struggle together, one in guard uniform. Nerishe dodges a knife, ducks under an arm, grappling against the larger guard.

"Stop!" I shout, knowing it's futile, hoping I don't distract Nerishe. I yank at the magic I can still feel in the air, only to have it yank back, burn me like scalding oil through my bones. I gurgle and wobble to my knees—the magic still won't let me use it like I used to. I try to get a grip on it, but it's slippery, painful. More magic fills the room—some of it from Orrin, but as the fighters break apart, I realize some of it is from the person in the guard uniform.

"Stop," I wheeze, and a vortex opens behind him. The pull of it screams in my body. Orrin shouts as he rushes past me, and raw magic flows from him, closing it. There's a shriek and a pop, and the vortex disappears, the assassin—and Nerishe—still on this side of it.

Which leaves us the problem of what to do with a cornered assassin. As the stranger struggles back to his feet, I think I can trip him by rolling into him if I have to, but Nerishe suddenly has him in a hold, the knife to his throat, breathing heavily.

"Who sent you?" she rasps. "Who sent you here?"

The assassin clenches his teeth, also panting from exertion. Blood slicks his hands, and magic still fizzes through the room. I can feel Orrin struggling to control whatever magic is humming in the room.

As the assassin thrashes in Nerishe's grip, the door bangs open against the wall behind me, missing my legs by a hair. I struggle to my feet as several guards rush into the room, followed closely by Connor and Hugh.

Everyone starts shouting, swords drawn, demanding Nerishe drop the knife.

"No wait, you don't understand," I yell into the din, knowing they won't listen to me but trying anyway. I step in front of the guards and hold up my hands. "It's not her fault!" I plead, looking at Connor, but his eyes widen at something behind me. He grabs my arm and pulls as I feel a push at my back, a tug, then I'm in Connor's arms and everyone keeps shouting.

He keeps an arm around me, giving orders, until Hugh's takes over. Connor pats down my back as he examines me, my face still pushed into his chest. "Are you hurt? Did he hurt you?" he keeps asking. "Gods all, Rhiannon, never stand between people with swords and knives, what were you thinking? Dorei save us." And he hugs me tighter, shuddering.

When he finally lets me turn around, I find blood and slowly organizing chaos.

The assassin is very dead. I shudder and cringe away from the blood, but bodies don't bother me as much as they used to. As much as they should. The part of me that should be horrified about the body decides to be horrified that I'm not horrified enough. It probably looks the same from the outside. I swallow hard and Connor tightens his arm around my shoulder.

Nerishe appears wounded, perched on the bed, blood seeping from under the hand she presses against her side. Orrin leans against the corner of the room at the head of the bed. Hugh stands in front of him, cupping his face, speaking in low tones. I can't hear him over the soldiers asking Nerishe questions, but Orrin's face is grayish, matching how I feel. He shakes his head sharply. I think he's sending his thoughts instead of trying to speak. Right now I wish I had that option. I hear a faint whisper of a buzz but whatever magic came to me during the vortex earlier hasn't decided what it's doing in me yet.

Julianna pushes her way into the room, Linnet in tow, crowding it further. "What happened? Hugh? Tell me," she demands brusquely, pushing people aside to get to Nerishe immediately. The guards move to stop her but she has her royal face on and they back away at a look.

Julianna glances briefly at the assassin on the floor. "One of ours?" she asks Hugh. Hugh looks at Connor in question.

Connor takes a deep breath. "That's our uniform, but I don't recognize him." Everyone looks grim, and the shouting has quieted. Several guards glare at Nerishe.

"What about the dead guard outside?" one barks.

"She was assigned here today," another answers.

"I didn't kill her," Nerishe mumbles sullenly, looking more and more gray herself. Julianna stands next to her, ignoring the blood on the floor that seeps into her hem and slippers.

"I never said you did, Anouk Nerishe. Why don't you lie back and let me see," she says gently.

"I'm afraid to move, Highness," Anouk slurs. "I can't let go, it feels deep."

"I know, I know, I feel it," Julianna singsongs a little as she helps Nerishe reposition and lie down. Her magic fills the room, tingling on my awareness like whispers, like many-legged insects. "Oh oh oh, it's not the worst, Anouk. You can take your hand away, I've got you." The magic burrows into Nerishe, sharpens, and I shudder.

Connor, who let me go for a few moments, looks over at me, gives more orders to the guards, and returns to my side. "Turn around, let me make sure," he orders me.

I don't know what he's talking about, but I do what he asks. I find myself staring at Linnet, who has kept quiet all this time. She glares at me—her worried angry glare. I can tell she's having a conversation with Orrin and Hugh through sending—I can almost hear it—but she glares at me while she's doing it. At least she's not yelling out loud about how we disappeared through a vortex and ended up here. That's probably not something to bandy about.

I feel Connor's hands on my back again, tugging at my dress. His hands touch bare skin and I startle—there's a tear in my dress, just below my shoulder. I do feel a sting, now that I'm thinking about it. The scars under the sting quiver a little, shift, itch. Shift more.

"Stars above, Rhiannon," Connor says. "This could have—you're just lucky they weren't faster. What would possess you—no. Don't answer that. Just—just don't answer that."

The tension ratchets up in the room just at that moment, and everyone looks toward the door. I turn in Connor's grasp to find Alexander standing with more guards in the doorway. He looks frustrated and surprised.

"What is the meaning of all of this? Guards, report!" he commands. The three who came with Hugh and Connor look to them first, which infuriates Alexander. "I said report!"

"Report in the hall, please, everyone. I need quiet and space," Julianna says firmly from beside Nerishe.

Alexander flushes more deeply with rage, and I watch Julianna sigh and look up, pleadingly, at Hugh.

Hugh smiles gently at Alexander. "The room is far too small, Highness. Let's all step into the hall and sort everything out." Hugh steps more firmly in front of Orrin, moves toward Alexander and the door with his palm open in invitation, but Alexander glares at him.

"Do you dare countermand my orders?" he spits. "I said, 'guards, report!'"

One of the guards steps forward, clearing her throat. "Your Highness, it seems either this guard attacked the prisoner, or the prisoner attacked the guards. When we came in, the two...guests were in the room with the prisoner and the prisoner held this guard with a knife to their throat."

"The guests?" Alexander asks, but he's looking at me. There's honestly no room for me to move anywhere, so I stay where I am, face blank, magic and reaction still seeping through my veins. I hold back a shudder from Alexander's glare. Connor's body is warm at my back, his hand at my waist, squeezing.

"And why were there any guests in this room at all?" Alexander demands, his voice brittle with fury.

Julianna straightens up from over Nerishe and turns around, pushing a guard out of her way. "Alexander, honestly, take everyone into the hallway. I'm stepping on this poor person's corpse here as it is. I'm trying to save this woman's life. If you can't be useful, then go away!" Her hands are bloody and her voice sharpens against every word.

Alexander's chin hardens as he glares at his wife. But he jerks his head over his shoulder to the door, and stalks out of the room.

Hugh and Connor exchange glances and gesture for everyone to leave the room, the guards making an uncomfortable wall of metal and leather to slide past. I grab Linnet's hand and try to keep her behind me once we're all out into the hall, staying well back from the other body. The guards who came with Alexander take position outside the door, avoiding the dead guard, and come to attention. I wonder if they were supposed to be here before or if someone abandoned their post.

"Now perhaps someone would be so good as to tell me what the hell is going on here." Alexander stalks toward me and looms. "Why are you here? What did you do?"

I shake my head, not sure what I can tell him that won't make everything worse. I don't even know what Orrin told the others.

Alexander isn't precisely wrong, after all. Orrin and I did do something. I just can't be sure what it was, and I don't want to explain it here, now, with my stomach roiling and my mind in shock and not sure who in this hall is with us and who would rather we disappear permanently.

Prince Alexander is likely in the latter group.

"Alex, dear, there's a perfectly good explanation," Hugh tries to be soothing.

"And I am waiting to hear it. What did this witch do, lure the guard in to be murdered by the prisoner?"

"Don't be ridiculous, Alexander," Connor snaps. "Rhiannon didn't lure anyone anywhere."

Alexander glares at him. "Ah, cousin, of course you are here. Perhaps you set all of this up. Perhaps it's you who are the traitor, after all. Just like your brother."

Everyone shifts uneasily at the viciousness of his tone. Connor stands straighter. "If that is your opinion of me, Highness, take it up with your father."

"My father," Alexander starts nastily, "wouldn't know—"

"Careful," Hugh breathes, as footsteps echo down the hall.

King Peter approaches with another contingent of

guard, along with Marchioness Boucher. I try not to laugh with caustic exhaustion. We only needed that to add to this mess.

Everyone hastily bends knee as the king strides up. He takes in the scene with a glance, then turns and enters Nerishe's room, Boucher a step behind him. I hear Julianna tell them she's very busy right now, thank you, and then Boucher and King Peter step into the hall again.

"You may report, Connor," he says.

"My king, shouldn't we hear from–" Boucher begins, but the king holds up a hand.

"Connor?"

Connor bows and begins telling the king that he was alerted to a problem by Orrin, although he doesn't say how. That he and the Duke of Haverston gathered several guards and rushed here to find that Captain Nerishe had subdued an assassin, but that at their arrival the assassin broke free and attacked one of her visitors. "At that time, Captain Nerishe killed the assassin. The captain was wounded at some point in the attack before that, sire. Which is why we summoned Princess Julianna."

"And why would you summon my wife as a Healer when the kirche has ordered her to–" Alexander starts, but the king waves him quiet.

"Visitors?" Boucher asks. "Who authorized visitors for Nerishe?" Her eyes glitter. She radiates fury, but she doesn't so much as glance at Orrin or me. Her attention stays on Connor, but an answer comes from further down the hall.

"And why shouldn't Captain Nerishe have visitors? Good afternoon, Your Majesty," I hear, and we all turn.

Duchess Marguerite walks down the hall toward us, and I watch Hugh's face lose color and gain it again in rapid succession. "Did you not get my very detailed message?"

"Your message was inadequate, Marguerite." Lady Boucher's voice could cut glass.

"I think you mean, 'Your Grace,'" Marguerite answers. "And that was not his response to me. Do you claim that His Majesty was lying? Your Majesty? Is what Marchioness Boucher saying true?" She looks at King Peter with an innocent expression.

"I would never call the king a liar. You are twisting words again, Your Grace," Lady Boucher spits.

"A tactic you should be entirely comfortable with, Lady Boucher," Marguerite says calmly.

"I will not have you interfering in this –" but the king raises his hands for silence, glaring, and she stops talking.

King Peter takes a deep breath. "I believe I would like to have this conversation somewhere other than this hall. I command everyone to keep their own counsel, about absolutely everything, until I reconvene you. At my discretion. You are all, every one of you, to keep quiet. Am I understood?"

"Of course, Your Majesty," Marguerite says. "I will bring Captain Nerishe's wife to see her, as I told you."

The king clenches his jaw. "Marguerite..."

She raises her eyebrows. "Your Majesty?"

He stares silently for a moment. "Yes. Do it." He glares at nearly every person in the hall, last and hardest at Marguerite. "I want to see you—all of you who were witnesses—in the map room at the top of the hour, and I will have a full report at that time. So I have ordered," he barks, and sweeps down the hall, his guards sweeping after him with barely a hesitation.

Lady Boucher wears a much more sinister glare, mostly aimed at Hugh and Connor, but she snarls a ghastly "follow" to Alexander. He complies without complaint or even looking back, which is concerning, and they both sweep after the king.

We're left in the hall with Marguerite, Hugh, Connor, and various guards. And Linnet, still clenching my hand in hers.

Marguerite takes a deep breath and turns to all of us. "Well, that was bracing, wasn't it? Hello, Hugh dear. I take it something awful has happened. Since this person seems to be deceased, and there's blood everywhere. Please tell me Captain Nerishe is all right. I really do not want to have to tell her dear wife anything else."

Hugh rubs his hands over his face. "In there, Mother. With Juli." Marguerite pats his face and gives him a quick kiss on the cheek, smiles at the rest of us distract-edly, and steps past the guards at the door to peer in.

"Can I help, Juli darling?" she says quietly. Julianna gives a sharp laugh, but not in humor, and says some-thing in a low voice. Marguerite nods. "I'll leave Linnet here for you, dear, in case you do need help. The rest of us will go clean up and get ready to report. Send Linnet if you need us."

"Mum," Hugh starts quietly, but Marguerite shakes her head just slightly at him as the rest of us stare at her. She gestures to the guards still standing with us in the hall—those who came with Connor and Hugh and those by the door who came with Alexander.

Connor turns to the guards at the door. "Who was

scheduled next on the duty roster?" he says quietly. They glance at one another, then admit they don't know.

Hugh sends one guard to find the duty roster for the rest of the day, instructs several to bring stretchers to remove the bodies, and relieves the guards at the door, replacing them with two different guards whose names Connor approves.

As he and Connor confer, Marguerite takes a moment to hug Linnet, Orrin, and me. "Let's get you away, children. Linnet, I expect my daughter will find a reason to send you to me before long. Find your way quickly when she does. But I want you here for a bit longer to keep an eye on things for her, all right? Connor will know whom to trust here, so you will be safe," she murmurs quietly, the four of us in a small huddle.

"Get yourselves cleaned up and come to my rooms—they're just across the hall from Hugh. Don't dawdle."

Connor comes up behind her, hearing the last part. "Orrin, go with Hugh for now. Your Grace, could you stay with them? I will take Rhiannon to the infirmary and then we'll find you."

He takes my hand and pulls me along behind him the opposite way everyone else is going. I look over my shoulder at Linnet, but she's fine, I suppose. I look back to keep my feet because Connor walks fast.

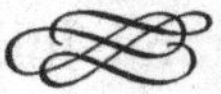

CHAPTER 30

"I'll take you the back way to the infirmary to avoid as many people as possible. But we really need to get a closer look at your back," Connor says, his steps brisk and his grasp of my hand firm.

Other than a little sting, and the odd feel of the parted cloth, my back doesn't really hurt. "I don't think it's serious," I say, but he's not listening. I think I would know if it were serious—I can feel my scars shifting under the cut and they don't care.

Is it worrisome that I know if my scars care? Is it worrisome that they might care? Likely it is. I put that aside as something to fret about later.

I want to slow down, but I'd have to pull my hand free to slow Connor at this point, and his hand feels far too good in mine right now. I need the comfort. The events of the morning are catching up to me. My heart still pounds, and under my skin the magic sizzles.

We rush through several sets of halls and stairs, my breath coming short, my long-injured lungs working too hard. It's normal for Connor, but that doesn't make it all right.

"My lord," I say forcefully, tugging at his hand, breathless.

He turns, a bit surprised, a bit exasperated. "What is it? Rhiannon, I don't want to wait much longer for a real Healer to look at you, and Julianna is busy, you may remember."

"Don't patronize me," I snap. "I don't need or want a Healer."

"I'm not trying to patronize you. Don't be difficult, Rhiannon. We need to make sure the blade wasn't poisoned," he says, sounding a little breathless himself.

"It wasn't poisoned, Connor. And I don't want a strange Healer looking at my back. Please."

He blinks a few times, then closes his eyes. "I just want to be sure you're safe, Dorei help me," he grits out. "I keep seeing that knife come out of the assassin's sleeve, and it's all I can do to..." He takes a deep breath. "I just want to be sure." His jaw is rigid. "How can you be sure?"

"My magic might not be exactly the way it was, but I can tell. The scratch isn't bothering the magic or the scars it's crossing. They don't care," I say, knowing it's the wrong thing to mention as soon as I do.

"What do you mean, they don't care?" He asks, raising his eyebrows.

"I can, I can simply tell it's fine. I'm fine," I stammer, trying to avoid sounding crazy. Or demon-tainted.

"But –"

"Connor," I say, putting my hand on his chest. "I'm all right."

He covers my hand with his and lowers his chin to

his chest. Sighing deeply, he brings my hand up to kiss my fingers. My stomach flutters, but I try to pull away.

"Stop. It's not fair, Connor," I say unhappily.

"What isn't? None of this is fair," he says, putting his hand on my waist and stepping closer, resting his forehead on mine. I hate how good it feels.

"You...this. Pushing me away, drawing me close. It's not fair. You have to choose." He closes his eyes, squeezing my hand.

"You're right. This isn't right," he says quietly.

"I should say not, Lord fitzWellan," a voice says from the stairwell.

Connor shifts quickly to stand in front of me, his hand on his sword hilt. I peer over his shoulder to see the ambassador of Indranah standing there, arms crossed and expression disapproving.

"Your Excellency," Connor says carefully. "How nice to see you again." He relaxes not at all, but he does let his hand drop minutely away from his sword.

Ambassador Acarla snorts. "I doubt that, as you've avoided me since I arrived, and I've just caught you canoodling in a hallway with exactly the unsuitable person you were told to avoid."

Connor stiffens further, and so do I. "I don't know what you mean. About any of it," he says in an icy tone. "I'll thank you to keep your tone civil."

"This is civil. You've been warned, Connor, son of the dira Anya. Your grandmother the ranee was most specific in her instructions for you. And she had many other instructions regarding this...personage." The ambassador sneers just a bit—just enough to know that I've been sneered at by someone important. His tone is icy. "I would not take the orders of the empress lightly, young diran."

"I do not take orders from the empress at all, as she is not my sovereign," Connor says, his voice remote as the night sky. "Good day to you, Ambassador."

"Do not say good day to me, Connor Jana. We have not yet finished this conversation."

A deep, unsettling crawling begins in my skin—like prodding a bruise, a pulse of prickling nausea and cold sweat. And it's coming from the ambassador—this time I'm sure of it, the threads of it feeling like his expression, like the sound of his voice. I take a deep breath and step around Connor, reinforcing my barriers to drive him off as I can. The crawling feeling subsides when I do, and the ambassador raises his eyebrows.

"This conversation is very over. And so is your inspection of me. I do not consent to any magical examination by you. Stop at once."

He looks taken aback. With a growl, Connor puts his hand on the hilt of his sword. I shake my head. "Don't make it worse," I murmur.

The ambassador regains his icy sneer. "I've done nothing at all to you. But the ranee demands some explanations regarding your magic."

"I am not Indrani—you don't get to treat me as if I owe you anything. The empress is not my sovereign, either."

"What is it you think to do with your life now, young woman?" the ambassador asks me.

I blink at him. "I mean to live it, Excellency," I say, keeping my tone to icy civility.

"And how do you think to do that, with everyone so very interested in your...abilities? What kind of life do you think you will have?" Connor makes a growling noise, but I wave him quiet. For a wonder, he subsides.

"Will you join your kirche?" the ambassador continues. "Will you give up the barony to the clergy, live a holy life of orders?"

"That is not my path, Excellency." I think I do well to repress a shudder.

He smiles. "Of course not. If it were, you would already have claimed a spot as an acolyte, not persuaded your...friend...away from his."

I glare at him. "My friend has not been persuaded by anyone. He is perfectly capable of making up his own mind."

"Ah, but is he? Are you? Are you so very certain that your minds are your own? That is a very great deal of magic power the two of you have coursing through you, is it not? Are you so sure you're the ones in control?"

"I don't know what you mean," I say, deadpan.

"That, then, is a problem. A very great problem."

"I have nothing further to say to you, Excellency. Good day."

"I believe I have more to say to you, young woman."

"No, you don't," Connor interjects. "I've had enough of this. If you have messages for me, relay them to the liaison. I will not speak with you any longer, and I will not stand for you harassing Talarians without cause."

Ambassador Acarla draws his frame even straighter, if that's possible. "I have cause, as you and your king know. I have great cause. You will not shirk your duties so easily. What of your grandmother? What of your grandfather? What of your family, Diran Connor? You have many responsibilities. You cannot walk away from them without consequences."

"Lord fitzWellan is more responsible than you have been a day in your life," I spit at him.

Magic crawls over my skin with a blossoming shudder, burrowing up behind my temples. Sweat prickles under my arms as the Sight unfurls in me again. I can hear Acarla's thoughts in tiny snippets. I might regret it, but I don't want to listen to him abuse either of us any longer. I reach along the new pathway I feel shuddering along my spine.

He's doing his job, but he's not entirely an honest person. He is dipping into funds not his to pay for something personal. I can't quite tell what, but he is zealous partly because he's covering for something. I look in his eyes and I see disdain and anger and fear.

"You aren't an honest person, are you, Ambassador? Your hands are not as clean as they should be. I think you should leave before all of your secrets become common knowledge, and the very dutiful people around you have great cause to tell your superiors and your empress how you've been thieving."

Connor puts his hand on my arm to pull me behind him, warning me off, but I've said what I wanted to say. The ambassador's face darkens and his eyes narrow.

"You are demon-tainted, and I will see you exterminated like the vermin you are," he hisses.

"No demons are here but you," I snap, and the man whirls away in a flurry of his ridiculous short cape—which is too warm for the weather—stalking down the hall.

Connor, still a bit ahead of me with his other hand on his sword, drops his chin to his chest. "I'm not sure that was wise," he mutters.

Shaking, I move away and slump against the opposite wall. "Probably not." Not that I'm not grateful to have the Sight back, but I'm worried I'll regret pushing that man.

"Was that actual magic you just used?" he asks.

I shrug, bite my lips. "Maybe a little. I...think it's back now. At least partly."

He sighs, rubbing his forehead. "You can't keep making enemies, Rhiannon. I can barely keep up with the ones you already have." He looks back at me, shakes his head. "We need to have someone look at your back, still. We don't have a lot of time."

"Connor, can't you do it? I'll have Julianna check it as soon as I can, I promise."

I feel fluttery just asking him, but I really don't want a kirche Healer to look at my scars or touch me right now. And Connor is...well, he's not safe. But I'd rather he touches me than any stranger. Or anyone, I acknowledge in a tiny voice to myself. He looks at me, closes his eyes, and nods.

"All right. Follow me," he takes my arm again, and we set off in a slightly different direction. This time we end up at his rooms, closer than I would have guessed from where we just were. He hesitates, then draws me inside.

Our rooms are just down the corridor, but he brought me to his. I don't know whether to be encouraged or dismayed.

"Turn around, let me see," he says as he closes his door. The outer room is decorated in sumptuous forest greens and burgundies, the dark wood of bookcases and a table and chairs, a comfortable couch in front of the fireplace. Shadows darken past the open door of his bedroom. I turn toward the window to show Connor my back.

His hands are gentle as he moves the fabric away from the wound. His fingers brush my skin, raising goosebumps that travel from my crown to my toes. I try to keep my breathing even. His breath falters. "It's not deep," he murmurs. "The bleeding has stopped. This gown is a loss, though."

"Linnet will figure out some use for it, or the seamsters will," I say inanely.

"It doesn't look inflamed. Do you feel lightheaded? Nauseous? Weak?"

Nervous laughter falls from me, and I shake my head. "Not from the scratch," I say, then bite my lip, glance over my shoulder at him.

He groans softly. His breath fans my neck, my cheek. He leans in and his head rests on my other shoulder, his hands gripping my arms. "Rhiannon," he rumbles. "I am trying so hard. Please stop throwing yourself into danger. And please," he gulps. "Ah, please," he says, and he kisses my neck. I shudder, and he draws me against him, wraps his arms around me. "Please keep your distance, my Rhiannon. I do not have much strength left," he whispers, his cheek on my hair.

I fight tears, and I feel him fighting them, too. "You keep saying to keep my distance," I whisper. "But then you touch me, and here we are again. If you really want me—but maybe it really is that I'm too difficult, too broken..."

"It's not you, lovely. It's nothing to do with you. I swear it...I swear. It's all me. I am too old, and too weary, and bound to too many oaths. I can't put you in any more danger than you are already. I want you to have every option open to you. Don't pick me. I'm the one who isn't good enough."

"Connor, that's just ridiculous," I push away, turn to face him. He passes his hand over his eyes, shakes his head.

"I know. And it doesn't matter. Let me clean that for you," he says, gesturing to my shoulder.

I let the tears fall. "No. I'll have Linnet or Duchess Marguerite help. Please just leave me alone." I brush past him, and he doesn't stop me. I slip out into the hall.

I knock on Duchess Marguerite's door—I'm sure it's her door—carrying a dress to change into. I didn't pass anyone in the halls, for which I'm grateful. Linnet opens the door and looks at me. "What did he do!" she snaps, yanking me inside.

"I don't want to talk about it. Can you just help me?" I indicate my still-untended shoulder.

The duchess looks over from where she stands speaking with Princess Eleanore and Lauren, Anouk Nerishe's wife. "Oh, dear." She sighs. "All right, let's take care of Rhiannon's issue," and waves us into the bedroom, following and taking some gauze out of a drawer.

"Let's get you out of the gown and cleaned up, then. It looks as if a light bandage should do it." She gets closer in and looks at the wound. "It doesn't appear to be deep. Didn't Connor take you to the infirmary, dear?"

"I told him not to," I say quietly. My eyes sting, but I'm not crying now. I take that small victory.

"Ah. Well, Juli can take a quick once-over later. I think you'll live." She smiles at me as she and Linnet help me out of the torn gown.

"I'm going to kill Connor," Linnet says conversationally, and I can tell she's been sending to Hugh and Orrin. I shake my head.

"Let it go, Linnet. Can we just focus on getting through this audience?"

Marguerite sighs as she wrings out a cloth for my back over the basin on her washstand. "There is rather a lot going on. I'd prefer not to add to the bloodshed, Linnet dear. And while Connor is bullheaded and likely being ridiculous, we do require him to be functional and present in this current situation. So no killing him, and that's final. But I'll have a word with him later."

"Please don't," I say, the war with the tears getting harder. Just—please don't." I don't want him hearing from everyone else about all of this. It's hard enough. I want to sink into the ground and hide forever as it is.

Marguerite clucks her tongue. "As you wish, then. Here we are, all cleaned up. I'll leave you to dress." She pats my cheek and kisses my forehead, leaving me to Linnet's tender mercies.

"I still think I should kill him."

I sigh through shuddering breath. "He gets to make decisions, too. And his is to...not be with me. Or something. So let's just deal with the next crisis on the list, please."

"Fine." She helps me into the russet and cream gown, which clashes a little with my frizzing hair but is otherwise completely respectable. She glares at it. "You should have worn the gold. Or the pale green. This isn't good enough to see the king, Rhi. Honestly."

"It's silk. What's wrong with it?"

"It's too heavy for today, and it's a day dress for sitting in a room and embroidering with family, not a command appearance before royalty. Here, let me fix your hair. And wear this." She takes off a gold necklace, and I see her gown is one of the more elaborate ones, a linen damask in deep royal blue. Of course, the weaving on it is exquisite.

"I honestly thought this was good enough," I say unhappily.

"It's just not your best, Rhi. And the golden cotton is so pretty on you."

"I'm not trying to be pretty, Li."

"You're not trying to be accused of witchery, either. But this will have to do. Bend down. Press this to your face." She somehow produces hairpins and tames my hair into a braid, as I press the wet, cool cloth to my eyes.

"You'll do," she says, as she smooths the fabric of the gown. "It's a good color for your skin tone, but you need to remember to stand straight so it flows right. Don't hunch." She scowls at my appearance one last time. "Don't let them know you did...what you did. Don't tell them about that. And don't do it again."

"I wasn't trying to do it the first time," I say, grasping her hand. "And I don't know that I get to deny that it happened if the king commands me to tell him everything. I think I'm not supposed to keep secrets from him." My heart starts to pound. "I'm not sure what to do, Linnet."

She launches herself at my waist and hugs me fiercely. "Stay alive. Don't do anything stupid."

I laugh a little wildly, hug her back. "I'll try."

Eleanore opens the door without knocking. "You'd better go. It doesn't do to keep Father waiting. But...be careful. The Butcher is up to something."

"Anything specific?"

"Just—something involving Connor. That's all I

could charm or eavesdrop, but it's not going to go well for you if she has anything to say about it."

"Wonderful," I say.

"I'll keep digging," she says, and returns to the sitting room.

"Linnet," Marguerite calls, "would you be so kind as to accompany Princess Eleanore as she escorts Lauren to her wife? She should be by her side, and I've no wish to make her wait." Marguerite smiles at Linnet as we return to the sitting room. Over by the windows, Eleanore charms a tense and worried Lauren into a small smile.

"I don't know why I can't just come with you," Linnet says.

"Because you weren't commanded to appear before the king," Marguerite says.

"I was—he said everyone!"

"But you didn't see what happened, you only showed up after the attack, with Julianna. He said all witnesses. Which means I'm going to keep you out of this as much as possible, so that not absolutely everyone in our party is in trouble with the king. You will go with Lauren to Julianna and Anouk and keep an eye on everyone there for us. Thank you, dear."

Linnet grumbles but leaves with Lauren and Eleanore. I watch her go with trepidation, but I'm not sure who it's for.

"Time to make an accounting, child. Best foot forward." Duchess Marguerite waves for me to follow her, and we make our way to the map room, as ordered. On time.

Hugh, Connor, and Orrin await us in front of the open doors. On either side, a guard stands at attention.

Voices drift out from inside. We all look at each other, then Marguerite takes her son's arm.

"You shouldn't be here, Mother."

"Not now, dear. Chin up, let's be our charming selves." He rolls his eyes as they turn to walk in together, the rest of us following like reluctant ducklings.

King Peter stands with Cardinal Robere, Prince Alexander, and Marchioness Boucher, and as an unpleasant surprise, Ambassador Acarla. The walls of the map room feel close and oppressive as we walk in.

It's only a medium sized room, not meant for large groups. Much of the space is taken up with a large table covered in various types of maps. Bright tapestries hang on the walls under the high windows, and there's only one chair, currently unoccupied. The patterned marble floor adds to the minor chaos of color and confusion. A heavy, dark rug lies under the table and chair. The room is designed for one person to intimidate and interrogate anyone else within.

We walk toward the king and bow or curtsey at Hugh and Marguerite's cue. King Peter beckons us forward, then turns to the ambassador.

"Thank you for your attention, Ambassador. I will speak with you tomorrow."

"I think I should like to be present for this audience, Your Majesty," Acarla says, smiling a little.

The king simply gazes at Acarla, waiting.

"I think my ranee might be quite interested to know my opinion on these matters and would be unhappy to learn of my omission."

King Peter remains silent, his impassive expression like carved stone. Alexander, watching with impatience, looks angry and about to break in, but when Boucher shakes her head at him, he subsides. Peter continues to gaze implacably at Ambassador Acarla.

"Really, Your Majesty," Acarla begins, but the king's raised hand silences him.

"Your eagerness does you credit, I'm sure, Ambassador. But your audience for today is finished. I will have a comprehensive statement to give to your ranee at a later time regarding information she's requested. You may go now."

Acarla's face darkens with rage, humiliation, or both. He bows carefully but without real deference, then sweeps past us, half-cape swinging. I watch out of the corner of my eye until I'm sure he's gone.

King Peter motions for the guards to close the doors, the mild boom reverberating out in the hall. We all bow to the king once more. Robere smiles at us a little, although everyone else stays grave.

The king nods at our bows. "Now, Connor, I will have your report."

"Yes, Your Majesty," Connor says. "I was with Hugh when we were alerted to a problem in the prisoner's room."

"By whom?" Alexander barks.

"Alexander, I will ask you to keep quiet," the king orders. Alex glares at his father as if he'd like to bite him but shuts his mouth.

"Orrin Beaudreau alerted Hugh, Your Majesty," Connor says.

"How was this accomplished?" Marchioness Boucher asks quietly, but the king allows it with a nod.

"By sending through magic, my lady," Connor says shortly. "As you're aware they are both able to do." Her mouth tightens, but King Peter motions for Connor to continue. "Orrin informed us that a guard was attacking Captain Nerishe and that the guard was using dangerous magic. To what purpose he could not ascertain."

"Is this accurate, Orrin Beaudreau?" King Peter looks at him, and Orrin nods grimly.

"Yes, Majesty." Orrin looks a little gray still, but I don't know if the reason is magical or emotional in nature. Both seem equally likely.

"Hugh and I commandeered several guards and hurried to the scene. When we arrived, we found the guardswoman Forrest dead at the door, and a person in a guard uniform had been subdued at some cost to Captain Nerishe. It was unclear who was the original aggressor, and the guards with us jumped to the conclusion Nerishe was at fault. Rhiannon Owen stood between us and Nerishe, to try to explain. Which is when the assassin broke from Nerishe, pulled a second knife from his sleeve and attacked Miss Owen. I was able to remove her from harm's way, while Captain Nerishe stopped the attack by stabbing and killing the assassin.

"Captain Nerishe was gravely wounded during the attack. Princess Julianna arrived with Rhiannon Owen's sister, also summoned through magical sending. The Princess began to help Nerishe, which is when Prince Alexander arrived."

"Why were those two with the prisoner? Who gave leave for that?" Boucher demands.

King Peter turns to her, raising his eyebrows. She bows a little. "Apologies, sire. I merely wonder why Rhiannon Owen and Orrin Beaudreau were allowed to flout your orders in such a way. It is surely suspicious activity, at the least."

"I would like to conduct this inquiry, Marchioness Boucher. If you cannot keep quiet, I will ask you to leave."

Boucher's eyes widen just a little, but I see it, and then she sees me seeing it, and I look away because that woman is frightening. She bows deeply, I assume glaring, but I'm not looking directly at her so I can't be sure. The king doesn't want us to talk about how we got there —did someone tell him about the vortex already? Or does he have some other reason for keeping us from answering that question?

King Peter turns and walks to the chair, lowers himself down into it. "Orrin and Rhiannon, was the guardswoman dead outside the prisoner's room when you arrived?" he asks.

"Yes, Majesty," we say in a ragged duet.

"Hmm. Was the door closed?"

"It was open, Majesty," I say. He motions for me to continue. "We heard someone cry out as if hurt, so we entered the room and we saw the guard fighting Captain Nerishe."

"But you didn't see who began the fight?"

"No, sire. But Captain–"

"That will do for now," he says, cutting me off. I bite my tongue and curtsey a little.

"Hugh," King Peter says, "what have you learned about this guard whom Captain Nerishe killed?"

"No one recognizes him, sire. We suspect him to be a spy. Another was supposed to be on duty today with the guard who was killed."

The king frowns. "I want to speak with that guard."

"We aren't able to locate him as yet, sire," Hugh says.

King Peter's eyes narrow. "Either he was in on it, or he's murdered somewhere. I want to know which. As soon as you do."

"Yes, sire."

"Did you find out anything else?"

Boucher steps forward. "I have information indicating that the attempt on Captain Nerishe's life was ordered by someone here in this room."

The king turns his head to look at her. "And who is that?" he asks.

"Connor Valcourt, brother and son of traitors," she hisses. "He planned an assassination under your roof, at his brother's direction, to keep her from confessing to you of his perfidy." She looks smugly furious. Or furiously smug. I bite my lips hard.

Connor keeps his face bland. "Valcourt is the name my brother took in exile. My name is fitzWellan."

"Your name is traitor!" Alexander yells.

"Alexander, please be quiet," King Peter says, his voice mild, but the look he gives his son shuts Alexander up again. Strangely, Boucher looks pleased at the exchange. Robere shares a worried look with Hugh.

"I have not spoken to or communicated with Stephen in any way these past ten years. I do believe my brother was behind the attempt on the captain's life. But I knew nothing of it until it happened."

"You were in charge of the duty roster!" Alexander shouts again. "You signed off on the change in personnel, you arranged for the spy. A spy in our own house. You've met with Nerishe in secret a dozen times since you all arrived! We all know it was you. We all know you're a traitor and a murderer! Just like you murdered my brother!"

The shout echoes off the walls. King Peter's eyes close and he shakes his head. "Alexander, that's enough. Not another word from you. I do not have time for wild accusations."

The prince shudders in fury, his face beet red. But he stops talking.

"It is strange that an assassin was able to make their way so deeply into the castle," Duchess Marguerite says in a pleasant voice. "But it seems more likely that Stephen has had spies in place for quite some time than that Connor decided to kill Captain Nerishe here in the castle. He could have killed her before they arrived in Corat if he wanted to do so. It just isn't plausible. Do be sensible."

"He could want to keep his hands clean for once, Your Grace," Boucher hisses. "Your very obvious bias for him makes you unreliable here."

"And your obvious bias against him doesn't do the same? Really, Yvonne."

"Listen," Boucher starts, but King Peter holds up his hands.

"Enough. Enough bickering. Connor fitzWellan, Earl of Dorward, I have faith that you are loyal to Talaria. You have sworn an oath to me. Are you forsworn?" He gestures to Connor with his right hand out, fingers and seal ring extended. Connor drops to one knee and presses the ring to his forehead.

"I am not forsworn, Your Majesty. I swear it on all I hold dear." A part of me is angry that we are going through this—I doubt Lady Boucher will be mollified by his swearing fealty yet again. But he didn't hesitate, and his face is as impassive as I've ever seen it. The king accepts his oath and gestures for him to stand.

"There's an easy way to find out if this plan was Connor's, isn't there, Father? Just have one of the freaks here scry it for you," Alexander says in a spiteful, venomous tone. He grabs at Orrin's shirtfront and hauls him to his toes. Orrin grunts in surprise. Hugh steps forward, an exclamation on his lips, but Alexander shoulders him away.

"You have them here for something—shouldn't their witch magic help us out for once?" he sneers as Orrin wrenches away and stumbles back, but it's too late. The magic of an oncoming vision swirls in the room. Orrin's been holding it back, I realize. The low buzz in my bones, the ache, familiar enough that I'd ignored it, rushes brutally through my skin and takes us both, even as I try to step back.

The battle again. The courtyard. A soldier looking over his shoulder and screaming, baelfire in the air, demons twisting in the wind of a vortex. Ships in the harbor, the city on fire. A stone wall collapses, soldiers pouring in, all of them wild-eyed and demon-ridden. Alexander desperately fights off soldiers near the vortex, failing, falling. Death everywhere, everyone falling to swords and demons. Montmoore raises his hands, blood dripping from them. He turns around and sees me, sees us, his face contorted in rage. The magic all around us magnifies dangerously—I hear me, I hear Orrin, both of us chanting and weeping—*link up, link up*. The magic under my skin tries to link myself to myself, more than once. The vortex howls, Montmoore screams, pulls a knife from his sleeve and flings it...

We're back, Robere supporting me as I sag, Orrin

clutched in Hugh's arms. Everyone in the room stands frozen in shock. Orrin's shout echoes in the sudden stillness. He grimaces and I see him flicker again, which causes even more stillness for a crucial moment. A knife appears from nowhere, sprouting from his arm, a shallow hit that tangles in the fabric of his shirt, falls to the floor as he hisses in pain.

On my skin, power dances like an invitation, but I am not accepting any more today. I slam the magic down and away from both of us, as best I can through my tangled threads. I pull it from Orrin and push it out of the room. "No, you don't," I whisper. But the magic still grabs hold of me, and I See.

I See Boucher meet with the assassin, tell him, "Just get that spy out of my house, and I'll let you walk away." I See her speak to other guards one by one, intense or threatening or cajoling...speaking through a summoning stone that looks an awful lot like those Stephen uses— and then Orrin's arm wraps around my shoulders, his face pressed into my hair.

"No, no, not now, no," he whispers again, to himself, to the magic, to me. I feel a hard yank from the direction of Robere, and we are back in the map room surrounded by a very unhappy group of people. Magic is all well and good when it's contained and far away and you're paying for it. Not so much when a couple of upstart nobodies have more than anyone can safely control.

Especially when it's so obviously not under control.

"What was that?" Yvonne Boucher hisses.

"A very important question. I can't wait to hear the answer," drawls Alexander. "Father, what an interesting parlor trick your new protégés have for us. These magic freaks who you are so certain can help us. Is that one bleeding?"

Not much, but there is a rent in the fabric of Orrin's shirt, and definitely a solid knife on the floor at his feet.

I do not like the looks Orrin is getting from Yvonne Boucher.

I don't like the looks I'm getting from her, either.

King Peter's eyes narrow further, almost lost in the puffy wrinkles around them. I realize that he looks exhausted.

"I would like to speak with Orrin Beaudreau and Rhiannon Owen," he says quietly.

"Your Majesty, I don't—" Boucher begins, but the king simply stares at her, and she stops, her head rearing back a little.

"Now, I think," King Peter says.

Alexander waves his hands. "I want to know what's going on."

"I don't care, Alexander," the king snaps. Alexander's mouth opens, but he says nothing. "Right now I'd like to speak with these two, without all of these interruptions. I will have quiet." Everyone just looks at him. "By quiet, I mean get out. Everyone but Beaudreau and Owen."

"Father—"

"Now!" The king's harsh bark startles everyone into moving.

Hugh puts one hand on Orrin's shoulder, his other grabs my wrist. "I'll wait for you outside. You're all right?" He looks over Orrin's wound. I glance over and see Alexander casting a speculative eye on Hugh's open concern. Orrin sees Alexander glaring and glares right back.

"We're fine," he says, raising his chin. Hugh's hand

rubs up and down Orrin's back before he turns to leave. Alex stares hard at Orrin for a moment, then follows everyone else out. Only Connor and the guards are left.

"You too, Connor." King Peter turns to his maps, expecting to be obeyed. Connor eyes the guards. "They'll be on the other side of the door," the king says. "With you. Go."

Connor bows to the king and gives me an inscrutable stare, then exits. The guards follow him out and close the doors.

King Peter sighs. Orrin and I keep our sweating hands clasped. Peter looks at us and shakes his head. "Relax, please. I'm not going to have you murdered in the map room." I just stare at him. "Or at all. For Dorei's sake, child. Your glare could crumble plaster. You've spent too much time with Marguerite."

I curtsey deeply. "I believe I learned that from my mother, thank you, sire." I say, keeping my voice mild.

He snorts. "I believe it. It appears your magic has returned, Rhiannon Owen."

I bite my lips, nod a little. "Some, Majesty. I'm not sure."

"'Some,' she says. After flaunting it in front of people I don't want privy to it, she says some of her magic has returned. There are things I would wish, young woman."

Orrin's face is stone. "What is it you wish, sire?" he asks.

The king sighs, shakes his head. "Too much. You need someone to look at your arm, so let's do this quickly. What was your vision, then? I'd like to be the first to know this time, since its revelation has put paid to several of my delicate plans."

"The attack—in the harbor, the courtyard. Here. Soon." Orrin keeps his words terse.

"How soon?"

Orrin looks at me. I can feel the tension radiating off of him through his clenched hand. I shake my head—I only know that it's soon.

"I still can't tell for certain. The weather was warm. I got the feeling that it was coming, this is looming over us and we need to prepare. There was magic—a lot of it —I could feel the spells filling the air, and there were far too many ships in the harbor, crowding in our ships. Things were on fire. The city was on fire. They—they were past the breakwater, and they had...it ..." he breaks off, looks at me.

"I'm not sure either," I say. "We're not familiar with this harbor. But it seemed like a blockade? They were obstructing the harbor. And they had a lot of cannon."

"How many ships?" Peter asks, visibly trying not to shout.

"I couldn't tell. The smoke was too thick. There were explosions and people screaming, and I just—I couldn't tell. We saw the courtyard, with soldiers fighting. We— Orrin and me—we were trying to stop Montmoore's spells. At least, I think that's what we were doing."

At this Orrin starts to tremble, something he's been holding back, trying to ignore. I feel my own reaction trying to set in. The magic still creeps along my skin, trying to dig in and tell me news I don't want to know.

"It was a different this time," I whisper.

"Different how?" the king snaps, no longer holding back.

"The vortex was...bigger. They were sending soldiers through not just from the ships in the harbor, but from further away. It takes so much power to make the vortex that big, but the demons they were using to create the power get loose. And I think—there were more people dead."

"Who was dead?"

I shudder. "Alexander," I whisper. "Connor. You."

Orrin lowers his head to his chest. "Hugh."

I shudder with him. We were both almost dead. We were trying to draw magic from everywhere in desperation. So much magic. "I don't think any of us were going to last much longer," I whisper.

Peter stares at us, his lips a thin slash on his face. "Then we stop it. I can close the harbor today." He stands and starts to pace. "I will change the outcome of this, and you will help me." His turns to stare at us, his eyes burn into mine. "You will help me, do you understand? I will not let this nation fall into Fanthas' hands—or Stephen's. I will use every advantage I can. I need you to be my advantage."

I swallow hard.

"I need to be able to count on you. You say you're fighting in this vision. That you are in mortal danger. That all of our lives depend on changing this. Are you with me? I need to hear you swear it." The king's glare burrows into me. "I know you have suffered at the hands of Montmoore and my oldest nephew. I know you both have your doubts about me. But I will protect this kingdom—and everyone you care about—for as long as I draw breath. Swear to me you will do everything in your considerable power to stop this vision."

Orrin shakes his head a little, but, lips gray, speaks the words our king demands. "I swear I will do what I can, Your Majesty. I want to stop this vision from coming true with all my heart."

I nod jerkily, sweating. "Me too...I swear it," I croak.

He turns to the map of Corat at the table to our right. "Where were you—where in the harbor were you seeing from?"

Orrin and I look at the map. The canals and bridges and harbor all mapped out, the streets marked in ink, and some of the buildings...it bewilders me, and I can't place it.

"Here," Orrin says, and I look closer. Yes, that could be it. That would make sense given the direction the ships were coming from.

"They came through a vortex, like the one we—like ..." I break off.

"Like the one you two went through earlier today, you mean," King Peter says.

"Yes," I whisper, swallowing hard.

"And that assassin was trying to open one to...what? Escape?"

"I think so," Orrin says weakly.

"How did you stop him? Cardinal Robere says you stopped him." Naturally Robere already told him.

"I reached for a closing spell, and I...honestly I just yanked the magic out of it," Orrin answers. "He wasn't expecting it, and I'm not sure he was the source of the spell. It felt like it was coming from somewhere else."

"Such as the one in your vision?"

"Yes," I nod. "The ships come through a massive one, and there are many soldiers aboard. Then there are several vortices from the ships, sending more soldiers through to shore. And then the battle we've been Seeing for months. It is soon, I can feel it."

Peter studies the map, makes some marks with a pencil. "You can send your vision to Cardinal Robere?" He asks.

"If you wish, sire," Orrin says.

"Do so," the king orders. "You're dismissed. Send Cardinal Robere back in with Connor and Hugh. And I suppose I'd best have Alexander and Lady Boucher, as well."

We bow carefully and walk toward the door as he continues to study the map.

"One more thing," he says, and we turn to look back, bowing again, but he still studies the map. "I am aware that Lady Boucher does not trust you and is looking for ways to discredit you. Try not to give her any more opportunity."

Orrin and I glance at one another, eyes wide. "Yes, Your Majesty," I say. "She, I should tell you..." I stop, worried.

"What is it?"

"She, she was...I think she knew about the assassin. I think...I think she let it happen. She may have—she seemed to have made some kind of deal," I say, not sure how else to interpret what I Saw.

King Peter looks up, his face a blank mask. "You Saw this? In a vision?"

"Yes, I—that's what it looked like," I tell him.

His eyes narrow. "Ah. Please share that vision with the cardinal as well." He looks across the room at the wall for a moment, then turns his basilisk gaze to us again. "You may go," he says, waving us away.

We bow once more and gratefully escape.

Into an argument.

"Your interference will not be tolerated, Your Grace," Lady Boucher hisses.

"I should think it is your interference that everyone concerns themselves with, Marchioness," Marguerite says, slightly less than calm.

"Perhaps we should remember to treat each other with respect and tolerance," Robere says in a harried voice. Boucher turns on him.

"I've had enough of your preaching, Cardinal," she snaps, and then everyone notices us standing at the open door.

"Here are the witches now," Alexander begins, but the king's voice booms from behind us.

"Attend," he says simply, and Boucher, Alexander, Connor, Hugh, and Cardinal Robere all turn to enter the map room. Not without some glaring all around—Hugh glares at his mother once as he leaves us. Alex glares at everyone.

Cardinal Robere's voice comes to us. *Send me the vision, please, Orrin.* It's the first sending I've heard in many weeks, and my knees almost buckle with the emotions I feel—relief, worry, a wild grief I try to ignore. I let the guards close the door behind us and lean a little on Duchess Marguerite's arm as it comes around me. Orrin sends the vision, and through a scratchy, itchy feeling, I See what he sends.

Orrin looks at me when he's finished.

Did you get that, too? He sends to me quietly. I just nod, blinking. Marguerite's voice breaks into my conscious mind and I realize she's speaking to us.

"Not the time to wool-gather, my darlings. Time to retire to our rooms, shall we? Come with me," she says, pulling me along with her. She reaches out her other hand for Orrin, and we walk with calm deliberation down the hall. "We'll have to look at your arm, young man. Quite a day for knife wounds, isn't it?"

I take deep gulping breaths, resigned to reconciling my changing state once again, as she serenely guides us away from the king and whatever is happening behind us.

CHAPTER 31

The day has already been ridiculously long. But we only just now have time for lunch. A tray sits on the table in my sitting room, and I fall on it like a starved animal. The small, buttered sandwiches are particularly good, and the tea is excellent. I barely remember to save some for Linnet.

I crawl out of the russet gown and into the gray day dress that Linnet lets me keep for "quiet days." Today has not been quiet so far, but I can hope the rest of the day follows the edicts of the dress.

Itchy restlessness papers over a deep lonely ache in my bones. I cross the hall and knock on Orrin's door.

Come in, he sends, and I take a deep breath and enter.

You see, I try sending, *some people know how to knock on a door.* It feels hard, pushing through weeds or tangles but he smiles at me.

So it's back, he sends, and I wince, sore and tired from using magic again.

"Some of it. So it would seem," I shrug. I don't know how to feel, other than utterly exhausted. Orrin pulls me in for a hug. We embrace for a few minutes, taking comfort in each other's presence, breathing.

"I can't believe this day," he mutters into my hair. "I can't believe any of it. I don't trust that we're safe here, Rhi. I think we need to make plans to get away. If we survive—I don't know that we could stay in this country."

I step back a little, blinking. "Get away where?" I ask. "I don't know where we'd go."

"My family will help us hide, get out. We could go to Indranah, maybe."

"They hate us in Indranah already," I say, thinking of the ambassador.

"Not if they don't know who we are. We'd be in hiding."

"And what of everyone here we'd be leaving behind? What about Hugh?"

"He'd just have to understand," Orrin croaks. "As will everyone else. They'll live without us."

"Will we, though? Don't tell me you're not smitten with Hugh. I can tell."

"Rhi—don't."

"I don't see why I shouldn't. You know you two need to talk about this. About your reasons for wanting to go —as well as any reason to stay. One of which might be that he loves you and will protect you!"

"Talk to him the way you should talk to Connor, you mean?" he snarks.

I flinch. "We...did," I say, and look down at my hands. "It didn't go very well."

Orrin sighs, shakes his head. "He's stupid, then." He hugs me again. "I'm sorry."

I shrug in his embrace. "He has his reasons."

"They're stupid reasons."

"Maybe, but he's sticking to them. But don't you see, that's you in this situation," I say as I pull back. "Your reasons for keeping Hugh at a distance are just as stupid, because you don't want to take the chance that he might actually love you," I rant.

Orrin pushes his hands through his hair and starts pacing, ranting right back at me. "You mean His Grace, the Duke of Haverston? That Hugh? Hugh Maximillian Gerard Theroux, who is one step below royalty, brother-in-law to the crown prince, distant cousin to the king, in charge of an entire duchy, who works as a soldier and a spy at royal discretion? My reasons for keeping him at a distance are not stupid."

"He loves you. I know he does," I say.

"Does it matter? How do you think this is going to go, Rhi?" Orrin snarls. "He'll just declare he loves me, and everything will be all right? We'll be protected and safe, and he'll tell his duchy that they get some nameless failed acolyte as spouse for their beloved duke?"

"Orrin," I say, but he makes a sharp, cutting gesture.

"He's a duke, Rhi. He has obligations, an heir to secure, and all of these, these...rules that he must adhere to. He's not some shopkeeper who can adopt an heir or have a husband or—or –"

"He hasn't exactly been celibate all these years. And I've been told he hasn't always been careful, either," I put in quietly.

"What?" Orrin spins, his hands in his hair.

"He can easily secure an heir, is what I mean. Children he's been quietly caring for—some of them his, I understand."

I keep my tone dry. While it's true that the spell to

stop or prevent conception is difficult, and the herbal remedies hit or miss, it seems to me that men of uncertain virtue somehow tend toward fertile women.

"Rhi, that's not –"

"If that's your only objection, then I'm sure a solution could be found. But have you even asked him?" I feel a perverse sense of irritated accomplishment—if my own obstacles to happiness are insurmountable, I'll be damned if my friends' are.

"It's not my only objection."

"What does Hugh say to any of this?"

"I..."

"He hasn't asked me. Not yet," Hugh says from the doorway.

Orrin's face goes slack, horror in his eyes. "Oh, no."

"Which I suppose is fair, since I haven't asked him, either," Hugh continues.

I fold my arms. "So you've both been stupid." Letting out a deep sigh, I turn to go, but Orrin's grip on my arm stops me. "Orrin, don't you think–"

"Stay. Here." He hisses, his face dark with anxiety.

"I really think..." but his hand only tightens, so I nod. I will stay, if he wants it.

Hugh clears his throat, clearly uncomfortable. "I'm sorry to interrupt," he says as he enters the room, shutting the door behind him. "I came to check on your arm. I—Orrin, I am...it's true, I have not been celibate. Nor have I always been discreet. Although rumors of just how debauched I am are rather exaggerated."

"Because of him," Orrin says. I bite my tongue, hard. We all know which him he means.

Hugh's face turns shiny with sweat. "Yes. I have managed several...delicate matters for my prince in the past. I do not deny it." He spreads his hands. "I have spent—I did spend—too much time in love with him. He once returned the favor. But he is...not a constant man."

"And you are?" Orrin asks, his own eyes on the carpet.

"No one has ever required it of me. I have made certain of that."

"And if someone did?"

Hugh takes another step forward. Orrin's grip on my arm tightens to bruising and I wince. Hugh ignores me in favor of the man he's wooing. "I could be constant," he offers. "I have no idea how to be in love anymore, Orrin Beaudreau. But I am willing to risk it. All of it. If you will risk it with me."

Orrin's breath turns fast and harsh with suppressed sobs. Several tears fall heavily to the carpet. He looks up at Hugh. "I don't know if I can. There is already so much —too much. I don't know if I can handle anything else."

"I would like to help. Wouldn't a burden shared be easier?"

"I won't be your little kirche toy. I won't be your magical talisman."

"I would only ask you to be my love." Hugh's voice is low and rough. "I only ask that we try. Everything else can be figured out."

Orrin laughs. "Only a noble would think everything would be so easy. Why would the king accept you courting me, staying with me? He requires direct heirs of everyone else or their lands revert to the crown or another family."

Hugh shakes his head. "King Peter needs me too much."

"And what if Stephen wins?"

"Then I won't be a duke, and none of your objections to my station will matter. If we're in exile, we could do what we liked."

"Not all countries would accept us as l-lovers." Orrin gives in and uses the word, but not without some stumbling.

"I have friends in some that would."

"Would they still be your friends if you weren't a duke?"

"I suppose we would have to find out." Hugh stands ever closer to Orrin, and I try to shuffle a little bit back. Finally, Orrin releases me. I grimace as blood returns to abused skin.

Hugh spares me the smallest glance, and I don't need magic to know that he'd like me to go. But it was Orrin asked me to stay. I'm not sure I should abandon him yet.

Orrin hugs himself, trying to keep the feelings and magic in him quiet. I feel the power swirling in the room, as agitated as Orrin is.

"I don't want to fall in love with you," he whispers. "You're too dangerous. You might die or decide you were wrong about me or–"

"I can't promise you I won't die," Hugh says, his voice a sandpaper parody of its usual smoothness. That roughness, more than any of his words, convinces me at least of his sincerity. "But I am not wrong about you, Orrin. You are lovely to me, and kind, and smart, and the best man I have ever known. If you do not want me, I will leave you be. That's your decision. Mine is that I want to be with you."

Orrin's harsh breath echoes in the otherwise silent room. I can feel his indecision in the air, see it in his trembling. He looks at me, a pleading, desperate look. But I can't interpret what he wants.

"Do you want me to stay?" I ask. He just looks at me helplessly.

"Orrin, my heart," Hugh rasps, "I will do whatever you want. We can do nothing about this if you'd rather. I can wait—I'm happy to wait. You don't have to make this decision now. You don't—I don't want you to do anything you don't—you're unhappy with." He swallows, holds out his hand. "You can—you can have me, any time. I'm not going anywhere." He rumbles, his voice lower and rougher than ever.

"I don't know, I don't know what I want. Everything is too big—the magic, the politics, the danger. And you, you're just—I don't know if I am—I'm not—I'm only..."

"You're perfect. There is nothing about you I would have different. And I will wait—I can wait. Whatever you need, Orrin."

I back slowly toward the door as the space between them narrows. Orrin sways forward as Hugh steps slowly closer. Hugh's hand reaches up to cup Orrin's face, and Orrin leans into it, his eyes closing.

I feel for the doorknob behind me, trying to fumble quietly, tears starting in my own eyes.

"I want this, for now," Orrin whispers. "For now, I just want this," and Hugh's arms close around him.

"Then you shall have it," Hugh says, and I slip out of the room into the hall, closing it softly and leaning on it.

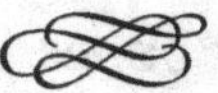

CHAPTER 32

The halls of the palace echo around me as I trudge to the chapel in the early morning light. I'm meeting the cardinal there for my lesson. He's also going to grill me again on how we safely traveled through the vortex four days ago, but I can't tell him what I don't know. We have worked on spells and the mechanics of the vortices, but what we know is that they are dangerous and require a lot of power.

Orrin shared his version of the vision with us, and I shared mine, relearning how to use my magic in its new pathways. It's stronger in some ways, but harder to manage than ever. Discovering how to work with Orrin again is important, I know, so we have spent most of the last few days either in the chapel or in Orrin's rooms, linking and unlinking, drawing power to try small spells such as sending or calling light. My magic links to everyone very quickly now, and even when I'm not linked I feel everyone again—voices in my head once more.

Hugh and Orrin have been standing very close

together while we work. It's the small joy that I'm holding on to, amongst all the worry.

We know the battle is coming soon, but not exactly when. So many things we don't know, including how we could possibly change the outcome, and the scars on our skin aren't giving easy answers. Mine still move under my skin, echoing in my bones. It's eerie and unsettling, and sometimes I think I can almost hear them whispering in my mind. Which might make it demons—I will ask Robere today to check again.

I take a breath as I enter the royal chapel, smelling the familiar kirche smells of books and stone. It overwhelms me with its ornate exaggeration. The carved stone pillars and fancy woodwork practically shout money and power. Larger than Haverston's by at least twice, it's mainly meant for the royal family and palace inhabitants. The Sonnenist cathedral in the middle of the city is where most, if not all, large kirche functions take place in Corat—coronations, royal weddings, or ignominious abdications.

Such as the forced dethroning of King Edouard, before King Peter took the crown. That was before I was born. Edouard was a terrible king, so the official story goes, and Talaria would have been lost to Fanthas long since had Peter not humbled and bested him in both political and actual combat.

Given all the knowledge I'm gaining of politics, it seems likely that some or all of that is a lie. King Peter should have expected discord and intrigue, given his conduct getting the throne in the first place. Or maybe that's just how courts and kingdoms work. Constant strife and intrigue and betrayal.

Such as the betrayal by Gerald, King Peter's brother,

which ended with Gerald's execution and Stephen vowing revenge. That did nothing to calm the courtly waters. The consequences of that act affect us all still.

I appreciate the beauty of the tapestries and statues here, though they do little to calm my nerves. This chapel has honored its history while rebuilding from castle to palace. The stones of the floor, the walls, have been in place for hundreds of years. Centuries of worship for the Star Lord and Dorei—all built up and decorated and burnished by the turning of so many seasons.

But I don't like meeting Robere here. The two other priests who serve the palace have no liking for me and make it known in various ways. Today it's Bernard striding up to me as I dawdle in the pews. He denies that Robere is here or that he left any instructions. Denying that I have a right to be here at all. The royal chapel is supposed to be open to all palace inhabitants, but Bernard would throw me out. I don't like this priest, this pale, scrawny man in front of me who screws up his face in such a sour way.

"I doubt His Eminence has time for you," he says, sneering. "You've taken up far too much of his time already. Perhaps Corat isn't the place for you."

I just blink at him, trying to keep my face neutral. I won't back down to any more bullies, but I just want to get on with the day. "I'm here for my counseling session with Cardinal Robere," I repeat, as calm as I can. "I wasn't informed of any changes, so I'll wait here."

"Why should the cardinal take any time to inform you or your ilk of anything?" the priest demands. "What could he possibly be counselling you about?"

Ah. My ilk. I suppose that was inevitable. Despite my

anxiety, or maybe because of it, I feel a hot anger start in my gut and spread. "My sessions with Cardinal Robere are no one else's concern," I say, spacing my words out distinctly.

"But they are my concern, young witch," I hear behind me in a courtly drawl. I recognize Alexander's voice and spin to find him uncomfortably close.

"Your Highness," I say curtly, dropping an abbreviated curtsey.

"Rhiannon Owen." He looks down at me, his own color high, his blond hair shining icily in the morning light from the windows. His nostrils flare, and I can tell that he's furious, although his expression is blankly pleasant. "What do you speak to Cardinal Robere about so very often? I believe an order from your prince is not so easily dismissed."

I take a deep breath, trying to keep my emotions from taking over. "There is no order above that of our maker, Highness. Nor do your orders supercede those of the king. I must protest that your order is capriciously cruel if you want me to go against my religion and my king all in one sweep."

I send a plea to Robere to help me, to hurry, but I don't have any control of my magic today, and I'm afraid I've blasted it to everyone. Everyone I have any connection to, anyway. Loudly. That I don't hear anything back could mean I didn't send it at all or that I can't receive sendings at the moment. It doesn't make me less anxious, not knowing which.

"Surely the king's orders do not refer to me," Alexander says with an angry smile.

"I don't know, Highness. Surely you can find out whatever you would like to know from the king, your father," I say. But King Peter hasn't told him much since we've come here or for months before that. I can See it, suddenly—See how the king is slowly shutting him out, as Boucher uses him more and more and undermines their relationship. But undermines it to what purpose? And why would Alexander want to help her against his father?

"I'm asking you now," he snaps, his smile growing sharp.

"I would hate to accidentally countermand the king, Highness. And you are aware a counsel with clergy is protected by kirche law."

The priest sniffs in outraged disdain. "Do not quote kirche law to the prince, witch! Your kind are not–"

"That is enough, Bernard," interrupts a very welcome voice from behind me. I look over my shoulder to see Robere walking between pews in a deliberately calm manner, his pale robes swaying.

Bernard stiffens. "Your Eminence, this–"

"I heard you quite clearly, Bernard. You knew my orders here. I will speak with you about it later. Go to your afternoon duties and prepare for late services. You are dismissed," Robere says and waits for Bernard to leave. The priest doesn't seem happy about it, so I don't think he'll manage to be any more courteous to me at any point in the future.

Robere turns a very civil smile to Prince Alexander. "Your Highness, how good to see you. May I help you with something?"

Alexander's expression is not what I would call perfectly civil in return. More predatory. "Cardinal. I would speak with you now."

"Ah, of course. Perhaps, Rhiannon, we could reschedule our counseling session," he says to me.

"I think she will come with us, Cardinal," Alexander says, and motions for us to follow him to the largest star chamber, the only one with a door, that I've been meeting with Robere in. It's safe to do some spells in, with Robere's magic to shield us.

I don't want to go into it with Alexander there. But I follow, glancing at Robere a little desperately. He nods at me, taking my hand and putting it on his arm. We pace slowly after Alexander's quick-stepping form. He stops at the door and turns to us, impatient. Robere smiles at him placidly, but my own expression is probably less serene.

"Ah, Alexander," a voice rings out from the doorway of the chapel. "Just who I was looking for," Hugh strides in, breathless, a bit sweaty. His face is cheerful and smile wide, charm on full display. "I was hoping to find you, my dear. I–"

"Not now, Hugh," Alexander growls. "You I will deal with later."

Hugh blinks at him, but ventures gamely on. "I'm not sure I understand, Alex. But I do need to–"

"Enough. I'm done listening to your blather. And I'm done with your false assurances and charm. Don't think I don't know about you and the little witch boy," he hisses. "If you think you can weasel your way into my good graces after that sort of betrayal, you're sorely mistaken."

Connor enters the chapel behind Hugh, who's stopped in shock halfway in. "It's not as though you had any good graces to begin with, Alexander," Connor says sharply. "And who exactly is he betraying? Your wife? Oh no, that's you who betrays her," he growls, his voice low and furious. Robere slowly draws me up the aisle away from all of them, one step at a time, as Alexander faces his one-time friends, his face blotchy, flushed.

"And there he is, the great hero from the traitorous family, whom we can trust so deeply because why would he let a little thing like his own family taint him?"

"Your family, too," I say, probably stupidly. Robere's hand tightens on my arm, and I can hear his dismay in his harsh exhale.

"What?" Alexander snaps, turning to me sharply.

"Your family, too. Your uncle, your cousin, your family." I take a quick breath, and then deliberately curtsey low. "Your Highness."

"You little witch, don't think I've forgotten about you," Alex starts, but Connor interrupts him.

"You're only upset because the king isn't sure of you any longer, Alexander. Why wouldn't the king be sure of you, his own son? What have you been doing to erode your father's trust in you?"

Alexander's face purples with his swelling rage, and I'm not sure that was a smart comment by Connor. But then, neither was mine.

"Don't play stupid, Connor. You and your little menagerie of freaks can't keep this up any longer. I want to know exactly what sort of treason you're playing at, and I will have it now. My father will—"

"I do think that's quite enough, dearest," Julianna says darkly as she enters behind Connor. Soon everyone will be here, I think, and feel a giggle start deep in my lungs. We can have a festival. Robere puts his arm around me as my shoulders begin to shake. I try to get a hold of myself, but my nerves are telling me it's to be tears or uncontrolled laughter, so it's hard work.

Alexander vibrates with rage, but Julianna just walks up to him and grabs his arm. "Come with me," she snaps. "I'm tired of these scenes."

I can see the moment he loses it and raises his hand. It will happen before anyone can stop him with words or get close enough to intercept. I don't know what Julianna will do. Hugh will challenge him. Connor will kill him, I think, and then everything will be so. Much. Worse.

I use my panic, the gathering magic around me, and I push. Push hard, push so hard the stones around us creak, and everyone cries out as the floor bounces once, twice, three times. Right under Alexander and Julianna. They both lose their balance and fall into the pews. By the time they get their balance back, Connor and Hugh stand in front of Julianna and Connor's hand is on his sword.

Alexander stands up, shaking, color still high. "You dare," he says, but he's lost in fear and confusion, and I hear Eleanore's uneven tread rushing into the chapel, feel her magic buzzing along my runes although it's not focused on me.

"No, Alex, no!" she shouts. She hurries to him, her cane thumping quickly across the stone floor, and our magics mingle in the air around me. I can see the strands of it, intertwining, boiling together, and I pull mine back, away, try to drain it down so I don't interfere with whatever she's doing.

I hope that priest from before is well and truly gone, or we are giving him quite a show.

"Alex, you're bespelled, you're bespelled right now

and I need to fix it," she gasps at him, and he stares at her. "It's that witch," he snarls, and she shakes her head frantically.

"No, no, it's not. It's Boucher who is bespelling you—you have to listen to me," she says, trying to cajole him into believing her. Her magic swirls around him. She's bespelling him, too, I think, even if she's not lying about Boucher.

"What are you, no—Eleanore. No," he shakes his head. "You've been spelled, it's you. They've magicked you, too," he says, and he takes her face in his hands, kisses her forehead. "I have to stop them," he mutters, and pushes her behind him. "I will stop you," he starts to yell, but Robere stands behind him suddenly. I don't remember him moving. He drops his hand heavily on Alexander's shoulder.

"You need to rest, my prince," he says quietly, and does something with the magic around us—something that makes Alexander blink twice and sway on his feet. "Rest," Robere says again, and Alexander slumps forward as Robere catches him and eases him into a pew.

Robere looks around at all of us. "Well, that was exciting," he says blandly. "What should we do now, do you think?"

"What was that before, that shook everything?" Julianna asks, dazed.

Connor looks at me, his eyebrow raised.

"Me," I whisper.

Everyone turns, shock on their faces. Connor just nods. "Ah." He takes a deep breath. "We should..."

Linnet rushes into the chapel with Orrin right behind her. "We should all get out of here, is what we should do. There are soldiers coming," she gasps out as she skids to a stop behind Julianna. "I don't know whose orders they're under but I don't think we should be here to find out."

Julianna looks like she might object, but Connor hoists the unconscious Alexander over his shoulder and nods to Robere to lead us. We follow him to the side of the chapel and out the door to Robere's chambers.

"We should likely not stay anywhere nearby, either," Robere says, and leads us out of his sitting room through a hallway to another door. He peers out into the main hall, waits a moment for the sound of marching footsteps to pass the corner, then motions us to follow.

Hugh takes the lead as we rush through the palace halls. I feel dizzy and achy and tired, magic still buzzing under my skin. Linnet looks sharply at me as I stumble, takes my hand in hers. "Keep it together," she mutters and hauls me along. I nod, but I worry I just tore everything apart.

CHAPTER 33

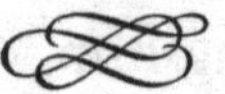

We make it to Julianna's rooms without too much fuss, despite the terrifying possibility someone will see the limp form of the prince and come to some very interesting conclusions. Some of which might even be correct. That would be disastrous.

"I think we're about to be in a lot of trouble," I say quietly as Connor lays Alexander down on the bed. Most of us crowd in the sitting room doorway as Julianna fusses over her unconscious husband. Connor stares at him grimly, shaking his head.

"I have a few ideas," Linnet says.

"No," I say "We are not doing whatever you have in mind." Her face is a bit too bloodthirsty.

"He's a bully," she says.

"He's a royal prince," I hiss at her.

"He is a bully, though. You're right about that," Connor says quietly as he walks toward us. Eleanore smacks his arm with her free hand as she passes him, but she doesn't contradict him.

"He's gotten worse," Julianna says. She pushes his hair off his forehead and sighs. "It's so much worse than it ever was."

Eleanore takes her brother's hand and sits on the bed, letting her cane lean against the headboard. "It has to be because of what Boucher does to him. I know it's her. I think she's hurting him, changing him. He never used to be this bad. Even though he was thoughtless sometimes, he wasn't mean like this, or ..." she trails off.

"Unbalanced?" Linnet says.

Eleanore's mouth pinches, but she nods. "Yes." She looks up at Robere, who stands at the far side of the room. "I think—I think I can reverse some of it with my magic. But she's pushed him a lot lately. And I don't know if he'll let me. If he'll believe me."

"He'll want proof," I say.

"He might not believe you, even with proof," Hugh says. "People don't, always."

"We need something. Something that will make him want to believe it," Connor says slowly. "We need to tell the king, one way or another. But he definitely won't do anything without proof. And there's no guarantee he'll believe us, either."

"Do you think Boucher is doing this to the king, too?" I ask.

Connor shakes his head. "How would we know? I don't think so—I've been keeping an eye out, and I've had people looking into it since you mentioned it was a possibility. But we need proof that anything is being done at all, to Alexander or anyone, and I don't have any. Yet."

"And there's the question of what the magic has been

doing to his mind," Robere says, pushing through into the bedroom. "I want to look into that more closely, with your permission, Your Highness," he says to Julianna. "He would likely benefit from your insight, as well."

She nods unhappily. "He hasn't wanted me near him much, lately. I will look, but I can't do anything without consent—if not his, then his father's."

"Juli—he's unconscious. He's your husband," Hugh protests.

"That's not ethical, Hugh, and you know it."

"If he were in his right mind," Hugh starts, but she cuts him off.

"I can't do anything to him without consent, and I won't coerce or trick him into it," she insists. "I'd be just as bad as the Butcher."

"Juli..."

"No," Alexander says hoarsely from the bed. He blinks rapidly, starts to sit up, but Eleanore soothes him into lying down again. "No," he says more forcefully, and turns onto his side to crouch a little, weight on his hands and flank. "No spells," he hisses. "No witches doing spells, no..." and he heaves a breath that sounds like the precursor to vomiting.

"You're sick," Eleanore says to him. "You've been made sick by someone you trusted. It isn't me, but I know how they did it. Look at me, Alex," she says. "I'm not doing any magic. But I know someone did magic on you," she insists.

"Witch," he snarls again, and she shakes her head

"Not who you think. It's someone else."

"It's her," he whispers, staring at me. I hold my hands open in front of me.

"I swear on the stars of my family, I have never harmed you," I say.

He blinks, confusion marring his pretty face. "Witch," he says again but without conviction.

"Should he be this weird right now?" Linnet asks.

Orrin and I exchange a glance, and without a sending or any speech, he nods and pulls Linnet further out of the room. No reason to give a definitely enraged, maybe insane prince my little sister as another target.

"Hey!" she protests, but she lets him maneuver her. I'm glad I didn't try it.

"He should be considerably more coherent, it's true," Robere says quietly. "My spell may have caused whatever hold Boucher has on him to backfire somehow."

"Are we certain it's Boucher?" Hugh asks.

"I am," Eleanore insists. "Someone is pushing him, and she's been telling him to distrust everyone."

"He does act very strangely around her," I say quietly. "She orders him around in a way I don't think he'd take if she weren't manipulating him. I can't prove anything, but I've felt her doing something."

Eleanore sniffs, nods her head. "It's her. I'm fixing this." She swipes her arm across her eyes.

"Alex, listen. Listen to me," she says, catching her brother's face in her hands. "I want you to let me do something right now. I want to take the magic off you. Will you let me?" He stares at her, brow wrinkled in concentration. "I think I can do it, with help. Can I do it? Can I try?"

He shudders, closes his eyes. Nods once.

"OK, then we're doing it. Help me," she says, looking at Julianna and Robere, but not saying their names. "He said yes, and I need help."

Robere nods briskly, walking to her side. Julianna wipes under her eyes briefly before taking Eleanore's hand across her husband's huddled form.

The magic moves fiercely, coming up fast, surrounding and calling to me. I have to hold my boundaries firm to keep from burning into their spell. The Sight shows me the threads of their power weaving over the prince.

Julianna's healing magic flows up around her, joining with Robere's steady power. Eleanore's magic bursts forth in ribbons of flashing copper, wrapping around Alexander. Julianna's blue threads and Robere's pale red ropes weave into her spell, an uneven but strong warp to her weft. The air grows dense with it, seeking out a dark, burrowing blankness that lies deep inside Alexander. The magic latches onto it, sticky, pulling, and he cries out in pain. Julianna's thread finds its way into the blankness, illuminating it, the shape of it.

I close my eyes and lean back, Connor's arm around me. I turn into his shoulder to keep my balance, stay out of the working. I can still See it in my mind.

With a flash, Robere's fine ropes sink into the blank magic, obliterate it. I raise my head from Connor's embrace and look at the bed. Alex thrashes once, twice, arches up with a hoarse cry, and then goes still. The blankness is gone from him, and all the other magic wraps him, then fades. His face looks peaceful, but he's unconscious again.

"Do we know if that worked?" Hugh asks.

"Boucher's spell is gone. But I don't know what it did to him," Robere says, his face a bit gray. "I didn't think it would be so insidious, but it's been in there for a while. I think it's lucky none of us tried it alone, or it might not have worked. And I don't know how much longer he'd have been sane, in any case." He looks up at Connor. "We must definitely tell the king."

"Obviously we will tell the king. But I cannot lay it on Boucher's doorstep without proof. And we risk having him blame others in these rooms without more proof they didn't do it."

"I will give evidence that they could not have," Robere objects.

Connor's hand tightens on my shoulder, but otherwise he keeps his face calm. "He is a king, and his son was harmed. I want to find more evidence of who it was before he makes decisions about who it might have been."

"Connor," Julianna starts, but something in his gaze stops her, because she subsides. "Maybe you're right. I will keep him here, and we'll just let it be known that he was injured. I'm healing him, but he'll need bed rest for a few days. That's all we can give you, Connor. Peter won't appreciate being kept in the dark at all, but he might forgive a few days if you get good information about it. More than that risks all of us far more than just the king deciding someone here is to blame for the spells—it might push him into thinking everyone here is. And a king who is only surrounded by liars is..."

"I know the risks," he growls. "I know every risk. That's my entire life's work, knowing risks. And I'm telling you, this is the only way forward that keeps R-, that keeps everyone out of trouble."

I feel him realize how hard he's squeezing me. and he releases me suddenly, taking several steps away and out of the bedroom.

"I have some ideas on where we can expand our

search," he says, his voice like gravel. "The soldiers we hid from in the chapel were searching for someone or something—Linnet, Orrin, did you see who was in charge of them?"

Linnet, in the next room, shakes her head. Orrin takes a deep breath. "I didn't see anyone. But I...know that Marchioness Boucher was counting on His Highness to start something in the chapel."

"You know this?"

Orrin nods. "It's all connected, in lines, in circles." His voice goes dreamy, and my bones tingle. "Boucher searches for what she needs to start her plans. She's fishing—she's trying to catch little fish to bring her bigger fish." I ride along the top of the vision, and I can See ghosts of his brain—whispers, blurry fish tangled in nets. I shudder, fear rushing through me. I'm pretty sure we're some of the fish.

"Boucher is working with someone else?" Connor asks. Orrin looks up, eyes coming back, wraps his arms around his middle.

"I think so. I...sometimes everything is bound up in riddles and metaphor. Boucher is working very hard to catch us—all of us. She wants something, but I don't know what it is."

Connor and Hugh exchange glances. "I intend to find out. Rhiannon, Orrin—I know everything is up in the air. Try to stay together, stay out of everyone's sight. Stay away from Boucher."

Orrin and I nod.

"Linnet, I need your help," Connor says, and Linnet looks up, eyebrows raised.

"My help? You never need my help," she says.

Connor's lips quirk. "Please. Find Duchess

Marguerite. Get her somewhere private and tell her what's happened. See if she can find out anything else. She's good with oblique information. Tell her to keep you with her. We'll need you to be able to send information from her while we're separated."

Linnet tilts her head, considering. "All right."

I catch Connor's eye, thanking him in my head for at least keeping her with the duchess. He gives a tight smile and turns to Cardinal Robere.

"Your Eminence, I would appreciate it if you could find out what spells might have been used on the prince. If they can be traced to whoever placed them. If there's any way to prove it."

"I will," he says. "I have some thoughts on it."

"Juli, I know you'll stay with Alex. I know you can't send to anyone but try to send someone with a message to Hugh if Alex wakes up. Try to keep him with you if he seems...unstable."

Julianna looks up from her husband, her hand on his on the bed. "I'm not letting him go anywhere if he's not well enough," she says, her voice flat.

"Understood."

"What about me?" Eleanore demands.

"I want you to find your father, Your Highness. If you can, find out what he knows. He may know more about this than we do—but I don't want to precipitate any rash decisions. Don't push him—it could backfire."

"I know how to deal with my father," Eleanore says with contempt. "And I know not to use magic on him. I have lived here my whole life."

"Of course," Connor says with a bow. "I defer to your expertise. But please get word to one of us if you learn anything significant."

She nods.

Connor turns to Hugh. "Hugh, will you join me?"

Hugh, who's been holding Orrin's hand, looks up. "Yes, of course," he says, and cups Orrin's face for a moment. "I'll find you later," he says to Orrin, and then gestures for Connor to take the lead. They leave Julianna's rooms, the rest of us standing awkwardly in silence.

"Guess we're not telling the king, then," Linnet says. "Does anyone know where Duchess Marguerite is?"

Robere shakes his head, looks speculatively at Alexander. "She could be in her rooms, but otherwise I'd try with Anouk Nerishe." He turns to me. "I think I'll come with you, Rhiannon, if you don't mind," he says. "I want to discuss what happened in the chapel today. Let's remove to your rooms, shall we? Orrin, will you come?" He looks at Julianna. "Your Highness, may we take our leave?"

Julianna takes a deep breath. "Yes, please. I will stay here with Alex. The nursery maid will be here with Atarah soon, and it would be best if you were gone."

We follow Robere out. The halls of the palace don't seem safe, but then they never did.

CHAPTER 34

Robere thinks our runes continuing to shift might hold the key to how to defeat Montmoore in the coming battle. He thinks my uptick in managing the power, in moving the stones of the castle, is because the runes have rearranged themselves again. We discuss it alongside the vision and the demons, and what banishing spells can do if you can control them. The banishment needs a Word of power, which is the spell with will and magic behind it. Robere tries to show us how to use one, but Orrin and I feel itchier and itchier as the day passes. The day melts into afternoon, with neither of us able to concentrate any longer.

"What do you mean, itchy?" Robere asks. "I need a clearer explanation." But all I can give him is the buzz in my bones. His voice starts to buzz there, as well, and the air.

Something is coming.

I send to Linnet, but she isn't answering, or my magic is broken again in a new way.

"Orrin, what am I feeling," I gasp out, but he's reeling

under his own visions, and we're being pulled into the hot, sucking void of magic in the courtyard, the battle before us.

"What are you doing, you two?" Robere shouts. "Do not start a vortex here!" But the vision is too strong, and we See: we See the courtyard, a vortex forming, and people coming out of it, in front of the king. The king, who is with Eleanore and Duchess Marguerite, and Linnet. I scream as the man I'm sure is Stephen runs through the vortex, sword out, a knife in his off-hand, the bodyguards too far away.

Stephen works fast, and though Duchess Marguerite grabs King Peter, he stumbles back just too late, a sword wound in his side. Linnet screams and grabs Eleanore but soldiers are pouring in and I See her as she falls trying to get Eleanore out, Duchess Marguerite trying to guard them but they have no weapons. The bodyguards are still running in and I start to run toward them but Orrin grabs my hand, tugs me in a different direction, yelling.

"Not yet not yet not yet!" he shouts, and Robere has my other hand, and we fall into another vortex, dizzying, violent, it tugs us as I join his chant to take us back, back before, when it hasn't happened yet.

The slip-scrape of the swirling storm, and we rush out into the courtyard as King Peter enters from the other side, Eleanore beside him and Duchess Marguerite and Linnet behind. "Get back!" I scream, gasping. "It's now, it's coming now!"

I can feel Orrin sending to Hugh, to Linnet, but I can't make it work, I can't hear what they're saying in this moment. I can only try to pull enough magic to me so I can do something to stop this slaughter before it happens.

The king stands near the north end of the courtyard with Eleanore, pushing her behind him. He draws a knife from his belt and Marguerite draws one of her own, stands beside him. Linnet takes Eleanore's hand and tries to go back out the door they just entered, but it won't budge.

"It's locked!" Linnet yells.

Someone inside the castle has betrayed us.

A storm-colored swirling nothing forms in the middle of the courtyard. Stephen jumps out of his vortex, landing in a crouch, sword out, knife in his off-hand. Before he can stab the king or my sister I ram into him with all of my strength, magic still buzzing along my bones, and he goes down in a heap, a shocked look on his face. I stumble over him while he lies stunned, turn and run for the king.

I can feel all the iterations of our visions around, all the times we've been here, and the magic is thick. Stephen shakes his head and scrambles up as soldiers in Fanthas livery tumble from the vortex behind him, pouring into the courtyard. Richard Montmoore exits with them, still pushing magic into the vortex. I hear rumbling and crackles like rolling thunder as he works to keep it open. It's so powerful this time, that others can actually see it and feel it.

Robere and Orrin and I stumble back, further toward the king, all of us retreating from the widening spell. It grows, impossibly large, roaring like a typhoon. Robere, watching Montmoore, holds still and takes a deep breath, grounding himself.

"Get back," he says. "Protect the king."

I'm still dizzy and sick from traveling back through time. Orrin feels the same—I See through his eyes, through mine, through everyone's. Too many minds with too loud thoughts.

Robere shouts a spell and brings his hands together, creating a shield of magic. It's the same spell I tried before at Dorward, but then I only lit the grass on fire. I try to emulate the cardinal's skill as we back toward the king, who yells orders and demands I cannot parse. I say the spell, I think, I move my hands, and I feel the air around us push away and back. King Peter falls to one knee, still shouting, and Robere glances over his shoulder at me, shouts instructions I can't hear.

Orrin pushes magic to me, around me, and I try to shape it. We link arms, say the spell together, and the shield forms, thick and pulsating. Standing just in front of the king, we look for a way to close the vortex down.

I don't want this reality to happen like all the other visions. Other iterations of me flicker in and out of this moment, open-mouthed with horror—ghosts of this future I have to change. They're fuzzy along my magic. Versions of Orrin, of Montmoore, of death and destruction flicker along my skin, along the skin of the world. It's all overlapping and I blink to bring the actual present into focus.

Soldiers flood into the courtyard from the south side wearing Talarian colors, Hugh and Connor in the lead. The Fanthan forces range between us, but at least the king isn't the only target now. Connor screams his brother's name and fights his way to him, the sounds of clashing swords and yelling of soldiers competing with the roaring vortex.

Robere, Orrin, and I are the only protection for the

king, and Eleanore and Linnet and Duchess Marguerite. Hugh leads a charge toward us, shouting, "To the king! To the king!" They fight their way through the flash of swords and the sudden bangs of small arms and muskets. Smoke fills the air in the courtyard.

Montmoore points his finger at Robere. "You can't interfere now, you old blasphemer! It's too late!"

None of our visions had Robere in them, I realize. Because we didn't know we could move through the vortex on purpose. Because we shouldn't have been able to, probably, and we brought him with us this time. We've changed something at least. But all our out-of-control magic combined doesn't feel like enough to defeat Montmoore's monster vortex.

"This is madness, Richard!" Robere shouts. "You'll never be able to maintain this. It's a sin against the sky!"

"It only takes a little blood," Montmoore chuckles. "And so much will be spilled today. What a pittance for so much power," he says, his face blankly pleasant. I shudder in revulsion.

"The demons have driven you power-mad, you fool," Robere spits back, and I'm sure it's true. But the spell is massive, and he's firmly in control. How many people died already to give him this much?

Robere and Montmoore both raise their arms and chant spells over the shouting and clanging of battle, magic clashing between them. The swirl of power surrounds them both.

Orrin and I maintain the barrier, but it's not perfect. Our concentration is only so good, and several soldiers push through. Then several more.

I hear fighting behind us. I sense King Peter's strength waning as he fights, but I have to concentrate on keeping the rest of the Fanthans out. One of his bodyguards staggers into place in front of me, her sword out, blood-spattered and breathing hard.

Waiting.

Orrin and I hold our ground in front of the king and Duchess Marguerite. Keeping the shield spell firmly in my grasp, I risk a glance over my shoulder. King Peter slashes at a Fanthan soldier, shouting orders. Marguerite has a long knife and a bloody arm, and Linnet, behind her, has a knife in one hand and a flame in the other. I can feel her in my runes, linked and pulling power. Several of the bodies around her have burns. Eleanore uses her cane against someone's head with her other hand on the wall for support. They are all still alive, so far.

"Get out the gate!" I shout at them.

"It's locked! Get it open for us!" Linnet shouts back. "Otherwise shut up and stop this!"

I grimace at her but turn back toward the fighting. We have to close that vortex.

Orrin looks around, sends to me. *I think I know how to reverse it. It might grab everyone who came through and send them back. It's like the closing spell from before, but with a twist.*

The shield wobbles and I grab desperately at it, try to firm it up. *If you can do it without me, I'll try to hold the shield,* I send back. *If you can't, I don't know. We'll have to think of something.* Sweat rolls into my eyes. I shudder, try to breathe, try to think through the noise. Shouts and screams and the roar of the vortex over everything, while Robere and Montmoore fling spells at one another that crawl along my bones.

Orrin pushes the full weight of the shield onto me, so

I expand my power into it to keep it steady, keep soldiers from getting past as best I can. Orrin starts to pull power into himself, and I feel a weaving of his magic into something complex and beautiful. The magic swirls around him and he starts to wrap the vortex in his power. He's looking for a way in.

Montmoore growls a word and tries to stop Orrin, but Robere flings something at him that takes him to his knees. I feel the vortex wobble. Montmoore's power flares, tears into all our minds, and we flinch back. In my head I hear a rending, a great moan, and the chittering of demons.

"No!" I shout with Orrin, both of us feel our hearts stutter at the sound. Orrin tries to gather the vortex's power to him, but the magic shifts and bucks at his spell.

Montmoore is losing control, his face gray and contorted in fury. "This is your fault! You did this," he snarls at us. He grabs the arm of a soldier near him and draws a knife from his robe. The soldier jerks away from him, horrified, but stumbles and Montmoore plunges his knife into his arm and then his chest as he falls.

"Stop this!" Robere yells, just as gray-faced and exhausted, and runs at him. "Stop it, you demon-mad heretic!" He leaps on Montmoore and wrestles him to the ground, trying to keep him from casting any more blood spells. They scramble at each other for the knife and roll into the expanding vortex. Before I can scream again, the vortex swallows them both.

Demons chitter and shriek, baelfire swooping out of the opening of the vortex. Which has indeed reversed, as we hoped. But not the way we wanted it to.

A swarm of demons descends on a Fanthan soldier.

My runes burn with his screams and the demons' shrieks. I hear whispers among the screams and shouts, between the orders and the magic and the clanging of swords, the report of small pistols and chanting of spells. Whispers that send atavistic fear to freeze my spine. I can almost understand them, but I don't want to. I watch them overwhelm defenders and attackers alike, pulling them down, feeding on them.

Orrin screams a spell—the power behind it pauses the chaos. The demons hang, suspended and pulsing, purple smoke smearing the air. Orrin screams out again, and I grab his hand, offering up what power I can. He pushes against the demons—Go Back, the spell says. He throws power behind his words and drives it against them. They falter into the vortex, scattering like leaves before a wind. They do not go easy. Not all of them are gone.

I let him use the power welling up in me, bubbling as I scramble for any more I can find. The vortex pulls people in—snagging the soldiers nearest to it as I think frantically what else we can do to stop it. There's so much power fueling it, more than Orrin and I can fight alone.

It feels malevolent; it feels like a trap. The shape of it changes—it's not a tunnel through to anywhere anymore. *Montmoore closed it on the other side,* I send to Orrin. *Why is it still open here?*

There's nothing in there but chaos and demons, he sends back grimly. More soldiers near it disappear, swallowed by the expanding, pulsing vortex. I can't hold the shield with the power I'm sending to Orrin, and it falls from my grasp as I sink to my knees, gasping. I twist around to see Fanthan soldiers surge in against the king's bodyguards. King Peter shouts and I yell to Linnet to get back, but she won't be able to hear me over the battle.

A sword comes down toward her and Eleanore, and she tries to turn it with her knife. The sword bites into her shoulder and I scream as she falls. Eleanore stands over her with her cane up, shouting. I reach out with all the magic I have left, and the ground around them buckles, shakes. Eleanore falls over Linnet, and the soldiers around them fall down, along with the king and Duchess Marguerite.

The gate behind them pushes open, and Prince Alexander surges through. He takes in the situation, sheathes his sword and hauls his sister back. He picks up Linnet and hands her to someone behind him. "Get them out!" he shouts, and wades into the fray.

Rhi, I need you, Orrin sends, and I'm torn. I want to run to my sister, but I can't leave Orrin to do this alone. I'm not sure we can even manage this together.

I stagger to my feet and grab Orrin's hand. Tears drip down my cheeks and I'm gasping through sobs. I stare at the vortex, which dips and wobbles and gobbles people down as they try to escape. Demons attach themselves to the stricken to keep from being scattered before Orrin's power.

You need to stop this thing, I hear from Hugh, as if we don't know. I glare at nothing, I don't even know where he is. It's so hard to see individual people in all the chaos. Everything devolves into a mass of movement. The line of defense is gone—it's only soldiers fighting each other or fighting to flee the demons and the vortex.

Orrin and I try to force the demons back into the void without much success, the power of his earlier spell gone now. The vortex should have collapsed without

Montmoore directing it, but it has fed too much on power and rages uncontrolled. I can barely stand, but I'm feeding Orrin whatever power I can find as he wrestles with it.

Connor appears in front of us, blood smeared across his face. "Rhiannon," he says, his voice gravelly from battle. "It has them. The king is in there, and Alex ran after. I have to get them."

"The king," I say stupidly. "In the vortex? When? He was—Linnet is hurt, and I can't—I don't know what to do," I whisper.

"Stop this thing. Get us out," he says, and he takes my face in his hands and kisses me once, hard. "I believe in you. Both of you. I'm counting on you because you have to come find me."

"What?" I yelp, but he caresses my cheek once and then runs into the vortex.

"Wait!" I scream, and I hear it echo.

I hear it echo through time, through all the iterations of me, and I feel them. Us.

We have so much power together. I reach into it, past it, and grab all of the power I can for Orrin.

"Link up, link up," I chant, linking to myself over and over, to every version of me. To every Orrin, every iteration of us, and reach out to touch the people in the vortex—stuck in time, stuck between time, the lost and wounded and Connor and everyone. I try to link to them all and pull them back to me.

Orrin focuses on the demons. He pushes magic at them in shattering gusts. "Go," he commands, banishment in the spell, and they rise up in a glittering mist of crackling baelfire.

"Go," he commands again, with all the power of every

time we've been here behind him, and they pulse away, toward the vortex. Toward all the people.

I try to pull the people back, but it's hard to do both. So I let them go to get the demons away first. "Go," we say together, Orrin and I, and push. A perilous shriek arises, a feeling of loss so great I almost vomit, and they hurtle into the vortex and vanish.

The vortex closes in on itself with a great rushing snap.

With everyone still stuck inside, between times and places.

"No!" I scream, running forward. Or I try to, but my legs won't hold me past a few steps. "No," I cough, falling forward, gasping. Orrin collapses next to me, sucking air. My head rings like a bell.

"Orrin," I hear from our left, and Hugh runs over. Captain Nerishe follows him, bloody and filthy from the fight, skin gray under the grime. Hugh kneels next to Orrin, pulls him in, checks him over, patting his face.

"I'm all right, all right," Orrin wheezes, and Hugh hugs him close, kissing his temple.

Nerishe looks me over. "Can you get them back?" she asks. I tremble everywhere, in every inch of flesh, everything hurts as I try to open up a link, a spark of magic, anything. We need to get them back. Of course we do. But the magic we've been wielding thins out and burns us back and is gone.

"I have to," I say, voice a ruin. "But we can't. Not—not yet. I need..." I don't know what I need. But I'll figure it out.

"You need to rest. Just a guess," she says flatly.

"Just wait, Rhiannon," Hugh says. "We can get them back. They are in Fanthas, now, with Montmoore.

Fanthas will ransom them back to us," Hugh says, but there isn't a lot of hope in his eyes.

"I don't think they're in Fanthas," I say dully.

"What do you mean?" Nerishe and Hugh focus on me, and I flinch.

"The far side closed with Montmoore and Robere. Robere is in Fanthas, probably," Orrin answers. "The rest of the people, there wasn't anywhere for them to go, to get out. Unless we can open it again, they're lost in between...everything." His voice creaks, bleak and scratchy.

"Including the king? And Connor and Alexander?" Hugh's eyes widen, horrified.

"Everyone after Montmoore," I answer. Hugh blanches, but Nerishe just looks grim.

"I have—I have to find Linnet," I say, trying not to sob. "She'll be with Juli, with the wounded."

I struggle to my feet, every bone a stone weight. I look over the bloody courtyard, everyone left staring at nothing or trying to help the wounded. I nod, letting the tears fall. "I need to find her," I whisper, and Captain Nerishe, limping, leads me away.

CHAPTER 35

Linnet is still alive. But she won't be healed any time soon—the sword did not do her any favors. Julianna staved off blood loss and infection, but she's still seriously injured, and there are only so many Healers to go around. I go outside, to get some fresh air, away from the stifling hall being used as a hospice. Eleanore promised to sit with Linnet for a little while— the princess is not badly injured, only sore and bruised. I need to get away from all the voices and the panic.

The panic follows me outside. I have to get them back.

Orrin and Hugh and a limping Captain Nerishe find me leaning against a wall in the sun, trying to breathe.

"You're going to have to run," Nerishe says without preamble. "You can't stay—they're coming for you now."

I can't comprehend her words. I can't parse the meaning. "Who is coming? What—why?" The evening sun glows golden on the steps just outside of the court-yard. Sweat and drying blood and the ache of everything has tightened into a giant itch that is me. It is the only thing keeping me from floating away in frantic dread. The smell of death, of sweat, of the city in the summer hangs in the air like a pall. I try to breathe but the air is so thick.

"Everyone is coming, now. And they're going to blame you for all of this. You are the ones who are stuffed full of this magic, it's you who are dangerous, and Indranah wants to take you. Talaria is going to let them. You have to run, now. I'm taking my wife and running, quickly, before they get themselves in any order. It's now or never."

Hugh looks at Orrin, whose face has gone blank and stony. I know it's fear. I can feel it—can almost taste it. It's the same as mine.

"But we have to try to get them back. I have to be here, where it happened—I have to—I can't leave Linnet. I promised. And the vortex—you run," I say to Orrin. Because I think I know how to link to those stuck in the vortex without him, and I can't let him be taken again. I'm the one with the connection to Connor. I can feel him, stretched thin and far away, but I know he's somewhere. I tell them. "You go, Orrin. Run—go as fast as you can. Get away from all of this, get out. They shouldn't have both of us, anyway. I can maybe convince them to let me keep trying."

Nerishe shakes her head. "They won't. I'm going— and I'll take whoever else is coming."

Orrin and Hugh look at each other. "You'll have to stay," Orrin whispers.

"How can I stay without you?" Hugh says in an agonized whisper. "How can I leave Mum and Juli to face this without me?"

"Your Grace, this isn't going to be a good place to be

for anyone close to this magic," Nerishe says. "Marchioness Boucher is going to look to blame you, since the earl is missing. We all should get out. Your mother even told me you should go." She looks hard at me. "You should come too. You should get out of here. They won't treat you kindly. They won't thank you for saving them."

Hugh looks at her grimly. "I'll get you out of here, take you somewhere safe. But I can't leave this mess to my mother alone. We have a short window to get you out, so let's go." He puts his hand on my arm. "Rhiannon, are you sure you need to stay here? Do you think you can get them back?"

Tears fill my eyes, so he's just a blur against the light. "I have to try. I have to at least do that. And it has to be here—I think I have to be here, to draw him back. How else can I reach him? Or the king? I know Connor's not dead. I can feel it. And I can't leave Linnet—not again. She's in with Julianna now. How can I leave her?"

Orrin hugs me, kisses my forehead. "Find me if you need me," he says.

Hugh hugs me hard, then steps back, nods to me, and takes Orrin's hand. Nerishe leads them away. Then I turn back to the hospice and go inside. I will help Julianna for as long as my body holds out or until they drag me away.

When Duchess Marguerite finds me some time later, I'm leaning against a wall. Julianna sits with her head in her hands, blood covering her to the elbows, streaked on her face, in her hair. Me too, I suppose.

"Rhiannon, where is my son? Where is Orrin?" Marguerite asks.

I look at her blankly. "They left. They left when you said to go."

She holds herself very still. "Who said I told them to go?" she asks quietly.

I just shake my head, fuzzy and stupid with exhaustion. "Anouk Nerishe? She said you said..."

Marguerite's face is blank. "Ah. This might have worked with all of you here, but just you—you should have run with them. They are coming for you."

"Who is—"

Marguerite pulls me to my feet and leads me to another door, but she is too late. Soldiers come in behind her with Ambassador Acarla, who points to me.

"There is one—the demon-tainted." A soldier with carefully gloved hands yanks me from Marguerite's grasp despite her protests, and I'm frog-marched away. I look back at Marguerite and Julianna, who are prevented from following by more soldiers.

When I'm dragged before Yvonne Boucher, I'm babbling and I know it. "I swear by Dorei I'm not possessed—I don't even hear them much, the demons. They're asking to go home, but that's not what I did, that's not what we were doing. We were trying to stop the attack, we just collapsed the vortex to stop them–"

I realize that there will be no king to appeal to. He is gone in the vortex, and Yvonne Boucher is apparently taking power.

The enormity of the day takes my breath all over again. My stomach clenches hard, my limbs shake. How do I manage this, now everything has fallen apart? How do I buy enough time for Hugh and Nerishe to get Orrin away? How do I get the king back?

The stomp of a lot of boots takes me by surprise as I'm dropped by the soldiers and fall shakily to a knee. I look around, look back up at Boucher, at the ambassador, wondering how I'm going to explain that I want to try to get back the prince and the empress' grandson. Both of her grandsons, though I suppose the ambassador might only care about the one.

"Enough, Rhiannon Owen. I've heard enough." I open my mouth, but her stony face, the grim triumph of it, makes my eyes blur, dries my throat.

"Please, my lady," I whisper.

"Enough." She lifts a hand and the ambassador steps forward. I glare at him, and he glares right back.

"It is arranged, my lady." He looks coldly down at me. "They will take this...baggage."

I look wildly around. Where is anyone to speak for me? Where is Eleanore? Where is Duchess Marguerite? Julianna? The bootsteps belong to soldiers in a uniform I don't recognize, but the heraldry looks Indrani.

"You will keep searching for the other one? It's not impossible that Stephen Valcourt and Fanthas have taken them," the ambassador says.

"N-no," I stammer. "You don't understand! Stephen is—and the king! They're in the vortex, too! They're lost in there. We have to—Connor is lost in there. Alexander, all of them. It took them. It took...Please. I must –"

The Indrani soldiers are coming for me. A soldier approaches me, her face grim and unyielding. She holds a set of manacles, in dull iron, carved with runes. I scramble to my feet.

"You are raving—the demons are raving," Boucher grits out. "Take her—it. Take it. For my king's death, for my prince's death, I will see you pay."

"They are not dead. They are not dead," I insist in a whisper. "I know where they are."

"They aren't anywhere—you saw to that, demon-tainted," Acarla snaps.

I stare at him, pleading. "Maybe not. Not yet—but I can still get them out. Let me try to reach them! I can get them out." I can almost See it, the magic fizzing on my skin like wine, like friendly lightning. Boucher stands in front of me, suddenly, her eyes open wide in denial as she feels it, too.

"No," she says to me, but I have to try. She yells and tries to grab me, but I can feel the spell, how it fits together. Everyone falls back from the heat as I open my channels wide and take in the magic, let it out again.

Yvonne Boucher strikes to stop me, but she's too late. I release a barrier against her—she falls back, cursing.

The power swirls around me, and I feel that part of my soul that is connected to Connor twitch, spark, flare up and align.

A thin vortex spins open in the middle of the room, charcoal dark churned with the color of a sunset storm, pulsing with lightning and demon whispers. I can almost taste the thickening miasma of magic. The connection snaps taut.

"Connor!" I scream, and I can See him, deep in the fog. I scream again, and this time he turns, a dark form in all the roil. "This way! To me!" I scream and open my hands to him, praying to a god I don't believe in anymore.

A figure staggers out of the vortex and steps from the fog. But when I can see him clearly, the face is not Connor's. It's Stephen who's come out of the vortex, his sword bloody.

As is his side. He falls to his knees out into the room, and I scream for Connor again. I try to pull on the link I can feel to people in there, further in, further lost. The connection wobbles, falters.

"No!" But the spell can't hold. I don't know how to hold it alone. It shatters against its own weight and shatters me, too.

When I scramble up from lying prone, I am surrounded by frightened guards, and a scowling Boucher steps forward to slap my face.

"You can't even get the right prince back, you stupid heretic." She turns to the soldier.

"Give me those shackles," she commands.

"Please no, you can't—I have to try again—you can't!" I plead.

"Just watch me." She yanks my arms in front of me, and all I know for a time is pain. The last thing I see before I pass out is Stephen's gray and grave face...

AUTHOR'S NOTE

I have so many people to thank, as always, because while writing is a task you mostly do independently, if you want to keep writing – to keep going when you doubt yourself, to write at all well – you need a heap. A heap of friends and family and writing buddies who cheer you on and keep you sane, and also to find your heaps of mistakes and help you fix them.

These past few years were very hard on me in many ways; writing at all was tough for much of that time, so I really needed my heaps of folks.

Thank you to Marti McKenna for being my editor for this book, keeping me honest about my story arc and comma usage, and helping me find the thread I lost in the middle somewhere. Without you I'd still be wandering around in palace hallways, hoping for a plot. (With a LOT more semicolons; I still really like them.)

Thank you to Angie, again, for being a kick-ass artist and making such a gorgeous cover. Seriously, you are amazing, and I love it so much.

Thank you Aynjel for your willingness to read iteration after iteration of the same dang scenes, helping me get to a point where there even was a book to edit. For squeeing with me about specific cinnamon roll moments (you know which) and loving my characters almost as much as I do.

Thanks to my friends and family for asking "when's the next book coming out," even when what that elicited was a groan. It's now! Here it is! I'm writing the next one already, I swear! Thank you all for caring enough to ask, and for being actually interested in the answer.

I'd like to thank my cats for being fuzzy and imperious and ridiculous creatures, because we all need some of that sometimes. We lost Medea while in edits for this book, which was devastating as losing a beloved pet always is. She was a helper, sitting on my lap or laptop or burrowing in wherever she could, and her purrs and complaints worked exactly as she intended. I don't know that she helped with plot per se, but she helped me be a person, which is always needed.

Last but not least, and for always, thank you Scott: for being my publisher, my copyeditor, my cheerleader, my IT person, and my business manager. But most of all, for being my love. We might not quite fit the trope of the grumpy one being soft for the sunshine one, but we're close, even if sometimes we switch places.

ABOUT THE AUTHOR

Lindsey S. Johnson lives in the Pacific Northwest with her significant other and several fuzzy little monsters known as cats. When not engaged in day job or word tinkering, she dances, sings, bakes, and has been known to spend time staring pensively at nothing or randomly muttering to herself, although she claims that also counts as writing.

A Tangled Vision is her second published book, the middle part of The Runebound trilogy. You can find out more about the upcoming finale online, at

www.lindseysjohnson.com

9 781954 394056